GW01458336

Hannah Hooton grew up in Zimbabwe studied Writing and Film at university, and was awarded the McLeod Prize for graduating top of her year. Her lifelong involvement with horses and the racing industry has brought an added authenticity to her books.

Praise for Hannah Hooton

'Reminiscent of a Tom Sharpe novel, but funnier.' *The Racing Post*

'Well-paced and the kooky characters absolutely believable. I laughed a great deal.' *The Romance Reviews*

'Group class and makes the grade on my shelves.' *Love the Races*

'Everything from a great storyline to some hot romance! The female Dick Francis.' *The Filly Forum*

'A great combination of mystery, thrill and romance. Get this book. Seriously. You will not regret it.' *Forging Fiction*

Also by Hannah Hooton

At Long Odds
Aspen Valley Series:
Keeping the Peace (#1)
Giving Chase (#2)
Share and Share Alike (#3)

Making the Running

(Aspen Valley Series, Book 4)

HANNAH HOOTON

Copyright © Hannah Hooton, 2015

All rights reserved

The moral right of the author has been asserted.

No part of this publication may be reproduced, stored in a retrieval system, or transmitted in any form or by any means without the prior permission in writing of the publisher. Nor be otherwise circulated in any form of binding or cover other than that in which it is published and without a similar condition including this condition being imposed on the subsequent purchaser.

All characters and events in this publication, other than those clearly in the public domain, are fictitious and any resemblance to real persons, living or dead, is purely coincidental.

ISBN: 978-0-9929853-5-6

Published by Aspen Valley Books, 2015

Acknowledgements

Making the Running was somewhat of a step into the unknown for me, and one of its themes in particular posed challenges. I would like to thank those who shared their experiences and helped to make this book that little bit more authentic, and I hope that I have handled the storylines inspired by them with tact. It is important to mention that the events in this book are not a manual on what every addict goes through, but a fictional version of what is possible.

As ever, my thanks to my wonderful editor, Michelle Foster, and my BETA readers, Michelle Knight and Kelsey Kissel. Much of *Making the Running*'s research was completed in previous novels or date back to my own experiences in racing yards, with the exception of a few facts. For those, my thanks extend to Dan Skelton.

And last, but by no means least, thanks to Harriet Jones and the rest of the Jones family, who introduced me to murder mystery parties in a way that made it impossible not to include in the story.

1

'AND FONTAINEBLEAU FORFEITS the lead!' The commentator's voice bounced off Stratford's grandstands and echoed across the course. 'Apollo's Prayer takes it up and goes on to win by two – make that three – lengths...'

Kate's hopes deflated. It would have been too good to be true anyway. Exchanging wry smiles with those beside her, she picked up the lead rope that she'd dropped in her excitement and went to collect her charge.

Fontainebleau's nostrils were as wide as ice cream scoops, gulping in the cool October air as Kate loosened his noseband and offered him a water bucket. She used her sleeve to wipe the worst of the mud away from his eyes and smoothed out the thin chestnut wisps that constituted his poor excuse for a forelock.

'Fontainebleau, the eternal bridesmaid,' she murmured. 'Come on, fella, step up to the plate. I'm never going to get to Cheltenham this way.'

By the time Kate unlocked the front door to her and her sister's Helensvale flat that evening, she was desperate for a hot bath and the luxury of curling up on the sofa in her dressing gown to watch TV.

The air was humid and thick with Saskia's Molton Brown bath oils and Kate made a silent prayer that her sister hadn't used up all the hot water.

'Saskia?' she called, tossing her rucksack on the dining room table and pulling off her mud-caked boots.

Only the sound of a hairdryer and Taylor Swift responded.

With a sigh, Kate padded across the faded carpet. She thumped on her sister's bedroom door on her way to the bathroom. The hairdryer was silenced and seconds later, Saskia's door was opened.

'Kate? Is that you?'

'In here,' she replied, kicking Saskia's dirty clothes towards the laundry basket.

Saskia appeared in the doorway. Even with a green face pack and her bangs in rollers, her beauty was evident. At twenty three, she was four years younger than Kate. Tall, leggy as a week old foal, she didn't need so much as to flutter her long lashes and toss her rich chestnut mane to make guys fall at her feet. By contrast, Kate was stocky with Minnie Driver curls that turned Diana Ross at the faintest hint of moisture, and a bosom that no bra seemed capable of supporting. The only thing they had in common, it seemed, was the surname Creswell.

'Thank *God* you're home,' said Saskia, all drama. 'You have to come out with me tonight.'

Kate spun the bath taps. 'I'm knackered, Saskia. I've been at Stratford all day.'

Saskia curled her lip at the condition of Kate's clothes and took a step back. 'What were you doing? Mud wrestling?'

'Font hit the crossbar again. I don't think he'll ever win again.'

'Well, I hope that hasn't put Jack in a foul mood,' replied Saskia.

Kate gave her a withering smile. She'd got Saskia the job of Aspen Valley racing secretary just a couple of months ago. She knew Jack wasn't the easiest boss in the world, but he was good at what he did, and Saskia was stroppy enough to deserve getting as much as she gave.

'Where are you off to?'

Saskia followed her out of the bathroom and into Kate's bedroom. 'Leonie's having a dinner party, but Viv's cancelled at the last minute.'

'Not Leonie,' said Kate. 'You know how trying I find her.'

'Please? I already said you'd step in.'

Kate unhooked her dressing gown from behind the door and looked at her sister. 'Saskia,' she groaned.

Saskia sensed weakness. 'Pleeeease, Kate. Come on. Leonie has some awful yuppie called Nicholas she wants to set me up with. I can't face it alone.'

Kate opened her mouth to object then shut it with a sigh. 'Fine. But I still need to have a bath – *if* you've left me any hot water.'

'Of course,' said Saskia cheerily. 'I bathed early so it had time to reheat.'

'Very thoughtful of you.' Kate gestured to Saskia's green face pack that was starting to crack. 'You better get that stuff off before it does damage, Princess Fiona.'

* * *

Saskia and Leonie greeted each other with enthusiastic air kisses.

'Sweetums, you brought your sister,' squeaked their host. She flopped a pink-taloned hand on Kate's shoulder and rolled her eyes. 'Thank you for making up the numbers. Although,' she lowered her voice, 'bloody Ignacio cancelled when he heard Vivien wasn't coming, so it wouldn't have mattered if you couldn't make it.'

'My pleasure,' replied Kate with a wry smile as she shrugged off her coat.

'Oh no,' said Saskia. 'Are you at odd numbers again?'

'No, thank God,' Leonie replied. 'Darling Nicholas saved the day. His brother Benedict said he'd come, though when I don't know. Now, you *must* meet Nicholas,' she said chivvying them out of the hall into the lounge.

Four heads turned at their arrival. Leonie towed Saskia over to one of the three men in the room. Saskia grabbed Kate's wrist and pulled her along too.

'Nicholas, I'd like you to meet Saskia Creswell. Saskia, Nicholas Borden,' said Leonie. 'Saskia's a racing secretary. Nicholas manages an investment firm in Bristol.'

Dressed in chinos and a navy blue blazer, Saskia's suitor looked like a member of the chess club. His brown hair was meticulously combed and his cheeks appled as he smiled a greeting at them.

'Pleasure to meet you,' he said, shaking Saskia's hand.

Saskia smiled helplessly and gave Kate a desperate look. 'Here, have you met my sister? This is Kate.' Saskia practically pushed their hands together.

Leonie shot daggers at Kate. 'Nicholas, won't you be a dumpling and make Saskia a drink? Kate, come over and chat with Declan.' She steered Kate away and pointed out her boyfriend who was fiddling with the gas fire. 'He always likes to talk horse.'

No introductions were needed. Declan was a partner at the Helensvale Equine Clinic, and their paths had inevitably crossed since Kate's move to the area two years before.

'Declan,' Leonie hissed. 'What are you doing? I can't do everything myself.'

'Tryin' not to get us blown up,' he said in a rich Irish brogue, watching Leonie quickstep out of the room.

* * *

A quarter of an hour later, Leonie announced dinner was ready to be served and would they please all make their way into the dining room.

Everyone shuffled to find their place cards. Kate found herself between Declan and a seat allocated to the absent Benedict.

Leonie followed them in, carrying plates of smoked salmon sushi rolls, and Kate caught her pouting at the gap beside her.

'I'm sorry, Nicholas,' said Leonie. 'We're going to have to start without Benedict.'

'I'm sorry he's letting you down like this.' He held out Saskia's chair for her.

Kate noticed her sister still wore a look of helplessness. She grinned across the table at her. She was surprised at Leonie's choice of suitor for Saskia. They were best friends after all. She should surely realise Saskia preferred her men on the rough side.

Wine was passed around and Kate put her hand over her glass as Nicholas offered her some. Saskia swallowed half of hers in one gulp and was ready for a refill by the time the bottle came back.

Declan gave his sushi an experimental poke with his chopsticks. 'What the feck is this?' he muttered.

Kate sympathised. Sushi would be a first for her too. She dipped the first roll in her bowl of soy sauce and whipped it into her mouth before it could fall out of her chopsticks. Her taste buds screamed in rebuke and she forced it down her throat. Tonight was going to be harder than she'd envisaged.

Leonie, with Declan's assistance, was clearing their empty plates and soy bowls when the doorbell rang. 'Declan, will you get that?' she said. 'I need to get those futomakis out of the fridge.'

'Can I help?' Saskia appeared eager to extricate herself from Nicholas's company.

'No. You stay where you are,' said Leonie in a tone that wasn't to be argued with. 'Nicholas, won't you distribute the sake before it gets cold?'

Nicholas was caught staring at Kate's Grand Canyon cleavage. To give him his due, his cheeks flamed red and, looking flustered, he sloshed the Oriental drink into everyone's ochoko cups. Kate didn't know whether to be embarrassed or amused.

Without meeting her eye, Nicholas offered her some sake. Kate wasn't sure she could stomach much more exoticism.

'Does it have alcohol in it?' she asked.

'I think so. Don't you drink?'

Kate was about to answer when the new arrival walked into the room accompanied by Declan. Kate's mouth fell open a notch. Dressed in hip-hugging blue jeans and a creased T-shirt stood a most appealing sight. Dark-haired with crinkly eyes and a lopsided smile that showed off a good set of pearly whites, he looked the sort any critical mother-in-law would approve of. Kate took in his broken nose and weather-beaten brow, deciding he was more sexy than handsome.

'Sorry I'm late. Couldn't find a place to park,' he said, clasping his hands. 'Where do I sit?'

2

KATE GLANCED ACROSS at Saskia to gauge her take on this new addition. Saskia was giving him a lazy once over.

Leonie came into the room balancing the next course in her arms and sucked in her cheeks at the state of the new guest's casual attire.

'Welcome, Benedict. I'm Leonie. You're just over there next to Kate.'

Kate felt like she'd won the pools as Benedict slipped into his place beside her.

'Ben de Jager,' he said, holding out a large, vein-popping hand.

Kate's gaze travelled from her own pale hand to his contrastingly brown one, over the leather wristbands, and up the defined contours of his arm.

'Kate Creswell,' she gasped. She looked across at Saskia.

Her sister had her chin planted in her palm, elbow on table, listening in sulky silence to Nicholas. Kate's gaze snagged on Nicholas. She fish-mouthed for a moment – they were *brothers?* – then remembered her manners.

'Kate, are you going to hog our new guest or are you going to introduce him to everyone?' Saskia spoke up.

Kate gave her a patient smile. Not satisfied to have just Nicholas for company, she was intent on stealing the attention of Kate's dinnermate as well. 'Ben, this is my sister, Saskia. Nicholas you know, presumably—'

'It would be awkward if they didn't,' cut in Saskia. 'How do you do, Benedict?' She held out her hand across the table, oblivious to her sleeve sloshing in a dish of soy sauce.

'Just Ben,' he corrected, shaking her hand.

'Benedict does sound awfully formal for such a casual guy,' Saskia said, running her sapphire eyes over Ben's chest.

Kate could almost feel her sister's magnetic energy pulling his focus away.

'Inherited from my grandfather,' he replied. His gaze strayed to Nicholas, who looked even less brotherly than before. 'That's about as far as the similarities go.'

His expression was teasing, but Kate recognised a spark of defiance in his eyes, challenging. Ah, she knew that look. She was no stranger to sibling rivalry.

Halfway through the main course, Kate's stomach decided sushi was definitely not to its liking. She put her chopsticks together and eyed Ben tucking into his dinner with zest.

'Do you want mine as well?' she whispered.

'Not a fan of sushi?' replied Ben.

Kate gave an embarrassed smile as her gut voiced its disapproval. 'Would appear not.'

Ben shrugged and transferred Kate's leftover sashimi and sushi rolls onto his plate. 'It's good for you. The Japanese are amongst the healthiest people in the world because of it.'

'I'll take your word for it.'

Ben gave her a quick wink and popped another roll into his mouth.

Conversation around her was strong with Saskia and Leonie dominating the debate on East Asian medical practices, but Kate couldn't concentrate. Her stomach churned and her mouth felt parched. After her initial glass of water, Leonie had forgotten she didn't drink alcohol.

She'd eyed the bottle of ginger ale Ben had brought with him.

'Would you like some?' he asked.

'Yes, please.' She watched him pour, his hand steady, calloused fingers contrasting with his soft grip around the thin crystal, and found her mouth less dry after all. 'Do you not drink?'

Ben shook his head as he topped up his own glass. 'Not alcohol at least.'

Ben pinged up another couple of points on her estimation board. 'So, Ben, what do you do?'

'I ride horses,' he replied.

Kate's estimation board trilled as a jackpot was reached. 'You do?'

'And you?'

Kate blushed unnecessarily. 'I also work with horses. I'm a groom, over at Aspen Valley Racing Stables.' For once, she wished she had some fabulously grand job that made people's eyebrows shoot up in admiration.

His eyes travelled back to Saskia who was lamenting the cruelty of whale hunting. 'Is your sister involved in horses?'

Kate stifled a sigh. *Another one bites the dust.* 'She's our racing secretary.'

Ben nodded in approval. 'How do you enjoy Aspen Valley? I've heard Jack can be a bit of a tyrant.'

'He's all right. He just doesn't suffer fools gladly. I've only five horses, which is fair.'

'He seems to go through secretaries quite regularly.'

'He married one of them,' Kate replied. 'I believe Pippa flatly refused to work for him and bed him at the same time.'

'And Saskia? Is she married?'

'God, no. Saskia's too much of a whirlwind to think about that.'

Ben nodded, a thoughtful look on his face.

Kate decided to surrender gracefully. This Ben de Jager seemed a nice sort. He might even be good for her sister.

During the lull before dessert, Kate decided she could take things no longer and excused herself to go to the bathroom. That sushi really wasn't sitting well with her. Dare she risk going to the loo? Her stomach gave a rumble like a stalling jumbo jet, signalling a imminent Code Brown, and her mind was made up for her.

A few minutes later and feeling much better, Kate looked around for some air freshener. A new queasiness filled her as it became apparent there wasn't any spray in the room. She flapped her hands to no avail and cringed. God, this was too embarrassing. Standing on tip toe, she tried to open the window. Her heart sank when the handle stuck fast.

'Please, no,' she breathed.

Bordering on panic, she struggled with the latch, jiggling it back and forth. With a clunk it jerked open, pulling Kate off balance. Nameless toiletry bottles tumbled out of the window and she winced at the sound of breaking glass on the patio deck below. The chill of the October air seeped into the room. She stood tense, unsure what to do next.

It was just her luck to get the trots at Leonie's dinner party. Leonie would never forget *or* forgive. On the bright side, she wouldn't have to attend any more dinner parties.

With no air freshener to hand, Kate chose the next best thing. She poured half a bottle of perfumed bath oils into the basin and filled it with hot water. She sighed with relief. The less than aromatic smell of her evacuations became overwhelmed by steamy clouds of lavender. She'd give it a couple more minutes.

Kate felt unnecessarily guilty returning to the party. Leonie was too busy dishing out a very exotic looking fruit salad to notice. It appeared Ben had taken advantage of the break between courses to swap places with Nicholas. Kate's heart sank a fathom. Then she noticed Leonie's glower at her disrupted table settings and almost forgave Ben for dumping her in preference of Saskia's company.

She slipped into her seat and Nicholas greeted her with a pleasant smile. She noticed Ben's place card had been tampered with and now read 'Benedick'.

'Is that a lavender perfume you're wearing?' he asked.

'Uh – yeah,' she said with a laugh an octave too high.

Nicholas misread her awkwardness. 'I apologise if you were expecting Ben for company.'

'No, I'm used to it,' she replied, gesturing to Ben and Saskia in deep conversation. 'Saskia has this effect on every man she meets.'

'No, no. You've got it wrong. I asked Ben if we could swap.'

Kate looked at him in surprise. 'Really?'

Nicholas looked bashful as he spooned through the kiwi fruit in his dessert bowl. 'Leonie will be disappointed, I know.' He sent her a mischievous grin. 'You don't mind, do you?'

Kate was too shocked to oppose him. 'No, not at all.' Afraid that this implied she was somehow insulting his brother, she added, 'I mean I was enjoying talking to Ben, but he was much more interested in talking about Saskia. And, well, so is Saskia, so this seating plan works much better.'

Nicholas laughed. 'I fear Saskia and I weren't quite on the same wavelength.' He looked at her in a way that made her feel she was the only one in the room and smiled. 'So, Kate, tell me. What does a lady such as yourself do to keep occupied? I think I heard you say earlier that you own racehorses?'

Kate hesitated and tried to recall when and to whom she'd told such a whopper.

'You told Ben you had five?' Nicholas prompted.

Kate twigged, and had a sudden reckless urge not to give the same old tired truth. 'That's right,' she said with a coy smile. 'I've five at Aspen Valley.' It wasn't a complete lie, after all. She spent so much time with them that they did feel like they belonged to her in a small way. Unofficially. In a non-financially draining way. Maybe.

Nicholas's face lit up. 'What a coincidence! We've just moved some of our lot to his yard.'

Kate began to have second thoughts about her imposture. 'Oh?'

'Well, they're my father's horses really. I'm his racing manager.'

Kate tried to work out which horses they owned, but Aspen Valley had too many new recruits to choose from. 'Do you race under de Jager or a partnership name?' she asked.

Nicholas frowned. 'God forbid, neither. Our horses are registered under my father, Bill Borden.'

'But Leonie said— I thought Ben— aren't you brothers?'

Nicholas's hazel eyes took on a steely sparkle. '*Half* brothers.'

Kate blushed at his clipped words. 'Sorry. I didn't mean to make assumptions.'

His expression softened. 'I should be the one apologising. Ben does ride our horses, so I guess it is kind of a Borden-de Jager partnership. It's my father's ambition to win with his two sons at his side, preferably at Cheltenham Festival.'

Kate immediately warmed to their father. 'Mine too. Cheltenham's just so...' She paused to think up the right word, to imagine what it would feel like to lead up a horse at the biggest jump racing festival in the calendar. 'It's where dreams come true.'

Nicholas smiled. 'You ever been?'

'Only as a spectator. You?'

Nicholas nodded. 'March's schedule is always planned to accommodate Cheltenham. Dad's been in the game for a long time. Never won any of the big championship races though.'

The dinner party soon began to wind down. The dishes had long since been dispatched to the kitchen, the table was littered with empty bottles of wine and sake and, thankfully, Kate's stomach hadn't objected to the dessert.

She was in mid-sentence when she felt a kick on her shin. Saskia gave a discreet jerk of her head and a meaningful look.

'I think I've just been given my cue to wrap things up,' Kate said to Nicholas.

'Oh.'

She was encouraged to see disappointment wash over his face. 'But I've really enjoyed this evening.' She hesitated then found the courage to be bolder. 'The latter part especially.'

Nicholas's smile broadened. 'Me too.' He fiddled with his napkin and cleared his throat again. 'I really mean that. Can I – I mean if you're okay with it – can I see you again sometime? Maybe we could do this again?'

Kate felt a warm rush of blood in her belly and she glanced over to see if Saskia was listening. 'Just the two of us?'

'Just the two of us. I'd like to suggest Saturday, but we're racing at Wetherby that day. How about next week?'

Kate narrowed her eyes. 'Who do you have running at Wetherby?'

'A couple of potential Festival horses as it happens. The Whistler in the Charlie Hall, and another in one of the undercard races.'

Kate began to feel ill again. 'Called?'

Nicholas gave her a puzzled look. 'Goodness, you really are into your racing. D'Artagnan's his name. I don't suppose you'll be there as well?'

Kate gave a half-smile half-grimace. 'I might.'

3

KATE RAN A cloth over d'Artagnan's clipped grey coat and down his wooly legs.

'I wonder if we're going to see your daddy,' she said, smoothing out his forelock with fingers that trembled. 'You've got to do your best, you hear? You want to make a good first impression.'

D'Artagnan butted her shoulder with his nose then tried to eat her cap. For his debut appearance on a British racecourse, the French import was remarkably laidback.

Kate took heart from his attitude. 'That's the only way we're gonna book our ticket to Cheltenham. Okay?'

From the confines of the stable, Wetherby Racecourse seemed a long way away. The winner of the last handicap hurdle was announced over the tanoy, fading in and out as the autumn breeze changed direction. Much closer was the deep muffled voice of her boss, Jack Carmichael, in the neighbouring stable talking with The Whistler's lass.

Kate wetted a brush in the water bucket and tried to smooth down her charge's wayward mane. In her eagerness to get d'Artagnan to his show-stopping best, she'd pulled his mane too short and now it stuck up like an eighties punk rocker's.

They both flinched at the sound of her mobile phone ringing. Kate dropped the brush and fumbled through her pockets to silence it. She tutted when she saw the caller ID.

'Mum, I'm working,' she hissed into the phone.

'Katie, you're always working. Don't you get weekends off like normal people?'

'Not when one of my horses is running. What is it?'

'The heating's not working and the fridge is defrosting itself.'

Kate closed her eyes and tried not to sigh so her mother would hear. 'Have you paid your gas and electricity bill?'

'Of course,' replied her mother without pausing to think.

'Are you sure?'

'Well, aren't they supposed to send you a final reminder before they cut you off?'

From the background came her brother's bored voice. 'They already did.'

Kate frowned. 'Is that Xander? Why isn't he at football practice?'

'Katieeee,' said her mother. 'Stop asking questions. What do I do about the fridge?'

Kate became aware of the Aspen Valley trainer's voice growing louder as he moved outside The Whistler's box. At the same time she realised she hadn't patterned d'Artagnan's rump yet and snatched up a stencil from her tack bag.

'Put newspapers down on the floor and ring your gas supplier,' she whispered. 'I've got to go—'

'But it's the weekend. They probably won't turn us back on until Monday.'

'Buy some candles then and get a takeaway. I've got to go. Bye.' She cut the call without waiting for a reply and stuffed her phone back in her pocket just as Jack arrived at the stable door with d'Artagnan's tack.

'Everything okay?' he asked as he let himself in.

Kate concentrated on brushing diamonds onto d'Artagnan's quarters. 'Yeah, just about done...'

'Good, good. Kate, this is d'Artagnan's owner, Mr Borden.'

Kate's heart skipped a beat. Please let it be Mr Borden, Snr, she prayed. Feeling foolish, she turned back to the door. Damn, maybe she should go to church more often.

Nicholas jerked back in surprise and Kate blushed.

'Hello again,' she said.

'You two know each other already?' said Jack.

It took Nicholas a moment to regather his composure. 'Er – yes, kind of. I think. He-hello, Kate.'

'Hi.' Kate's cheeks burned, and keeping her eyes averted, she tossed the stencil back into the bag and readjusted d'Artagnan's noseband. While Jack secured his saddle, the grey rested his chin on Kate's shoulder, sending gusty sighs down her ear canal.

Nicholas remained in the doorway, not speaking, but not moving away either. Kate gave him an apologetic smile. Poor man, she couldn't blame him for looking a little dazed.

Nicholas's gaze flickered downwards from her eyes, paused on her chest, then dropped to her feet. His cheeks pinked and he cleared his throat.

Nicholas was obviously a boob man.

'You've – er – got something on your – um...' Still staring at her feet, he gestured to her left breast.

Kate looked down to see a hay and grass-seasoned string of drool making its slow descent down her red Aspen Valley jacket, courtesy of d'Artagnan.

'Oh!' Kate gave a high-pitched laugh of embarrassment that startled d'Artagnan and provoked a dark look from Jack. She wiped her jacket clean with a cloth and just to be sure, mopped d'Artagnan's lips as well.

D'Artagnan tried to eat the cloth.

'Anyway, I should probably let you get on,' Nicholas said, still addressing her feet. 'My father will be wondering where I am.'

Saddled and booted, d'Artagnan jogged around the parade ring. He snorted with each breath and leaned in on Kate. Glad of the distraction, Kate pushed back, digging her elbow into his shoulder to steady him. What had she been thinking? She should have fessed up the other evening when she'd realised the inevitable. But it'd been so long since she'd last been asked out on a date. Was it so wrong to want to savour the moment? No, but it did now make her feel rather pathetic.

Jack boosted d'Artagnan's jockey into the saddle and the horse's jog became a *passage* any dressage rider would be impressed by.

'Hi.'

Kate looked back at Ben de Jager smiling down at her, giving her that same feeling one got when discovering an extra cube of chocolate in the wrapper.

'I hear someone's been telling porkies,' he said.

Kate turned the same shade as her cap and jacket and resumed her tug of war with d'Artagnan. 'More of a loss in translation.'

'Aha.' He sounded less than convinced. 'How's this punk been behaving?'

Kate let out a grateful sigh for the change in subject. 'A bit flighty now. Not sure if it's a good thing or a bad thing though. This is our first outing together.'

'Mine too,' he said. 'How's Saskia doing?'

Well, at least he'd asked about d'Artagnan first.

'A bit flighty,' she said with a dry smile. 'Not sure if it's a good thing or a bad thing.'

They followed the string of horses out onto the woodchip chute that ran alongside the home straight. D'Artagnan cantered on the spot.

'Look after my boy, okay?' she said, unclipping the lead rope.

'You talking to me or d'Artagnan?' asked Ben, a devilish twinkle in his eyes. 'Wish us luck.'

D'Artagnan gave a small rear and took off with a propulsive fart.

'Good luck,' Kate said to their departing figures.

Frankie, fellow Aspen Valley stable lass, was waiting for her by the rail and together they walked back to the parade ring where they could watch the race on the big screen. Kate liked Frankie. Small, blonde and freckled, she was as tough as any lad, and unassuming, despite recently marrying racing's hottest property, jockey, Rhys Bradford. They were also both taking part in Helensvale Am Dram's production of *Cinderella* that Christmas.

'You had a bet?' Kate asked.

'Nah. You?'

Kate shook her head and watched the horses cantering down to the start on the big screen. D'Artagnan's grey colouring stuck out amongst the more rustic-coloured horses.

'Probably just as well,' Frankie said.

'You never know. D'Artagnan might be the next Desert Orchid.'

Frankie laughed. 'Not if his jockey is anything to go by. What do you make of him?'

'He seems nice enough. And cute. Haven't seen him ride before though.'

'He used to be pretty good. Won the amateurs' title a few years back.'

Kate stared at her. 'Seriously? I've never heard of him.'

'Unsurprising. He disappeared from the scene as quick as he appeared. Just like that.' Frankie snapped her fingers. 'The only reason I've heard of him is because he and my brother were fighting out the title. Seth called him a plum because his daddy bought all the certainties for him to ride.'

'You think d'Artagnan's better than twelve-to-one then?' Kate said. 'Maybe I should nip over and put a fiver on.'

'I wouldn't. Since this Ben de Jager's come back, he's barely ridden a winner. Rhys reckons he goes out of his way to ride no-hopers. Some sort of rebellion against his father, sounds like. That's why Rhys is on The Whistler in the Charlie Hall. He's odds-on to win.' Frankie became distracted as the screen showed the horses lining up behind the tape. 'Here we go.'

Kate's attention wavered. D'Artagnan broke the line and caused a false start. Ben got a bollocking from the starter once they'd all returned and the tape had been redrawn across the course.

She bit her lip. From the brief moments she'd had with Ben de Jager, he hadn't come across as a trust fund baby or a rebel. Maybe he'd just lost the knack, she wondered. Even so, one didn't go from being champion amateur to a fumbling idiot.

The horses approached the start once more in a semi-orderly group and the starter released the tape. Kate's heart quickened with the thunder of the cavalry charge. Above her, the blare of the commentator's call ricocheted off the grandstand.

'Looks like Lyrical Lord is going to take them along, leads by two lengths to Faire le Pont in second on the inside of Good Will Hunting, running keen. Slalom Flyer tracks those with Life of Brian on his outside and d'Artagnan scrapes the paint off the rail in sixth...'

Kate gripped her lead rope as the field approached the first fence. A hiss of birch and all contenders were safely over. Against the multi-toned green of the racecourse's rural backdrop, d'Artagnan's grey figure was the first to catch the eye. Over the remaining four jumps in the backstretch, the twelve horses streamed over, pace steady, jumping accurate. Kate knocked her knuckles together. So far, so good. Ben was keeping d'Artagnan tucked in and the grey had settled in behind the others.

Lyrical Lord showed the way around Wetherby's sharp home turn, increasing his lead to four lengths. The crowd cheered the horses over the open ditch in front of the stands. D'Artagnan spring-heeled the jump and landed alongside Slalom Flyer.

'Over the eighth and favourite Faire le Pont gets in a little close to that one,' drawled the commentator. 'All the others are safely over as Good Will Hunting moves up to share the lead with Lyrical Lord. Next is a plain fence – d'Artagnan had to reach for that one, loses a length. They pass the post and head out for their final circuit; Lyrical Lord and Good Will Hunting heading affairs to Faire le Pont, Life of Brian, Slalom Flyer, d'Artagnan, and Sweet Medici brings up the rear as they make the turn into the backstretch.'

Kate scrutinised her horse's progress. Ben stood motionless in his stirrups and, meeting the tenth fence, d'Artagnan jumped out of his hands in a bold arc. Kate's breast swelled with pride. What a magnificent jump that was! Seven from home and Faire le Pont began to pile on the pressure. Good Will Hunting's challenge was short-lived and he was soon passed by the favourite. The pace increased, and legs making their seasonal debut began to feel the strain. Life of Brian was the first to wave the white flag and an awkward jump, five out, put paid to his claims.

Kate chewed her lower lip and beat a rhythm with her heel. She hadn't had a winner for eighteen months. If Ben and d'Artagnan kept going the way they were, that statistic could change. She dared to hope.

Faire le Pont took the lead and, heading for the home turn, began to turn the screw. Ben kept d'Artagnan on the inside, saving ground, reducing drag by tracking Lyrical Lord. But Kate could see Lyrical Lord tiring. He scrambled over the fourth last and Kate's gaze darted to the next open ditch.

'Take him wide, Ben,' she breathed. 'Don't risk it.'

Telepathy didn't appear to be Ben's forte and he kept d'Artagnan snug behind his emptying rival. Kate's blood turned icy as a thought occurred to her – he wouldn't lose on purpose, would he?

Over the third last and Faire le Pont was pushed into a long stretch over the open ditch. In second, Lyrical Lord wobbled. D'Artagnan, still on bridle, pegged his every stride.

'Take him wide!' yelled Kate. Her words were lost in the roar of the crowd. She whipped the air with her tangled lead rope. 'Take him wide, Ben! Goddammit!'

Lyrical Lord got in close to the open ditch and parted the birch with a hefty thump. D'Artagnan took off only a stride behind. The fence dragged Lyrical Lord's impetus from him and he almost slowed to a trot.

Kate twisted her body sideways, willing Ben to do the same. Faire le Pont was still within striking distance. They still had a chance, if only Ben would allow it.

D'Artagnan landed and bumped into Lyrical Lord's backside. Kate swore and turned away. She was going to give Ben such a bollocking when he got back, owner's son or no owner's son. The crowds continued to cheer and with her back to the race, Kate glowered up at them.

'Kate! Kate! You might want to see this!' shouted Frankie, wrenching her round.

D'Artagnan was clear of Lyrical Lord, thundering in pursuit of Faire le Pont like a warhorse charging into battle. Faire le Pont rose over the final fence looking petite by comparison. The bulk of d'Artagnan loomed on his outside, broad dappled shoulders juddering as his tremendous stride ate up the ground.

Kate's adrenalin went galactic. 'Go on, d'Artagnan!' she screamed. 'Go on, my boy!'

Ben rocked in his saddle, fanning his whip alongside d'Artagnan's giant body. His presence seemed to intimidate the slighter-built favourite and six strides from the post, d'Artagnan put his head in front. Kate hollered until her lungs hurt. She punched the air and did Bojangle kicks as she ran to fetch her winner.

In the winner's enclosure, Ben accepted his father's hearty backslaps as he unsaddled. Kate wrestled with a buzzy d'Artagnan. Out of the corner of her eye, she noticed Ben and Nicholas exchange a decidedly curt nod. Ben slipped the saddle off d'Artagnan's slick back and was herded into line next to Kate for the winning photograph. Formalities over, he stole a peck on her cheek.

'Well done,' he said with a playful wink. He walked away to be weighed in before she could reply.

Kate felt like her stomach had been switched to zero gravity. D'Artagnan brought things back into perspective by stamping on her foot. With a wince, she pushed him off and returned to her duties. She pulled a rug over his steaming back and noticed Nicholas glowering at Ben's departure.

'Congratulations,' she said.

Nicholas looked at her, as if noticing her for the first time, and beamed. 'Thank you. You too. You deserve the credit.' He cleared his throat and stepped closer to speak privately. 'You know I should be cross that you lied, don't you?' he said.

Kate squirmed in her boots. 'I'm sorry. I guess I wanted you to think I led an exciting life. Being a lass is far from glamourous.'

'But I do find you exciting.' He sent another fleeting glance in Ben's direction and lifted his chin. 'Will you still have dinner with me next week?'

Kate stared at him. D'Artagnan head-butted her and knocked her off-balance. 'You sure?'

'Very sure,' he replied, keeping a wary eye on a fretful d'Artagnan.

'Great! I mean, yes, please.'

4

SITTING OPPOSITE NICHOLAS in Helensvale's local pub-restaurant, The Golden Miller, the following Saturday, Kate could hardly breathe. The saucy underwear that Saskia had bullied her into buying (not that anyone other than Kate was going to see it tonight) cut into her ribcage.

Nicholas smiled at her from across the board game-sized table. 'You're looking very lovely tonight,' he said.

'Um, thanks. So are you.' Well, sleeveless cardigans were never going to make her weak at the knees, but it made Nicholas look homey. Homey wasn't a bad thing. Kate, on the other hand, felt terribly sirenesque in her dusky pink Grecian top. Saskia had insisted her boobs were her best asset and she should use them to maximum effect.

Kate tried to take a deep breath. God only knew how she was going to breathe after their meal.

'How's work?' Nicholas asked.

'Okay, thanks. D'Artagnan and The Whistler both came out of their races fine.' She paused as Nicholas nodded amicably. 'But you probably know that already.'

'Jack did mention it in his report, but it's good to hear it from someone even closer to the ground, so to speak.'

'Was your father pleased with d'Artagnan's win?'

'Sure. Mind you, it wasn't all that strong a race.'

Nicholas's indifference punctured the bubble Kate'd been floating on all week, and she bit her lip. 'Were you very disappointed with The Whistler?'

Nicholas shrugged. 'We know he's better than that. It was the slow pace that scuppered him. Third place is still pretty good for a seasonal debut though, in that kind of company.'

Joey, the ponytailed barman, sauntered over with two menus and their drinks as conversation lagged. Kate frowned down at the list and daren't look up.

Dating never used to be this tricky, did it? She was too out of practice.

'What are you going to have?' Nicholas asked.

'The broccoli and cheese on ciabatta, I think.' It sounded safe even if a little more adventurous than her usual diet.

'And for mains?'

Kate panicked. Was he expecting to have a full blown three course meal? 'I'll just have that for mains, thanks,' she replied.

Nicholas grinned. 'I like your style. Save room for a bigger dessert, right?'

Kate gave a weak laugh. Jack Carmichael would not be a happy camper if she pitched up to exercise his horses ten pounds overweight. Joey returned to take their orders and their menus and Kate was left to fend for herself again. Nicholas gave her an encouraging smile.

'So how many horses do you have to look after?'

'Five. D'Artagnan's by far my best.' She hesitated, wondering if she sounded too much of an ass-kisser.

Nicholas chuckled. 'Doesn't say much for the rest of your lot. Who looks after The Whistler?'

Kate tried hard not to take offence. He didn't understand, after all. 'Frankie Bradford.'

'Relation to Rhys?'

'His wife. She's got a great stable of horses. The Whistler and Dust Storm, and then, of course, Ta' Qali. You'll have heard of him.'

'I'd say everyone's heard of him after last season,' said Nicholas. 'If he wins at Cheltenham this year, Hollywood will probably give him his own star on the Walk of Fame.'

Kate couldn't help a sigh of envy escaping.

Nicholas raised an eyebrow and tried to catch her eye. 'Why so sad, Batman?'

Kate laughed at herself. 'I'm not sad. I've just always dreamt of taking a horse to Cheltenham. And there Frankie is with two major contenders. Maybe even three, if The Whistler is as good as everyone thinks he is.'

'Well, I don't know if The Whistler is Cheltenham material yet, but I could have a word with Jack if you like? Maybe you and Frankie could swap horses.'

'Oh, no.' Kate was mortified. 'No, I couldn't do that. That would just be so low.'

Nicholas shrugged. 'Okay. Just say the word if you change your mind.'

Dilys Jones, wife of the pub landlord, delivered their food to them and stopped for a chat. She was no stranger to Aspen Valley Stables. With her Welsh foghorn voice, her visits never went unnoticed. She was, of course, one of ten joint owners of Ta' Qali, and, added to their thrilling previous season, the syndicate's reality show was tipped for a television award nomination. Dilys was close to delirium at the prospect of walking the red carpet and receiving a BAFTA from Benedict Cumberbatch.

'She's quite the character, isn't she?' Nicholas said after Dilys finally left. He scooped a forkful of lamb shank into his mouth, still smiling.

'She's a nightmare at the races apparently. Jack won't allow her near Ta' Qali beforehand because she upsets him.'

Nicholas snorted. 'Poor Jack.'

'Having said that, it's nice to have owners who are enthusiastic.'

'You'll like my father then. He eats, sleeps and breathes jump racing. All sport, really.'

'Is he how you and Ben got involved in racing?'

'Me, yes. Dad and I work well together. I manage one of his firms in Bristol.'

'Sounds serious work,' said Kate, thinking she didn't know the first thing about investment banking.

'It's not for the faint-hearted. I mean, I might be the boss's son, but one still has to be on the ball. There's a lot of responsibility involved in investing other people's life savings.'

Kate recognised the slight defensiveness in his tone. 'It can't be easy running an investment firm and managing his racing.'

Nicholas cut through his meat and his knife screeched against the plate. 'It's as close to a sportsman as I'll ever get.'

Kate stopped chewing. So maybe that was the cause of the animosity between him and Ben, rather than Ben just being the better looking one. 'How many horses does your dad own?'

Nicholas shrugged and concentrated on gathering the last scraps of food on his plate. 'More than he needs, less than he used to have.'

Putting her knife and fork together, Kate tried to imagine what life would be like owning more horses than could be counted. To her surprise, she wasn't filled with envy. Owning that many horses she'd never get to know them as individuals and it was that experience that kept her in the game. It was the small things, like the way d'Artagnan would dunk his deflated football into his water bucket then spring back in mock surprise when he was splashed.

The thought made her smile and she heaved as big a sigh as her bra would allow. She didn't need hundreds of horses. All she needed was d'Artagnan.

Her thoughts were interrupted by a dull pop and suddenly the vicelike pressure on her ribcage lessened.

Horrors! Kate froze, not daring to breathe.

'Of course Ben doesn't help matters,' continued a blissfully unaware Nicholas. 'Dad wouldn't have half so many horses if Ben didn't ride.'

Kate tried to keep a straight face. 'Really? Mmm. I'm just going to pop to the loo.'

As she went to stand up though, Dilys reappeared carrying two desserts.

'You sit yourself right back down,' their patron blasted. Kate sat. 'I've two special treats for two special customers.'

Kate looked down at her bowl of wafer biscuit and hot caramel drizzled over three scoops of ice cream. 'I've just got to go to the Ladies,' she said.

'Nonsense!' said Dilys. 'This will all be melted if you leave it.'

Kate could feel her left boob slipping from its cup. 'But—'

Nicholas was already tucking into his. 'This is delicious, Dilys. Try it, Kate.'

Dilys beamed and waited expectantly for Kate to sample the dessert. 'I made it especially.'

With each breath she took, Kate could feel gravity pulling on her chest, but she couldn't escape the melting ice cream. She scooped up a spoonful of dessert and nodded in exaggerated appreciation.

'Mmm.'

Her sudden movement unleashed her left boob's bid for freedom. She daren't look down. Instead she looked at Nicholas, who had suddenly gone pinker than her top. He, in turn looked down at his plate. The top-tiered scoop of his ice cream tumbled off its place and Nicholas's ears turned scarlet.

'Excuse me,' Kate gasped and made a dash for the loo.

Saskia screamed with laughter throughout Kate's story. 'Was it broken or did it just come undone?'

'It was broken.'

'Oh my God. What did you do?'

Kate regarded Saskia's enrapt expression. If she'd thought she'd get any sympathy from her sister, she was mistaken. Sat on the sofa in their living room and clutching a hot toddy the morning after, Saskia had never looked less sympathetic.

'I used a safety pin to piece it back together.'

'Lucky you had one. What did Nicholas say?'

'Nothing. I think he thought I had a bodily malfunction rather than a wardrobe one.'

Saskia screamed with glee. 'That's even worse.'

'Tell me about it. Apparently, I managed to upset Dilys as well.'

'Is that what Nicholas said? What an arse. It's not like you could have helped it.'

'No, he didn't say it out loud,' Kate was quick to defend her date. 'He's a lot more subtle than that. But I could still tell.'

'Did you kiss him?'

'No.'

'Didn't he make a move?'

'No, Saskia!' Kate laughed. 'My bathroom debacle probably put him off.'

'What a turd,' said Saskia supportively. 'Are you going to see him again?'

Kate shrugged, remembering how she and Nicholas had stood on the pavement outside the pub and said their goodbyes. He'd planted a quick kiss on her cheek and bade her goodnight. 'Probably not. Anyway, what would he want with a girl like me? He's so rich, he could have any girl he wants in the West Country.'

'Not me,' Saskia said, drawing her knees up and blowing on her drink. 'I'm saving myself.'

Kate arched an eyebrow at her sister. 'Who's the lucky guy?'

'Jack.'

'Jack?'

'Yes. Jack Carmichael.'

Kate's eyes widened. 'Saskia, no!' she said, appalled.

'What's wrong with that?'

'Well, he's married for a start.'

'Exactly. And who is he married to?'

'Pippa.'

'Who used to be his secretary. He's obviously got a thing for girls in the office.'

'No, no, Saskia. Don't. You'll end up losing your job and making a fool of yourself.'

'No, I won't. Jack's just asking to be seduced. I can tell.'

'Has he said as much?'

Saskia pulled a reluctant face. 'Well, no, but he's never particularly forthcoming in the verbal department. I bet he's a tiger in the sack.'

'Saskia! Stop!' Kate covered her ears, not sure whether to laugh or cry. 'Please don't do anything silly. Jack might've married his secretary, but now they've got a daughter together. You don't want to split up a family, do you?'

'She's only a baby. It'd be much easier now than if she was older.'

Kate realised Saskia was being serious and she raised a finger at her younger sibling. 'Don't even try, do you hear? Everyone at the yard worships Pippa. If you managed to seduce Jack and take her place at Aspen Valley, there'd be a mutiny.'

Saskia groaned and put her drink down and got up. Even hungover and wearing Peppa Pig pyjamas, she still looked gorgeous. Kate's confidence in Jack's loyalty to his wife wavered.

'Why do you want to seduce Jack, anyway?' she asked.

Saskia flicked through their DVD shelf and shrugged. 'He's hot, he's successful, and he's got to be rich.'

The doorbell rang and Saskia, already on her feet, went to answer it. 'Shit!' she hissed. She leapt back from the door and needlessly hid behind the wall.

'Who is it?'

Saskia looked at her with panicked eyes. 'You have to talk to him. Tell him I'm not here!'

'Who?'

'Shhh!' Saskia looked around for an escape. There was none. 'Shit. Don't let him stay long.'

The doorbell rang again. Saskia, fleet on her glitter-painted toes, dashed into the corridor leading to the bedrooms.

Kate threw aside her cushion and got up. 'Saskia, for goodness' sake, who—' She stood on tiptoe to see through the spyglass. The fish-eye distorted image of Ben de Jager greeted her from the landing.

5

'BEN! HI,' KATE said, opening the door. 'Come on in.'
Ben shuffled his hands in his bomber jacket pockets and took a hesitant step forward. 'Hi, Kate. Er – is Saskia home?'

Kate heard the click of Saskia's bedroom door closing. 'No, sorry.'

Ben's face fell. 'Oh. I probably should have called ahead, but she said to pop round whenever, and I was just passing, so...'

Oh, she did, did she? Kate had a mind to blow her sister's cover. But no, she couldn't hurt Ben like that. There was one way she could make Saskia pay though.

'Why don't you come in, anyway? Have a cup of tea. I wouldn't want you to have made a wasted journey.'

'Well, I was just passing—'

'Nonsense!' Kate ushered him in and closed the front door.

'Are you sure? Do you have company? I thought I heard voices.'

'Be careful who you tell that to,' she replied.

Ben made a small attempt to laugh at her joke and Kate cleared her throat.

'Television,' she explained. 'Now, tea or coffee?'

Ben followed her through into the narrow kitchen. There really wasn't much room for one person, let alone two, one with broad shoulders, the other with big boobs. They shuffled around each other like teens in a dance hall as Kate filled the kettle and found two unchipped mugs.

'Is Saskia likely to be back soon?' asked Ben.

'Maybe.' Kate kept her eyes on the tea-making. Saskia was going to kill her for this. 'Might be worth waiting around to see.'

Ben shed his jacket, showing off a pair of mesmerizingly toned arms. Saskia would change her tune when she saw them. Realising what she was doing, Kate blushed.

'Do you take milk? Sugar? Do you like it added before or after the hot water? I don't mind, but I know some people prefer it a certain way.'

Ben shook his head. 'As it comes. Three sugars. Hey, how does Moses make his tea?'

'Pardon?'

'Hebrews it.'

Kate laughed shrilly, more from nerves than at the joke.

Drinks prepared, they returned to the lounge. Ben took his place on the threadbare sofa, his back to the front door and corridor. Kate sat in her usual shabby armchair and only then noticed Saskia's half-drunk hot toddy on the coffee table. Lord, she hoped Ben wouldn't notice it. How was she to explain the whisky hangover cure when he must know she didn't touch alcohol? She needed to distract him, but oh! what to say?

'Weather's been good lately, hasn't it?' she settled on.

Ben nodded. 'If you ignore the ten mils of rain we had last night.'

'Ah, yes. Still, better that it rains at night than when I'm at work.'

'The perils of working with horses,' said Ben with a grin.

'Yes, especially grey horses. I put d'Artagnan and the others out the other day and thought he'd escaped when I went to bring them back in. Not a grey horse in sight. The blighter had given himself such a mud bath, even his eyelashes were caked.'

'Probably getting himself ready for Glastonbury.'

Kate giggled. 'I wish he wouldn't. It's not much fun getting him clean. And his tail stays yellow no matter how often I wash it.'

'I know the feeling,' Ben said with a small laugh.

Kate regarded him curiously. Did he know the feeling? Truly? As far as she was aware, millionaires' sons usually got somebody else to do the dirty work. She decided not to challenge him. Instead, she blew on her tea and smiled. 'Oh.'

'No, really, I do,' Ben insisted. 'I have a racehorse rehab stable – it's only small. We've got six in right now – well, nine if you include the three in livery – but that's plenty mud to clean off.'

Kate almost dropped her drink. 'A racehorse rehab stable?'

'Yes. Or a retraining stable, whichever name you prefer. We're just a small outfit, but every little helps.'

'Gosh, that sounds wonderful. What do you retrain them for? Eventing? Dressage?'

Ben looked much more at ease than he had just a few moments ago, and he beamed at Kate's genuine interest. 'Depends on the horse. Some just want a quiet life hacking. Others miss the pizzazz of the racecourse, so need something a bit more competitive.'

Kate thought of all the horses she'd ridden in her career. So many personalities, yet they were all trained for the same discipline. 'It must be fun working out what suits which.'

Her mobile phone bleeped on the table and she reached for it. There was a message from Saskia.

What are you doing? Get rid of him!

'I'm being terribly rude,' said Ben. 'I didn't ask if I was keeping you from your plans. I can go—'

'No, no. That was just Saskia.'

Ben looked hopeful and Kate's annoyance at her sister stepped up a level. How dare Saskia disappoint him like this?

'She's on her way home. Shouldn't be long.'

Twenty minutes later, Ben was still ensconced in conversation with Kate. She had almost forgotten the purpose of keeping him in the flat when a movement in the corridor caught her eye.

Saskia tip-toed out, and safe from Ben's view, gestured at Kate to wrap things up.

'Would you like another tea?' Kate asked.

'Lovely. Let me,' said Ben, rising to his feet.

Saskia fled back to her bedroom.

With fresh tea brewed, Ben settled back down on the sofa to continue their conversation. 'You must come out and see the place. Like I said, it's not huge, but there's plenty to do. Horses to be schooled, paddocks to be harrowed.'

Kate brightened. 'You'd let me ride?'

'Of course,' he replied, as if this was a given. 'You do ride, presumably?'

'Yes, but I don't know much about dressage and stuff. I've only ever ridden racehorses.' The first time Kate had sat on a horse had been her first day at the Racing School in Newmarket nine years before.

Ben winked at her. 'If you can school d'Artagnan over fences at Aspen Valley, you're more than qualified to ride my lot.'

Saskia reappeared behind him. With her tongue cinched between her teeth, she held her shoes aloft and crept like a cartoon cat burglar towards the front door.

'Does Saskia ride?' Ben asked, making Saskia freeze.

Kate blinked, trying not to focus on Saskia behind the sofa. 'Horses? No.' *Men, yes.*

'That's a pity. She could've come to help as well.'

Saskia stuck her finger in her mouth and pretended to gag. Ben looked at his watch and frowned.

'Where is she? You must have got that text half an hour ago. I really shouldn't keep you any longer.' He began to make motions of departure.

Saskia was still a few feet away from the door. Kate met her stare of panic. Even if she got to the door, he would certainly hear it opening and closing.

'What sort of music do you like?' Kate blurted. 'You really must hear this girl I found the other week.' She fumbled for the power button on the hi-fi on the coffee table.

'I really should be going,' said Ben. 'I've disturbed you long enough.' He collected both their empty mugs and frowned at Saskia's abandoned hot toddy before picking that up as well.

Kate's ears burned. Out of the corner of her eye, she saw Saskia gingerly turning the door handle.

'Just listen to this. She's got a fabulous voice. Such soul.' Kate didn't even know what CD was in the player. She pressed Play and hoped for the best. The introduction to 'Roar' bounced around the room.

'Katy Perry?' said Ben dubiously.

Kate gave an over-bright smile and nodded. 'Such soul, don't you think?'

'Um... Well—'

Oh, God, she was never going to live this down.

'Look, I appreciate you accommodating me like this, but I really must get moving. Will you tell Saskia I called round?' He stood up with the mugs in his hands and turned just as Saskia was backing out of the door.

Kate held her breath.

Ben's face broke into a wide lopsided smile. 'Saskia! You're back!'

Saskia froze in her cat burglar hunch then assumed a dazzling smile. 'Ben! What a surprise!' she said, opening the door wide.

Ben strode over to her, but, with his hands full of mugs, hesitated from giving her a hug. Saskia leaned forward, placing a hand on one broad shoulder, and kissed him on the cheek. 'How lovely to see you. Have you been waiting long?'

'No, no. Just a few minutes.'

Saskia shot Kate a venomous look before resuming her charmed facade. Katy Perry roared through her chorus of champions and tigers. Ben's brow creased at the sight of Saskia's shoes in her hand.

'I prefer to take them off before coming inside,' Saskia said.

'Oh, yes. Sorry,' Ben muttered, glancing down at his CAT boots.

Saskia nodded to the mugs he held. 'Were you leaving?'

'Well... I was, but now you're here—'

'Don't let me stop you.' Saskia darted over to the sofa to retrieve Ben's jacket and held it out to him. 'I'm up to here with Sunday chores.'

This time it was Kate's turn to shoot her daggers.

'Oh,' said Ben. 'Yes, of course you are. How silly of me. I must also get on.' He turned to Kate and clumsily exchanged finger hooks with her. Saskia's hot toddy sloshed onto the carpet. 'I'm so sorry.'

Kate's heart went out to him and she gave him a warm smile. 'The carpet's a mess as it is.'

Ben looked grateful. He bunched his jacket in his hands and smacked his lips together. 'Right. Well, thanks. I'll see you both soon, no doubt?'

Kate nodded. 'D'Artagnan's already bouncing about looking for fences to jump, so Jack will probably have him on course pretty soon.'

Ben backed out of the flat, not quite able to look Saskia in the eye. 'Splendid. See you then.'

With the door closed, Kate and Saskia glared at each other.

'What the hell are you doing?' Kate demanded.

'What am I doing? What the hell were you doing? I had to sit in my bedroom for an hour while you two babbled on about bloody racehorse rehab. I was dying for the loo.'

'It serves you right. Why did you invite him round if you didn't want to see him?'

'I didn't know he was really going to pitch up, did I? Who does that, for goodness' sake?'

'And then to send him out like that,' said Kate, warming to her task. 'That was mean, Saskia.'

Saskia gave her a sour look. 'Oh, bugger off. You're not my mother,' and flounced back to her bedroom.

6

A COLD SPELL the following week saw the last of the autumn leaves fall. Come Wednesday, Kate was glad to get into the sweet, musty warmth of d'Artagnan's stable to muck out and saddle up. The big grey greeted her with his customary nose-butt and treated her to a silent but violent outlet of gas when she walked around him to unhook his rug.

'What a charmer,' she drawled, wrinkling her nose.

D'Artagnan turned his head to look behind at her and appeared to smirk.

'Watch it, sunshine, or I'll tell on you. I'm seeing your daddy tonight,' said Kate, brandishing a body brush at him.

D'Artagnan tried to eat the brush.

Nicholas had called on Monday and suggested they dine in Bristol tonight. Apart from the fact she didn't know what she was going to wear (how was one supposed to look sexy when the temperature outside was close to freezing?), she was looking forward to it. It couldn't be worse than the last date.

An hour later, as dawn crept over the hillside, Kate guided d'Artagnan high-stepping onto the path to the Gallops. In a neighbouring paddock a flock of geese had taken a respite from their migration. D'Artagnan watched with interest, ignoring Kate's request to circle at the foot of the hill.

'Kate, come on!' yelled Frankie, waiting astride Bold Phoenix.

Kate sawed on d'Artagnan's right rein and bounced her heels off his ribs. D'Artagnan flicked an ear then, with a snort, deigned to give his attention back to his rider.

Bold Phoenix fretted to follow the pair of horses setting off ahead. He pawed the ground in anticipation and snatched at the reins.

'Oy, come on,' Kate muttered to her horse. 'Where's your head this morning?'

Bold Phoenix gave a half-rear.

'We're off,' said Frankie, unable to hold him any longer.

With a lead, d'Artagnan showed a little more enthusiasm, and strode out in a steady rhythm. The frigid wind burnt Kate's cheeks as she cajoled him for more speed. D'Artagnan wouldn't be rushed though, and he completed the workout without breaking a sweat.

Maybe it was the heavy going. Maybe he still hadn't recovered from his race. Maybe he was just having an off-colour day. All the possibilities ran through her head as she and Frankie walked back down the hill and past Jack's Land Rover parked at halfway.

Jack waited for them, hands tucked deep in his pockets as he leaned against the vehicle, collar rucked up around his neck.

Kate could see where Saskia was coming from. Anyone who didn't find Jack ruggedly attractive needed a CT scan, but that wasn't excuse enough to try split him up from his family.

'Did that feel as bad as it looked?' he asked.

Kate nodded. 'He just felt lethargic the whole way, even from the get go.'

Jack chewed his lip as he studied d'Artagnan snorting dragon plumes of fog from his nostrils. 'It's probably nothing. Just give him a check over before you put him on the walker. Take his temperature.'

'Sure. I think he's just having one of those days.'

Jack pushed himself away from the car. 'Can't afford to have many of those if he's going to Cheltenham,' he muttered as he opened the door.

Kate pulled d'Artagnan to a halt. The wind, whistling in her ears, must have distorted his words. 'What did you say?'

Seeing Kate's look of shock, Jack's customary frown softened and he gave a half-smile. 'I said he'd better get his act together if he's going to join The Whistler in the Gold Cup.'

Later that evening, Kate practically ran from her car to the entrance of Lo Russo Italian Restaurant on Bristol Harbour promenade. Nicholas was relaxing on a leather couch in the soft-lit lounge, gazing out of the window. Kate couldn't contain her elation and hugged him tight before he'd even managed to stand.

'Thank you,' she whispered in his ear. 'Thank you so much.'

Nicholas laughed and disentangled himself. 'I'm guessing Jack has already told you then.'

Her eyes filled with tears. 'Oh, thank you, Nicholas. I can't tell you how happy this has made me. D'Artagnan will do you proud, I promise.'

'Touch wood,' said Nicholas. 'The Whistler's good, but...' He gave a sceptical shake of his head and Kate squeezed his hands.

'I know d'Artagnan hasn't done as much, but he can be just as good. I know it.'

Nicholas gave an awkward chuckle, probably uncomfortable with her gratitude. 'Just out of interest, what exactly did Jack tell you?'

'That he and The Whistler would both be in the Gold Cup.' Kate gave an ecstatic sigh and plonked herself down on the couch beside him. 'The Gold Cup,' she murmured. 'Gosh, I would've been happy with an entry in the Ryanair or even the Festival Handicap, but the Gold Cup – *wow*.' Kate could almost burst with pride that d'Artagnan's potential was being recognised.

'Right. Yes, well – um – even if it doesn't work out, you can still say your horse played a part in the Festival. And that's what you wanted, wasn't it?'

Kate laughed. 'Yes, but the Gold Cup? You've gone above and beyond anything I could've wished for.'

Nicholas shrugged like it was no big deal. 'I wanted to make it special for you.'

Kate hugged him again. His minty cologne filled her sinuses as she gave a great sigh of contentment. Knowing Nicholas would be too much of a gentleman to take advantage of the situation, she smoothed his hair away from his forehead and trailed her fingers down his cheek.

Nicholas's gaze flickered from her eyes to her mouth. 'And I mean that, Kate. You are special to me.'

She leaned forward and kissed him. His lips were soft, almost childlike. No stubble grazed her skin, and, stealing a peek, she saw his eyes were closed, long choir boy eyelashes fanning his cheeks. 'Thank you,' she whispered.

Nicholas cleared his throat and darted an uncomfortable look around. 'You're welcome.' He caught the eye of a waiter. 'Let's get you a drink, shall we? What would you like?'

'Orange juice, please.'

'You sure you don't want anything stronger?'

'No, thanks. I'm not a big drinker.'

Kate's mobile phone rang as Nicholas placed their drinks order. **Xander** lit up the screen. Mumbling her apologies, she cut the call without answering.

'Sorry. My brother,' she explained.

'Ah, yes. They do get a bit bothersome, don't they?'

'He's not that bad. He's only fifteen.'

Her phone rang again and she laughed. 'I take that back.' She cut the call once more and pocketed her phone. 'I'm sorry. You don't ever want to meet my family.'

'I hope I will one day,' replied Nicholas with a smile. He looked at his watch. 'Shall we go see if our reservation is ready?'

They were shown to their table and Kate tried to put her brother's phone calls out of her head.

'How has your week been otherwise?' Nicholas asked.

'Cold.'

'Can't be particularly pleasant working outside at this time of year.'

Kate shrugged. It was the rain that she really didn't like. 'It's not so bad when you're on the move the whole time. You warm up pretty fast.'

Nicholas took her hand and ran his thumb over her calloused fingers. 'Poor things must take a real battering.'

Kate flushed. Nicholas's hands looked more feminine than hers, soft and well-groomed. She imagined they hadn't done anything more strenuous than count out bank notes. 'I do use hand cream when I can,' she said. 'But it's not the sort of thing you think of to do in between mucking out and riding.'

'You should treat yourself to a day at the spa. My mother goes every week to one in Bath. I'm sure she could get you a discount as a member's guest.'

Kate blushed even more. She subtly withdrew her hand and buried it in her lap. 'That would be kind.'

Nicholas regarded her for a moment, his lips parted in anticipation of a question, but he appeared to change his mind, instead looking down at his menu.

'Are you going to The Golden Miller's Halloween party this weekend?' Kate asked.

'You mean, come in fancy dress?'

Kate nodded. 'It's a laugh. People come in some crazy costumes.'

'I don't know. It's not really my cup of tea,' said Nicholas, not able to meet her eye.

'You don't have to go to extremes if you don't want to. My costume's hardly going to win any prizes.'

Nicholas gave a hesitant smile. 'I'll think about it, okay?' and took refuge behind his menu.

Kate's mobile vibrated in her pocket, letting her know a message had arrived. Nicholas was still glued to his menu, so she gave in to curiosity. Xander didn't call very often.

Instead it was from Saskia.

Xander keeps trying to call me. Doesn't he know I have a life?

Kate bit her lip. It was even rarer for Xander to call Saskia. A feeling of unease wormed its way into her gut.

'Nicholas – um – would you excuse me for a minute? Just going to pop to the loo.'

Nicholas looked up, his gaze snagging on her chest, which she couldn't blame him for considering the last time they'd played out this scene. 'Don't you want to order first?'

'I won't be a minute.'

In the safety of the Ladies, Kate redialled Xander's number.

'Hey,' came her brother's droning voice.

'Everything okay?'

'I can't wake Mum up and I'm hungry.'

'Can't you make something for yourself? Noodles or a sandwich or something?'

'There's no food.'

Kate pinched the bridge of her nose. 'Can you order a takeaway?'

'No money. Can you come over?'

'Now isn't a good time, Xander. I'm on a date.'

'Oh, okay.'

Kate sighed. 'Try wake Mum up again. She can't be that bad.'

'I'm trying. She's still sleeping.'

'Give her a shake.'

'I am. She's not budging.'

In the mirror, Kate saw her eyes widen in panic. 'What do you mean exactly, Xander?'

43

'I'm shaking her and... *Mum!*' Xander yelled, then quieter to Kate, 'See? No response.'

Kate stilled. Maybe her mother's condition was more serious than she thought – than either of them thought. 'Okay. I'm on my way.'

Nicholas was waiting, his menu folded away, when she returned.

'Everything okay?' he asked when he saw her expression.

'I just spoke to Xander. I'm sorry to be a pain...'

'Is something wrong?'

'Just a bit of a family crisis. I—' Kate hesitated, hating to be such an inconvenience.

Nicholas gave her a sympathetic smile. 'Do you need to go?' he said.

'I don't want to, Nicholas. It feels so terribly ungrateful to leave, but...' She chewed the lipstick off her lower lip, torn between loyalties.

'It's okay. You should go.'

Kate knew she had to take the out he was giving her. She unhooked her handbag from the back of her chair and looked at him, her expression anguished. 'I'm so sorry, but I think I should. I'll explain everything to you – just not quite yet.'

7

XANDER ANSWERED KATE'S knock at the door. Curly haired like Kate, he stood a foot taller, but with an awkward stoop like he hadn't quite mastered his gawky frame yet.

'You okay?' she asked.

Xander shrugged and closed the door behind her. Kate walked through into the lounge in search of her mother. The room was messy, but vacant. 'Where is she?'

'In her room.'

Kate jogged up the stairs and paused outside her mother's door. The same fear she'd felt over the phone coiled up her throat. She opened the door and switched on the light.

The limp figure of her mother lay fully clothed across the bed, snoring softly. Relief that she was alive swiftly turned to anger. Kate walked over and shook her by the shoulder. Val Creswell didn't stir.

'She's out cold,' said Xander from the doorway. 'Been this way since I got home.'

Kate moved around the bed and kicked over a wine bottle half-hidden by the bed's frilly base. It spun across the laminate floors into the wall. Another half jack of gin stood empty on the bedside table.

She gave her mother another shake to no avail. Leaning close to her ear and trying not to breathe in the toxic BO, Kate yelled at her mother to wake up.

Val groaned and lifted a limp hand over her face to shield the light from her eyes. 'Turn th'light off,' she mumbled. She tried to roll onto her side and Kate grimaced at the state of her hair.

'Xander, turn the light off,' Val said again.

Xander reached for the switch, but Kate held up her hand. 'No, leave it on. Mum, wake up. We need to talk.'

Val appeared to have fallen asleep again with her arm resting over her eyes. Kate's patience evaporated and she snatched up the gin bottle and emptied the last inch over her mother's face. Val sat up, coughing and yelling. She glared at Kate through bloodshot slits. 'What the hell are you doing?'

Kate folded her arms and stood over her mother. 'I can tell you what I *was* doing. I was on a date with a really nice guy when I got a call from Xander saying that you were so drunk he couldn't wake you up. I thought I was going to find you dead!'

'Exaggerating,' Val mumbled, using her duvet to blot the gin from her eyes. She staggered to her feet and pushed past both Kate and Xander to go to the bathroom. Kate cast a look around her mother's bedroom as they waited. Apart from the two bottles she'd already spotted, she couldn't see any other signs of alcohol.

'How often do you have to cook for yourself?'

Xander shrugged. 'Paul's mum lets me stay over with them sometimes.'

Val reappeared from the bathroom. She'd splashed some water on her face and looked surprisingly alert.

'Mum, this has got to stop,' Kate said.

Val ignored her and rooted through the jumble of accessories on her dressing table to find a hairbrush and sat down on the stool with a bump.

'Mum, listen to me. Your drinking is out of control.'

Val gave her a thunderous look in the mirror's reflection. 'Just because I like a tipple does not mean I am out of control.'

'Look at yourself though. Look at Xander—'

'What's wrong with me?' said Xander.

'Nothing's wrong with you,' replied Kate. 'I mean for her to look at what she's *not* doing. It's not right that you should go to Paul's to get a decent meal. Mum, you need help.'

Val turned round to face Kate and held up her hairbrush in a threatening manner. 'I do not need help. I never needed it before, and I don't need it now.'

'But your drinking—'

'Keep your nose out of my business!' snapped Val. 'I know what I can handle.' She turned back and tugged her hairbrush through her greasy hair.

'Mum, I just found you passed out on your bed. Is that what you call handling it?'

'I was having a snooze. I'm allowed to do that, aren't I?'

'You were drunk.'

'Do I look drunk to you?'

Kate had to admit that, apart from her mother's physical appearance, she didn't actually seem that intoxicated. Her speech wasn't slurred, her balance seemed rock solid and her eyes, bloodshot though they were, appeared focused. But the sallowness of her skin, the dullness of her hair, the reddening of her nose all pointed to the same thing.

'Maybe not now,' Kate relented. 'But a drunk is what you're turning into.'

Val's lips curled back in a snarl, but she couldn't hold Kate's gaze. 'I'm not a drunk. How dare you call me that?'

So infuriating was Val's denial that Kate wanted to scream. She clutched her head and turned away. 'Dammit, Mum! How can you be so blind? So stubborn? You need to get help. Go to an AA meeting. Something!'

Val threw her hairbrush down, scattering the items on the dressing table. Kate and Xander both jumped. Val swivelled round on her stool and fixed Kate with a furious glare.

'I am *not* an alcoholic,' she spat. 'If all you've come round for is to insult me then you can piss off again. I don't want to hear your self-righteous bullshit.'

Kate's throat tightened and she swallowed hard. She tried to keep calm, to remain rational, but her breath came out in a shuddering stream of hurt. 'Fine, if that's the way you want it to be, then fine. Xander and I are going out for dinner.' She looked at her brother for his consent.

Xander's dubious expression told her he wasn't going to risk making any decisions.

Kate took his wrist and marched him to the door. 'Just don't expect him to bring home a doggy bag for you.'

8

KATE'S MOOD HADN'T improved by the next morning at work. Even d'Artagnan's attempts to relieve himself in the wheelbarrow didn't cheer her up when all he achieved was to knock over the whole load.

She heaved the soiled straw back into the wheelbarrow while the big dappled grey stood at the back of the stable, his deflated football held between his teeth like a comfort blanket. He tossed the ball in her direction. The ball rolled to a drunken stop against her foot and Kate stopped. D'Artagnan looked hopefully in her direction and she sighed.

'I'm sorry, baby,' she said. She leant her pitchfork against the barrow and stepped across the box to fuss him. She scratched him beneath his punk mane then beneath his gullet where she knew he enjoyed it most. D'Artagnan stretched out his head and closed his eyes, silvery eyelashes brushing his charcoal-smudged eyes.

Kate smiled. 'You look like you're going to start purring in a second,' she said.

A tutting at the door made her pause. She turned to see, of all people, Ben de Jager, leaning his arms on the stable door. A teasing smile tweaked his lips.

'This what you get up to all morning? It's a wonder you get any work done.'

D'Artagnan opened an eye to inspect the intruder and gave an exasperated snort when Kate stopped her scratching.

'TLC is part of the package,' Kate replied, nevertheless returning to her duties. 'What are you doing here?'

'Jack's running Laughing Stock on Sunday; wants me to school him beforehand.'

Kate nodded. 'Tricky customer. Billy hits the deck at least once a week riding him.'

'Great,' came Ben's dry reply. He dug into a pocket and held out a plastic bottle.

'What's this?' she asked.

'Blueing shampoo. It'll help with his yellow tail. Add some corn starch to the mix to prolong its effectiveness.'

The unexpectedness of the gift and the thought that not only had he been paying attention, but had acted upon it, touched her. 'Thanks, Ben. This is lovely,' she stammered. 'See, d'Artagnan?' she said, holding out the bottle for the horse to sniff.

D'Artagnan tried to eat the bottle.

Ben grinned. 'Is Saskia here yet?'

Kate glanced at her watch. It wasn't yet eight o'clock. 'Not yet, I wouldn't imagine.' She paused, remembering how Saskia had treated Ben when last he'd come to visit. 'And you're better off leaving it 'til after you've ridden. The office is always manic first thing.'

'I'll do that. See you on the Gallops,' he said and took his leave.

Kate rested on her pitchfork and watched Ben's departure. She shook her head. Saskia was a fool to turn him away. She must have a chat with her.

Kate waited until she had a lull between exercise lots before sneaking into the racing office. Saskia was at her desk, talking to a client on the office phone while also texting on her mobile.

Smiling down the phone, Saskia cheerily ended her conversation. 'Arsehole,' she said in an about turn to the replaced receiver.

'Who?'

'Mr Cox. Thinks he's God's gift thanks to bloody Dexter. It's not like *he* had to do anything special to win those Champion Hurdles.'

'Well, this season's Festival might bring him down a peg. Frankie could start a brass band with her trumpet blowing about Ta' Qali. She reckons he's never been better.'

'She's only saying that because she owns a leg.' Saskia pouted in thought. 'I wonder if I should buy a racehorse. Seems to be the way to go.'

'The way to go where? Bankrupt?'

'Well, look at Frankie. She nabbed Rhys through Ta' Qali. And Leonie told me practically the entire syndicate were hopping in and out of each other's beds last year, Eoin and Dilys being the exception. And then there's Pippa. It was through Peace Offering that she hooked Jack.'

Kate laughed and held up a finger. 'Don't go there, *please*. Besides, you can't afford a racehorse.'

'Yes, I can,' said Saskia. 'Well, probably not a whole one, but a hoof at least.'

Kate raised an eyebrow. 'Might you care to pay your share of the rent with that hoof money first?'

Saskia looked away and started tidying her desk. 'You'd think you'd cut me a break, being family and all.'

'And that's another thing we need to talk about: family,' said Kate. She'd let Saskia's overdue rent slide for now in view of more pressing concerns. 'Or more precisely, Mum.'

Saskia still couldn't meet her eye. 'What about her?'

'Xander called me round last night. I had to ditch Nicholas mid-date—'

'Couldn't have been that upsetting.'

'Shut up, Saskia. You don't know him. I had to go sort out Mum. Her drinking is out of control.'

Saskia looked at her at last. 'You sure? You know how you overreact.'

'I'm not overreacting. She'd drunk so much, she was comatose. I thought she was dead.'

Saskia threw up her hands. 'What do you want me to do about it? The stupid cow never bloody cared about anything I did, so why should I care about her? You practically raised me, not her.'

'There's Xander to think of,' she replied. 'He has to deal with it all on his own. I had to take him to KFC last night because there wasn't any food in the house.'

'Okay, so she needs help,' said Saskia. 'What's that got to do with me?'

'I think she should go to AA.'

'Well, I doubt she'll want me there. It's not like she held my hand when I needed it.'

Kate masked a sigh. She didn't blame Saskia for her bitterness. They had grown up with an absent father and a mother who couldn't handle his cameo appearances in their lives. Kate had flunked her exams and taken the earliest opportunity to move out. The Newmarket Racing School had been her saving grace, but it meant Saskia had had to deal with their mother – then struggling to cope with the demands of a six-year-old Xander – by herself.

'Well, there's the thing. She says she doesn't need help. She doesn't think she has a problem.'

'There's your answer then. There's no point in trying to help someone if they can't admit they have a problem. Isn't that Step One?'

Jack's entrance interrupted Kate's reply. He looked frozen. Saskia's face lit up.

'Coffee, Jack?'

Jack nodded. 'Please. Any messages?'

'Only Mr Cox wanting to come see Dexter work.'

Jack grunted and flipped through the mail in Saskia's in-tray. 'I'll work out when he's due his next fast piece and let you know.' He paused over a pink envelope and lifted it to sniff. His nose wrinkled in distaste.

'More fan mail?' said Saskia with a coy smile. 'You can't blame them really.'

Jack looked unmoved. 'Send whoever this is a thank you letter and leave it at that.' He dropped the envelope, scowling at his perfumed fingers and wiped them on his jacket like they were stained with dung.

'Gosh, you're so patient with them all,' said Saskia. 'I don't know how you do it, juggling owners, fans, media, and running such a successful business at the same time.'

Saskia's flattery made Kate's toes curl. She looked at Jack for his reaction. Jack, tearing open a letter postmarked the British Horseracing Authority, didn't appear to be listening.

'Not to mention a family as well,' Kate said, sending Saskia a murderous look.

Jack looked at Kate as if noticing her presence for the first time. 'Did you want me for anything?'

'No.' Kate shook her head. 'Just passing on a message from Ben to Saskia.'

'Ben's riding Laughing Stock out in the next lot,' said Jack. 'You're on Chic Shadow. Appreciate it if you stick close, show him the way.'

For a moment, Saskia looked terrorised by the knowledge Ben was in situ, but managed to turn it into a brilliant smile for her boss. She flicked her chestnut hair over her shoulders like a shampoo model. 'I'll go get that coffee, shall I?'

Jack gave a vague murmur of thanks and wandered through to his office still reading the BHA letter. His door clicked shut and Kate sprang into action.

'Saskia, what the hell?' she hissed. 'Stop it.'

'No, you bloody stop it. Mind your own business.'

Kate bit her lip. 'You're wasting your time. Jack is already taken, can't you see?'

Saskia ignored her and flounced across the reception to the kitchenette to make Jack's coffee. Kate followed her.

'Ben wants to see you.'

Saskia groaned as she refilled the kettle. 'Oh God, no.'

'What do you have against him? He's a nice guy. He's good looking—'

'If you like the run-over-by-a-tractor look.'

'That's not fair. He *is* good looking,' said Kate, 'and he's got fantastic arms—' Kate paused to savour the mental image and Saskia frowned at her. 'But that's beside the point,' she hurried on. 'He runs his own business, he's obviously keen on you—'

'I suppose he is heir to quite a bit of dosh,' mused Saskia.

Kate bit back her curt reply. If Ben's inheritance drove Saskia's affections away from Jack then so be it. She tried to think of more of Ben's redeeming features. '*And* he doesn't drink,' she said, remembering his ginger ale at Leonie's dinner party.

'I don't want to get myself lumped with some tea-totalling bore,' said Saskia.

'Being tea-total doesn't make you a bore. I'm not a bore, am I?'

Saskia gave her a dubious look, and Kate irritably dismissed it. 'Whatever. Ben isn't boring. If you just gave him half a chance, you'd see that for yourself.'

'If he's so great, why aren't you dating him?' said Saskia, pouring the boiled water into a Jockey Club coffee mug.

Kate shifted in her boots. 'Because I'm dating his brother.'

Saskia sent her a wicked grin. 'Have to make sure we split that inheritance then, eh?'

Kate relented enough to see the funny side and she shook her head at Saskia with a weary smile. 'Just be nice when he comes in to see you, okay?'

* * *

Kate met Ben by the mounting block and together they rode to the schooling paddock. Laughing Stock, a skittish chestnut, bucked the whole way. Ben carried on chatting while his mount performed circus tricks, his balance unfaltering.

'I hear you and Nicholas have been seeing more of each other,' he said.

'We've been out a couple of times,' replied Kate, unwilling to commit. 'He's a nice guy.'

Ben gave an indifferent shrug. 'Yeah. He's all right.'

Jack called them over and gave them instructions as they readjusted their girths. 'I know this is your first time aboard Laughing Stock, so stick close to Kate. He likes company and Chic Shadow's unlikely to do anything stupid.'

With the rest of the small string behind them, Kate and Ben set off for a warm-up canter across the paddock. Above them, the hill blocked out the buttery morning sunshine, leaving them in the chilly shade.

Laughing Stock plunged forward in a rocking horse canter and blew out great, foggy snorts. Ben stood up in his stirrups and rocked with him.

They finished their warm-up lap and approached the first schooling fence. Chic Shadow popped over without any qualms, but Laughing Stock treated it like Becher's Brook. Ben sat back as the chestnut gave a rocket-propelled buck.

'Let's pick it up a bit,' he yelled.

Kate pushed her mount along. Chic Shadow flicked an ear at his errant work partner and puffed to keep up. The fifty shades of greenery skirting the track sped by in a blur. Over the second fence, Laughing Stock was a couple of strides clear and, on landing, Ben skilfully brought him back under control.

'When're you coming to visit my stables?' he said, raising his voice above the wind.

Kate's stomach lurched in delight that *he* wanted *her* for company. She was quick to remind herself of the fact that he fancied Saskia, and this was no more than a platonic gesture, probably even a ruse to get closer to her sister.

'When you invite me properly, I guess.'

'Ha! You waiting for a royal invitation in the mail? Come by anytime. When is your next weekend off?'

'This weekend.'

The third fence delayed Ben's reply and the horses jumped in harmony.

'Even better then,' he continued on the other side. 'I'm only going to get half my lot exercised on Saturday because of Ascot racing, so come by then. I'll be there most of the morning.'

Kate thought about it for a moment. See? He was only inviting her because it would make his life easier. Having said that, she *was* curious, and she did quite fancy the idea of helping out. 'Deal,' she replied.

9

THAT SATURDAY, KATE drove away from Helensvale with the peals of bell practice at the church drifting through the window on a mild autumnal wind. Her rattling Ford, fondly known as Harrison, splashed through the puddles on the undulating country road, passing high holly hedges bordering fields from which she could detect the not unpleasant odour of organic fertiliser.

Skewered atop a battered sign for Thistle Lodge Stables was a carved pumpkin, reminding Kate she must stop by the craft shop on the way home to get some fabric for her costume. She trundled down the cobbled drive, winding between bare-branched birch trees. In a clearing away from the road, a block of stables stood with its back facing a double-storey cottage with a mossy slate roof.

Kate breathed in the smell of soggy bark and fermenting birch leaves. She was about to approach the cottage when she heard the sound of human life coming from the other side of the stables.

In the middle of a small U-shaped yard, Ben hosed down a horse's muddy legs, singing along to 'Friends In Low Places' on a radio hanging from the eaves. The horse nodded its head, as if to the beat of the melody, clearly enjoying the attention.

Kate put her hand to her mouth to mask her smile. 'Hello.'

Ben whirled around. 'Hey, Kate!' He lifted the hosepipe in greeting and Kate made a hasty sidestep to avoid being splashed. 'Oops. Sorry.'

Under full length leather riding chaps, Ben's blue jeans were highlighted in the most inappropriate areas, and despite the low temperature, he was wearing a grubby white T-shirt that showed off his broad chest and arms. Kate wished Saskia was here to see him.

'Give me a minute to finish off Miranda here and I'll be right with you,' he said. He plugged his thumb over the hosepipe and fired a jet of water at the mare's hindlegs and tail.

Kate stood to the side to avoid the splashback and looked around the yard. It was a modest build, which, when she looked closer, was showing the strain of a low budget.

Kate hadn't expected a millionaire's son to be holding up his guttering with chicken wire or using baling twine to reinforce door bolts. But the yard was swept clean and, although she knew there must be a muck heap somewhere nearby, she couldn't smell anything except fresh wood shavings and damp earth.

'Switch off the tap for me, won't you?' Ben asked.

Kate hastened to assist then followed him over to the adjoining bullring where he swung the gate shut and unclipped Miranda. Instead of wheeling around and bolting around the tight corral, the mare stayed put, pitching her ears forward and breathing gustily over her master.

'I haven't got any,' Ben said holding out his empty palms. 'Sorry.'

'Here,' said Kate, taking a carrot from her jacket pocket. 'If she doesn't mind it second-hand. Tried to give it to d'Artagnan and he spat it out. He'll eat everything else, but he's the first horse I've come across who doesn't like carrots.'

Miranda wasn't a picky eater and she crunched through the treat, eyes sparkling. Ben smiled as he let himself out of the bullring.

'Come on. I'll introduce you to the rest of the gang.'

'And this guy,' Ben said, slapping his hand on the half door of the fourth stable, 'is one you might be familiar with. Used to live at Aspen Valley.'

At the sound of his voice, the horse came to the door. He was a handsome chestnut with a thick forelock and a pendant star spilling down his forehead.

Kate gasped. 'Is this South of Jericho?'

'Or Jerry, as he's now known,' Ben replied, nodding.

Kate reached out a hand to stroke the gelding's nose. 'I did wonder where he'd gone.'

'He had colic surgery. Not necessarily career-ending, as you well know, but his owner had had enough.' He rubbed the gelding beneath his flaxen mane and patted him. 'He's got a bit of a fragile constitution, has old Jerry. Touch wood, he hasn't had any problems with us. Should be ready to find a new home in the New Year.'

'Doing what?'

'Eventing, I reckon. He's a great all-rounder. Did you ever ride him at Aspen Valley?'

Kate shook her head. 'No. He was out of my league, sadly.'

Ben gave her a mischievous smile. 'Do you want to have a go here?'

Sat astride Suddenly Seymour, a dark bay with long dopey ears and a liberal white snip dribbled over one nostril, Ben led them over to a pegged out twenty-by-forty manége within a vast wilderness paddock. Kate felt like a million dollars aboard South of Jericho. The gelding walked out with a forward stride and crested his neck. Unusually for an ex-racehorse, he had a 'soft' mouth, and responded to the lightest of touches to the reins.

As they walked along the fence to the arena, Kate spied a rusty mobile home tucked beside the stables.

'Anyone live there?' she asked.

'Me.'

Kate hesitated. 'So who lives in the house round the front?'

'Fiona. She rents that and three of the boxes.' Ben grinned at her puzzled expression. 'I own the property, but retraining racehorses doesn't exactly bring in a lot of cash. Fiona's contribution helps pay for a lot of the overheads.'

'But I thought—' She didn't want to make assumptions, but she thought surely with a father like Bill Borden, Ben shouldn't have to live in a dilapidated caravan.

'I wanted to do it myself, you know? I haven't been what you'd call the exemplary son. I—' He hesitated and sighed. 'Anyway, what say we do twenty minutes flatwork then tackle some cross-country fences?'

Kate nodded, smiling to mask her intrigue. Not an exemplary son? What did that mean? Her conversation with Frankie at Wetherby races flashed into her mind. She'd said Ben was 'rebelling' against his father, but he didn't strike her as being particularly rebellious, unless this was his idea of defiance. Mind, Frankie had also described Ben as being a 'plum' riding armchair winners for his rich father, and Ben was certainly not that.

Ben had already set off to work Suddenly Seymour at the far end of the school. Kate gathered her reins and pushed Jerry into a trot.

After a couple of circles during which Kate was aware her horse was not collecting himself like Ben's was, she realised she was being watched. Kate tensed, and Jerry sped up.

'Shoulders back,' Ben called out to her. 'You've been riding racehorses too long. Sit up straight.'

Kate did as she was instructed, ever conscious that, by squaring her shoulders, her boobs bounced even more.

'You want to *squeeze* with your inside rein. *Squeeze* with your legs. Slow your rising. He's going too quick. You want him to round his back, get that inside bend. That's better!'

Kate felt the immediate response from Jerry as she applied the aids. His nose tucked in and she could feel him driving forward with his hocks.

'Now, maintain the impulsion, squeeze with your outside leg behind the girth, inside on the girth.'

Kate carried out the commands and, miraculously, South of Jericho knew what she was asking and half-passed across the diagonal. She laughed in delight at this coded language between species.

'You should be a teacher,' she called back.

'Sorry, I didn't mean to boss you around.'

'Not at all. I haven't a clue how to ride flatwork. Where did you learn all this stuff?'

They trotted in opposite circles to each other and Ben waited for their next pass to reply. 'My grandfather. He was a dressage instructor.'

'Gosh. I used to think of dressage as just a bunch of fancy tricks, but this feeling of contained power is just extraordinary. It's not like the power you get on the Gallops, when it's so often a tug of war. Jerry hasn't pulled at all, I feel like I'm holding all his power in my fingertips.'

'"Where grace is laced with muscle and strength by gentleness confined,"' quoted Ben with a smile. 'Jerry's probably giving you a warped perspective. He's the best in the yard.'

'How can you bear to let him go?'

Ben shrugged. 'That's the nature of the business, unfortunately, and I have to pay the bills.' He ruffled Suddenly Seymour's black mane. 'This guy's going to miss him the most. Seymour's got a bit of a crush on Jerry. He has a thing for redheads it would seem.'

Kate grinned. 'Like his owner.'

Ben gave her a heavy-lidded look. 'Except I prefer females, and generally of the Homo Sapien variety.'

* * *

Twenty minutes later, Ben led the way out of the arena and into the paddock. Jerry knew what was coming and snorted with every jig-jog stride he took.

'It's a beautiful setting,' said Kate. 'How many acres do you have here?' The paddock disappeared behind copses of trees and into dips and valleys, making it difficult to estimate.

'Six in total. I was lucky to get it, even if it does still need a bit of work.'

'Can't you ask your father?' Ben threw her a sharp look and she was quick to continue. 'I mean, not to give you the money. I appreciate you want to do it yourself, but he could loan you some.' She peeked at him from beneath the rim of her helmet, wary of what toes she might be stepping on.

Ben looked grim. 'When my grandfather died, he left me some money. And this is what it paid for. I want to do it for him. *With* him.'

'You were close to your grandfather?'

'Yes,' he replied. 'My grandparents raised me.' A fleeting nostalgia swept through his eyes, but then something else – almost a flash of guilt – replaced that emotion. It was gone in a blink. Ben pointed to three cross-country fences up ahead. 'You ready to rumble?'

Kate nodded.

'Okay then,' said Ben. 'We'll have a practice run. Nice and simple, nothing too complicated. I've just got to fix this.' He jumped off and re-plugged a white flag into the ground on the left of the three brush fences. 'Important to train eventers to jump between the flags as much as anything.'

'Which one are we jumping?' said Kate. 'There's three.'

'Yes. Novice, Intermediate, and Advanced,' he explained, pointing to each of the different sizes. 'Seymour's still a bit wet behind the ears, so we're sticking to baby jumps. Jerry's probably ready for Advanced, but he's not done cross-country with anyone except me, so you might want to stick with Intermediate. That okay with you?'

Kate nodded, appreciating that he hadn't recommended Intermediate because he wasn't sure of *her* level of competence, the more likely reason.

She collected her reins. Jerry snatched at the bit and jig-jogged forward.

'Wait a sec,' said Ben, holding out a hand. He gestured to her stirrups. 'You might want to lengthen those. Otherwise you could end up using the ejector seat.'

Kate lengthened her stirrup leathers by a couple of holes and looked to Ben for approval.

'A couple more.'

'More?' She wrinkled her nose. 'I'll be losing my irons if I make them much longer.'

Ben grinned at her. 'Rubbish. You've been riding racehorses too long.'

'I don't think Jerry's willing to stand around much longer.'

'Here. You do that one. I'll do this one.' He pushed her thigh back so he could pull on the leather and adjust the buckle.

Kate nearly lost her balance as the warmth of his arm penetrated her jodhpurs. With a snap he pulled the leather taut and planted her foot into the stirrup. 'How does that feel?'

Kate nodded, and was tempted to ask if he'd care to do the same to the other leg, just so her knees could be equally jellified.

10

THE GOLDEN MILLER'S Halloween Party that night was in full swing by the time Kate and Saskia walked through the cobwebbed doorway. Weaving their way to the bar, Kate was already regretting coming as Batwoman as her homemade wings slapped unwitting zombies and vampires every way she turned. Saskia, intent on winning Best Dressed, had gone all out with her blue spandex *Avatar*-themed jumpsuit, but was leaving a trail of blue make-up on everyone and everything she touched.

Eoin, the pub landlord, sweated through his blood-stained bandages as he handed the girls their drinks. 'Six eighty, please,' he puffed.

'Leonie!' cried Saskia, conveniently removing herself.

Kate rolled her eyes and took out her purse.

Mindful of her wings, she stood on the foot-rail to search the sea of cleaver-sliced heads for a familiar face. It wasn't an easy task when the entire pub resembled a *Waking the Dead* meets *The Avengers* set.

In defeat, she returned to ground level and carried her and Saskia's drinks over to her sister's party. Leonie was dressed ready for a new term at Hogwarts while her boyfriend, Declan, Aspen Valley's main veterinary support, looked a fright in a Freddy Krueger jersey and hat. Nursing a Bloody Mary, he looked bored with his company and greeted Kate with a warm, albeit slightly scary, smile.

'Howsa goin', Kate?' he said. He regarded her costume and nodded. 'Batwoman?'

'Yes,' she replied with relief. Her costume had been put together more through her own creativity than with any loyalty to the traditional character, and it was good to know she was still recognisable.

Saskia took her drink from Kate and said, 'Although Batwoman didn't have wings.'

'Well, it's convincing enough to me,' replied Declan.

'Do you recognise mine?' Saskia said, jutting out one hip and posing, felinesque.

Declan frowned and pulled a doubtful face.

'She's Neytiri from *Avatar*, of course,' Leonie tutted.

'Never heard of it,' he replied, sending Kate a conspiratorial wink.

A hand slipped around Kate's waist and she jumped, more in surprise than in fright, as Dracula sidled up beside her. Ben grinned, fang-toothed, from behind the upturned collar of his cape. 'Good evening,' he murmured.

'Ben,' Kate gasped and choked out a laugh. 'Good grief.'

'My, my, my,' murmured Saskia, regarding his costume with a luxuriant arching of her spine that was intended to provoke a similar surveyance. She looked him up and down and Kate noted the satisfied pout on her sister's mouth. Saskia liked dangerous men and one couldn't get much more dangerous than Dracula. Kate had to admit he carried off the claret waistcoat and frilly white shirt very well.

'Have you heard from Nicholas?' Kate asked. 'I still don't know if he's coming.'

'I'm here. Sorry I'm late.' Nicholas appeared from the crush of people and he immediately spotted Ben's hand around Kate's waist. Ben dropped his hand at his brother's frown and took a step closer to Saskia and Leonie.

'You came,' Kate said as he pecked her on the cheek. His nose was cold from the outside air. 'I didn't think you would.'

Nicholas held his arms wide to reveal his rather safe costume. 'You said we didn't have to go to extremes. You look terribly mysterious though.'

Kate wanted to use the same excuse, but the words refused to come. Nicholas was certainly dressed differently, in a white tunic over beige chinos and what appeared to be an LED tube light hanging from his belt, but beyond that she hadn't a clue who he was meant to be.

'Luke Skywalker, right?' Declan saved her.

Nicholas beamed. 'The very one. How are you, Declan?' He shook the vet's hand with the both of his then looked around with satisfaction. 'This looks an interesting party, doesn't it?'

Interesting, definitely, but a couple of hours later, it was verging on rowdy too. A group of zombies that Kate recognised from Aspen Valley were trying to play volleyball with a carved pumpkin across the bar-restaurant partition and glasses and bits of pumpkin were flying everywhere.

Kate, Nicholas, Declan and a couple of Declan's friends sought refuge at a table and were laughing their way through a game of *Sixty Seconds* at which Nicholas was surprisingly good. Saskia, Ben and Leonie had disappeared, although Kate did catch a glimpse of Ben ordering drinks. The bar lights warmed his already olive skin tone (he certainly had the best tan Kate had ever seen on a vampire) and his eyes crinkled as he laughed with Eoin. Eoin looked to be persuading him to take part in the Best Dressed competition, which was struggling for attention as the 'voters' were too busy having a good time to watch the contestants parade.

Kate cheered when Saskia sashayed her way down the wobbly catwalk. Her pose and pout was met with appreciative wolf-whistles from drunk wizards and zombies. Kate's workmate, Billy, was next up, sporting a Grim Reaper-slash-Scream outfit. After stumbling up the steps in his swathes of black sheets, it was to no-one's surprise when he went arse over tit and landed face-first on a bottle-strewn table, nearly taking out Snow White's eye with his plastic sickle. In fact, it got the biggest cheer of all the contestants.

'Are you going to take your chance?' asked Nicholas.

Kate shook her head. 'I can't compete with this lot. Are you?'

'No way.' His laughter faded and his expression became grim. 'Oh, look who is though.'

Ben had mounted the steps to the catwalk and was doing a dramatic show of whipping his cape around to hide his face then revealing a sparkling canine. He stopped at the end of the catwalk and jutted out a sexy hip. The female contingent whooped in appreciation as he met them all with dark and smouldering looks. Laughing, Kate clapped as Ben took a bow and leapt from the stage in a whoosh of satin cape.

With the last contestants paraded, Eoin laboriously climbed the catwalk steps to announce the winner, his bandages by now falling away to reveal a red and sweaty face.

'The winner in our women's category is—'

Someone somewhere beat the bar to create a drumroll.

'—Nefertiti,' Eoin announced.

The Golden Miller cheered in approval. Saskia looked even bluer than before.

With Nefertiti dispatched with her complimentary bottle of booze, Eoin asked for quiet again. 'And the winner of our men's category is—'

Cue drumroll.

'—Dracula!'

About ten different Draculas cheered at the news. The only one who wasn't fighting his way to the stage was Ben, who was having too fine a time laughing with friends.

'No, no! Not you lot. Him!' Eoin said, pointing at Ben.

Hands pushed a surprised-looking Ben to the stage and once he realised what was happening, he cheered as well. He lifted his alcoholic prize in a victory salute, showing off a lithe and athletic figure beneath the cloak. The overzealous screams of the pub's female population made Kate's eardrums quake.

Kate returned her attention to her table, but out of the corner of her eye, she spotted Ben pouring his bottle of champagne into Saskia and Leonie's glasses. She noticed Nicholas watching as well. 'Ben looks like he's having a whale of a time,' she said.

'Yes. Doesn't he?'

'He must be shattered what with racing all afternoon and we were schooling his horses all morning.'

Nicholas frowned. 'I thought you had the weekend off.'

'No, I visited Thistle Lodge Stables this morning.' She faltered as Nicholas tensed. She glanced across at Ben again, seeing him tap the champagne bottle against Saskia and Leonie's glasses in a toast. 'Just to help out. Ben's got a horse I used to know from Aspen Valley.'

Nicholas patted her hand in a feeble attempt to reassure her. 'Of course. Will you excuse me for a moment? I must just pop to the Gents.'

Kate looked back at the board game, which Declan and his friends had abandoned. She and Nicholas had been winning, mainly thanks to Nicholas's prowess, but also to the gradual deterioration of the other players. With every drink Declan sank, the more incomprehensible his Irish accent became.

'Kate!' he hollered from two feet away. He bumped across to sit in the chair beside her and lolled an arm across her shoulders. 'I could fix you up wit' one of my brot'ers, you know. They're new to town, like, and t'ey could do with a grand girl like yerself.'

Kate smiled. 'Thanks Declan, but I'll pass. I'm not really on the market as such.'

'Are you not now?' he said in surprise. 'Who is the lucky fella?'

Kate paused to see if he was being serious, but his expression was one of complete ignorance. 'Er – Nicholas? You know, the guy I've been with all night?'

Declan looked delighted. 'Is that right? I was after t'inking you were just friends, so.'

Kate supposed he had a point. Nicholas hadn't so much as laid a finger on her knee all evening. 'How many brothers do you have?' she asked (there was no harm in having a back-up plan).

'Four,' he said, holding up three fingers then correcting himself. 'An' all workin' in the good business too.'

'Which is?'

'Hoss racin', of course. Kian, he's the brains behind the whole t'ing. Settin' up camp over Bracken Fields way. Wants us to do the whole lot, breedin', racin' and—' Declan paused, as if sure there was a third cog to the wheel, but quickly gave up, '—and breedin'.'

'That sounds very ambitious.'

As Declan got stuck into telling her all the plans they'd made to establish an O'Keefe racing empire, Kate's gaze strayed back to The Golden Miller's crowds. It had slimmed, somewhat, with the conclusion of the Best Dressed competition. The draft from the door opening and closing was making the tea-light inside the table's carved pumpkin flicker and her eye was drawn to the entrance.

To her surprise, she recognised Nicholas and Ben standing outside in the cold. They were arguing. Kate craned her neck, but the door swung closed again and blocked her view. She looked around to where she'd last seen Saskia. Her sister and Leonie had their heads together in an intense gossip session only interrupted by refills of Ben's champagne bottle.

'I'm not sure Bracken Fields will ever be big enough to require my full-time attention, but it's a nice t'ought, do you not t'ink so, Kate?'

'Hmm?' she said at the mention of her name.

The young vet looked at her expectantly, if not entirely focused.

'Um, yes. Absolutely.'

Nicholas was back five minutes later with fresh drinks. There was no trace of his argument in his expression and no sign of Ben anywhere either.

'Everything okay?' she said.

Nicholas beamed. 'Yes.' He tapped his beer against her lemonade and took a sip. 'Reckon I'm going to have to take a taxi home after this one.'

'I could give you a lift?' suggested Kate.

'I live the far side of Bristol. I couldn't ask you to go all that way. Thank you though.'

Kate became uncomfortable under his gaze as she realised there was an alternative. No, she wouldn't be bullied into inviting him back to her flat. Not that he was bullying her, not in the slightest, but the option had now been presented.

She wasn't ready to take that next step. Hell, they hadn't even kissed properly yet and the thought of Luke Skywalker undressing Batwoman and vice versa didn't lend much romance to the deed.

They were just finishing their drinks when Saskia weaved her way over to their table.

'There you are. Leonie and I are going clubbing in town. Will you drop us off?'

'Town as in Bristol?'

'Yes.'

Even though she'd been happy to drop Nicholas off just a few moments before, Kate was not so inclined to do the same for her sister. 'I'm not your taxi service, Saskia.'

Saskia pouted. 'Where's Ben?'

Kate had a mind to tell her not to use him as a taxi service either, but thought better of it.

'Tell you what,' said Nicholas. 'Why don't we three share a taxi? I'll pay.'

No amount of blue make-up could mask Saskia's horror. 'You want to come clubbing too?'

'No,' Nicholas laughed. 'I'm going home to bed, but we can detour through the city centre. It won't be a problem.'

Saskia swayed and exchanged none-too-subtle glances with Leonie. 'And you'll pay?'

Nicholas nodded.

Saskia shrugged. 'Okay then. Thanks.'

Nicholas took out his mobile phone to call a taxi company while the girls finished off the champagne.

* * *

They bid Declan and his mates goodbye and stepped out into the frigid air.

'Where *is* Ben?' Kate said, rubbing her arms. It felt more like the depths of winter than autumn.

'Gone home, I expect,' Nicholas replied.

Kate was dying to know what their argument had been about. Apart from natural curiosity, she'd like to put Nicholas straight if they'd been arguing about her visiting Thistle Lodge Stables. Then again, she'd sound awfully arrogant to presume it was all about her.

'How long will the taxi be?' she asked instead.

'About two metres, I should think. Maybe a bit longer.' A small smile tugged at his mouth.

Kate snorted. 'Ha, ha. How many minutes will it be, smart ass?'

'Ten minutes. Where's your car? There's no point in you freezing with us.'

Kate pointed down the street in the vague direction of where she'd parked and Nicholas took her arm.

'I'll walk you.'

Knowing what must surely come next as they reached the semi-privacy of her car, Kate fumbled through her handbag for her keys. At last she got the door open. 'Right, well, that's me off then.'

Nicholas stepped forward and ran his hand up Kate's arm. His fingers were warm, but Kate still shivered. He leaned in, then began to chuckle.

Kate gave him a doubtful look.

'Sorry, it's just that this isn't how I imagined things to go,' he said.

Relieved that the awkwardness had been removed from their situation, Kate lifted her mask, making her face ten times colder.

'That's better,' murmured Nicholas, running a finger down her temple. 'Now I can see you properly.'

He cupped her face with his palm and kissed her. His nose was cold against her cheek, but his mouth was warm. Kate closed her eyes. As she responded, Nicholas increased the pressure and moved his body closer to hers. A long hard – *something* – pressed against her hip.

Crumbs, she'd underestimated him.

Nicholas's kiss faltered and he pulled away and looked down. Kate realised it was his makeshift light sabre.

Nicholas gave a nervous laugh. 'Sorry.' He winched his belt round, so the tube was no longer in the way. 'Can't risk breaking that or I'll be cooking in the dark for the next week.'

He kissed her again, long and slow, and Kate felt like a snowflake melting. Only the shouts from up the street where Saskia and Leonie were still waiting for the taxi interrupted them.

Kate pulled away reluctantly. 'Looks like your ride's here.'

Nicholas looked disappointed, but opened her door wide for her to get in. 'Yes. Safe journey home.'

Kate stepped in, not easy with batwings attached. 'You too.'

Nicholas was about to shut the door when he hesitated. 'Kate, I don't want to rush you into anything, and I don't want you to read too much into this, but—' He hesitated, making Kate hold her breath. 'Well, you see my parents are throwing a Guy Fawkes party on the fifth. There'll be a big crowd, so it's nothing too intimate, don't worry, and Dad always has a great fireworks display—' He grimaced and looked at her for the first time to gauge her reaction. 'Would you like to come along?'

Kate thought for a moment. Yes, it was a little early to be meeting the parents, but it didn't sound like a sit down meal where she'd be grilled about her suitability as daughter-in-law.

'I'd like that,' she said.

Nicholas let out his breath, fogging the air, and grinned. 'Great.'

11

FOR HER OWN peace of mind as much as anything, Kate decided to stop in on her mother and Xander once a week, just to check there was food in the fridge and the bills were all being paid. For her first visit, she bought a cheesecake by way of a conciliatory gesture. It wasn't the healthiest of meals, but would probably be better received than a bag of sprouts and broccoli.

When she arrived, she knew at once that something was up. Xander wouldn't meet her eye when she asked him how school was going.

'What's happened?' she said, fixing him with an eagle eye.

Xander shrugged. 'Nothing,' and bounded up the stairs to his room before she had a chance to press him.

Kate found Val in the kitchen, reading on her laptop. Kate was encouraged to see her mother looking fresh, her hair still damp from a recent shower.

Kate greeted her warily.

Val flicked her a curt look then resumed her internet surfing. 'Come back to take another bite out of me, have you?'

'I brought you this.' Kate put the cheesecake on the table beside the laptop and waited.

Val looked at the cheesecake for a long moment then looked up at Kate. 'Thank you.' Her words were forced, but Kate took it as progress.

'I'll put it in the fridge.'

Unsurprisingly, the fridge was almost empty and could do with a good clean. Kate wrinkled her nose at the smell and spotted an open can of hot dogs in brine that was a month past its use by date. As subtly as she could, she removed the can and drained it in the sink before her mother noticed.

'I asked Xander how school was,' she said. 'Won't be long before he takes his GCSEs.'

Val didn't look up. 'He's taking a break from school right now.'

Kate frowned. 'Study leave?'

'No. He got suspended last week.'

Kate stared at her. 'What?' she cried. 'What for?'

'Just acting a teenager.'

'Like how?'

Val closed her laptop and walked out of the kitchen.

'Doing what, Mum?' Kate said, hot on her heels.

'Katie, must you be so aggressive? It's no wonder we don't tell you anything. You get so uptight.'

Kate hid her white knuckles in the folds of her coat and tried to swallow her temper. 'Mum,' she said in as soft a tone as she could muster, 'Please tell me why Xander got suspended from school?'

Val shrugged as she took out her cigarettes. 'The school's overreacted, in my opinion. It's not like he set fire to the place.'

'What did he do?' Kate's voice was slow and steely.

Val finally met her gaze, but looked away again and lit a cigarette. 'He was caught smoking on school grounds.'

Kate was jolted by the insignificance of the crime. Her mother was right, the school had overreacted. Not that she endorsed Xander's behaviour, but still. There were worse crimes.

'Is this not the first time?' she asked. 'It does seem a bit harsh.'

Val lifted her cigarette to her lips, fingers trembling. She tried to meet Kate's eyes, then, with an impatient exhalation, retreated to the kitchen again.

Kate found her sloshing three fingers of vodka into a glass. She bit her lip. 'Has Xander been caught smoking before?'

Val splashed some orange juice and water into the glass and took a deep swallow. She closed her eyes and, without opening them, said, 'He was smoking weed.'

Kate felt like she'd been punched. She couldn't believe Xander would do such a thing. He was too *good* to stoop to such levels of rebellion. Val opened her eyes when Kate stayed gobsmacked. To Kate, she'd never looked less bothered.

'Xander is doing drugs?' she at last uttered.

'It's hardly drugs, is it?' said Val. 'A little weed never hurt anyone—'

'Mum, it's drugs!' cried Kate.

Val shook her head. 'See? Now you're overreacting too.' She brushed past Kate to go back into the lounge. 'The school is being bloody-minded, that's all. Like you say, Xander's got exams coming up. He needs to be at school, learning. They don't give a shit though, do they?'

Kate tailed her mother into the adjoining room, her arms outstretched in incredulity. 'Xander is caught doing drugs on school grounds and you think *the school* is at fault? Mum, in what world is that rational? I'm surprised he wasn't expelled. Where is he? Xander!' she called up the stairs.

Unsurprisingly, there was no answer. Kate jogged up the stairs and banged on his door.

'Leave him, Katie, for goodness' sake,' said Val from the base of the stairs. 'Don't be such a drama queen.'

Kate stared down at her mother. Was she being a drama queen? Was she overreacting? Should the fact that her mother was an alcoholic and her brother was on the road to becoming a junkie not cause her alarm?

Kate's blood ran cold at the thought of Xander failing his exams. What would happen to him? She'd failed her exams – without the help of narcotics – and only by sheer luck had she got a place at the Racing School. It had been Val's fault that she'd failed school, Val's fault that for years she'd gone around thinking she was stupid and talentless. If it hadn't been for the Racing School and her work placement in Newmarket, God only knew where she would've ended up.

'I am not being a drama queen,' she said, trying to keep her voice steady. 'And I am not overreacting, Mum. No responsible parent would sit back and think his behaviour is acceptable—'

'Oh, so it's my fault now, is it?'

'Yes! Christ Almighty!' Kate exclaimed, flinging her arms out. 'You're making excuses for your son while he gets suspended from school for doing drugs? Where is the parenting in that? And what sort of example are you setting him with your drinking?'

Val rolled her eyes. 'Here we go again,' she said in a sing-song voice. 'It's time to rip a few shreds off Mum again, is it? It's always my fault, isn't it Katie? Don't you ever get tired of blaming it all on me?'

The air was punched out of Kate's lungs in an exhalation of disbelief. With a furious gasp, she strode across the landing to her mother's bedroom.

'Hey, where do you think you're going?' Val squawked, thumping up the stairs in pursuit. 'Katie!'

Kate ignored her. She snatched up an empty half jack of vodka from the bedside table. Looking around for more, she caught sight of a bottle neck peeking out of a waste paper bin and grabbed that too, sending bunched tissues bouncing onto the floor.

'Katie, stop it. Hey! What are you doing?' Val cried when Kate pulled open her mother's wardrobe.

She tried to pull Kate away, but Kate'd had enough experience being pushed about by d'Artagnan for her mother to have much effect on her.

She wrenched open drawers that smelt of musty charity shops. At the back of the underwear drawer, she found what she was looking for. Her fingers closed around cold glass. With a sardonic smile, she pulled out the full bottle of cheap vodka and held it up to Val.

Val looked furious and snatched it out of Kate's hand. 'Leave me alone! Just go away, you horrid thing!'

'Why are you hiding bottles if you're not a drunk?' Kate challenged her.

'I was saving it. See? It's not open, is it?'

Kate shook her head in disbelief. 'And I bet you there's more, isn't there?'

She marched out of the bedroom with Val scurrying behind her and headed downstairs to the kitchen.

'Just stop what you're doing, Katie! This isn't fair. You gave me no warning. You can't just show up like this.'

Kate ignored her. She dumped the bottles she'd already collected in the sink and swung the cupboard doors open. The shelves were virtually empty. Kate reached behind a fat bag of rice, the only edible item going, and felt around. No bottles there. She looked around for more potential hiding places and noticed Val's eyes flicker towards the breadbin.

Kate unearthed another vodka bottle and added it to the sink.

Val looked close to tears. 'Why are you doing this? Stop it, Katie!'

Kate turned on her in exasperation. 'No, *you* need to stop it. I'm just trying to show you what you're doing to yourself. And to Xander! Have you stopped to think what effect this is having on him?'

'Xander's just fine.'

The horrors of Kate's own childhood came back and she clenched her teeth. 'Xander is not "fine". He needs a mother. We all needed a mother!'

'You turned out all right, didn't you? Got yourself a cosy little job—'

'You call this all right?' interrupted Kate, gesturing to herself. 'And this?' She pointed to where she knew a scar was above her eye. She shook her head in sadness. 'You have no idea, do you?'

'Things haven't been easy on me either, you know.' Val's face contorted in self-pity. 'I didn't ask for all of this. And if you bloody cared so much, why did you leave us?'

Kate spied an empty bottle poking through the top of the kitchen bin. She stepped closer. Yes, she could definitely smell it more now. 'I left because I wasn't going to let you drag me down with you. I'm sorry you had to raise us by yourself, I'm sorry that man only ever stayed around long enough to knock you up—'

'Don't speak about your father like that.'

'I'll speak about him however I see fit. He's been no father to me,' Kate retorted. She opened the bin lid and shook her head at its contents. 'I left because I wanted to get away from this!' In one swift movement, she heaved the plastic bin up onto the counter and emptied it into the sink. The clatter and crash of breaking bottles drowned out Val's scream of anger. She attacked Kate with her fists. Kate used the bin as a shield against the blows.

'Stop it, Mum!' she cried. 'Look at what you're doing!'

Val froze, chest heaving. For a moment she looked like she was going to cry, then her eyes turned a fiery shade. 'Get out!' she yelled and flung her hand towards the door. 'If you've got nothing nice to say then get out! Just get out!'

Kate trembled. A lump swelled in her throat and she pursed her lips to stop them quivering. Why was she bothering when this was the abuse she got in return? She threw down the bin, not caring when the cupboard door it hit fell off its hinges. She snatched up her handbag and lifted a warning finger to her mother.

'You'd better watch out. You do whatever the hell you want with your life, but I'm not going to let you ruin Xander's. Social Services will get involved and you'll be in a whole lot deeper shit if you're deemed an unfit mother. No more benefits—'

'Oh, bullshit,' Val spat. 'This is nothing. Social Services have got bigger fish to fry.'

Kate hated to admit that Val was probably right. A fifteen-year-old boy smoking a bit of marijuana wouldn't even register on their radar when they had babies with broken bones to deal with.

'Then I will go to them,' said Kate, summoning her courage. 'I'll report you. And I'd like to see how well you dry out in a prison cell. We'll see if there's a problem then or not, won't we?'

Val's lip curled in distaste. 'What kind of daughter are you, eh? Willing to send your own mother down? Get out, you little bitch.'

Kate didn't need to be told twice. She turned back by the door and met Val's putrid look with one of steel. 'If Xander fails his exams, then I will kick up shit. And you'd better bloody believe it.' She glanced up at the stairs. 'You hear that, Xander?' she called.

Xander didn't respond. It didn't matter to Kate. All that was important was that her mother had heard her.

12

GIVEN HER FAMILY drama and a heavy fall she'd taken that morning, Kate wasn't much in the mood for any more fireworks, but she'd promised Nicholas she'd attend his parents' Guy Fawkes party. Nicholas ushered her into a surprisingly modest reception room on her arrival and Kate rethought her presumptions of how wealthy bankers lived. The decor was classy without appearing gaudy and the high Victorian ceilings kept the room, full of guests, from feeling cramped.

'Kate, I'd like you to meet my parents, Bill and Nora Borden,' said Nicholas, gesturing to a couple near the fireplace.

'Evening!' boomed Bill Borden above the chatter. Tall and rather eccentrically dressed in a purple, crushed velvet suit, he reminded Kate a little of Bill Nighy. He held out his hand and Kate had the discomfort of offering him her left. They exchanged an awkward hand-squeezing shake.

'Sorry, my right is out of commission,' she said holding up her bandaged right wrist.

'What happened?'

'I fell off one of my horses. Well, not one of *my* horses. Actually, he's yours, but I exercise him for you,' Kate babbled.

Bill gave her a strange look.

'D'Artagnan?' asked Nicholas.

'No. Laughing Stock. I was helping fill in for one of the lads.'

Laughing Stock's regular rider, Billy, aka the Grim Reaper, had broken his wrist in his catwalk fall at The Golden Miller. Jack's mood had gone from dark to pitch black when Kate had followed suit, albeit with just a sprain.

'Not much to laugh about,' said Nora, rolling her pearl necklace anxiously between her fingers. In contrast to her husband, she was dressed in a demure cream suit that offset her mahogany-toned bob. She had watery hazel eyes and features that Kate recognised a lot of Nicholas in.

'Are you all right?' she said, touching Kate's arm. 'Is there anything we can get you?'

Kate shook her head with a smile, feeling more embarrassed than anything. 'I'm fine, really. Just a slight sprain.'

Nora smiled kindly. 'Nicholas has told us so much about you.'

If that was meant to reassure her, it had no such effect. 'Oh, dear,' she heard herself say.

Bill gave a hearty laugh. 'Nothing but good things. He's been like a teenager in love.'

Nicholas turned puce. '*Dad*,' he said out of the corner of his mouth.

'So you work at Jonny Levine's, is that right?' Bill asked Kate.

'No, Dad. Laughing Stock's with Jack Carmichael,' Nicholas patiently explained. 'The same as The Whistler.'

'And d'Artagnan,' Kate added. 'I look after him.'

Bill Borden looked mystified until Nicholas provided, 'French bred grey gelding, staying chaser, won at Wetherby last time out.'

'He's such a treat,' Kate gushed, trying to override her embarrassment that he didn't even know his own horses. 'And I'm so grateful you're giving him his chance at Cheltenham.'

'Ah, yes.' Bill tapped his nose and nudged her with a gangly elbow. 'All part of the master plan, if you know what I mean?'

Kate didn't know, but she smiled obediently. 'It's been an ambition of mine – as Nicholas has probably already told you – to take a horse to the Festival,' she said.

'Mine too, mine too,' Bill replied. 'And it's a tough road to get there. A tough sport all round, as you well know.'

Nora shook her head. 'It is so awfully dangerous. No place for a woman, if you ask me.'

Kate didn't respond.

Nicholas came to her rescue by putting an arm around her. 'I doubt Kate will always work in racing, Mum. Will you, Kate?'

Kate hesitated. That wasn't much of a rescue, come to think of it. 'Er – well—' She hadn't really thought of wanting to do anything different.

'Or at least not in the same capacity as you're in now,' Nicholas compromised.

Kate twisted her fingers together in discomfort. 'Well, perhaps in the future. But for now I'm enjoying it,' she said.

Nicholas gave her a puzzled look. 'But I thought you said you found it boring.'

Kate laughed in surprise. 'Boring? Goodness, no. It's far too demanding to get boring.'

'But at Leonie's—' He hesitated, then shook his head.

'Do it while you're young and fit,' said Bill, punching the air and nearly spilling his red wine.

'What about children?' asked Nora. 'You have to do that while you're young and fit as well and I can't imagine you'd be able to do both.'

Kate's mouth dropped open. Wow, Nicholas's parents didn't beat about the bush.

'Mum,' said Nicholas. 'Give Kate a break.' He gave Kate's waist a quick squeeze and removed his arm. 'I'll just go get us a drink. What would you like? Coke? Cranberry juice?'

Kate didn't care. She was just relieved that conversation was over. 'Cranberry juice sounds lovely, thank you.'

With Nicholas excused, Bill and Nora's attention fell on Kate once more, and she shifted uneasily in her black pumps.

'Do you not drink?' Bill asked.

'She's probably driving,' said Nora.

Kate hesitated. She hated it when people asked. 'No, it's not that. I—'

Nora's eyes widened in fear and Kate could see screaming illegitimate grandchildren running through her mind. She had the insane urge to giggle and tell Nora that no, the most intimate she and Nicholas had been was a snog.

'I just don't drink alcohol,' she said.

Bill looked puzzled. 'Is alcohol a problem for you?'

'No, no!' laughed Kate a little shrilly. That was a bit too close to the bone. 'I just don't like the taste.'

'Of course, of course,' said Bill with a frown. 'I apologise for asking.' He gave another small laugh, but this time it sounded more nervous than hearty. 'It's the obvious conclusion one jumps to, I'm afraid.' He took a swallow of his wine and glanced at his watch. 'I wonder where Ben is. He said he'd be here.'

Nora's mouth puckered up like a cat's bottom. 'So unreliable. Ah, Nicholas,' she said, her expression softening as her son reappeared with Kate's juice. 'I was just about to tell Kate how well you've organised everything tonight.'

'Fireworks start at nine o'clock sharp, and there's plenty to set off,' Nicholas said. He squeezed his mother's hand. 'I couldn't have done it all by myself though.'

Nora glowed.

'You have a lovely home,' Kate said, hoping to score back some brownie points.

'Perhaps Nicholas could show you around later. Do you live in Bristol as well?'

Kate shook her head. 'No, I live in Helensvale with my sister. The rest of my family live in Bristol, though,' she said then bit her lip.

'Really? Whereabouts?'

Too late. 'The other side of Clifton Suspension Bridge,' said Kate with an evasive wave of her hand.

Bill laughed. 'Kate, my dear, most of Bristol is on the other side of the bridge.'

'Around St Paul's way,' she said reluctantly. St Paul's was about as far removed from the Bordens' neighbourhood as one could possibly get.

To her relief, Ben entered the room just at that moment and neither Bill nor Nora seemed to register her reply.

'Ben!' Bill exclaimed in delight. 'We were starting to worry.'

Nicholas and Nora exchange dubious looks.

Ben clasped his hands and greeted them through a stiff jaw. 'Hello, Nora. Nicholas.'

Nicholas didn't reply. Kate felt his arm slip around her waist as Ben turned to her.

Ben's jaw relaxed. 'Hi Kate. You holding up?'

'Kate was just telling us about her family,' said Bill.

Ben's eyes twinkled. 'You didn't happen to bring Saskia with you, did you?'

'What does your father do?' asked Bill.

Oh, shit, thought Kate in despair. 'My parents are separated,' she said. 'We don't have much contact with him anymore.'

She couldn't quite bring herself to call that man her father. The last time she'd seen him was when she'd stumbled upon him packing a suitcase. She'd been eleven at the time. He'd tugged the zip shut, snagging it on a stray shirt tail in his haste, and had only noticed Kate in the doorway when he'd heaved it off the bed. His composure had faltered for a moment then his haste had returned. He'd patted her on the head as he'd passed through the doorway. 'Out the way there, Katie. Daddy's got to go away on business. Tell your mother I'll call her.'

But, of course, he hadn't.

'And your mother?' Nora asked.

Her mother had been devastated, seven months pregnant too. Kate chose her words carefully. 'She used to work at a magazine.'

'And now?'

'She – er – has... *difficulties*,' she said. 'She no longer works.'

'I've heard journalism is a very stressful job,' said Nora kindly. 'Do you share her writing talents? Being a writer sounds a much safer job.'

'Not if she were a war correspondent,' said Ben.

Nora's pencilled eyebrows steeped in disapproval. 'I'm not talking about that sort of journalism, Benedict.'

'Anyway, I'm not much of a writer,' blurted Kate. 'And my spelling's atrocious.'

'Nicholas could help you. He used to run the student newspaper at university. Didn't you, darling?'

Nicholas turned pink. 'I don't think Kate wants help with her homework, Mum,' he muttered.

'What's wrong with the job you already have?' Ben asked.

'Nothing,' said Kate. She glanced at the carriage clock on the mantelpiece and masked her sigh of relief. 'It's nearly nine o'clock, Nicholas,' she said. 'Do you want help setting things up?'

'Oh, no, it's all taken care of.'

'Oh,' she said with a weak smile. 'Great.'

Kate braced herself against the cold as she stood amongst the guests on the back lawn to watch the fireworks light up the sky. The Bordens hadn't scrimped on the show. For ten minutes, the sleepy suburb of Leighs Wood was turned into a war zone as bangs, cracks, and whizzes shook the quiet. The air became heavy with the smell of sulphur.

It was a terrific display, but Kate had to admit, as she cricked her neck back into place, that she was relieved when it was all over. She couldn't help imagining the animals cowering in fear at the noises and flashes.

She hoped Helensvale had gone easy on the celebrations. She hated to think of d'Artagnan and the rest of Aspen Valley Stables injuring themselves in their panic.

Everyone clapped as the last Catherine wheel faded to black and hurried back into the warmth of the house. Kate hung back, holding Nicholas's hand.

'You okay?' he asked, noticing her reluctance.

'I just want a quiet moment before we go back in,' she said.

'Anything wrong? If it's my parents, then please don't pay them any attention.'

Kate watched the last of the party ascend the stone steps and through the French doors before replying. 'I wanted to tell you—' She hesitated, unsure of how to say it tactfully. 'Nicholas, I like you. A great deal,' she added.

Nicholas gave a nervous laugh. 'Oh dear. I feel a "but" coming on. Look, if you think I've come on too heavy by introducing you to my folks—'

'No, it's not that. And there's no but. I'm glad to have met your parents. They're a fine example of why you're such a good man.'

Nicholas looked relieved. He squeezed her hand and lifted his other to cup her cheek. Warmed from his pocket, his fingers were comforting on her cold skin.

'I'm glad too,' he said. 'You're very special to me, Kate. I want to show you that.'

'You don't have anything to worry about,' she continued. 'I'm not going anywhere. I—' Oh no, her mental script was disappearing like the firework smoke on the breeze. 'You are the *only* one I'm interested in.'

'What are you trying to say?'

Kate closed her eyes in defeat. This wasn't working. 'Ben's a friend, but nothing more—'

'Ben?' Nicholas said in surprise and dropped his hand from her cheek. 'What does he have to do with anything?'

'I know you were upset the other night when you found out I visited Thistle Lodge, but you must believe me, it was just a friend helping out a friend. He's more interested in Saskia, anyway.'

Nicholas looked at her, brows pinched, lips parted in hesitation. 'Okay,' he said slowly.

Kate shook her head in frustration. He wasn't getting it. Not really. How could she make him understand he had nothing to fear from her friendship with his brother? 'Do you believe me? Please say you do.' She squeezed his hands. 'I don't want to come between you and Ben. I don't want you to fall out because of anything I do.'

'Kate, it's fine.'

Kate was confused. 'But what about the other night?'

'The other night?'

'Yes. Outside The Golden Miller, I saw you arguing—' She faltered when Nicholas's hold on her hands stiffened. 'I thought you...' She tailed off, suddenly very uncertain of her assumptions.

Nicholas shook his head and smiled. 'I'm sorry you saw us arguing. We weren't arguing about you.'

'Oh,' Kate said, wrong-footed. 'Okay.'

'It was nothing. Just some pesky thing. Siblings, eh? Don't you and Saskia ever argue?'

'Oh, all the time,' she said with a relieved laugh. 'My week isn't complete without a set-to with her.'

Nicholas kissed her and put his arm around her. 'I hope my parents haven't scared you away. My mother has a habit of putting the bootie in.'

'No, they're lovely. It's so nice that you get on so well with them.'

'I didn't realise your father wasn't around. Must have been tough growing up without him.'

'It had its moments.'

'What about your mother? You've met mine. I hope you'll introduce me to yours soon.'

Kate shook her head. 'You don't want to meet my mother.'

'Of course I do. She might think there's something wrong with me if you keep putting it off.'

'I'm not putting it off,' Kate replied. 'We just have a difficult relationship, that's all.'

'How so?'

Kate hesitated. After tonight's introductions, she was in no doubt telling Nicholas about her mother would be a mistake. 'It's a long story. Shall we go back inside? I can't feel my toes.'

Nicholas relented and they walked up the steps together.

13

KATE POPPED INTO the racing office to report a cut one of her horses had sustained during their morning workout. She opened the door and almost tripped over the threshold in surprise. Saskia and Jack were posing for a selfie, Saskia with a coy smile and Jack looking uncomfortable. Her sudden appearance didn't help and Jack pulled away and straightened his jacket. He treated them both to his default frown.

'Everything okay, Kate?'

Kate did her best to ignore what she'd just witnessed. 'Chic Shadow's nicked a heel. I've syringed it and cleaned it up, but thought I should let you know.'

Jack's frown deepened. 'Bad?'

'I don't think so. He's not lame.'

'Well, remind me tomorrow morning and we'll have another look before he does any work.'

'Sure.'

Jack gave an abrupt nod and exited the room into his office. Kate waited for the door to click shut before rushing over to Saskia.

'Saskia, you crazy fool,' she hissed. 'When is this going to stop?'

Saskia smirked as she reviewed the image on her phone. 'This is one for my Facebook profile, I reckon.' She held it out for Kate to see. 'We make a pretty handsome couple, don't you think?'

Kate threw a wary glance at Jack's door and brushed past Saskia to her computer.

'What are you doing?' Saskia said.

Kate clicked furiously onto Facebook and typed a name into the search field. 'I'll show who else make a handsome couple. Look.' She wrenched the screen sideways so Saskia had a full-on view of Pippa Carmichael's profile. Her background image was of Aspen Valley at sunset, but like Kate had predicted, her profile picture was of her, Jack, and Gabrielle.

Saskia pouted and snatched the mouse away to close the page. 'Lighten up, will you?' she grumbled. 'I've read Russian novels more cheerful than you. Just let me live my own life.'

Kate clenched her teeth. She couldn't get into a domestic with Saskia when Jack was in the next room. 'I'll let you live your life when you decide to grow up,' she said.

Without waiting for a response she turned on her heel and exited the office.

Kate's mood was not improved when d'Artagnan put in another lethargic effort on the Gallops. Jack called Kate over on her way back down the hill.

'Does he make any noise?' he asked. 'Could be his breathing causing a problem.'

'No, he sounds clean as a whistle.'

'Could be he's just not a good worker. Saves himself for the big days out.'

'When is his next big day out?'

'Haydock for the Betfair Chase.'

Kate sucked in her breath. The Betfair Chase would be her first Grade One.

'But if he carries on like this...' Jack said, shaking his head.

'Well, you say that—' Kate began then stopped herself. Who was she to give a champion trainer advice on how to manage his horses?

Jack raised an eyebrow. 'Yes?'

'I think – I think he's bored.'

'Bored?'

'Yes. He's a smart horse and smart horses get bored quickly. You've seen the toys he needs in his stable. I think cantering up this same hill every day is just making him bored.'

'Horses usually enjoy routine. It's safe,' countered Jack.

Kate looked down at her reins and mumbled, 'D'Artagnan isn't your usual horse.'

Jack puffed out his cheeks and looked out across the valley for inspiration. 'Tell you what,' he said at last. 'Take him for a spin around the estate.'

Kate stared at him. The estate he was referring to had to be the stately home on the other side of the hill. 'Aspen Court?' she said. 'Are we allowed?'

Jack shrugged. 'As long as we don't make it a habit, I'm sure they won't mind. You ever been?'

She shook her head. She'd seen glimpses of it on *In The Running*, the reality show that had been following the Ta' Qali Racing Syndicate, two of whom were members of the household.

'Then it'll be an adventure for the both of you,' said Jack. 'Go have fun, have a canter through the grove. Just follow the road over the hill. There's a gate beside the cattle grid.'

'You mean now?'

Jack gestured to d'Artagnan with distaste. 'Well, he's hardly had a workout.'

He started muttering about their chances in the Gold Cup, but Kate was already turning d'Artagnan around, lest he change his mind.

At the top of the hill, Kate halted her horse to look around. A brisk breeze lifted d'Artagnan's mane and seeped through Kate's jacket. She'd been up here plenty of times, but it had always been on foot to catch horses from the top paddocks and she'd always been in too much of a rush to stop and admire the view. Thunderheads skidded across the kingfisher blue sky, casting shadows across hedged fields that reminded Kate of a lumpy quilt slung over a slumbering giant. A shaft of sunlight turned one hill into emeralds and she could just make out a silvery line trickling across it – a stream or tributary of the River Avon – and she realised Thistle Lodge Stables must be near there.

For a moment, she yearned for the simplicity of Ben's world. No mother drinking herself into an early grave, no brother taking drugs, no sister sabotaging their jobs, no stress over the horses' performances at the races.

She looked to her left where, somewhere over the horizon, lay Cheltenham, and Kate remembered why she did what she did. For four days every March, the otherwise unremarkable Gloucestershire town became the epicentre of champions, where its heartbeat pulsed like earth tremors through the jump racing world. The skyline over the neighbouring county was black and a distant grumble of thunder rolled over on the wind.

Down below, Aspen Valley Stables looked toy-like. The tiles on one of the stable block's four extensions was a different shade of red to the rest, evidence of the extra stabling that had been built in the summer.

Stabling for a hundred and twenty horses, all filled, thought Kate. That had to be a mammoth task, and she was pretty sure the recent developments to the facilities had been in no small part down to Bill Borden's patronage. His horses accounted for about ten percent of those stables.

It was difficult to get her head round the man she'd met the previous night. He had been so – so *normal.* Kate didn't like to think she judged people before she knew them – or even at all – but the Borden contingent had come with a reputation that was hard to ignore: that the big shot investment banker owner wasn't afraid to flash the cash, that one of his sons 'worked' for his daddy and the other got to ride all the sales-topper winners.

Kate shook her head and shivered in shame. None of the Bordens – or the de Jagers – were like that. Sure, they had their problems, but money hadn't tainted them like she knew it did others. They'd accepted her, after all, hadn't they?

While Kate sat, lost in thought, d'Artagnan gazed out over the countryside. She ran her hand down his mane, which had thankfully grown out of the punk rocker style he had sported at the start of the season.

She leaned down and placed her cheek beside the warmth of his strong neck. 'Come on, fella. We're not going to get to Cheltenham standing around like this.'

The aspen grove that Jack had mentioned was dark and spooky. Even d'Artagnan had the woolies, shying at rustles in the undergrowth. A snap of a branch and a blink of shadow made them both jump. Kate clucked her tongue, hoping that a little speed would dispel the eerie whispers of the trees. D'Artagnan broke into a canter, his hoofbeats muffled by the soft carpet of fallen leaves.

Kate stood up in her stirrups and pressed her fists against her horse's neck. 'Come on, d'Artagnan. Let's stretch those legs.'

D'Artagnan flicked an ear, but declined to oblige. A sudden movement through the trees though, and d'Artagnan didn't need to be asked twice. Kate sat low over his neck. His hooves beat in time with her heart. There was definitely someone following them. But who, she couldn't think. Groundsmen perhaps? Maybe, but she was sure someone would have called out and asked what they was doing. Visitors to the estate? Kate had a nasty feeling the estate was closed to the public during winter. An icy thought turned her blood cold. Poachers? She'd heard about the killing of Aspen Court's prized stag.

Out of her peripheral vision she glimpsed shadows moving faster and the more insistent crackle of crushed undergrowth. She pushed for more speed. D'Artagnan responded willingly. Safety lay out in the open parkland, but the grove stretched endlessly before them.

'Come on, champ. Faster,' she called.

D'Artagnan's ears flicked back at the tremor in her voice. Suddenly a rush of tawny brown and tan burst out of the shadows. Kate cried out and d'Artagnan swerved hard, making her clutch his mane. Kate's eyes darted about her and an almost hysterical laugh of relief bubbled out.

D'Artagnan realised it at the same time.

The deer herd were running with them, behind them, on either side. Spindly legs leapt over tangled bushes. A couple jumped into their path to lead the way. Kate ducked her head beneath her elbow and saw more bringing up the rear. She whooped, and by the way d'Artagnan's ears pricked forward, she knew his fear had passed as well.

She soon found she didn't have to urge him on anymore. His blood was up and he wanted to stay with the herd. They hurdled a fallen tree trunk and Kate laughed again as the deer, just a couple of feet either side of them, bounded over as well. D'Artagnan puffed to keep up. The deer might be small, but they were swift, and soon Kate had to admit defeat.

As the light at the end of the grove filtered through, she slowed the big grey to a trot and watched the deer bound out of range.

D'Artagnan snorted and tugged at the reins, wanting to gallop on, but Kate brought him back as they reached the edge of the treeline. She patted his damp neck and grinned.

'Well!' she said. 'That's not something you do every day, is it?'

D'Artagnan shook his head in response, making her laugh. Out in the open, Kate glimpsed the corner of Aspen Court's honey gold walls beyond a sloping bank. It seemed a world away from her own. Maybe she would take a wander down and ask if they were open in the off-season. She'd heard that the local hunt met on the front lawns every season for a drag hunt. Perhaps that was something she and Nicholas could go see together.

Just as that idea appealed to her though, fat bullets of rain began to fall. The angry clouds she'd seen earlier had swept away the blue sky. They were in for a drenching.

With a sigh, she turned d'Artagnan to head back to the stables. She had work to do and they'd had their bit of fun for the day. What's more, the rain heralded a more insistent task to be carried out: she needed to sort things out with her mother.

14

VAL CRESWELL STOPPED short outside the entrance to St Paul's Community Centre and turned accusing eyes on Kate.

'What are we doing here? You said we were going shopping.'

'We are. I just thought we'd stop here for a while.' Kate took her mother's arm to guide her inside, but Val pulled away.

'You liar, Katie. Look at the sign. It says Alcoholics Anonymous!' With a humph, she stalked back down the path.

'Come on, Mum. Please,' Kate said, hurrying after her. 'Just this once. Do it for me if not for yourself.'

Val turned on her in anger. 'There's nothing wrong with me. Stop trying to tell me there is. Stop... *humiliating* me!'

Kate's patience wore thin. 'Do you think I want to do this? That I *enjoy* it?'

'I don't know, Kate. I don't seem to know you at all these days. You only bother to come round so you can point fingers at me. My life is hard enough, you know.'

'I know it is. That's why I'm trying to help you—'

'How can going to an AA meeting be helpful? I'm not an alcoholic!'

A hundred angry retorts jumped to the tip of Kate's tongue, but she swallowed them back. 'If you'd just go to this one meeting,' she said, her voice low as she became aware of the stares from passersby. 'You'll see it's nothing to be ashamed of.'

Val laughed hysterically. 'You're telling me *I've* nothing to be ashamed of? So says the daughter who left home at the earliest opportunity and didn't bother visiting for seven years. Who's ashamed of who exactly?'

Kate flinched at the home truth. 'I was working in Newmarket, which isn't exactly down the road. And seven years is a bit of an exaggeration. I came back most Christmases.'

'Oh, so now *I'm* the one who's exaggerating? You're the one accusing me of being an alcoholic just because I like the odd drink. You might think yourself too good for that – you with your prissy little attitude,' she said with a sneer and disdainful flick of her hand. 'But that doesn't make me an alcoholic!'

'Mum, please. I'm trying to help you.'

She put what she hoped was a reassuring hand on her mother's arm, but Val tugged away and set off down the street.

'If this is the sort of help you give, then I don't want it,' she flung over her shoulder.

Kate stood for a moment, sucking in a lungful of air to stem the tears that threatened. She felt like letting her mother go, leaving her to carve her own bottle-shaped coffin.

Why should *she* go to all this effort when Val was so obviously unwilling to help herself? Why should *she* feel guilty when she wasn't the one with the problem? Why should *she* put herself through this sniping and hurt when it wasn't her life in danger?

She should just let her mother get on with it and to hell with the consequences. She'd put up with twenty-seven years of this bullshit. There'd been no support network for her when she'd had problems at school, no guidance into adulthood, no chance of a carefree teenage life when she'd spent most of her time looking after her younger siblings—

Kate's thoughts screeched to a halt. There was Xander to think of. She couldn't leave her mother to the wolves even if she wanted to.

She ran down the street after Val. 'Mum! Mum, wait!'

Val carried on walking. 'I'm not doing it, Katie,' she said once Kate had caught up. 'I'm not going to sit there alongside a bunch of drunks and losers and have you try to convince me I'm one of them.'

Kate didn't know how to reply. It seemed a hopeless argument. 'Think of Xander.'

Val stopped. Kate looked away, unable to meet her mother's accusatory gaze, and sighed. Then from behind them, she heard her name being called. Kate recognised the voice before she'd even turned around and her heart flip-flopped into her shoes.

Ben jogged a couple of steps to bridge the gap between them. Kate glanced at the community centre, wondering if he knew its significance.

Val turned to Kate with raised eyebrows. 'A friend of yours?'

Ben reached them and gave Kate a warm kiss on the cheek. The smell of his aftershave made her light-headed.

'Hello. I'm Ben,' he said holding out his hand to Val.

Kate sighed. 'Ben, this is my mother, Val. Mum, this is my friend, Ben.'

'Hello, Ben,' Val said, turning on the charm. 'How nice to meet a friend of Katie's. I don't often get the chance.'

'I thought it was you back there,' said Ben. 'I called out, but you couldn't have heard me.'

Kate froze. What if he'd heard their conversation, witnessed their argument outside St Paul's? What if Nicholas found out and he put two and two together?

'You're the last person I expected to bump into in the middle of Bristol.' She tried to keep her tone light. 'Shopping?'

Ben held up a bag bearing the logo of Drayton Saddlery. 'Yeah, and meeting a friend.'

'Us too,' Kate said quickly. 'Shopping, that is.'

A short silence followed, whereupon Ben beamed at them both and said, 'Can I treat you to a hot drink and mince pie? There's a teashop just over there.'

'No, I don't think—'

'That would be lovely!' Val interrupted. She gave Ben a dazzling smile then turned it on Kate. Kate could see the hint of malice in her eyes. She was doing this on purpose. To punish Kate for 'humiliating' her.

'What about your friend?' Kate said. 'Won't you be late meeting him?'

Ben cleared his throat. 'Actually, it's a her – she's really more of an acquaintance than a friend – and I've just come from there.'

'You must be so busy though. And we really ought to get on.'

'Nonsense, Katie,' laughed Val. 'We've plenty of time.' She patted Kate's arm and gave Ben a patronising smile. 'A bit of a worrier, is our Katie.'

Ben looked from mother to daughter with uncertainty. 'Okay. Well, if you're sure.'

Babs' Teashop reminded Kate of her mother. Respectable on the outside, but tired and broken inside. Her arms stuck to the laminate table when she leaned on it and she only hoped the stained and faded menu from which she'd chosen from wasn't reflective of the currant bun she ordered with her tea.

'Do you live locally?' Ben asked Val.

'Not far.' She elbowed Kate and teased, 'But perhaps not as far away as Katie would like.'

Ben laughed obediently, but Kate noticed his brows knit. Oh God, why had she let herself be talked into this? There was no possibility of it ending well.

'If that was the case, I would still be living in Newmarket,' she said. 'I took the job at Aspen Valley to be closer to you lot, remember.'

Val pulled a face as if to say the good intentions of her daughter's move were negligible.

'How's d'Artagnan getting on?' Ben said diplomatically.

'Great,' Kate said, perking up. 'Jack had me take him for a spin round Aspen Court's grounds. We got caught up in a stampeding deer herd. He loved it.'

Ben laughed. 'Let's hope he loves the stampede of horses he's going to meet next weekend.'

Kate's stomach flipped at the thought of d'Artagnan lining up in the Grade One Betfair Chase. She knew they were still a long way from Cheltenham, and if he failed to deliver in the time between, Jack might very well pull him out. 'He'll leave them trailing in his wake.'

'That'll be the plan at any rate,' he chuckled.

Kate was aware of her mother becoming fidgety, no doubt itching for a tipple, but she ignored her. 'How's Jerry?'

'He's fine, yeah. Seymour's still smitten with him.'

Kate snorted. 'Can't say I blame him. How much do you think you'll get for him?'

Ben shrugged. 'That's not as important to me as where he goes. Little point in running a rehab centre if you're just going to throw them to the wolves again.'

Val tensed in her seat. 'You run a rehab centre?' she asked.

Kate almost laughed. By the look on her mother's face, she must think bumping into Ben was part of the grand plan.

'Yes, for ex-racehorses.'

Val laughed. 'What – do they get hooked on all the drugs that are pumped into them to race?'

'UK racing is – by and large – drug-free,' replied Ben. 'What my business involves is retraining ex-racehorses who still have plenty more miles left on the clock.'

91

'Ah, I should have guessed it had something to do with horses. You won't find any horsier girl than Kate.'

Val was saved from Kate's waspish reply by the arrival of their orders.

'Are you doing Christmas shopping?' asked Ben, breaking open sachet after sachet of sugar.

'Nothing specific,' Kate mumbled through a mouthful of currant bun. Whoever the baker was had been a bit heavy-handed with the baking soda, but otherwise it was rather tasty.

'Kate thought she'd surprise me with a morning out,' said Val.

Kate sent her a warning look.

'Lovely,' Ben beamed. 'Reminds me I need to do my Christmas shopping soon. I can't stand the last minute rush.'

'Do it online,' said Kate. 'That's what I do.'

'Oh, but going out and braving the crowds is part of the gift,' countered Val. 'Actually, visiting the stores shows that you care. Doing it online seems so impersonal somehow. You know what I mean?'

Ben opened his mouth, but made no sound.

Kate sympathised. 'Don't worry, Ben. You don't have to answer that.'

Ben closed his mouth. 'My problem is I never know what to get.'

'Depends on who you're buying for,' said Val. 'As a mother, I always liked a bottle of my favourite perfume.'

Kate stared hard at the remnants of Ben's empty sugar sachets. She'd never bought her mother perfume. Not only that, she knew her mother had always asked for a 'fancy' bottle of fizz.

'That's one present I don't have to buy, sadly,' Ben said, tinkering with his teaspoon in his coffee.

'Oh, I am sorry,' said Val, sounding genuine.

'She's been dead a long time. I never knew her.'

'That's so sad,' Val said, reaching across and squeezing Ben's hand. 'How awful for you not to have a mother.'

Kate's sympathy for Ben was suddenly overshadowed by resentment of Val's words. What sort of mother had she been to her?

'What do you reckon Nicholas would like?' Ben asked.

'Truly, I haven't a clue. I was going to ask you the same question.'

'Who's Nicholas?' asked Val.

Ben hesitated. His eyes flickered between Kate and her mother. Kate gave an almost imperceptible shake of her head.

'My brother,' said Ben. 'We're all part of the same horsey world.'

Kate gave him a grateful look and he responded with a wink of allegiance. He took a glug of his coffee – really, his hands were too big for the dainty china – and turned a charming smile on Val.

'So Val, you've heard about my horses. May I ask what you do?'

Kate's heart dropped. Hoping that if she finished her currant bun quickly it might hasten the others and get this dreaded 'tea party' over with, she shoved the last of it into her mouth.

Her mistake.

A crumb caught in her throat and she was overcome by a coughing fit. Ben ineffectually thumped her on the back while she coughed into her paper napkin. She reached for her drink only to realise she'd finished it already. Ben was quick to give her his. Kate took a gulp and dislodged the crumb, but her taste buds cringed at the sweetness of the liquid. She turned watery eyes on him. 'Thanks,' she croaked.

'I write,' said Val.

Ben's eyebrows shot up, impressed. Kate's shot up too, although hers reacted more in surprise.

'A writer, eh?' Ben said. 'Novels? Journalism?'

'Journalism,' said Val. 'A food critic for a magazine.'

'What a job to have,' Ben said with envy. 'I bet you had a great time growing up with only the best food, eh, Kate?'

Kate was tempted to say that actually, she'd done most of the cooking herself. That Val's 'working' lunches had usually involved a bottle or two of wine and, once started, Val hadn't seen any reason not to carry on for the rest of the day. Kate had a suspicion restaurateurs had grown wise to her mother's weakness and had plied her with even more booze so that they would get a glowing – if somewhat hazy – review.

Kate bit her lip and smiled. 'It was an interesting childhood, I'll give it that.'

Val glared at her. Kate noticed the tremor to her mother's hand as she replaced her cup in its saucer. Val also noticed it and was quick to hide her hands beneath the table. 'I think it's time I made a move,' said Val.

'Yes,' said Kate, gathering her bag and preparing to leave. But Val pushed her down.

'No, no, Katie. You stay here. I need to get back. I've work to do.' She pulled her coat on and smiled at Ben. 'Maybe I should review this place! It was lovely meeting you, Ben, and thank you for the coffee. Kate, thank you for your surprise gesture this morning,' she said pausing to pick the right words. 'It has been most enlightening.'

With Val gone, Kate faced Ben with a sigh. And *relax*.

Ben raised an eyebrow. 'So, what's the story with you two?'

The gentle tone to his voice caught Kate off guard and tears pricked her eyes. She looked down at her scrunched up napkin and blinked them away. 'I'm sorry. I'm being silly. It's just hard, that's all. You know how it is.'

'Sure.' Ben carried on looking at her. 'You want to tell me about it?'

Kate looked up and gulped. She really could do with an ally, just someone to dump all her grievances on. Ben wouldn't judge, and he had such a genuine look on his face — one that said he wasn't just asking because it was the polite thing to do or because he was nosy. He really did want to help her get it off her chest (God knew her chest was heavy enough).

She swallowed hard. 'Do you promise not to tell? Not even Nicholas?'

Ben held up two fingers. 'Scout's honour.'

Kate almost smiled. 'You're meant to hold up three fingers,' she whispered.

Ben looked at his incorrect salute, shrugged and put them down. 'I wasn't one for building campfires anyway. But I can honour a promise.'

Kate took a deep breath. 'Mum and I weren't really shopping...'

15

TELLING ALL TO Ben turned out to be surprisingly therapeutic. They'd sat in Babs' Teashop drinking endless cups of tea while Kate spilled out her fears and frustrations.

Kate had plenty of time to go over that day in her mind as Aspen Valley's lorry trundled east to Huntingdon where Fontainebleau was lining up in a midweek handicap hurdle. Her two work colleagues, Woody and June, were too busy pretending not to flirt with one another to notice the silence coming from her corner of the cab.

She'd taken a swallow of her cold tea once the last of her woes had been spilled, and Ben had nodded in thought.

'Sometimes a person has to hit rock bottom before they can start climbing up. They call it the ping-pong effect,' he'd said.

Kate couldn't bear to think of her mother getting any worse. How was she meant to sit back and let it happen? And to let it happen to Xander as well as their mother?

'Does Xander like horses?' Ben had asked. 'Send him round my place. It might do him good to have some male company, and I could always do with another set of hands.'

Kate had perked up at this suggestion. She couldn't think of anyone better to 'mentor' her teenage brother – apart from Nicholas of course, but since she couldn't tell Nicholas her family dramas he wasn't a valid contender for the title.

The only challenge now was to get Xander to agree. He'd never shown much interest in her job, but then again, he was fifteen, he didn't show much interest in anything but Man United or girls.

Before they'd parted, Kate had pleaded with him again not to tell anyone.

Ben had tapped his nose and winked. 'Mum's the word.'

* * *

Blue skies and white vapour clouds flew overhead as the sixteen runners circled the infield. Kate stood by the track's exit chute, fingers rat-a-tatting the plastic running rail. Fontainebleau was no superstar, he was approaching thirteen and hadn't won since his four-year-old season. That's not to say he hadn't come close over the years – Fontainebleau was Aspen Valley's unofficial bridesmaid, with two dozen runner-up prizes to his name. But they'd switched back to hurdles for today's outing and Kate was quietly hopeful of his chances. The sunshine that bathed the course wasn't strong enough to dry the ground out and, with the overnight downpour, her horse would love the boggy conditions. The starter climbed his platform and raised his yellow flag.

Kate's mobile vibrated in her pocket.

What do you say to a home-cooked meal Friday night? I do a mean oysters bienville. Nicholas xxx

Kate's attention flickered back to the screen in front of the grandstands. The horses were filing out of the infield and jogging towards the tape.

'Bugger,' she muttered and pocketed her phone.

The starter's flag fell and the tape whipped back. The sixteen horses set off at a sedate pace for the three and a quarter mile marathon. Kate's confidence grew. Fontainebleau wasn't a fast horse and the steady pace would suit his cruising speed. Kate picked out Rhys's pink jacket and yellow cap bobbing in a tightly packed midfield.

The field rapped the first two hurdles. A couple out back, short of room with a view, blundered over the second and the field lost one rider to the turf. Kate winced. She wanted the pace steady, but she wished the front runners would pick it up a bit so the field could string out.

'And it's Gin Rummy showing the way to The Great Pretender,' drawled the commentator. 'Hiroshima shares third with Run Rudolph Run and Streetlife on the outside. Then it's back to Quasimodo matching strides with Fontainebleau in seventh.'

The horses rumbled past the grandstands for the first time. Rhys's pristine silks were already splattered with mud. The runners swung right around the far turn into the back stretch and up the incline to the third.

Kate transferred her gaze from the course to the screen. She knocked her knuckles on the rail as the field closed in around Fontainebleau.

Rhys pulled down a set of muddied goggles, making Kate grimace. Fontainebleau would be getting it all in the face, poor soul.

The horses popped over the next. Fontainebleau pecked as he clipped heels with the horse in front of him. Rhys took a tug, but it was a hopeless case. They were hemmed in on all sides.

Kate cringed as they took the next. There was no opportunity for Fontainebleau to find a rhythm, and even though she was no jockey, she knew rhythm was crucial for this marathon task. The four frontrunners led the way over the fourth. Two of Kate's fellow grooms groaned in despair as a horse slipped on landing and brought down another. She wasn't enjoying the race. Thanks to the boggy ground, what should have been a fairly simple task was becoming more dangerous by the second.

The depleted field hurdled the fifth, rounding the turn without any major mishaps, and steered back into the home straight for the second time.

'The Great Pretender now takes over at the head of affairs,' called the commentator. 'Gin Rummy drops back. Run Rudolph Run—no, *Quasimodo* now moves into second...' While the commentator had the thankless task of distinguishing the jockeys' muddied silks, Kate kept her eyes trained on her horse. He'd found some room, helped by fallers and horses trailing out the back. She gripped the running rail in hope, encouraged to see Fontainebleau's loping stride take them easily over the ground.

The sixth and seventh came close together in front of the stands and the small crowd gave a muted cheer. Rhys lowered his posture and Fontainebleau moved up into fifth position.

Kate jigged up and down. 'Come on, Font,' she murmured. 'Let's break this duck once and for all.'

With the increase in tempo, the field streamed over the seventh. Fontainebleau was caught off stride. Kate sucked in her breath. Her horse reached for the jump, nose and toes touching. Kate willed him to clear the jump. Fontainebleau touched down off-balance and slipped on the ploughed landing side. He crashed down onto his shoulder and slid along the ground.

'And Fontainebleau is down! Takes a nasty fall!' cried the commentator.

Kate's knees gave way and only her hold on the rail kept her upright. The field corkscrewed around Fontainebleau's prostrate bulk and galloped away, abandoning him in the mud.

Teeth chattering, Kate waited for her horse to get up. For agonising seconds, he didn't rise. Then with a lurch of his head, he staggered to his feet.

Kate exhaled. She ducked beneath the rail and sprinted down the side of the course. Rhys was also on his feet, looking none the worse for his tumble, albeit a little muddier. Heart pounding in her ears, she watched him take Fontainebleau's reins and lead him forward. She braced herself for the staggering step of a broken horse. Fontainebleau took four even steps and she relaxed. He was okay.

Dusk had long fallen by the time Kate led Fontainebleau down the ramp and back onto Aspen Valley soil. The gelding walked gingerly beside her. Stiffness had set in after the three and a half hour lorry journey, and his adrenalin was no longer a sufficient pain reliever.

While he tucked into his supper, Kate swept a massage pad over his neck, shoulders and back. Fontainebleau stamped his hoof and swung his head round to pull a threatening face.

'Sorry, sweetheart. I know it's not pleasant, but it'll help, I promise.'

It was hard physical work, but in the cosy confines of the stable with the salty taste of horses and hay in the air and the yard outside deserted in the darkness, Kate was content.

The gurgle of a young child's laughter stopped her mid-sweep. A child? She poked her head over Fontainebleau's door. Next door, d'Artagnan was also looking out, football hanging from his mouth, ears pricked towards the adjoining row of stables. Kate followed his gaze.

Outside Peace Offering's stable stood Jack's wife, Pippa, holding a toddler up to stroke the yard's Grand National hero. Jack walked across from the office to join them. Kate moved back into the shadows, but couldn't stop herself from watching them. She'd only seen Gabrielle a couple of times since her entrance into the world last Christmas. Small pudgy hands slapped down on Peace Offering's forehead and she received a gentle telling off from her father. Peace Offering didn't seem to mind. He nudged the child's thick anorak, eliciting more giggles.

'Mind her fingers,' warned Jack. 'He'll mistake them for carrots. Come here, Gabs.'

Pippa handed over Gabrielle and Jack bounced her into a more secure position high in his arms. Gabrielle held out her flannel rabbit to Peace

Offering and squealed in glee when he took an ear between his teeth and tried to tug it out of her hands.

Kate sighed and leaned back against the doorframe. She'd only ever known Jack Carmichael, the businessman and trainer, and when he was feeling particularly iron-fisted, it was difficult to remember he was still a person behind it all. Yet here was no better example of who he was when he let his guard down. Laughter relaxed the lines on his forehead, and a smile released the grim set of his mouth.

She couldn't really blame Saskia for finding him attractive. And not just physically, so it was pointless saying one would have to be blind not to see it. It was in his manner – his total commitment to his horses, the competitive steel in his eyes, tempered with this softness for those whom he loved that Kate was now witnessing. But there was the key. *Those whom he loved* did not and should not ever include Saskia.

Even though she could see the strong bond between Jack and his new family, she also knew the might of Saskia's seductive powers. No man was immune, regardless of their marital status.

Gabrielle made a grab for Peace Offering's forelock and Jack was quick to ensure she didn't pull it too hard.

What a lucky little girl to grow up loved by two stable (in all senses of the word) parents. What would it be like to have a father? Not just for when she'd been a child, but now into adulthood? Would he have sat her down to discuss the serious business of career prospects and taxes and home-buying? What about when she married? Her 'fiancé' wouldn't have anyone to ask permission. Of course, the fact that that was old-fashioned and generally ignored in the modern world didn't matter. For Kate, not having a father made this one more thing she'd be denied. He wouldn't give her away at her wedding or make a speech at the reception or share part of the first dance with her. None of that would happen.

Kate shook her head. Gabrielle didn't know how lucky she was.

As her thoughts lingered on wedding vows and marquee receptions, she suddenly remembered Nicholas's text.

'Oh, shit,' she hissed.

Pulling out of sight of the Carmichaels, she retrieved her phone from her pocket. There was another message from Nicholas.

Or I can just do shepherd's pie if seafood isn't your thing.

Kate hesitated as she reread his earlier message and the penny dropped. She hadn't picked up on the subtext before. A romantic home-cooked meal would mean visiting Nicholas's house in Bristol. In the evening. Involving oysters. She didn't need to be Miss Marple to figure out what he had in mind.

'Sorry, been racing all day,' she murmured as she typed. 'I love seafood. What time?'

Kate and Saskia's landlady was waiting on the landing when Kate dragged her feet up the stairs to their second floor flat.

'Hello, Mrs Singh,' said Kate. 'Everything all right?'

The plump Indian woman folded her arms across her chest and glowered at Kate. 'You think I don't know what you're doing in there?' she demanded.

Kate paused, her hand on the balustrade. Mrs Singh lived in the flat directly above them and with walls like paper, it wouldn't have surprised Kate if she *did* know everything they did.

'I'm sorry?'

'You and your sister, you know what's written in your contract? No smoking, it says.'

'But I don't smoke, Mrs Singh,' she said, then, after a pause, added, 'And neither does Saskia.'

Mrs Singh's eyes blazed. 'I'm not a fool. I know what's going on in this building.'

Kate pulled out her keys and unlocked the flat door. 'I'm not doubting you, Mrs Singh. Maybe it's one of the other tenants, but neither Saskia or I smoke. It can't be us.' She opened the door and looked to her landlady for dismissal.

Mrs Singh tutted then waved a hand at her. 'I have my eye on you two. And if you do not know how to abide by your contract then I can find someone else who does.'

Kate closed the door behind her and leant against it. Had Saskia started smoking without her noticing? She didn't think so.

16

SEVEN O'CLOCK ON Friday night wouldn't have been doable if Nicholas's house hadn't had off-street parking for Kate to nip into two minutes past the hour. The house, semi-detached with period features, didn't appear particularly lavish, but Kate had a feeling houses in Clifton that had parking for two cars within its borders didn't come cheap.

Nicholas welcomed her inside, hair neatly combed, wearing white chinos and a diamond-patterned golf sweater. Kate nearly asked if he needed to see her membership card before entering, but thought better of it. Nicholas looked too nervous to see the funny side.

She followed him through to the open plan kitchen lounge, noting the neatness of everything. Framed photographs hung from the walls of Nicholas and his parents, Nicholas graduating, Nicholas receiving an achievement award from work. Kate didn't doubt Nicholas put his all into everything he did. A 'grinder' was what racing folk would call him. Her mind took a sharp decline into the gutter and she turned a snort of amusement into a cough.

'Hope you're not getting the 'flu,' said Nicholas, handing her a drink.

Kate shook her head. 'No, just a tickle.'

'Good, good. Make yourself comfortable then,' he said, gesturing to the room. 'I'll put on some music.'

There was an undisputable whiff of his mother's decorative influence in the soft furnishings, but that wasn't such a bad thing, Kate was quick to tell herself. It's just that cream lounge suites made her nervous when she was holding cranberry juice.

While Nicholas attended to the stereo, Kate took a closer look at the shelves of books and photos. She withdrew a random book to find out Nicholas's reading tastes then pulled a dubious face at Tony Blair's autobiography.

She couldn't help but notice that in all the photos of the Borden family – on holiday, celebrating Christmas – Ben was absent. Kate frowned, and only partly because James Blunt's simpering voice had suddenly filled the room. Ben had been absent from all the family photographs at Bill and Nora's house as well.

She stopped at a photo of a young chubby-cheeked Nicholas, school blazer straining around his middle. He was sat with three other boys in front of a chess board.

'You were captain of the chess club?' Kate said, reading the caption and raising a teasing eyebrow.

Nicholas gave an embarrassed chuckle and came to join her. 'I was going through a rebellious phase.'

'Do you still play?'

He shook his head. 'Never really enjoyed it, to be honest.'

'But you were captain.'

Nicholas shrugged and peered closer at the picture, squinting at the boys' faces. 'I wasn't much of a sportsman. And Dad wanted me to play something, so it was either that or the clarinet.'

'I bet it served you well,' she said. 'All that strategizing and tactical play can't be so very different from what you do now at your dad's investment firm.'

'It's not so much "Dad's investment firm" as it is just a company that he has a majority shareholding in. I mean, he doesn't really have anything to do with it. I run the shop—'

Kate regretted speaking. 'I know, I'm sorry,' she interrupted and hastily shoved Tony Blair back onto the bookshelf. She tempted him back into good humour with a smile. 'Anyone who can captain the chess team without even enjoying the game must be pretty darn smart.'

Nicholas gave her a repentant smile. 'Sorry. Touchy subject.'

His smile wavered as he spotted the book Kate had replaced, and with a quick frown, put it back in its correct alphabetical place. He smacked his lips together and raised his eyebrows. 'What say we head into the kitchen so I can check the food?'

Kate gave Nicholas ten out of ten for effort. The table was set with flowers and candles and while James Blunt wasn't exactly her first choice of music, she could see what mood he was trying to achieve. It turned out he was also an ace chef. Shrimp and mussel soup was followed by oysters succulent beneath their crispy coating of breadcrumbs and parmesan cheese. She closed her eyes in ecstasy. She could get used to this.

'Nice?' asked Nicholas.

Kate opened her eyes. 'Mmm. Delicious. A man of many talents.'

Nicholas gave his usual embarrassed cough-like chuckle. 'My mother's recipe,' he said, patting his mouth with his napkin (one made from starched fabric, not like the kitchen roll Kate relied on).

Over dinner, they discussed the next day's racing at Haydock where d'Artagnan and The Whistler were due to contest the Betfair Chase. Kate got up to clear the table once they'd finished. Nicholas beamed at her and sat back to allow his empty plate to be removed.

Kate was about to roll up her sleeves when Nicholas called through, 'Just pop them in the dishwasher. I'll switch it on later.'

A dishwasher! Goodness, she really could get used to this. As she bent to stack the plates and cutlery, a familiar movement in her nether regions made her heart sink.

'You've got to be kidding me,' she whispered.

She quickly finished loading the dishwasher and headed back into the lounge where Nicholas was lighting more candles around the room.

'Can I use your bathroom?' she said, hoping he wouldn't think it weird that she was taking her handbag with her. She could always refresh her make-up and use that as the excuse.

'Of course. There's one just under the stairs.'

Once safely locked in the WC, Kate pulled down her knickers and groaned. Yup, her period had started.

'Oh, for fuck's sake,' she muttered with unusual vehemence. 'Why now? Why tonight? Why not tomorrow? Stupid bloody—'

'Everything all right in there?' Nicholas's distant voice floated through the walls.

'Yes, fine!' she called back then lowered her mutterings as she sorted herself out. 'No, it's not all right. My stupid body has decided to say sod your romantic evening and aphrodisiacal food. Tonight ain't going to be *The Night*.'

Nicholas smiled from his position on the sofa and held out a bowl of strawberries. Kate went to sit beside him, remembering too late she hadn't refreshed her make-up. Oh well, he'd know soon enough why she'd taken her handbag with her.

With his arm stretched along the back of the sofa, Nicholas reached out and stroked her hair. 'I've had a wonderful evening.'

'So have I,' she replied. 'You've outdone yourself.' She tried to think of something else to say, but with Nicholas giving her come-to-bed eyes, she could think of nothing other than her period.

Nicholas plucked a strawberry from the bowl and fed it to her. Kate realised she probably should have just taken a bite rather than have the whole thing in her mouth. It was an impressive size considering the season must be just about over, and it made chewing with her mouth shut difficult. She swallowed, feeling about as sexy as a sow, and tried to counteract it with a smile.

Nicholas leaned across and kissed her.

Maybe that was far as he'd go, Kate thought hopefully. Nicholas wasn't a rip-one's-clothes-off-in-the-heat-of-passion kind of guy. Maybe tonight they'd only get as far as second base.

He pulled back to gaze at her, hazel eyes warm. 'How did you get that scar?' he said nodding to her right eyelid.

Kate instinctively reached up. 'When I was a kid,' she said with a nervous laugh. 'You know, just... messing around.'

Nicholas smiled and leaned forward to kiss her eye with tender lips. He fluttered them down her face to her mouth, where they became more urgent. He wound his arm round her and gently pushed her down onto the sofa. His hand crept round and found her breast. He squeezed it.

Ow, that hurt. It seemed the contact wasn't enough though and he delved beneath her blouse. Kate felt his shuddering breath on her ear. His fingers were hot on her skin as they uncupped her breast from her bra. His thumb grazed her nipple, making it harden in response. He pressed himself against her, and, hands trembling, unbuttoned her blouse. Her bra unhooked at the front and Nicholas stopped breathing as her chest was laid bare for his perusal. He swallowed. Kate could feel the unmistakable hardening of his erection pressing against her leg.

'You're so beautiful,' he whispered, his eyes never leaving her heavy breasts.

Kate's toes curled in embarrassment. Like a sculptor appraising his work, he cupped her boobs, stroking and teasing. Another shuddering breath escaped his lips and he leaned down to suck on one hardened nipple. Kate winced at the pain.

Nicholas wasn't holding back. He was like a starving infant, except one with a helluva hard-on. She tried to enjoy it, gave a moan to reassure him and threaded her fingers through his hair. Nicholas whipped one of her hands down to his crotch and pressed her palm against it. Heat burned through his chinos.

Before Kate could stop him, he unbuckled his trousers and crept his fingers up her skirt.

'No – Nicholas, wait.'

Nicholas unplugged himself from her breast. 'Am I going too fast?' he said. 'I'm sorry. You're just so lovely.'

Kate bit her lip and tried to pull herself into a sitting position. It wasn't easy with Nicholas half on top of her. 'It's my fault, Nicholas. I'm sorry. You've gone to all this trouble to make this evening special, you've been a perfect gentleman, but—' She looked down, saw her exposed chest, and tried to reassume some dignity.

Nicholas's eyes were wide with confusion and insecurity. She reached forward and kissed him.

'I can't, not tonight. My—my period has started.'

Nicholas's mouth fell ajar. 'Oh,' he said. 'Right, well, okay. Um...'

Kate cringed even further. 'There's nothing to say we can't carry on, but – well, you know...'

Nicholas shook his head and pulled back to do up his trousers and tuck his shirt back in. 'No, of course. Not for our first time.'

Kate gave him a grateful smile. 'That was what all the cursing you heard in the bathroom was about.'

Nicholas attempted a smile. 'I thought it might have been the decor.'

With respective buttons done up, they sat in uncomfortable silence on the sofa, listening to James Blunt shudder through 'Best Laid Plans'. Nicholas held the fruit bowl over his crotch until things had cooled down then held it out to her.

'Another strawberry?'

17

KATE WOKE THE next morning with d'Artagnan imprinted on her brain. She'd slept fitfully, falling in and out of the same dream, in which every conceivable and inconceivable disaster had befallen d'Artagnan's big day, and, for once, she was relieved when her alarm clock went off.

Saskia, whose car had failed its MOT earlier that week, grumbled as she was forced to leave her bed an hour earlier than usual and hitch a lift with Kate.

Aspen Valley was shrouded in thick cloud when they arrived. The security lights around the yard did little to penetrate the gloom and the sound of hungry horses banging their doors clung to the dense air.

Kate made a beeline for d'Artagnan's stable. He had his head over the door, his grey coat blending in with his surroundings.

'Glad I didn't have to fetch you from the paddock,' she said, rubbing him between his nostrils as she let herself in. 'I wouldn't find you in th—' Her words dried on her lips as she looked at him properly for the first time beneath the yellow glow of the overhead bulb. 'Oh, no, what have you done?'

His cheek bone and temple were grazed a livid red. Blood had matted above his eye and his forelock and mane were tangled with straw. A quick look at his torn rug, the dishevelled bedding and the scuff marks on the wall were answer enough.

Kate's heart sank. At some point during the night, d'Artagnan had obviously lain down too close to the wall and had injured himself trying to get up. She checked his legs and found more evidence of the struggle on his joints. She sighed and sucked her teeth in disappointment. D'Artagnan nudged her arm, as if in apology, and she reached out to stroke his neck.

'Poor fella. There I was thinking I'd had a bad night.'

* * *

Kate trudged over to the offices. The reception was bright and toasty. And empty. Kate paused for a moment. She *had* brought Saskia with her, hadn't she?

The sound of voices from Jack's office reassured her and she walked across the slate-coloured carpet, not stopping to take off her boots, and knocked on his door. At the trainer's command she entered his office, but stopped short at the scene before her.

Saskia was perched on the corner of Jack's desk, giggling as she took notes, stockings crossed, her skirt hitched up to show three inches too much thigh. She swivelled round to see who it was, and, safe in the knowledge it was only Kate, she let her balance teeter and had to right herself by grasping Jack's arm.

Jack looked up from his paperwork. 'Hello, Kate – Saskia, watch it,' he muttered. 'You're sitting on a letter that's to go to the Queen. I really don't see how sitting on the desk rather than the chair is going to help your back ache.'

Kate faltered. To her knowledge, Saskia didn't suffer from back ache. 'Bad news, Jack,' she said. 'D'Artagnan managed to get himself cast.'

Jack looked up. 'Bad?'

She nodded.

Jack closed his eyes and exhaled. He put his pen down and got to his feet. 'Let's go have a look at him then.'

Kate hung back so that Jack was out of the room before she confronted Saskia. Her sister straightened the creases out of the Queen's letter and spoke without looking up.

'Don't even open your mouth,' she said in low drawl. She finished with the letter and tossed it back onto the desk, then looked at Kate, lips pursed.

Kate clenched her teeth. She didn't want to be the spoil sport, the nag of the family – a trait she felt she was developing more and more in recent times – but at the same time, she couldn't stand aside and watch Saskia ruin everything.

Saskia sauntered past, sniffing the air and wrinkling her nose. Kate knew she was trying to wind her up. She hadn't been in the stables long enough to smell of them yet. Saskia, on the other hand, smelt like she'd been marinated in perfume.

'Kate? Come on!' came Jack's voice from the reception.

With a last glare, Kate pushed past Saskia and followed Jack outside into the cold.

Ten minutes later and d'Artagnan was declared too sore to race. Kate wanted to cry. The Betfair Chase was a popular Gold Cup trial, and there was at least half a dozen horses, including The Whistler, who would be lining up to deliver the first clue to the Cheltenham Festival puzzle.

Now d'Artagnan wouldn't be part of it. He would either have to wait until Boxing Day for the next major Gold Cup trial or enter a lower class race. The thought of him taking in a midweek handicap chase upset her even more. He could win by twenty lengths and the pundits would still doubt his ability. What did he beat, they would ask before tossing his chances of Festival glory onto the scrapheap.

Kate stopped herself mid-thought. She was just upsetting herself and d'Artagnan's wounds needed her attention. Not to mention the four other horses in her row who were yelling for their breakfast.

Midway through the afternoon, Kate quit trying to get the dirt out of bridle buckles and headed for the office. Saskia was watching a repeat of *The X Factor* while she worked.

'You're gonna have to switch over to the racing in a minute,' said Kate, closing the door on the cold behind her.

It was customary for the staff to crowd into the office to watch the racing if they had a runner in a Grade One event. The pain of having to watch the Betfair Chase from the stables rather than the leafy paddock of Haydock's parade ring was secondary to the pain her body was inflicting upon itself though. Her period weighed like a brick inside her and her boobs ached like hell. 'You got any Nurofen?' she asked.

Saskia dipped into her handbag and tossed a box of painkillers onto the desk. 'Pour us both a glass of water, will you? My hangover's kicking in.'

Kate fetched them two drinks from the kitchenette and between them they finished off the last of Saskia's pills.

'Need to get some more on the way home,' Kate said abstractly watching Simon Cowell rip into some poor middle-aged woman whose orange-shadowed eyes looked close to tears.

'What's the story with you and Ben?' Saskia asked.

'Me and *Ben*? Me and Nicholas, don't you mean?'

'No. Ben,' said Saskia. 'I had to ring him up to tell him he didn't have a horse to ride this afternoon and he wanted to know if you – and Xander of all people – would be visiting him tomorrow.'

For the first time that day, Kate perked up. 'He did?'

'Yes.' Saskia frowned at her. 'What's going on? I thought you were trying to set *me* up with Ben, not Xander.'

'I thought Xander should have a male role model in his life.'

'And you picked Ben?'

'What's wrong with Ben?'

Saskia pulled a face. 'Nothing, I suppose. I just find it odd when you're dating Nicholas. If you think Xander needs some sort of father-figure, I would've thought your boyfriend would be your first choice, not your boyfriend's brother.'

Kate hesitated. Saskia had a point there, but then Nicholas didn't know about her family. Ben did. But she couldn't tell Saskia that, not yet. She hoped Nicholas would forgive her for what she was about to say. 'Ben offered. Nicholas didn't.'

Saskia rolled her eyes. 'God, he doesn't give up, does he? He asked me out tonight.'

Kate unperked. 'And what did you say?'

'No, of course. I said I already had plans. And don't look at me like that. It's Saturday. Of course I've already made plans.'

Kate shook her head as the first of Aspen Valley's weekend staff tramped into the room. Saskia switched over to Channel 4 as the presenters went through the runners. She felt her heart skip a beat when she saw d'Artagnan's name greyed out and the words 'Non Runner' beside it. The presenter mentioned his absence wouldn't make any difference and Kate dug her fingernails into her palms.

'Knobhead,' she muttered.

The camera reached The Whistler, looking polished and sleek and a worthy favourite. To Kate's surprise, a short interview with Nicholas, acting as racing manager, followed. A wave of guilt washed over her. With all the morning's drama, she hadn't paid a single thought to the fact she wouldn't be seeing him today.

Nicholas darted a nervous look at the camera and squared his shoulders. When asked what he thought of The Whistler's chances, he came across confident, but modest.

'And what about the late scratching of d'Artagnan?' asked the presenter. 'How would you have rated his chances?'

'We're very disappointed that d'Artagnan won't be lining up. It'll be The Whistler out on his own today. Hopefully, there'll still be some pace in the race. That's what blew his chances in the Charlie Hall.'

A small cheer went up in the office as the field of seven horses jumped off for the three-mile Betfair Chase. Kate scanned the A-grade chasers for a pacemaker. None of them appeared particularly forthcoming, and, as they rounded the bend, The Whistler was snatching at the rumps in front of him.

Rhys Bradford had his hands full approaching the first fence. The Whistler jumped awkwardly and bumped the horse beside him. A few murmurs of concern rose in the office. They were going at such a dawdle that the camera tracking them chose to focus on the thicket of wintery trees in the background for more arresting viewing.

'Why doesn't Rhys just make the running and get on with it?' someone said.

''Cause The Whistler likes a tow, don't he?' another replied.

'Gotta be better than this farce. Look at him. He's gonna come down in a minute.'

Kate watched in tense silence. Somewhere in the Haydock grandstands, Nicholas would be watching with the same reservations. Victory seemed remote.

After The Whistler had fluffed his lines for a fifth time, Rhys pulled him wide of their covered position on the rail and rounded the front runners. A couple of staff cheered at the sudden move. The Whistler strode into the lead, picking up the pace and stretching his lead to four lengths before the rest of the field cottoned on to the raise in tempo.

Kate clasped her hands, hoping he would find a rhythm now.

The Whistler veered sharply inward and nearly left his jockey in the wing of the fence. Rhys gave him a tap down his neck with his whip and straightened the favourite out. The Whistler lifted his head and pinned his ears like a sulky mule and Rhys was forced to push him on.

Kate groaned with the rest of the Aspen Valley staff as their stable star allowed the rest of the field to catch up and by the twelfth fence he was back where he'd started, four behind, but a lot less enthusiastic than before. Rhys showed him the whip, but Kate knew, even with six more fences to take, their chances had flown. He might only have six rivals to beat, but they were select – Zodiac was a past Cheltenham Gold Cup winner, Canyon Echo had won last season's big novice chase at the Festival, and even China Blue, at forty-to-one, was no slouch. The Whistler couldn't afford to sulk in such company.

'What a feckin' plug,' Irishman, Woody, complained.

Billy, who mucked out The Whistler on Frankie's days off, defended the horse. 'He's not a plug. He just needs things to go his way.'

'Goddamn diva,' someone muttered as the race reached its conclusion.

The Whistler was pushed out to take sixth, no big achievement since the only horse he beat was pulled up anyway. He crossed the line a good twelve lengths behind the winner, Canyon Echo.

The staff left the office without waiting to hear the story of the race from the presenters. 'He's not going to win a Gold Cup acting like that,' someone grumbled on their way out. 'Not without a pacemaker at any rate.'

Kate felt awful for Nicholas. He considered the Borden horses' performances a reflection of his own abilities as a racing manager, and she knew he wanted to show his father he was capable. It was more important than ever now that d'Artagnan should prove his worth.

18

WITH XANDER IN tow, Kate paid Thistle Lodge Stables a visit the following afternoon.

'You sure you're okay with this?' she asked her brother as they pulled up behind the stables.

'For the hundredth time, I'm fine. Let's just get it over with.'

'You never know, Xander. You might enjoy it.'

'Twenty quid, right?'

Kate didn't like to think she was bribing Xander. It was more like insurance. 'For every visit, and as long as you help out and agree not to smoke any more dope.' Actually, it was more like blackmail.

Ben's welcoming grin as they arrived in the yard was enough to ease her anxiety. Xander hung back and dragged his feet.

'Come. We'll get you kitted out in some boots so you don't spoil those and I'll show you around,' Ben said, patting him on the shoulder.

Kate let them go and walked over to see Jerry, whom she'd spotted standing by the paddock gate with his mates. The chestnut pricked his ears and stretched his head over the gate when she took out a couple of deformed carrots that she'd got on discount from the local store. The other horses crowded in for a share and Suddenly Seymour flattened his ears at the others whenever they tried to get close. Only Jerry was excused from his snapping teeth. Kate smiled.

She was joined a few minutes later by Ben and Xander. Xander looked unimpressed with his dirty green Wellington boots and in very unfamiliar territory holding a head collar and lead.

'Kate, you take Jerry and Julio there with the white face,' Ben said, handing her a couple of halters. 'Xander, you grab Seymour.' He ducked beneath the fence and was soon lost among the six horses crowding around him.

Xander sent Kate a look of uncertainty and she gave him an encouraging smile.

'Come on. Nothing to worry about.'

'But I—'

'Come on, you two,' said Ben, re-emerging from the scrum leading three horses. 'You're going to have to move it if you want to ride while it's still light.'

Xander looked at him in horror. 'Ride? I don't know how to though.'

Kate ducked between the bars of the fence and slipped a head collar over Jerry's nose. 'Ben's a great teacher, don't worry.'

With the herd depleted and having watched Kate secure Jerry, Xander ventured into the paddock to collect the remaining horse. Seymour whinnied to his stable companion as they threatened to leave without him, but otherwise stood quietly for Xander to get himself organised.

With all horses at last locked in their stables, Kate followed Ben into the tack room.

He handed her a grooming kit. 'Take your time with Jerry. I'll give Xander a quick tutorial and we'll meet you in the paddock.'

'Ben,' Kate said, stopping him as he went to walk out. 'Thank you.'

Ben winked at her and gave her a smile that could melt a polar bear's heart. 'No problem.'

Dusk was falling by the time yard duties were completed. Kate watched Ben lock the feed room door and realised with a surprising heaviness to her heart that this was the end of the day's outing.

Of course, it was because of Xander's progress that had made the afternoon so enjoyable, not Ben, Kate told herself. She had a boyfriend after all, she wasn't allowed to enjoy another man's company like that. So yes, absolutely all because of Xander.

'You in a hurry to get home?' he asked.

Kate's heart lightened its load in anticipation and her cheeks warmed in shame. She looked to Xander for his reaction, but he just shrugged.

'What did you have in mind?' she said.

'Arcades and Icecapades is in town for the holidays if you fancy it.'

Arcades and Icecapades was a seasonal funfair in which arcade games, funfair stalls and an outdoor ice rink were crammed onto a tiny park in central Bristol.

Kate looked down at her dirty clothes. 'Right now?'

'Go home and shower first if you want.'

'Xander? What do you think?'

Xander shrugged again. 'Yeah, okay. Whatever.'

'I reckon we're in for some snow,' Ben said as they joined the throngs filing into the park a couple of hours later.

Kate groaned. 'More abandoned race meetings then. Mind you, not that it would make much difference to my lot.'

'How is d'Artagnan?' asked Ben.

'No worse for his ordeal. I don't know where Jack's going to send him next though if we're to get a race in before the King George on Boxing Day.'

'Maybe he'll go straight there.'

Xander gave them both a bored look. 'Can I go to check out the games?' he said.

'Go on then,' replied Kate. 'Just keep an eye on your phone for messages, okay?'

Xander muttered something unintelligible in teenage-speak and ducked into the crowds and hurried away.

'What does that even mean?' said Kate. 'I've never even heard that word before.'

Ben shrugged. 'It doesn't register on sound frequencies above a certain age.'

Kate laughed. 'Don't. You make me feel old.' She hesitated, but then curiosity got the better of her. 'How old are you, Ben?'

'Twenty-nine last August. Am I allowed to ask your age?'

'No.'

Ben grinned. They continued to walk, sidestepping distracted fairgoers and children chasing each other down the paths between the rides. They passed a burger stall and Kate's mouth watered at the aroma of frying onions.

'Ooh, that smells good,' she groaned.

'You want one?'

'Are you going to have one?'

'I've no rides for a few days, so I reckon I could manage it.'

Kate laughed. Usually on dates, it would be the woman watching her weight. Not that this was a date, of course. She and Ben were simply chaperoning Xander. Kate's inner cynic questioned Xander's whereabouts, but she pushed it away. Okay, so maybe she wasn't doing a great job of chaperoning, but that still didn't make this a date. Dates were excursions shared with one's boyfriend, not the boyfriend's brother. Lather, rinse, repeat. This wasn't a date.

Ben exchanged a fiver for two sausage and onion rolls and they tucked into their meals as they walked.

'So what do you think of Xander?' Kate asked.

Ben finished a mouthful before replying. 'He's a good kid.'

'I'm sorry if he comes across as a little – you know – *reluctant*.'

'He's just being a teenager. It would be uncool to be enthusiastic.'

'He got suspended from school for smoking dope.'

Ben glanced at her and laughed. 'Kate, you look like the sky's about to fall.'

'But it's serious, Ben.'

'Not necessarily. Kids are gonna push the boundaries. They're curious, they're going to experiment. I'm not saying let them do whatever the hell they want, but you can't wrap 'em in cotton wool.'

'I'm just afraid for him.'

'We'll keep him on the straight and narrow. Just keep bringing him back to the stables.'

Kate tried not to worry. 'Thanks.'

Ben glanced her way and nudged her with his elbow. 'Knock, knock,' he said.

'Who's there?'

'Nicholas.'

Kate smiled in anticipation of the punchline. 'Nicholas who?'

'Knickerless girls shouldn't climb trees.'

Kate snorted and shook her head.

At the end of the stalls was the ice rink. Skaters wobbled around, interspersed with shrieks of laughter as some overbalanced and landed in an untidy mess. Pop music blared from the speaker system. Kate watched young families holding hands, guiding and guarding their children between them.

'Do you fancy a go?' said Ben.

'I'm a terrible skater.'

'No, I didn't mean that.' Ben pointed to some arcade games. 'Over there. Looks like they have a racing game.'

Kate caught the devilish twinkle in his eye and threw the last of her sausage and onion roll into a bin. 'You're on.'

* * *

Kate decided that whomever had designed the horseracing game had never sat on a horse before. Used to d'Artagnan's broad bulk beneath her, her balance felt precarious atop the narrow plastic saddle. Beside her, Ben readjusted his seat with a grimace.

'Not the comfiest saddle I've ever sat on,' he said.

Kate flushed pink and looked ahead to the digital screen. A tinny whistle sounded and Kate gave a shriek as her 'horse' started to rock violently. The race was on.

Fumbling for a grip, she stood up in her footrests (of course, stirrups would have gone against health and safety) and tried to find the rhythm in her horse's jerky movements. On the screen, a rush of horses with very bad conformation steamed past her inside.

'Where are you?' She looked across and laughed.

Ben's screen was facing the pixelated grandstands.

'Damn thing doesn't have any steering – oh, here we go.'

His screen swung round the right way and Kate saw a horse with an arrow and a caption reading 'Player 1' labouring ahead.

'Ooh, that's me!'

Ben lowered his posture and began to drive his horse forward. Kate turned her attention back to her own race. Player 2 edged onto her screen as Ben overtook her. Kate pressed the Whip button and they turbo boosted forward. She edged her horse to the inside rail and passed a couple of the computer horses. A clock in the corner counted down the distance to the finish and her horse's energy levels.

'You're not getting away that easily,' Ben warned.

Kate laughed, upsetting her rhythm again, and nearly fell off. Player 2 poked its head back onto her screen. Kate pressed the Whip button again, but it didn't have the same effect as before. Ben's horse pulled ahead and Kate squealed in frustration.

Ahead the chequered flag waved (whomever designed this game *really* didn't know anything about racing). The leaders were dropping back, but Kate didn't think for a moment she'd beat them. More important was beating Ben. Ben pulled further and further ahead.

'How the hell are you doing that?' she cried.

Ben grinned across at her. 'I have a way with horses.'

All of a sudden, his horse started to slow.

'Oh, you're idling!' she yelled, pushing her mount harder.

'What? What the hell?' Ben jabbed frantically at the Whip button until a red light flashed on his screen. 'What? Disqualified for overuse of the whip? Bloody hell!'

Kate whooped as she passed Ben's slowing horse.

Ben was incensed. 'How can they disqualify me for overuse? It's just a computer. You don't even get that harsh a penalty in *real* racing!'

Kate laughed so hard, her body went weak. Her mount paid no consideration to her though and continued jolting. Unable to 'pull up', Kate's balance teetered.

'Ooh, I'm falling!'

With one more jerk she took a somewhat inelegant tumble from her plastic steed. Her horse carried on bucking on its stand. She tried to get back on, but it was impossible.

'Hey, what about the remounting rule?' Ben said. His horse walked over the finish line and he pumped the air in victory.

'What are you celebrating for? You got disqualified.'

Ben dismounted and puffed out his chest. 'So did you for falling off. But I still beat you.'

'You got disqualified before me, so technically *I* beat *you*.'

They argued good-naturedly as they left the racing game behind. Their path took them via the ice rink again.

'You sure you don't want to skate?' Ben said.

Kate shook her head. 'I'm useless. Do you skate?'

Ben leaned his arms on the railing to watch the proceedings. 'I used to. My opa used to take me to Holland when I was younger to visit the family. Near the town where they lived, there was a lake that froze over during winter, and he'd take me skating.'

'Of course,' Kate said, enlightened. 'De Jager. That's Dutch, is it? I thought it was German.'

Ben shook his head. 'Opa moved over here when he married Nan and set up his dressage academy.' He paused to watch a couple skate by, their bodies interlocked. 'I reckon he was good enough to ride for his country, but he never did.'

'And you're named after your grandfather, aren't you?' she said. 'Benedict doesn't sound very Dutch.'

Ben smiled without mirth. 'You've a good memory. Wrong grandfather though. Benedict was my dad's dad.' He paused to look at Kate. There was something in his expression that she couldn't decipher.

Not resentment or bitterness, but almost a wry sadness. 'It was my mother's parting gift, shall we say?' he said.

Kate didn't reply. What could she say? For starters, she didn't understand what he meant. A parting gift to whom? And why?

She thought of the 'parting gift' her own mother had given her when Kate had left for Newmarket. Like a name, it was part of her identity too, a reminder each day of their turbulent relationship.

'Hey, there's Xander,' said Ben, pointing across the way. 'Shall we go join him?'

'Do you think we should? He might not appreciate our company.'

Ben pushed himself away from the railings and pressed his hand against her lower back, sending the most inappropriate signals to her brain. 'We have one major advantage,' he said. 'We have money.'

Ben was right. Xander was quite happy to play arcade games with them providing they paid. After a while though, even he was becoming tired of the same games and they headed for the stalls for some more traditional fairground entertainment.

'How are your hoop-throwing skills?' said Ben, stopping in front of one stall.

'Neglible,' replied Kate with dubious honesty.

'Xander?'

Xander looked reluctant until he spotted the prizes on offer. 'Can we try get that tardis?'

'*Dr Who* fan, are we?' said Ben, handing over some money to the stall holder. 'Gonna be a tough one. That looks like the big prize.'

Xander was given half a dozen hoops. By the fourth, he was still no closer to winning his miniature tardis. The pegs were set in such awkward positions it was virtually impossible to hoop them.

'Why don't you just try for one of the smaller ones? You'd have a better chance,' suggested Kate.

'Because I want the tardis.'

Kate shrugged and watched Xander blow his last couple of chances.

'You want a go?' Ben asked her.

Kate shook her head. She didn't fancy looking any more foolish than she did already. 'I'll watch.'

Ben took his six hoops and got into position, shifting his weight from foot to foot like a goalkeeper anticipating a penalty kick. With a quick flick of his wrist, he let the first hoop spin away. It bounced off one of the props.

Kate raised an eyebrow at him.

Ben rolled his shoulders and puffed out his cheeks. 'I'm just warming up.'

She laughed at the intense focus on his face. His second hoop glanced off the tardis peg and they all groaned.

'Okay, come on. I'm going to get that thing,' Ben said, cricking his neck.

His next three shots missed.

'It's a farce,' he said. 'It's impossible to get the angles from here.'

The stall holder shrugged. 'I've given out four tardises already.'

Ben threw his last hoop. It looped through the air and caught on the tardis peg. Their cheers were premature though as the hoop's momentum spun it off again. The hoop tumbled off the props and landed on a teddy bear peg.

Xander exclaimed in frustration. The stall holder took down a teddy bear and gave it to Ben.

Ben held it out to Xander. 'Here you go, champ.'

Xander looked disgusted. 'Fuck, I don't want it. That's so gay.'

'Says the *Doctor Who* fan,' said Kate, giving him a stern look.

Ben took back the bear, passing it from hand to hand and looked from Kate to Xander to Kate. His gaze lingered on her, his expression awkward. The fogging of his breath lessened, and Kate's heart began to thud in anticipation.

He held out the prize to her. 'Bears should be loved too.'

Kate's fingers curled into the soft fur of the toy, and she hugged it to her chest, feeling stupidly happy. 'Thank you.'

Ben's gaze remained on her, and he gulped. Kate's pulse went from smooth to samba. With a final inhalation and a clap of his hands, he looked away. 'Right! Where to from here?'

Kat followed him and Xander down the aisles as they searched out fresh entertainment. His question lingered in her mind. Where to, indeed?

19

WHILE KATE HAD her misgivings over where she and Ben were headed, she was in no doubt of her direction the following weekend. And with the right man no less. She and Nicholas stood to the side of Aspen Court's front lawns to watch the Somerset Hunt gather for the day's drag hunt.

A soggy week had given way to fresh, but chilled, blue skies and the ground remained frosty where Aspen Court cast a shadow over the gardens. Most of the hunt members had sought out the sunshine though as they waited for the Master and his whippers-in to arrive with the hounds, laughing and chatting and enjoying the drinks and nibbles provided by the host.

Kate took a couple of photos of the scene. 'I'm so glad they still do it,' she said with a contented sigh.

Nicholas gave her a doubtful look.

'I mean, I prefer it as it is now, where no fox is killed,' she explained, 'but it's such a wonderful sight, such a strong tradition. Hunts have such bad reputations, but look...' She gestured to the horses, of all shapes, colours and sizes, all groomed to perfection with manes and tails plaited, and their riders equally well-turned out. 'Look how smart they all are. And see how the men tip their caps to the women, the etiquette, the pride. It's just so...'

'Jane Austen?' suggested Nicholas.

'Well, yes, in a way.'

The mournful low of a hunting horn drifted across the estate, soon followed the baying of hounds. The horses became restless as the sounds got louder, until from around the corner burst a magnificent splash of red, tan, black and white as the MFH and his whips arrived with the hounds.

The hairs on Kate's arms prickled and she snapped more photos. 'Isn't it beautiful?' she breathed.

'It's a great venue for an event,' replied Nicholas.

'One of the girls I work with, Frankie Bradford, got married here last year.'

'Yes, I know. I was there.'

'Oh!' Kate said in surprise. 'I didn't realise you knew each other.'

'We don't. I know Rhys well enough though. God knows he's ridden enough of our horses over the years.' Nicholas looked up at the honey-bricked stately home and sniffed in appreciation. 'I'd get married here.'

'Mmm,' Kate agreed non-commitally. She couldn't deny it would be a fabulous venue if one was to have a grand ceremony and reception. She'd never really imagined herself in that scenario though. Who would she invite? And even if her husband to be had hundreds of friends, she wasn't sure she'd want to risk her mother making a show of herself in front of so many. And Xander would have to give her away. He'd hate being at the centre of such attention, and a speech would be out of the question.

The hounds wove through the crowds of horsemen and foot followers, yelping and baying. With a short toot on his horn, the Master signalled for the hunt to move off.

Kate sighed as they cantered away to where the scent would have been laid.

'Gosh, d'Artagnan would love this. All the galloping across country and jumping hedges and ditches. No chance of him getting bored doing that.'

'How's he recovered from his casting incident?'

'Much better. He only missed a couple of days' work, but Jack—' She hesitated, a concern that had arisen over the past few days resurfacing. She didn't want to land her boss in hot water with his biggest owner, yet at the same time... 'Nicholas, do you think Jack is favouring The Whistler over d'Artagnan?'

Nicholas's brows knitted. 'How do you mean?'

Kate thought over the previous day's workout, where Jack had informed her d'Artagnan wouldn't be having a prep run before Kempton's Boxing Day meeting. 'Just that the King George is just around the corner and he's not prepping him like I'd have thought he'd need to.'

Nicholas shrugged. 'Well, The Whistler is the more fancied of the two.'

'Yes, but—' Kate sighed. She didn't want to come over all sentimental or to start using her relationship with Nicholas to influence business affairs. 'But you'd still expect him to train them both to a point where they're the best that they can be.'

Nicholas pulled his coat tighter around him as a breeze swept across them and grinned at her. 'I didn't realise you knew more about training than Jack Carmichael.'

Kate pouted. 'I'm just saying I don't think d'Artagnan is at the level he needs to be going into a Grade One race. I ride the horse, I do know something about training,' she added in defence.

'He was entered in the Betfair Chase, wasn't he? Jack couldn't help him getting cast the night before.' Nicholas smiled and patted her hand. 'I'm sure you've nothing to worry about. Just let Jack do his job. I have absolute faith in him. Now, shall we go inside and see if we can get some brunch? I believe they've opened a tearoom of sorts.'

Like a pulled muscle, Kate felt a twinge of impatience. Annoyance that Nicholas was being so dismissive of her concerns, frustration that there was nothing she could do but watch d'Artagnan line up at Kempton only ninety per cent fit.

Inside the warmth of the tearoom, they took the last available table and ordered scones and hazelnut lattes. The room buzzed with chatter from people who'd come to watch the hunt. Kate recognised Tessa Hawkesbury-Loye, Helensvale's pantomime director, serving customers and making the men blush with her outlandish flirting.

She came over with their order and her eyes lit up in recognition. 'Kate! How lovely to see you. Did you enjoy the meet?'

'It was beautiful. Looks like it's keeping you busy.'

Tessa rolled her eyes in dramatic fashion. 'This is nothing compared to the spin the Am Dram has got itself into. Bloody Tom has broken his leg falling off his motorbike.'

'Oh, God. Is he all right?'

'Well, no. He's broken his leg. I should think it hurts like a bastard. But that's not the worst of it. We're an Ugly Sister short now—' Tessa's name was called and she tutted. 'Got to run. And *then* find us another Ugly Sister.'

Nicholas looked bemused as Tessa hurried away. 'What on earth was that about?'

'The Helensvale Christmas pantomime. We're doing *Cinderella*,' Kate explained. 'Or we were. It's a bit close to curtain time to lose one of the big players.'

'But she said *Tom*.'

'We're doing it old-school gender reversal, so the prince is played by a woman and the ugly sisters by men.'

Nicholas laughed. 'Are you playing the prince?'

'No,' said Kate with a sad sigh. 'I'm the prince's pal, Dandini. Frankie Bradford's taking the starring role. I auditioned, but I imagine my boobs got in the way.'

Nicholas's eyes skidded south of her face. He turned pink and tried to hide his discomfort behind his latte. Kate tried not to snort. Then a marvellous idea occurred to her.

'Hey, what about you? Have you ever done any acting?'

Nicholas's blushes disappeared and he looked horrified. 'You're asking me to dress up as woman?'

'Well, it's a pantomime. People would understand you'd be doing it for the role. Come on, it'd be fun!'

'Goodness, no, Kate. I couldn't possibly,' he replied with a nervy laugh.

'You sure? You wouldn't have too many lines. You'd just have to flounce around like an ugly sister would.'

'Sorry, no. It's not my cup of tea,' said Nicholas in a strangled voice. 'You should ask Ben. He likes acting the fool.'

No love lost there, Kate thought. Did she and Saskia act the same way?

There was a moment of uncomfortable silence then Nicholas spoke up again, a forced lightness to his tone. 'So, anyway, it's my birthday coming up soon. The folks are throwing me a bash to celebrate my big three-o.'

Kate made an effort to eliminate Ben from her mind. 'When?'

'January twelfth. The party will probably be the weekend of, though.'

Kate beamed at him. 'Then I shall make sure I have that weekend off.'

Nicholas patted his mouth with his napkin then folded it onto his plate. 'What say we have a wander around the house when you're done, then head home?'

Kate paused. 'Home being...?'

Nicholas raised a teasing eyebrow. 'Will my place do? You could treat me to an early birthday present.'

Kate tried to ignore the metaphorical squealing of brakes in her mind. She was being ridiculous. She was dating Nicholas, and they were both adults. So what if he didn't ignite the same fire in her that a simple touch from Ben did? Ben was his brother; to deny him now, shamed her. Maybe more intimacy would set her on the right track. It would put her head in the right space. Besides, Ben wasn't an option anyway. He fancied Saskia. She should be grateful to Nicholas that he'd chosen her over her sister.

'I'd like that,' she said.

20

NICHOLAS'S BREATH ON her shoulder slowed until only a gentle wisp tickled her skin. Kate opened her eyes. It was useless even trying to sleep. She looked across at Nicholas, her lover now. Dark lashes covered the lines beneath his eyes. His lips lay slightly parted as every muscle and nerve in his face relaxed.

Kate looked up at the ceiling to soak in what had just occurred. It hadn't been a hugely successful coupling. Two people – one of whom she knew for sure was out of practice – moving at different rhythms, hyperaware of their new level of intimacy, self-conscious to the point of awkward, neither wanting to abandon themselves to the gloriousness of sex, but both still eager to show their appreciation.

The afternoon sun projected its rays through the latticed window and Kate watched the pretty patterns project across the Artexed ceiling. Shadows of leaves danced along the frame. Watching them bob around as they caught the breeze filled her with peace.

She shouldn't read too much into their love-making. First times were always a bit shabby. She darted a quick look at Nicholas again to make sure he was definitely asleep then eased herself away. Shivering, she pulled the blanket at the foot of the bed to wrap around her shoulders. She rose to her knees, using the window sill behind the bed to balance and lay her arms on the ledge and gazed out.

Across from Nicholas's courtyard garden was a row of well-maintained suburban houses. The mulberry vines that covered the patio pagoda down below extended up the brick walls of the upper storey. It was the leaves creeping over the window frame like peeping toms that were casting dancing puppets on the ceiling.

A rustling caught her eye and she leaned forward to look below. A bird – she didn't know what type; it was brown, so it wasn't a dove, she knew that much – was busy scratching amongst the tangled branches. Every few seconds it paused to look out, round black eyes alert to danger, its body momentarily poised before resuming its scrabbling. It paused once more, but this time the danger must have been nearer, for, in a flutter of feathers, the bird took off.

Kate gave a little gasp when she saw what it had left. Sat snug in amongst the vines was a small, perfectly woven nest and peeping out of the narrow opening were two speckled eggs.

She shot Nicholas a quick look, but stopped herself from waking him. He looked too peaceful and the eggs would still be there when he woke up. She turned back to the nest, resting her chin on her arms and smiled. Did she detect one of the eggs give a faint tremor of imminent hatching, or was that just wishful thinking? She wondered how long they'd been there. Were they hours away from hatching or weeks? How long did chicks take to hatch?

Kate sighed, and, leaning her cheek on her arms, looked back at Nicholas. She hoped she was making the right decision. She'd never had much luck with men. It wasn't a case of dragging a string of failed relationships behind her. She'd just never had very many. Two to be exact, which for a twenty-seven-year-old felt rather pathetic; one that had lasted eighteen months, the other only five.

This time would be different though, she was determined. She was in a different head space. She told herself she really wanted this one to work.

But hadn't she been the same at the beginning of those two measly failures? She and her new boyfriend had been caught up in a whirlwind of blissful selfishness, only interested in each other and sod the rest of the world. They'd never wanted to part company, even for a day, and when they did they'd texted each other to show they were in one another's thoughts. But then their halos had dulled until eventually the rust showed through. Partners' nuances and habits, which had been endearing to begin with, grated on the other's nerves. Unable to voice their grievances, in denial of the end of the honeymoon, they'd clenched their teeth and avoided the issue. Kate remembered the bickering, sniping over the pettiest things as an alternative to saying what they really wanted to say. And, instead of looking at flats to rent together (the latter relationship Kate had gone so far as looking for places with a spare bedroom aka nursery at one point), she'd found herself sneaking peaks at single rooms to rent. After that it had been just a matter of time.

Why did her relationships always fizzle out? She always started out with the best of intentions, full of positivity and happiness. It was like discovering a new favourite song. One would listen to it over and over again, revelling in the happy high it created, but then once that first rush of novelty and delight wore off, one would listen to the song maybe once a day. Then once a week. Before long the song would be lost in the music library and finally the day would come when the CD was thrown out completely because one didn't want to have to listen to it ever again.

Nicholas's nose twitched, the two fine lines between his brows deepened until he reached up and brushed a lumbering hand across his nostrils. His brow relaxed and he continued to sleep.

Would they tire of each other just like the others? No, Kate told herself. She mustn't have that attitude. Besides, things had changed since she'd last packed her things. *She* had changed. For the better, she hoped. She was more mature, she had more empathy, more patience. She and Nicholas weren't rushing into things – hell, Leonie's dinner party had been back in early October – slowly does it wins the race.

Perhaps that was it. Perhaps all she needed was moderation. Even if the thrills of new love threatened to overwhelm her, she would remain in control. If she ever got to the stage where she needed to buy two sets of toothbrushes, she would know it was time to back off.

She thought of her and Nicholas's conversation earlier about Aspen Court as a wedding venue. Most of her reservations would be about the ceremony itself, rather than what came after. Nicholas would make a good husband, she was sure. Dependable, responsible, and humble despite his fortune – *his fortune*; she couldn't deny that hadn't gone unnoticed. If security was what Kate craved then Nicholas had it in abundance. What worried Kate was if security was *not* what she craved.

With a sigh Kate allowed Ben to enter her thoughts. Why did she feel like she'd somehow cheated on him? It was a ridiculous idea. He knew she was dating Nicholas. He would have presumed they'd already slept together. Besides which, he didn't even fancy her. She doubted he'd even care. She had to concentrate on the man who *did* want her.

What could she get Nicholas for Christmas? She didn't know if he had any hobbies or what his interests were. Even racing, she suspected, wasn't his favourite pastime. Then there was his birthday to think about. Goodness, it was going to be an expensive few weeks.

Kate stopped mid thought.

Nicholas was turning thirty in January. Ben had told her the other night that he'd just turned twenty-nine. She looked at Nicholas with a puzzled frown. She'd presumed Ben was Bill's son from a previous relationship, but if Nicholas was the older of the two, and his parents were still together, that meant Bill Borden had to have had an affair. Right around the time Nicholas was being born.

And, Kate realised with dawning comprehension, that would explain Ben's mother's 'parting gift'. She'd named her baby after her lover's father, thereby ensuring Bill would recognise his illegitimate son.

Crumbs, and she thought her family was messed up.

When Kate lumbered her weary body into the flat later that evening, she found Saskia still up, watching television.

'And what time do you call this?' Saskia said with a grin.

Kate accepted her due with a smile. 'If Nicholas lived in Helensvale I wouldn't have come home at all.'

Saskia gasped. 'You've slept with him finally? Christ, that didn't take you long, did it?'

Kate shed her coat and plonked her handbag down on the table. The flat was freezing. 'Yes, Saskia, I've slept with him.'

Saskia sent her a mischievous wink. 'So what's he like? Are you ever tempted to put on a baker's hat?'

Kate frowned. 'What?'

'I imagine that's would it be like kneading all that dough around.'

Kate picked a cushion from an armchair and threw it at Saskia. 'Don't be horrible. Nicholas isn't fat.' Saskia gave her a look and she relented, 'He's just... well-cushioned. Besides, that doesn't matter. What matters is up here,' she said, knocking on her skull, 'and in here.' Kate knocked on her heart.

'And down here.' Saskia knocked on her crotch. 'Is he any good? I expect he's missionary style only, isn't he? Not really the adventurous type is Nicholas.'

'Saskia, don't be so mean. And I'm not going to tell you because it's none of your business.' Kate didn't particularly want to admit that no, Nicholas wasn't the most adventurous in bed, although he'd seemed quite partial to the cowgirl style. She had a feeling that, judging by the way he had grappled with her bouncing boobs, that that had been the appeal.

Saskia shuddered and Kate didn't ask what she was imagining. 'I'm going to bed.' She paused on her way out, noticing the curtains moving in

128

a draft. 'Is that window open?' She walked across and pulled wide the curtain. 'God, Saskia, no wonder it's freezing in here. Why—' She stopped and sniffed the air. 'Have you been smoking?'

'No.' Saskia didn't meet her eye.

'Bloody hell, Saskia.' Kate pulled the window shut. 'Do you want to get us kicked out of here? Mrs Singh is right above us,' she hissed.

Saskia looked sulky. 'Fuck's sake, Kate. It was just the one. Talk about overreacting.'

Kate pressed her lips together. She knew it wasn't just the one. After Mrs Singh had confronted her on the landing that time, it couldn't be just the one.

'Saskia,' she said in a level voice. 'I'm asking you nicely. Please don't smoke in here.'

Saskia raised her hands in repentance. 'See? That wasn't so hard, was it?'

21

A WEEK BEFORE Christmas, Kate paid another visit to Thistle Lodge Stables, again with Xander in situ. Her stomach turned over at the prospect of seeing Ben again. It was nearly a month since Arcades and Icecapades, and, given a choice, she'd probably prefer another month before facing him. But Xander had gone behind her back and got permission to visit again (when did he get Ben's phone number?) and she couldn't very well say no if it meant an improvement in Xander.

Ben greeted them from the tack room doorway and walked over, bowlegged and misty breathed.

'All right, Xander?' he said, exchanging hip handshakes with the boy. 'Hello, Kate. Ready to rock 'n' roll?'

Kate made an indecipherable noise.

'Well, the horses are already in,' said Ben. 'Xander, you stick with Seymour. Kate, Jerry for you?'

'Yes, please.'

'Good stuff. I thought we should take advantage of this dry spell and put him over some cross-country fences, if that's okay with you?'

Kate didn't know what she'd been expecting, but cool nonchalance hadn't been it. Maybe she'd imagined the whole thing. She'd had so much time to go over that evening that perhaps she'd blown it out of proportion.

She laughed in derision at herself. Whilst she'd been tying herself in knots for the past month, Ben had been going on his merry way, probably fantasising about Saskia.

Jerry bounced down the path from the schooling arena to the paddock. His mane flapped in a silken fringe along his bowed neck, his mouth soft on the bit, the rocking motion of his stride as comfortable as a cradle.

Suddenly Seymour, desperate not to be left behind, trotted to keep up.

'I'm not going to be jumping, am I?' Xander said, his voice juddering as he was jostled in the saddle.

'Not unless you want to,' replied Ben.

Xander shook his head. 'Not if Seymour's going to act like a pothead.'

Ben raised an eyebrow at him. 'I thought you liked potheads.'

'I'm not a pothead,' he mumbled, looking embarrassed.

Ben swung his leg forward to check Miranda's girths. 'Good,' he said. 'Because potheads are bad news, no matter which way you look at it.'

Xander regarded him from beneath frowning brows. 'Haven't you ever smoked?'

Ben swung his leg back. 'Once,' he said. He winked at Xander as he urged his mount into a trot. 'But I never inhaled. Kate?'

'Never,' she said with a firm shake of her head.

'No, you turnip, I wasn't asking you if you'd smoked dope. I was going to ask you to lead the way.'

'Oh. Which course am I doing?'

'Stick with intermediate.'

Kate shortened her reins. She could do this casual demeanour just as well as him. In fact, she'd show both of them just how indifferent she could be.

'Say, Ben. Have you ever done any acting?'

Ben gave her a funny look. 'That's a bit of an odd question. Acting *up*, perhaps. Acting, not so much.'

'It's just that Helensvale Am Dram are putting on *Cinderella* for the Christmas pantomime and one of the – um – *actors*—' Maybe she should broach this gently considering how Nicholas had reacted to dressing in drag, '—has had to pull out suddenly, and, well, Nicholas said that you might fancy helping us out.'

'Doing what?'

'Playing an Ugly Sister?' Kate grimaced in anticipation of his answer.

Ben laughed. 'And there I was thinking you needed an understudy for the prince.'

'Could you do it?'

Ben looked thoughtful for a moment then he broke into a grin. 'Okay. Why not?'

'Really?'

'Sure. Is Saskia going to be involved? I will, if she is.'

Kate felt like she'd been kicked in the gut. She swallowed hard and nodded. 'Sure she is.' Well, she would be once they'd had words.

'Great. Just let me know where and when I'll be there. Do you want to show the way?'

Jerry was more than happy to do so. The rocking motion of his canter became steeper as he anticipated Kate's command.

She wasn't going to let herself be disappointed. She had no right to be disappointed.

She touched her heels to his ribs and like a cannonball he shot forward in the direction of a roughly pruned holly hedge. Kate stood up in her stirrups, using her mount's pricked ears as a target guide.

Jerry lengthened his stride and took off in a fluid arc. She looked back as they landed. She could see Ben hanging onto Seymour's head as the gelding tried to follow his buddy. She squeezed her reins, felt Jerry respond.

'You coming?' she yelled over her shoulder.

'We'll meet you by the brook,' Ben called back. 'Carry on.'

Kate didn't have to be told twice. She needed to get away. The wind rushed through her clothes, icy fingers grappling. Her eyes watered, making the sunshine sparkling on the dew turn to chandeliers when she blinked. The rush of elements gave her release.

Jerry bounded over the next couple of fences like they weren't even there. Kate envied his future owner. He was perfect in every way.

The path led them over a log pile and down a bank to the brook. Before Kate could heed Ben's words, Jerry was splashing through the shallows.

Kate squealed as the icy water sprayed up to soak her jodhpurs. She only just had time to grab a handful of chestnut mane before they were plunging up the other side of the bank and into a sparse copse of conifers.

This was further than Kate had come before and she had only Jerry to rely on to guide the way. She thought she heard Ben shout, but, when she looked over her shoulder, he and Xander were out of view. She considered pulling up, but Jerry was having too good a time to pay much heed to her aids.

She spotted a couple of flags through the trees and around a bend loomed a small upturned dinghy. It was a bit bigger than the other fences they'd faced, but there was no alternative fence, so Kate pressed on.

Jerry pricked his ears and took off a good four feet from the obstacle. He arced through the air, taking Kate higher than any steeplechase fence, and touched down on the soft bed of pine needles.

Kate couldn't keep the smile on her face from spanning ear to ear. She gave Jerry a hearty pat down his neck as he sped on in search of the next pair of flags.

The next jump was a dry stone wall, not all that high, but made wider by the fallen stones around it. Jerry saw a stride and cleared it without losing impetus. They swung left, following a path marked by white washed bands around the tree trunks.

A deceptively small jump came into view and Kate steadied her mount in suspicion. Three strides out she spotted the steep drop on the landing side. Jerry lifted off and she leaned back in her saddle, letting the reins slip through her fingers. For a moment, it felt like they were suspended in midair then they were falling, falling, steeper and further down. Jerry's hooves hit the ground and jolted Kate off balance. Her crotch connected painfully with the pommel. She felt gravity pulling her out of the saddle, but then sheer determination not to make a show of herself in front of Xander and Ben kept the partnership intact.

Jerry cantered on, a little more cautiously now, and Kate swivelled round to look back at the drop fence where she'd left her stomach. From this angle it didn't look that big, but by God, it felt at least ten feet on top.

The markers led them over a couple more fences before swinging back towards the brook. Ben and Xander were waiting on the opposite bank. Jerry slid down the slope and Kate dug her knees into the rolls of her saddle to stop herself slipping forward. With a giant leap at the base, Jerry jumped halfway across the brook and landed with a mighty splash, making Kate shriek again. To finish off, they galloped up the opposite bank and hurdled the log up onto flat ground again.

Ben cheered as she pulled up. 'How did he go?'

'Like a superstar,' Kate gasped, rubbing her hand up and down her horse's neck. Jerry snorted and tossed his head. 'That was amazing.'

'I'm not surprised. I haven't finished building the course on that side of the brook. Everything over there is Advanced level.'

Kate choked out an apology, but she was too thrilled to make it sound convincing.

Ben just laughed. 'Humour me for a while. Miranda's still learning the ropes.'

Half an hour later, the trio unsaddled in the yard. Kate refrained from asking Xander how he'd enjoyed his first taste of jumping. It seemed every time she pressed him for progress, the more inverted he became. Everything Kate said was met with an indifferent shrug or a mumbled 'okay'.

She led Jerry away from the others, forgetting Seymour's attachment to the chestnut. Xander gave a shout as his horse pulled free. A chaotic scrabbling of metal shoes on concrete, the thump of bodies and indignant equine squeals followed. Kate turned just in time to see Miranda lining herself up to double barrel Seymour.

'Xander!'

Ben saw Xander's vulnerability at the same time. He leapt forward and pushed the boy out of the way as Miranda let fly. The force of her hooves connecting with his shoulder spun him round. Ben groaned and went down on one knee.

'Ben! Are you okay?' Kate hurried back with Jerry trotting wildly beside her.

Ben held up a hand, but was too winded to speak. Xander stood in the middle of the fracas looking blindsided. Kate passed him Jerry's reins and rushed over to lead Miranda away to a safe distance. The bullring was nearby and Kate jogged the mare over and turned her out.

Ben was on his feet when she returned.

'Are you all right?' she said, 'Did she catch the bone?'

Ben flexed his shoulder and grimaced. 'Shit,' he grunted. 'I don't think so. Ugh, it's okay.'

He walked over to Xander to relieve him of one of his charges, but his steps faltered.

Kate was beside him in an instant to steady him. 'Come sit down,' she said, guiding him over to the mounting block.

'I'm fine, really. Just a bit dizzy,' Ben said, reluctantly allowing himself to be led aside.

Kate ignored him. Once she had him sitting, she unzipped his jacket partway and pulled it back so she could see beneath the muddy scuff marks. Specks of blood oozed through his white T-shirt. Kate saw all she needed to for now.

'Right. Where's your first aid kit?'

Ben winced as he shrugged. 'I've got a few bits and pieces at the house.'

Kate tutted. One of the first and most crucial lessons she had been taught was to always have a first aid kit handy in a stable yard. 'Come on then. Let's get you cleaned up. Xander,' she said, turning to her brother. 'Are you all right with those two?'

Xander nodded, looking more than a little guilty.

Ben saw his expression and he summoned a smile for him. 'Hey, don't beat yourself up. It wasn't your fault.'

The mobile home was gloriously warm compared to the chilly temperature outside. Kate sat Ben down at the breakfast bar.

'Have you got antiseptic? A dressing?'

'It's not as bad as all that, is it?' Ben said, peeping beneath his jacket. A grunt and a grimace later and he'd answered his own question. 'Bottom drawer on the end.'

Kate riffled through the arbitrary assortment of fishing line, gardening gloves and microwave manuals, and pulled out a bag of medical supplies. She filled a bowl with warm water and mixed it into a saline solution.

Ben unzipped his jacket and Kate pursed her lips as she tried to decide how to get at the wound through his shirt. Blood had seeped further inland.

'You're going to have lose the shirt,' she said. 'Can you lift your arms up?'

Ben looked at her in dispute and she gave him her best matronly look. He did as he was told, sucking in his breath at the pain. Kate tugged his shirt up to reveal a toned abdomen and broad chest. The breath evaporated from her lungs.

Mindful of his shoulder, she eased his shirt over his head and slid it off his upstretched arms. She heard Ben swallow and felt his breath on her skin. Their eyes met and for a moment she forgot what she was doing.

She dropped her gaze first and concentrated on his injury. It looked like Miranda's hooves had missed his shoulder bone, but she had still managed to plant one angry welt on the soft tissue around it and another on his pectoral muscle. The skin was grazed, but apart from bruising it didn't appear to be serious.

She reached for a cotton ball to dip into the saline solution and dabbed it on Ben's chest. The excess water ran down his body and he winced. Kate raised an eyebrow at him.

'It stings, okay?' Ben said in defence.

Kate leaned in to clean the wound of dirt and Ben parted his thighs to give her more room. A quick glance down at the half-naked man in grubby blue jeans and chaps was enough to bring a hot flush over her.

Telling her hormones to get a grip, she applied an antiseptic cream. She rubbed it over the wound, unable to ignore the intimacy of the gesture. Ben watched her eyes as she worked and she tried to keep her face expressionless. Her fingers trembled as she secured a dressing over the worst of the graze, but, once done, they seemed to take on a life of their own.

She watched them linger on Ben's chest. His deep breaths pushed against her touch. She looked up. Ben's lips were parted, his eyes dark. Kate felt a tug of arousal in her groin. It would be so easy to lean in just a few centimetres more. Too easy.

The sound of boots scraping on the wire rack outside gave Kate enough time to step back before Xander burst through the door.

'How's it look?' he said. His face fell in disappointment. 'You've already covered it up.'

Kate nodded and went about tidying up. Too damn right it was already covered up. And whatever had just happened between them – covered up was exactly how it was going to stay.

22

CHRISTMAS DAY WAS something of a non-starter for Kate. She would pop over to her mother's later for Christmas turkey leftovers and to exchange gifts, but for the most part, she had work to contend with.

In the warmth of The Whistler's stable, she kept a firm hold on his head collar while Frankie ran the clippers over his coat in preparation for the following day's King George VI Chase.

'Sorry to have roped you into this,' Frankie said. 'He's just such a diva. Won't let me tie him to the wall and there's hardly anybody else here to help.'

As if to prove her point, The Whistler rolled his eyes as the clippers buzzed around his ears.

Kate didn't mind. It beat scrubbing water troughs any day.

'He's so bony too, which doesn't make it any easier,' Frankie continued. 'You wouldn't think he was an ace three-mile chaser, would you?'

Kate ran her eye over the bay gelding. He wasn't a pretty horse, especially when only half-clipped. Narrow shoulders led to a long back. He was about as different to d'Artagnan as a thoroughbred could get. 'He's not the best-looking,' she agreed. 'But he's athletic in a nerdy kind of way. Like the equine version of Eddie Redmayne.'

Frankie laughed. 'More like Eddie black mane. Do you think Eddie's a bit of a diva too?'

'He's in the right job for it.'

Frankie chuckled as she meticulously shaved the hair around The Whistler's saddle patch. 'What about d'Artagnan? Which Hollywood hunk is he? Jamie Dornan? He *is* fifty shades of grey, after all.'

Kate laughed. 'No! Eww. D'Artagnan's got more charm in one hoof than Christian Grey has.' She thought for a moment. 'George Clooney,' she settled on. 'But from his younger days.'

Frankie's shoulders shook with laughter. 'Oh, bugger, I've gone too close there.' She brushed the stray hair away to reveal an uneven saddle patch. 'Never mind. No one will notice.' She and Kate exchanged mischievous grins.

'Did you hear we've got a new Ugly Sister?' Kate asked.

'We do?'

'Yeah. Ben de Jager.'

'D'Artagnan's jockey? Gosh, how did that come about?'

Kate opened her mouth to respond, when Frankie waved the clippers at her in excitement.

'That's what I was meaning to tell you,' she said, her eyes lighting up. 'You remember me saying how he disappeared from the racing scene after he won the amateur's title? Well, Rhys was telling me the other night it was because he was banned!' Frankie looked joyous over this juicy piece of gossip. Kate didn't see the funny side.

'Banned for what?'

'Rhys wasn't totally sure. Something about being caught with alcohol or drugs in his system. You know how they have those random tests in the weighing room.'

Kate shook her head. 'Impossible. Ben doesn't drink.'

'Must have been drugs then,' Frankie replied with a shrug. She moved round to The Whistler's offside and began clipping again.

Kate's brain buzzed as loudly as the clippers. Ben caught doing drugs? That was like saying the Pope liked to samba on Saturday nights. It just didn't suit his persona. And anyhow, hadn't he warned Xander against drugs?

'That can't be right,' she said. 'Ben's not like that.'

Frankie glanced distractedly her way and shrugged again. 'Just telling you what Rhys told me. And he would know.'

'It must be a rumour. Racing's rife with drug accusations.'

Frankie lifted an eyebrow. 'There's usually a basis for those accusations.'

Kate shook her head vehemently. 'No. Not this time.'

'If you say so. Hey, are you plaiting tomorrow? I'm in two minds about doing The Whistler.'

Kate didn't want the conversation to linger on Ben any longer than it had to. The guilt of her moment with him in his home had been triplicated by the opening of Nicholas's Christmas present this morning –

a day out at a spa, complete with massage and makeover. All she'd got for him was socks (which, in her defence, he had asked for) and a deluxe edition DVD of *The Wolf of Wall Street* (which he hadn't, but Kate thought it was up his alley).

'Well?' Frankie prompted.

Kate snapped back to the present. 'Oh, I doubt it. My plaits always come out lumpy and uneven.'

Ben, a drug taker? No, that couldn't be right.

23

MID-MORNING ON BOXING Day, the Aspen Valley lorry splashed through the slushy puddles through Kempton Park's gates. Kate and four other staff jumped down from the warmth of the cab to unload their horses. It was a thrilling sight to behold. First, Ta' Qali and Dexter, the yard's two prize hurdlers, tramped down the ramp in their red rugs and bandages, set for battle in the Christmas Hurdle. They were followed by the up and coming Shenandoah, entered in the Kauto Star Novices' Chase, then a couple of useful handicappers who would feature in supporting races. Last to exit the lorry were d'Artagnan and The Whistler to contest the King George.

D'Artagnan was on his toes, nostrils popping at the London track's unfamiliar smells.

Frankie led the way to their boxes. She was only meant to be looking after Ta' Qali, of whom she also owned a share, and Billy, recovered from his broken wrist, was tending The Whistler. But because she knew her horses better than anyone else, she fussed around them both.

'Make sure you oil his hooves again,' she ordered Billy. 'But only do it at the last minute, otherwise he'll get bits of sawdust stuck to them in the stall. And be sure to allow plenty of time to stencil his rump. He gets antsy about it. Have you remembered his ear plugs?'

'Give it a break, Frankie, will you?' said Billy. 'Just pay attention to Ta' Qali and leave us alone.'

Frankie looked offended. 'I was just trying to help, Billy. The King George runners have to parade in front of the stands and the place is going to be packed. He needs his ear plugs.'

'I know,' snapped Billy, in a rare show of impatience. 'And at this rate I'm going to be the one wearing them if you don't quit it!'

Kate kept her nerves to herself. She slipped into d'Artagnan's box and placed a hand on the grey's neck. Her fingers trembled.

'It's just the cold,' she murmured to d'Artagnan as she shook the tremor out. 'I'm not that nervous. I know you can do the job, eh, fella? You just run like you did at Wetherby that time, just slip in somewhere midfield. Let the others do all the hard work up front. You and Ben just find some cover and wait until two out before making your move, okay?'

D'Artagnan had his head over the door, watching the activity outside, but his cocked ear told Kate he was listening to her.

'You show what you're made of and we'll be well on our way to Cheltenham, you hear?'

The Christmas Hurdle was one of the most anticipated races of the season so far and Kate would have liked to take ten minutes to find a spot to watch it from. But the King George was immediately after it, so she and Billy had to make do with listening to the commentary echoing from the grandstands.

'Are you Team Ta' Qali or Team Dexter?' Kate asked as they stood outside their stalls to catch the call.

Billy shrugged. 'Dexter, I guess. He's the reigning champ and he won it last year.'

'Yeah, but Ta' Qali beat him in Ireland.'

'By a nose.'

Kate grinned. 'Sounds like they're about to jump off.'

The whole yard seemed to hold its breath for the next four minutes. The racecourse might only be a few hundred yards away, but the echo of the commentator's cry and the roar of the crowds made it feel miles away.

'Coming to the last!' Nick Stone's call drifted over to them. 'It's Ta' Qali by a head! Dexter's battling back!'

Kate and Billy clung to each other, in their mind's eye picturing the two Aspen Valley horses tackling the final flight.

'Ta' Qali makes a mistake! Dexter's going on! It's Dexter all the way! Ta' Qali's coming back for more, but he can't bridge the gap. Dexter's going to win it! Dexter lands his third consecutive Christmas Hurdle! It's a length back to Ta' Qali and Mountain Dew runs on for third...'

Kate exhaled. Billy pumped a fist in triumph.

'Wait for the rematch at Cheltenham,' Kate said. 'Ta' Qali will get his own back then.'

Billy grinned and strutted back to The Whistler's door. 'No chance. Dexter's unbeaten at Cheltenham. It's his lucky stomping ground.'

Kate's gaze rested on d'Artagnan looking out over his door. Would Cheltenham prove lucky for him? 'We'll see.'

Kate hadn't reckoned on what she would say to Ben once he was astride d'Artagnan. Her mind had been too full of the race ahead, but here he was, looking very sober in his two-tone blue silks and wearing the white cap that signified he was the second string of the two Borden horses.

'Hi,' she managed to eek out. She'd spotted Nicholas and his parents standing in the centre of the parade ring, but he'd either not seen her or felt it was inappropriate to wave because he was yet to acknowledge her.

'Hi,' replied Ben. His goggles hid his eyes and his mouth barely lifted. It was difficult to tell whether he was suffering from race nerves or Kate nerves. 'Merry Christmas.'

'Merry Christmas. Did you have a good day?'

'Not bad,' Ben said with a shrug. 'You?'

'Not bad.'

They were starting to sound like each other's echoes.

She turned her attention back to d'Artagnan. The grey was taking the preliminaries well and when she slipped his rug off his loins, she was pleased to see he wasn't sweating.

The third of eight runners, Kate led d'Artagnan out of the paddock and down the chute onto the track for the parade. D'Artagnan snatched at his reins and jogged sideways. Ben whistled to him. Kate glanced up at Kempton's yawning grandstand, black with people standing shoulder to padded shoulder in their thick coats and scarves.

'Hey, Kate?'

Kate's heart leapt at the gruff mention of her name. 'Yes?'

'What did Jeff Bridges say when he met the three musketeers?'

Oh, he was just going to tell her a joke. 'I don't know.'

'All for Tron and Tron for all.'

Kate suffered a serious sense of humour failure.

D'Artagnan broke into a crab canter when he felt the lush carpet of turf beneath his toes, and Kate had to use her whole weight to keep him in line. Canyon Echo, the Betfair Chase winner, was set free by his handler in front.

'Okay, let us go,' said Ben.

Kate didn't want to. Letting go meant there was nothing more she could do. Reluctantly, she relaxed her grip. D'Artagnan fretted further.

142

'Kate,' Ben said, his voice sterner, yet somehow more gentle. 'Time to let go. It'll be okay.'

She looked up, saw the sympathetic turn of his mouth, and took a deep breath. She patted d'Artagnan on his neck and stepped away.

'Good luck.'

Kate and Billy bagged a vantage spot in the chute where they had a clear view of the winning post and the panoramic screen. Kate wound her lead rope around her knuckles as they waited for the horses to assemble at the start. Her heart quickened when she spotted the starter climbing his rostrum. The grandstand hummed in anticipation.

The starter's flag fell, unleashing a wave of sound from behind her and the eight runners plunged forward. D'Artagnan's conspicuous grey head poked into the lead. Kate twisted on her heels and gritted her teeth.

'Steady up, Ben,' she muttered. 'Take him back.'

Her words were lost in the roar of the crowd. D'Artagnan led the way to the first of the eighteen fences and stood off the wall of birch for a stag-like leap. The rest of the field followed in his wake, with The Whistler sharing stalking duties with Finsbury Square. Kate tugged on the white rail, willing Ben to take a pull. But d'Artagnan strode further clear and by the first open ditch, had increased his lead to five lengths. Ears pricked and the bit firmly between his teeth, the grey skirted the far turn unchallenged by his rivals.

Kate groaned. 'Come on, fella. What are you doing? Take it easy,' she said.

With her heart leaping into her throat, she watched the big screen as the field tackled the four fences in the back stretch. With d'Artagnan setting such brisk fractions, The Whistler was jumping well. Canyon Echo galloped off the pace, with only the old veteran chaser, Zodiac, behind him.

The horses swung right into the homestretch for the first of their two circuits. D'Artagnan got in close to the next fence, brushing through the birch, but lost little momentum. Kate wondered how much longer they would last going at such a frenetic pace.

The ground shuddered beneath her feet as the horses neared her vantage point. The crowd cheered them on. She willed d'Artagnan to settle so that Ben could take him back in the field. He needed a chance to refill his lungs before the real battle began. She watched closely as the grey galloped past. He didn't appear to be pulling anymore. In fact – Kate's mouth fell open – *Ben was pushing him on.*

'Ben, what are you doing?' she yelled. She bumped shoulders with Billy as she jumped up and down in frustration. 'What is he doing? They're going to be dead on their feet at this rate!'

Billy's eyes didn't leave his runner. 'I don't know, but The Whistler's still going strong. Aspen Valley's still in with a chance.'

Finsbury Square closed the gap on the lead to two lengths and The Whistler stuck close by in third, travelling rhythmically beneath Rhys Bradford. 'I don't care about Aspen Valley!' she cried. 'I care about d'Artagnan. What is Ben playing at?'

Billy ignored her, sucking in his breath as The Whistler thumped the next fence. Kate was at a loss. By the close-up on the screen, she saw, without doubt, Ben kneading his hands alongside d'Artagnan's neck. The grey extended himself willingly. He thundered down on the open ditch which he'd spring-heeled on their first lap, but his energy reserves were diminishing and he had to reach for it. The untidy jump brought Finsbury Square alongside him and Kate grimaced. She could see her Cheltenham Gold Cup dreams swirling down the plughole.

Over the next four fences, d'Artagnan slipped back in the field. Ben bumped low in his saddle, urging his mount on, asking the impossible. Finsbury Square, with The Whistler in close attendance took up the lead. Canyon Echo strode past d'Artagnan like he'd just joined the race.

Turning for home, the horses were met by a cacophony of noise from the crowd. Rhys pressed the button on The Whistler and the wiry bay drew up alongside Finsbury Square. Two out and he was in the clear with Canyon Echo and Zodiac the only ones making up late ground. Trailing in sixth, d'Artagnan made a clean, but weary, jump. The track was a-tremble with thundering hooves and stamping feet as Canyon Echo ate into The Whistler's advantage. The Whistler cleared the last jump, receiving a celebratory roar from his fans, and plugged on up the run-in. Canyon Echo and Zodiac collided in midair in their pursuit. Both faltered on landing; Zodiac's jockey was jolted out of his saddle, putting him out the race. Canyon Echo's impetus was sucked from him, allowing The Whistler to canter over the line for a comfortable victory.

Billy warrior-yelled and leapt into the air. He pulled Kate into a rough embrace, his cheery gasps hot on her ear. Kate half-heartedly returned his hug. Over his shoulder, she watched the remainder of the field finish the race. Canyon Echo bagged runner-up, followed by a loose Zodiac, Moroccan Velvet, Finsbury Square, Pharoah's Gold and the only reason d'Artagnan didn't finish last was because Lombardo was pulled up before the finish.

Kate was fuming as she met Ben coming into the chute. D'Artagnan was awash with sweat, his body stained steel grey. The blood vessels on his neck bulged like wriggly worms beneath his skin. He was blowing hard, poppy-red nostrils distended, his eyes bright with adrenalin. Ben was equally out of breath. He let the reins go slack and relaxed in his saddle as Kate took control of his horse.

'What was that all about?' she demanded.

Ben pulled his goggles down around his neck, leaving angry etchings on his cheeks. He wiped an arm across his nose, leaving more mud on his face than had been there before. He looked too exhausted to rise to Kate's challenge.

'Just following orders,' he replied.

'What? Whose orders?'

Ben didn't answer immediately. He reached down to smooth d'Artagnan's mane back onto the right side and shook his head. 'The owners'.'

Kate stared at him, trying to decide if she'd heard him correctly. The jubilant crowd was making it difficult. 'But I don't understand,' she stammered. 'Why would anyone give you those orders? His race at Wetherby showed us he was better held up. Why would you make the running with him?'

They drew to a halt in the unsaddling enclosure and Ben kicked out his stirrups. He looked down at her, his expression dispassionate. 'That's something you should discuss with the racing manager.' He dismounted and steadied himself against his horse as he tweaked his bad shoulder then unhitched d'Artagnan's girth.

Kate didn't have the chance to reply. She unbuckled d'Artagnan's breastplate so that Ben could take his saddle and go weigh in. D'Artagnan dunked his nose into the water bucket she held out for him, blowing bubbles as he continued to puff.

At the other side of the paddock, The Whistler was being led around, his silken winner's rug sticking to his steaming body. Around him, the

Bordens were enveloped by a shower of backslaps, handshakes, and hugs. Their laughter hung shrill in the damp air.

Kate waited for Nicholas to turn their way, to pay some sort of credit to his other horse, but to no avail. She was left with his tweed-jacketed back to her. D'Artagnan withdrew his head from the bucket and slopped a mouthful of water over her arms. The chill on her skin only intensified the cold she already felt inside.

'Come on, fella. Let's get you home.'

24

KATE WAS EARLY to arrive at The Golden Miller the next evening. She sat at the bar watching the sports news and keeping an eye on the door. She felt sick to her stomach as they showed highlights of the King George.

On cue, Nicholas stepped through the doors and the locals gave him a congratulatory cheer. Nicholas accepted it with awkward modesty and turned his wide smile on Kate. She struggled to return it. Her teeth clenched when he kissed her hello.

'Hey, Eoin?' Nicholas raised a finger to attract the landlord's attention. 'Give us a Carlsberg, will you?' He leant an elbow on the bar and gave Kate a cheerful smile. 'You all right for a drink?'

'I'm fine, thank you.'

'How was your Christmas?'

'Do you mean Christmas Day or the overall holiday?' she replied.

His smile turned to bemusement. 'Well, either, both. I don't mind. Were they very different?'

Kate took a deep breath, ready to confront him when Eoin returned with Nicholas's order. He took the credit card offered to him and waited while the PIN machine processed the transaction.

'Well done for yesterday,' he said, looking at Nicholas beneath his caterpillar eyebrows. 'Wish we'd had some of that luck in the Christmas Hurdle.'

'Ah, yes, a shame about Ta' Qali,' replied Nicholas. 'Still, second isn't bad, is it? He ran a great race.'

Eoin grunted in reluctant agreement. 'Would've been a whole lot greater if he hadn't mucked up the last hurdle.' The PIN machine disgorged a receipt and, in one swift movement, Eoin tore it off and handed it and Nicholas's card back to him. 'Enjoy.'

Nicholas took a sip of his beer and gave an exultant sigh. 'Nothing like a cold lager, eh? I've had enough champagne these past forty-eight hours to last me a year.'

Kate looked at him in disgusted wonder. Was he trying to rub it in? Did he not know what he had done? Not just to her, but to d'Artagnan as well.

'What?' he said, catching her expression.

'Don't pretend you don't know, Nicholas,' she snapped.

He looked at her in surprise. 'What have I done?'

'Yesterday's King George!' she said, then made a conscious effort to keep her voice down. 'You made d'Artagnan make the running just so The Whistler could win.'

Nicholas rotated a shoulder and cricked his neck to avoid Kate's gaze. 'Come on, Kate. Speculate to accumulate, you ever heard of that?'

'I don't have time for your poxy business sayings,' she said. 'What you did was wrong. It was unfair!'

'Kate,' Nicholas said, placing a hand on her arm. 'Please don't be this way. Try to see things from my perspective. I'm a racing manager – my job is to create as many winning opportunities as possible—'

'You made d'Artagnan lose!'

'—and going into a race like the King George – a race where there was no discernible pace from the other runners – we had to make a decision. The Whistler had a favourite's chance of winning if they went a decent gallop, as he proved, but without it his odds would've been double figures. Even on his best form, d'Artagnan's chances of winning were going to be slim.'

'You used him, Nicholas. I know you've got a business to run and everything, but d'Artagnan is not one of your company commodities. He's a real person. And you used him!'

Nicholas let on a first trace of impatience. He let his hand drop. 'Sorry, Kate, but d'Artagnan isn't a person.'

Kate bit her lip. He didn't understand what she was trying to say. 'He is a *being* and he's better than you give him credit for. I know. I ride him every day.'

'And Jack trains him. He said our best chance of winning was to have d'Artagnan as a pacemaker.'

'He was hedging his bets,' she argued. 'He doesn't care which horse he wins with. He just wants the accolade to add to his CV.'

Nicholas held his arms out wide. 'Then everyone's happy—'

'I'm not!'

'Everyone who matters,' Nicholas snapped back.

Kate stopped in surprise. She inhaled sharply and fumbled for her bag. 'That's it. I'm out of here,' she said, hoisting herself off her stool.

Nicholas made a grab for her arm. 'Wait, Kate!'

She shrugged him off and marched to the door. She no longer cared about the curious stares that followed her exit.

A brisk breeze blew down the High Street, making her whole body prickle with goosebumps. Eyes down and hands planted in her jacket pockets, she headed for her car.

'Kate!' Nicholas hurried after her. 'Will you just listen for a minute, please!'

He stopped in front of her and took her arms. The wind swept the ghosts of his shallow breaths away as he prepared his defence.

'You *do* matter,' he said. 'I'm sorry. That came out completely wrong. I didn't mean a second of it. Of course you matter, you matter so much to me. What I meant was you don't have a stake in d'Artagnan like Jack and I do. *He* needs the winners to keep his business going. *I* need the winners to keep my father happy. I don't mean to trivialise the role you play, because I'm well aware you play a vital role in the whole thing, but your stake in d'Artagnan is an emotional one.'

'And is that so wrong?'

'It isn't wrong, but it won't pay the bills.'

Kate's lip trembled. A wave of resentment washed over her. 'What do you know about paying bills?' she said. 'You've never had to worry about them before. Your family have so much money they don't even know what to do with it all. Hell, your father doesn't even know who trains his horses!'

Nicholas's expression darkened and he pointed a finger at her. 'That is unfair, Kate. Yes, my father indulges in racehorses, and yes, he has the money to do so, but don't make out we know nothing about counting the pennies.'

Kate flushed red with shame. 'Whatever! I don't care about your shrewd business moves! What I do care about is d'Artagnan. How is he going to justify his place in the Gold Cup after today's performance?'

Nicholas's anger was replaced with discomfort. With a gasp, Kate realised why.

'You're going to use him again, aren't you? You're going to use him as pacemaker for The Whistler in the Gold Cup.' She threw out her arms. 'Nicholas, I don't believe you!'

'Come on, Kate. I've tried to explain it to you. What does it matter if he's the pacemaker or not? You said you wanted a runner at Cheltenham Festival. Well, I got you a runner at the Festival.'

'I wanted a runner who would be racing on his own merits,' she cried.

'Well, I'm sorry that isn't going to happen. If I could make things different, I would. But I've got to go with what Jack advises. If he says The Whistler could win the Gold Cup with d'Artagnan as pacemaker, then that's what we have to do.'

'It's not, though! You're the owner. You get the final say.'

'A good owner listens to his trainer.'

'Then why can't you use some other horse to set the pace? Why d'Artagnan?'

Nicholas held out his arms in resignation. 'You need something with a bit of class to impact the pace in a race as hot as the Gold Cup. And he is classy, I do recognise that.'

'Obviously not enough,' she muttered, pulling her car keys out and walking round to the driver's door.

'Please try to see things from my viewpoint,' Nicholas continued. 'If I could have it any other way, I would. But Jack said—'

'I need to go,' she interrupted him. 'If we stay here any longer we'll say something we'll regret.' She bit her lip. Probably too much had been said and done already.

Nicholas stood on the pavement and watched helplessly as she unlocked the door. 'Kate, don't let this come between us.'

'I have to go,' she said primly before climbing in and ending the conversation with an unhealthy slam of the door.

Saskia was oblivious to Kate's mood on her return home. As Kate rid herself of her winterwear, Saskia pondered what she would buy with the Debenhams voucher that Jack had bought her for Christmas.

'It's difficult to decide,' Saskia said. 'I mean obviously I'll have to get something he'll like, something sexy, but since I only see him during office hours it seems a bit inappropriate.'

'Hasn't stopped you before,' Kate said, bending to pick up the mail that Saskia had left on the mat.

'I have to find a way of seeing him out of the office. Somewhere where he'll see me as a woman, rather than an employee.'

Kate flicked through the pile of junk mail. 'If that voucher is anything to go by, then I'd say he recognises you as something more than an employee. I didn't get one.' No, all she'd got from Jack for Christmas was a pacemaker.

She paused over a hand-delivered letter addressed to her and Saskia. A Christmas card perhaps? She flipped it over. The envelope didn't look very Christmassy. She teased open the flap.

'I did make an extra effort at the Christmas party,' said Saskia. 'But matters weren't helped by Pippa being there.'

'I told you, she's part of the team at Aspen Valley. You'd be lynched if – oh, shit,' Kate interrupted herself as she read the enclosed letter.

'What?'

Kate closed her eyes. What next? Was this some sort of test from God? '"For the attention of Miss Kate Creswell and Miss Saskia Creswell,"' she read. '"This letter serves as notice that the fixed-term tenancy at the aforementioned address will not be renewed at the end of the current term and you are to vacate the premises by the date stated below as per the requirements set out in the Residential Tenancies Act 1986."'

Saskia stared at her, wide-eyed. 'Shit. What date does the tenancy end?'

Kate held up the letter for her to see. 'Twentieth of January.'

'But that's not even a month away,' cried Saskia. 'They have to give us more notice, surely.'

Kate read the conditions of the act and shook her head. 'Nope. Not according to this. They can chuck us out with twenty-one days' notice.'

25

SASKIA LET OUT a frustrated sigh and stomped through to the flat. 'Stupid bitch!' she yelled up at the ceiling. 'She's done this on purpose, you know that?'

'Saskia, keep your voice down. She'll hear you.'

'Good! I want her to hear.' Saskia crashed around the kitchen as she prepared two mugs of coffee, slamming the cupboard doors and nearly breaking the mugs as she thumped them down on the counter.

Kate looked around at the remnants of the party Saskia had thrown yesterday while she had been at Kempton. 'Do you think maybe your party had something to do with it?'

Saskia turned wild eyes on her. 'Are you blaming this on me?'

Kate didn't fancy another confrontation so soon after Nicholas's. 'No, no. Although...'

'What?'

Kate shrugged. 'She knows you've been smoking in here. I don't know what went on yesterday, but maybe it was the last straw.'

Saskia pouted, arms folded across her chest as she waited for the kettle to boil. 'Stupid bitch,' she muttered again, this time a little tearfully.

Kate wandered back into the lounge and sat down. A wave of tiredness settled over her. She read the letter again. She shouldn't be so surprised. Mrs Singh had warned her.

Saskia returned with their coffee and put Kate's down on the table next to her. 'What are we going to do now? You're all right. You've got Nicholas to move in with. But what about me? I've got nowhere.'

Kate took a deep breath. Life had sure chosen the wrong time to fall apart. 'I doubt I'll be moving in with Nicholas. Not after tonight.'

A fine drizzle was falling as Kate led Fontainebleau around Chepstow's parade ring. The rangy chestnut hated the wet about as much as Kate did and kept bashing his head against her. After four laps of the ring, her arm felt like tenderised meat and she was beginning to question her loyalty to Fontainebleau.

'Come on, Font,' she muttered as another blow knocked her sideways. 'Give it a break.'

The gate onto the course was opened and the horses filed out. Fontainebleau swung his head and a buckle on his bridle ripped the sleeve of her red Aspen Valley jacket.

'Little bugger,' she said, rubbing her arm.

'I'll take him from here,' said Rhys from up top.

Kate sent him a grateful smile and unclipped the lead rope. Rhys clucked his tongue and the chestnut jogged through the gate and loped away to the three-mile start.

Kate looked around the grandstand where it was a wonder anyone could see anything, there were so many umbrellas up. There was no place for her to take refuge from the rain, so she rucked up her collar and took her place by the rail.

'Kate!'

Kate looked around and spotted her boss's wife, Pippa, sheltering beneath a huge golf umbrella, and gesturing to her to join her. Kate jogged over and took cover.

'Thanks.'

'No problem. Not the most pleasant of ways to spend the day,' Pippa replied.

'Font's not too keen on the weather either.'

Pippa grimaced in sympathy. 'I know. Does it make me a bad person for cheering at the weather forecaster last night? Peace Offering does so enjoy a good slog through the mud.'

Kate smiled and shook her head. Pippa's horse Peace Offering was their sole representative in the Welsh National. 'Where's Gabrielle?'

'At home giving the babysitter a hard time. Jack wanted her to come along. Can you believe he's already bought her a horse? Bless him. Gabby's only just turned one. It'll be retired by the time she can even grasp the concept of horseracing.'

'Which horse?' Kate asked, going through her mental file of Aspen Valley residents.

'Shenandoah. Jack picked him up at the sales in Ireland.'

'Oh, yes. I know the one.' Shenandoah was hard to miss. Officially dark bay, but closer to black, he had a flashy white face and white stockings that reached over his knees and hocks.

They watched the horses canter down to the start on the big screen in silence. Kate felt a little awkward standing shoulder to shoulder with Pippa. Even though the boss's wife was a popular figure in the yard, Kate didn't know her all that well. The person she did know well was Saskia, who was busy trying to tempt Jack away. She wondered what Saskia would say if she saw them on television together. Having said that, after a night on the razz, she doubted Saskia had even tumbled out of bed yet.

'Jack told me you were a little upset on Boxing Day,' said Pippa.

Kate shrugged, in an attempt to appear unbothered. 'A bit,' she said, then when Pippa raised an eyebrow at her, she relented. 'Okay, maybe more than a bit. But I suppose I don't really have the right. I'm just d'Artagnan's lass. It just took me by surprise when Jack had him make the running.'

'I know, I'm sorry,' Pippa replied. 'I hope you won't hate Jack too much for it. He wasn't happy about the arrangement.'

Kate gave a mirthless laugh. 'But it was his suggestion that they do it.'

Pippa frowned at her. 'Far from it. He doesn't like using pacemakers, but the owners insisted.'

'You sure?'

'Oh yes. I remember him having a good moan about it at the time.'

Kate pursed her lips. She wanted to shake Nicholas. This time he'd gone too far.

The horses jogged towards the tape, but neither Kate nor Pippa were paying attention.

'Jack's been terribly stressed this season,' Pippa mused. 'What with Simon leaving last year, he hasn't had an assistant trainer to help share the workload. And it just seems to be getting worse. He's been so distant lately. He won't talk about it though. You know what Jack's like.'

Kate tore her eyes away from the screen to look at Pippa. The trainer's wife's brow was furrowed in concern. For the first time Kate noticed the dark shadows under her eyes.

Could Jack's distance have anything to do with Saskia, she wondered? And, despite claiming work stress was the culprit, did Pippa suspect something else was the cause? Kate couldn't think of any other reason why she would confide in her otherwise.

'He is very busy,' Kate agreed. 'But I know having your support makes it bearable.'

Pippa sent her a grateful smile and readjusted her hold on the umbrella. Raindrops cascaded over the rim as it swayed. 'I hope so, although it's not always easy. Not when he's never home.'

The start of the race intercepted any chance of reply. For a second Kate hated Saskia for disrupting the Carmichael family bond and for putting her in this situation.

Half an hour later, Kate was as dirty as if she'd run in the race herself. Fontainebleau hadn't run badly and had stayed on to take third. Still the bridesmaid, Kate thought, but it was a better result than Huntingdon. She washed him down and pinched some hay from his hay net to dry him. Fontainebleau snapped long yellow teeth at her every time she took some more.

'It's your own fault,' she told him. 'Perhaps if you didn't like ground deep enough to swim in then I wouldn't have to wash all this mud off you – most of which is now on me.' She slung his rug over his back and gave him a pat. 'Right. I'm out of here. I need a hot drink and then I'm going to watch Peace Offering. Are you going to behave while I'm gone?'

Fontainebleau pulled at his hay net and ignored her.

Kate looked in on Peace Offering next door where his lass, Emmie, was putting the final touches to her charge.

'I don't know why we bother,' Emmie said, seeing her at the door. 'I won't even be able to tell which one he is when the race is over.'

Kate grinned. 'Think of Rhys. He's got to do it six times over today. I'm just popping over to get a tea. Do you want one?'

Emmie looked at her watch. 'Ooh, that does sound good. If you're quick.'

Head down and hands deep in her pockets, Kate jogged away from the racecourse stables to the canteen. She looked a sight, she knew. Her hair was having a Diana Ross day, mud stained her clothes and no doubt her face as well, and her jacket was ripped. She wondered what Nicholas would think if he saw her like this. In a strange way, the thought was quite therapeutic. She imagined herself walking into his house, announcing her arrival home from work, trailing muddy footprints over his cream carpet and collapsing on his tasteful Nora Borden-styled couch.

She swung the canteen door open and nearly knocked the person on the other side flying.

'Oh! Sorry,' she cried, reaching out an apologetic hand. Her gesture froze as she realised who it was. 'Ben,' she said. 'I didn't know you were riding today.'

She mentally flipped through Aspen Valley's runners for the day to make sure none of them were Borden horses, but no, unless one of them had been sold recently, they all had other patrons.

Ben looked her up and down and hid a smile. 'Yeah, just the one. Dad's got Camber Sands in the Welsh National.' He paused, as if gauging her mood and readjusted the sports bag slung over his shoulder. 'He's trained up north, not one of Aspen Valley's.'

'I know that much.' Her reply was sharper than she'd intended and she grimaced. 'Sorry. I—'

She didn't know how to act around him. How much responsibility did he share in the racing tactics of the Borden horses? How much was he to blame for d'Artagnan's King George?

'Is Nicholas here?' she said.

'Somewhere, yes. He's got Dad and Nora with him.'

Maybe her hypothetical wonderings about Nicholas seeing her in this state were soon to become a reality.

'Anyway,' Ben said, changing his grip on his bag. 'I'd better get suited and booted.'

'Yeah. I've got to get tea as well,' Kate said needlessly. She moved aside to let him pass and he gave an awkward nod of thanks. He made a move towards the door then stopped.

'Kate,' he began. 'About the King George...'

'Don't, Ben,' she replied with a shake of her head.

'No, look. I just wanted to say sorry. It's a tough deal.'

'Did you know about it from the start?' she asked.

'Pretty much, yeah. But no one was deliberately keeping it from you—'

'Nicholas was.'

Ben shrugged. 'Well, that's as may be, but I wasn't.'

'Why didn't you say anything?'

'I presumed you'd have figured it out anyway with me riding him.'

'What's that supposed to mean?'

He gave a mirthless chuckle. 'Come on, when was the last time I rode a horse with half a chance of winning?'

Kate conceded this was true. 'Why is that?' she said.

Ben looked at his watch. 'I'll tell you another time. I've got to get going.'

'Sure. Well, good luck.'

Ben grinned. 'Thanks.' He pulled the door open and paused. 'I'll see you at rehearsal tomorrow?'

Kate gasped. With everything going on, the pantomime had slipped her mind. 'Gosh, yes. I'd forgotten about that.'

Meet me by the saddling boxes?

Kate pressed Send and waited for the message to confirm delivery. In moments Nicholas had replied.

Give me twenty minutes.

Fair enough. He'd come to watch the Welsh National anyway. Kate could wait twenty minutes. Half of her felt leaden with doom at the prospect. The other half, strangely, was looked forward to it with a kind of sick anticipation.

Welsh National over, Kate sheltered beneath the stables' overhang and watched Nicholas walk across the yard towards her carrying a Borden racing two-tone blue umbrella. Rain from the overflowing guttering splattered on the concrete floor in front of her.

'How'd you do?' Kate asked.

Nicholas regarded her with a wary expression. 'He fell.'

She'd been preparing for this conversation for the past twenty minutes, but that answer hadn't featured in her mental script. 'Oh. Is Ben okay?'

Nicholas's mouth tightened. 'He'll live. More's the pity.'

Kate's strained patience broke. 'Why don't you like him?'

'Why do *you* like him so much? Ben's no saint, Kate,' he said in a voice that made her feel about twelve. 'There are things about Ben that you don't know.'

Kate's memory pinged with her and Frankie's conversation while clipping The Whistler. 'Like what?'

Nicholas stepped closer so that he was sheltered from the rain, and closed his umbrella. He looked around for stray eavesdroppers before continuing. 'He—he—' Nicholas struggled to speak and he stopped with a sigh. 'Did you know he didn't even go to his grandfather's funeral?'

'Rubbish. He loved his grandfather!' Kate's mind whirred as she tried to think up possibilities why Ben wouldn't have been there.

'He does a lot of taking and not a lot of giving, okay? Now, I'm sure you didn't ask me over here to counsel me on my relationship with Ben. What did you want to see me about?'

Kate squared her shoulders and refocused. 'I thought we should have a chat.'

'Can't it wait until after the races? I'll buy dinner. You look a right state.'

'No, I wanted to get this over and done with. I spoke to Pippa Carmichael earlier.'

'Oh?' His reply was casual, but his eyes told a different story.

Kate nodded, pinning a happy smile to her face. 'Yes. And she mentioned a funny thing. She told me how Jack hated using pacemakers. Don't you think that's funny?'

'Kate, please don't make a fuss. We can talk about this later.'

Kate ignored him. 'I thought it was funny. Especially after you told me the other night that it was *his* idea to use d'Artagnan as a pacemaker. Or did I misunderstand?'

Nicholas cleared his throat and fiddled with his umbrella. 'It was more of a joint decision.'

Kate feigned enlightenment. '*Ohhhhh*. Okay. So, when Pippa said that you had *insisted* on d'Artagnan making the running, what she really meant was you and Jack had decided that together.'

Nicholas gave her a sad look and sighed. 'What do you want me to tell you, Kate?'

'The truth would be nice.'

'All right then. The truth is I am my father's racing manager. He enjoys winning. I get him winners. If he wants to win a particular race, then I don't care if we own half the field and that six of our horses have to lose in order for the seventh to win. Yes, I let you believe it was Jack's idea, but that was because I wanted to protect our relationship—'

'You didn't let me believe anything, Nicholas!' Kate retorted. 'You lied outright.'

'I didn't want it to come to that. I never intended to lie to you. I genuinely thought stepping d'Artagnan up into the big league would be enough for you.'

Kate didn't reply. He looked genuine enough. Maybe she *had* expected too much of him. Maybe she *had* forced him into a corner that meant he had to lie to get out of it.

For a moment, she entertained the idea of forgiving and forgetting. But how could she forget when Cheltenham was still to happen? How could she keep up a pretence that all was forgiven when she was nowhere close to accepting d'Artagnan's racing tactics?

'You told me how much you wanted to go to Cheltenham,' he continued. 'And maybe I'm wrong, but I didn't think you were that fussed about whether or not you won.'

'It's not about the winning, Nicholas.' Kate clutched her head in frustration. 'Oh!'

'What? Don't tell me it's about the taking part. No wonder you and Ben get on so well, you're both such bloody good losers.'

'Will you stop bringing Ben into this!' she cried.

'I can't help it. He's sucked himself into our lives so much it's impossible not to.' Nicholas's face flushed red with anger. 'You don't know what it was like, Kate, growing up with that—that *parasite*. He'd coerce Dad into giving him presents. I'd find them hidden away – a Liverpool shirt, a tennis racket, all sorts of games and gadgets – and I used to think they were for me. But they'd never materialise and I realised it always happened when Dad went to visit Ben. Do you know what that felt like?' Nicholas's eyes turned watery and he banged his umbrella on the ground, loosing a mini shower of raindrops. 'And don't think things have changed now we're adults. He's still doing the same thing, having Dad buy him all these bloody horses.'

Kate stared at him in surprise. 'I'm sorry you and Ben don't have the easiest of relationships,' she said levelly. 'But he has nothing to do with what *you* did to d'Artagnan and to me.' She shook her head. 'I can't do this anymore.'

Nicholas pulled an ugly face and banged his umbrella again. 'Fine, whatever. If that's what you want.'

Kate's heart drooped. She wasn't into emotional blackmail, but she realised a little part of her had hoped that if she threatened to end things with him he'd change his tune. She felt foul for thinking that, foul for expecting too much of him, and foolish for misunderstanding things for so long.

'Take care,' she mumbled and turned away.

26

'I DON'T SEE what's so special about Cinderella,' grumbled Saskia as she and Kate walked through Helensvale Community Centre's doors the next evening. 'The last time I lost a shoe at midnight I was accused of being drunk.'

Kate laughed. Saskia could mutter all she wanted, Kate didn't care. The main thing was she had agreed to help out with the Christmas pantomime.

Various members of the cast were chatting, sat on the stage or at long tables usually reserved for tea-serving at art and craft sales.

'Evening, Tessa. I've brought along a helper for you. This is Saskia, my sister.'

Tessa, the pantomime director, looked up from her seat on a table. She was using a chair as a footrest. 'All right, Saskia? Glad to have you on board. I take it this isn't our Ugly Sister?' she said to Kate.

Kate shook her head. 'Ben's our Ugly Sister. He said he'd be here,' she said, glancing around.

Saskia stared at her and Kate remembered she'd forgotten to include that particular detail when coercing her sister into taking part.

'We're about to get started, so he'd better hurry up,' Tessa said. 'You get those script changes I sent out?'

Kate nodded, attention zoned in on the director so that she didn't have to look at Saskia. 'Right here. I'll just go sort myself out...'

Tessa hopped off the table and clapped her hands. 'All right, people. Let's get started. We've got plenty to get through and I want to get the ball properly choreographed this evening.'

Eoin Jones looked around. 'Where's my ugly sibling?'

Tessa frowned. 'Shit.' She flipped through her notes. 'Okay, change of plan. Act One Scene Two: Prince Charming and Dandini are out riding in the forest and they bump into Cinders. Frankie, Kate, Rosie.' She looked around to check all three cast members were present. 'You're up first.'

'What do you want me to do?' asked Saskia.

Tessa deliberated for a second. 'Can you make coffee?'

Kate fled to the stage without daring to meet Saskia's murderous gaze. Frankie, the production's Prince Charming, was already on stage talking to Cinderella, aka Rosie, the pretty assistant from the local bookmakers shop.

Tessa called for quiet and Rosie scampered to the wings leaving Kate and Frankie to play out the first half of the scene using a couple of brooms for horses.

'I say, Dandino, I just wish I could be a regular guy sometime,' projected Frankie, trying to hold her broom between her legs while reading from her script at the same time. 'Then—'

'Frankie, for the hundredth time,' interrupted Tessa. 'It's Dandini, not Dandino.'

'Sorry, I do try,' said Frankie, looking repentant. 'It's just Dandino's a name my brain's more accustomed to.'

'Why?'

'Well, he's a racehorse, see—'

Tessa held up her script in surrender. 'Just try to remember, okay? All right, carry on.'

Frankie readjusted her broom and cleared her throat. 'I just wish I could be a regular guy. Then I wouldn't have to deal with awful screaming women like the Baroness's two daughters.'

'Imagine how One Direction feels,' replied Kate.

'Oh, I don't know. I don't think they're that great.'

'Oh yes they are!'

'Oh no they're not!'

Kate turned to the 'audience' for back-up and the cast members sitting at the tables obliged with the combined 'Oh yes they are!'

'I've an idea,' carried on Frankie. 'Why don't we swap identities, just for a while? You be a prince and I'll be you!'

'But Your Highness—'

'No, *Your* Highness!'

'All right then. I'll race you back to the palace, but don't forget royalty gets a head start!' said Kate and thundered clumsily across the stage riding her makeshift steed and making way for Prince Charming to bump into Cinderella out collecting firewood.

Not needed until Act Two, Kate joined Saskia by the drinks table in the corner. 'You okay?' she said quietly.

Saskia pursed her lips. 'Is this another of your attempts to get me and Ben together?'

'Actually, no,' she replied. 'We genuinely needed a replacement Ugly Sister after Tom did a leg.'

Saskia rolled her eyes as she waited for the catering urn to heat up. 'God, you're so horsey, Kate. Real people don't "do" legs, okay? Only your racing lot say that. Ordinary people say they've broken a leg.'

'All right, fine. Tom broke his leg and we needed a replacement. Ben said he'd do it.'

'So why am I here?'

Kate wavered. 'Because he'd only do it if you were involved.'

Saskia groaned. 'Why am I doing this?'

'Because you owe me big time. We're meant to be moving house in a fortnight and we still haven't even looked at any places.'

Saskia looked around the hall with distaste. Cast members wandered about, chatting and not paying the slightest attention to the action on stage.

'This is such a mess,' she said.

Kate was in silent agreement. Ben wasn't helping matters by not showing up. But hopefully, come the opening night they would have established some sort of order.

The door creaked open as the forest scene came to an end and Ben slipped in. He hurried over to Kate and Saskia, still wearing his work jeans and a T-shirt with sludge-coloured stains on it.

'Sorry,' he said. 'Jerry had colic.'

Kate's heart jumped into her throat. 'Is he okay?'

'Yeah, he's fine now. Wasn't a bad case, but you know what his constitution's like. Hello, Saskia.' He reached forward to kiss her on the cheek. Saskia froze away from his grubbiness, but only succeeded in burning herself on the urn. She leapt forward, making Ben beam at her forthcoming response.

'Right, well, you're about to go on,' said Kate, appalled at the jealousy that sprung up inside her. 'Let me introduce you to Tessa. She's our director. You're Ugly 1, okay? Eoin, over there, is Ugly 2.'

Ben and Eoin had everyone in stitches as they clamoured for the prince's affections. Poor Frankie was yanked from one side to the other as they fought over her. Ben pulled a stroppy face when Ugly 2 barged him out of the way to get the first dance. With a swift movement, he'd smacked Eoin over the back of his head with a handbag.

'Oi, steady on,' said Eoin, breaking character and rubbing his head.

Kate and the cast snorted as Ben turned from sulky dame to apologetic gentleman.

'Carry on, carry on,' yelled Tessa.

Ben whisked Frankie off her feet and out of Eoin's reach. 'His Highness should know how well his bride-to-be can waltz.'

'I'll remember this,' growled Ugly 2, shaking a fist.

'Well, they say elephants never forget.'

Frankie was in hysterics as Ben pranced her around the stage. His greater strength was obvious for all to see.

'Okay, everyone, get set for "Waltzing da Builder",' Tessa boomed.

Sat at the piano, Mrs Greenley, the local primary school teacher, pounded down on the keys, and Kate, dancing with a chorus girl, tried to contain her laughter enough to sing.

Ben broke into a moonwalk and the choreographed dance fell apart. The Wicked Stepmother, aka Dilys Jones, and her partner cannoned into Kate. Kate teetered on the edge of the stage and had to abandon ship, almost landing in Mrs Greenley's lap.

Tessa yelled for a stop and for the next ten minutes, the cast attempted to organise a routine in which no one fell into the audience – not an easy feat given the community hall's meagre stage.

Tessa at last called time and Kate sank into a seat, sweating. She took a glug from her water bottle and was glad to see Saskia smiling as Frankie and Rosie acted out a palace gardens scene.

'I told you it would be fun,' she said.

Saskia's smile disappeared. 'Pantomimes are just silly.'

'But you like panto.'

'Since when?'

'You watch The X Factor, don't you?'

Half an hour later, Kate was called upon once more to assist the prince in finding the foot that fitted the glass shoe.

'Oh, sweet prince – you handsome devil – look no further,' Ben said, strutting forward to the edge of the stage and pushing out his chest. You have found your bride for that shoe is mine.'

'No, it's not!' cried Eoin, muscling in.

'Oh yes it is!'

'Oh no it's not!' yelled the audience.

'Well, we shall see,' said Frankie. 'Dandino-*dini*, I promised that every maiden should have a try. Assist this lady with her footwear.'

Kate knelt before Ben and went to unlace his mud-crusted boot.

'Probably best just to pretend,' whispered Ben. 'I've been wearing these all day. Tessa won't want you falling off the stage a second time.'

Kate snorted and carried out the pretence. 'It doesn't fit, Your Highness,' she said.

Ben lay back on his chair, laying a hand across his forehead in a dramatic pose. 'It's the heat! The heat I tell you! It makes my feet swell so.'

'But it's Christmas outside,' argued Ugly 2. 'Here, let me try—'

'No, no! Then it must be from our flight from Ibiza. Those Ryanair cabins are never pressurised properly.'

A scuffle broke out as Eoin wrestled Ben from the chair. Ben's script went flying. At last, the balding landlord plonked himself down, looking worryingly purple in the face.

'You okay?' whispered Kate, still on her knees.

Eoin nodded, gasping to get his breath back. 'Not – quite as fit – as I used to be.'

They acted out the rest of the scene, and the cast whistled and clapped when Cinderella was finally reunited with her prince.

With the rehearsal at an end, Kate walked out into the car park with Saskia and Ben. A chilly breeze swept the rain into their faces. Kate pulled the hood of her jacket up.

'Can I treat you both to a drink?' she asked, feeling guilty and indebted in equal measure.

Ben shook his head. 'Thanks, I must head home. See how Jerry's doing.'

'Sorry, yes, of course you must. I hope he's okay.'

Under the glow of the car park's security lighting, Ben sent her a reassuring wink. 'I'm sure he is. He was starting to look his old self by the time I left earlier and Fiona said she'd check in on him.' His gaze remained on her for a long moment. 'He'll be okay,' he said gently.

The look in his eyes filled Kate with warmth and she nodded. She didn't want to be the person that worried about everything and everyone, even if she often felt that way.

Ben smiled at them both. 'I'll see you two next week. I'm coming round to ride a few lots for Jack.'

He jogged away to his muddy pick-up, side-stepping a slushy pothole with the nimbleness of a boxer. He'd make a great dancer.

'Well, he might not want a drink, but I do,' Saskia broke into Kate's reverie. 'Some mulled wine to warm us up would do.'

Kate followed her to the car, suddenly feeling much less inclined to go to the pub now for some reason.

27

A WEEK INTO January and Kate had little time to mourn her failed relationship with Nicholas. With the opening night just a week away, she had rehearsals to attend every night. She and Saskia also had to find a new place to live, and finding reasonably priced rentals in Helensvale was harder than she'd anticipated.

Finally, a flat within their budget popped up in her email alerts from the local estate agents, and Kate and Saskia took the afternoon off work to go view it.

'Who's this knobhead?' said Saskia, looking at the designer suit with Brylcreemed hair waiting for them outside the block of flats.

'Hush, Saskia. He might be able to lip read.'

They got out and the young man stepped forward.

'Hello. Jensen Llywelyn,' he introduced himself in a thick Welsh accent, and tucked his leather folder under his arm to shake Kate's hand.

'Kate Creswell,' she replied. 'And my sister, Saskia.'

Saskia batted her eyelashes at him and gave him the once over.

Jensen Llywelyn beamed at them both and rubbed his hands together. 'It's a bit chilly out here. Shall we go inside?'

Kate glanced up as they walked up the steps to the building's entrance. As far as first impressions went, they weren't off to a great start. Sooty dirt clung to the peeling cream facade.

Still, beggars couldn't be choosers. This was the only place on the company's website that was within their budget.

'No lift, I'm afraid,' Jensen said, tramping up the stairs. 'But it'll get you fit if nothing else.'

'What floor is it on?' Saskia asked.

'Fourth.' He paused and winked at Saskia. 'Penthouse suite.'

Kate tried to think positive. They had to move, so she might as well make the best of it. However, the smell of stale fish and chips mixed with diesel fumes did nothing to encourage her. Noticing the grime in the corners of the landing and on the iron balustrade, she avoided touching anything.

'And here we are,' said Jensen, unlocking a door on the top landing and swinging it wide for them to enter.

Kate's spirits plummeted back down to ground level. Inside, the smell of fish and chips was even more apparent. She tripped over a balding carpet into the lounge and looked around. The only window had one of its panes replaced with a square of MDF, making the room dark and feel smaller than it already was.

'This is definitely the place I saw on your website?' she asked.

Jensen beamed even wider, but couldn't quite meet her eye. 'Absolutely. I appreciate it's not in the best of conditions, but you have to admit, you'll be getting it for a bargain.'

Kate wandered through the flat, cold despair filling her gut. She and Jensen Llywelyn had very different ideas of what constituted a bargain. This place was thirty pounds more expensive than Mrs Singh's flat and wasn't half as fit for dwelling.

She stopped in the kitchen, where the grime imbedded along the tiling was the same colour as the manure heap at Aspen Valley.

'You must try to look at the bigger picture,' she could hear Jensen telling Saskia. 'A good clean and this place would look ten times better.'

With one finger, she hooked the yellowing net curtain aside to peer out of the window. Below was Helensvale's bus depot, which Kate supposed accounted for the diesel fumes in the stairwell.

She had to think positive, Jensen was right. With a bit of elbow grease the flat could be habitable. What choice did they have? It was this or nothing.

Holding her breath she took a quick peek into the broom cupboard-sized bathroom. She snapped the light off after only a couple of seconds, not even daring to look at the state of the loo.

She was starting to think that moving back in with their mother was a better alternative when she entered the first of the two 'double' bedrooms. One could probably squeeze a double bed in, but that was about it. She'd have to get into bed from the doorway. Then she saw the carpet stain in the corner.

'This place isn't fit to be lived in,' she exclaimed, going back into the lounge. 'It's revolting, and there's a stain in the bedroom that looks a bit too much like blood for my liking.'

Jensen had the decency to look guilty. 'I know it's not quite up to scratch, but with a little TLC, it could be very nice.'

'A little TLC? It needs a whole refurbishment!'

'Well, maybe the previous tenants didn't leave it in the best of conditions, but—'

'What did they do? Murder someone in the bedroom? I can't sleep in there! It looks nothing like the pictures on your website. Did you Photoshop them or something?'

Jensen's neck turned red and he made a show of clearing his throat and readjusting his Burberry scarf. 'I'm afraid, given your budget, there's not a lot else I can offer you.'

Kate looked at Saskia, who had her lip curled in disgust at her surroundings. 'Come on, we're not living here,' she said, taking her arm and propelling her to the door. 'I don't care where we end up, but it's not going to be here.'

Saskia pulled free and turned to the estate agent. 'Is there really nothing else on your books? We've just been so unlucky lately. Our landlady has given us hardly any notice at all – she's been so inconsiderate. We've just had the most rotten time, what with getting our notice, and then our mother being ill. We've had an awful Christmas.'

Kate shot her a wary look, but kept her mouth shut when she saw Jensen's wavering expression. Saskia gave him her best doe-eyed look and even summoned a few tears to make her sapphire eyes glisten.

'Well...' he began.

'You'd be such a hero if you could find something,' carried on Saskia. 'A man like you, brilliant at his job, caring for his clients. We'd be model tenants.'

Jensen hesitated and pulled at his scarf. 'Well, there is one place,' he said in a conspiratorial tone. 'It's not *actually* on our books as such. I'm a bit of an entrepreneur, you see, and I run a little business on the side – nothing that I shout about since it's also real estate, if you get what I mean.'

Saskia gasped. 'Oh, you are clever! I knew it as soon as I laid eyes on you that you were a man who knew his way about town. Didn't I say as much, Kate?'

Kate nodded dumbly.

Jensen smirked and almost struck a pose. 'I've got a two-bed terraced house on the High Street. It's not on the market just yet, but it will be in the next couple of days. And I'll be honest with you,' he said, spreading his arms at his surroundings, 'it's a palace compared to this place.'

'How much?' Kate asked.

Jensen paused to ponder. 'Well, the landlord has every right to put up the price with a new tenancy, but because I like you—both—and I trust you to be good tenants, I'll persuade him not to. The tenants in at the moment are paying fifty quid more than this place.'

Saskia gave a gleeful gasp and clapped her hands. 'Oh, thank you! You are such a hero. Can I hug you? You don't know how you've saved us.'

Jensen pretended to think about it for roughly a millisecond then held out his arms to Saskia.

Saskia made a big show of embracing him and wheeling him round so that she could face Kate.

Mouth agape, Kate shook her head and smiled in admiration. Saskia gave her a pouty smile in return and winked.

28

BACKSTAGE WAS IN chaos when Kate, Saskia and Frankie arrived for the opening night of *Cinderella*. Tessa shouted to cast members in between jabbering on her mobile phone.

'What's happened?' Kate asked.

'Rosie's come down with a bug.'

Kate stared at her. 'Cinderella's sick?'

'Yes, and I can't find her understudy.' She plugged one ear to listen to her phone. 'Well, I can't get hold of her. You're going to have to go round to her house – I don't know where she lives!' Tessa looked up and shouted, 'Anyone know where Wendy lives?'

'In a Wendy house?' suggested Saskia.

Tessa glowered at her. 'Anyone? Shit. This whole thing's going to pot.'

'I can do the part,' said Saskia.

Kate and Tessa looked at her in surprise.

'You?' Kate said.

'I pretty much know the part from prompting in rehearsals. It's hardly rocket science.'

Tessa grabbed her by the shoulders. 'You mean that? Oh, you good girl! *Good* girl! Kate, will you help Saskia with her costume?'

'You sure you can do it?' asked Kate as they hurried towards the racks of clothes and the makeshift make-up tables.

'Sure. And what I don't know, I can just ad lib. How hard can it be?'

An hour later, Kate slipped on her buckle shoes and headed for the wings. The hall was quickly filling up with families.

'How's it looking?' a voice from behind her asked.

Kate jumped, her nerves already stretched tight. She spun round, expecting to see Ben, but was instead faced with a buxom dame in full make-up and ball gown.

'Good grief!' she laughed.

Ben grinned and attempted a wobbly curtsy. 'I'm channelling my inner-trannie. What do you think?'

'You look fantastic – or as fantastic as an Ugly Sister should look,' said Kate noting the amount of grease paint that had been needed to cover Ben's tan, and the fake beauty spot above one heavily rouged cheek.

They moved aside to allow the set builders to vacate the stage and Tessa clapped her hands.

'Five minutes, everyone!'

Saskia was born to perform. Perhaps not to sing, as they were soon to discover, but as far as acting was concerned, the audience were none the wiser to the last minute swap. Kate was so busy worrying about Saskia that she gave herself no time to stress over her own part, and even saw the funny side when Prince Charming continued to refer to her as Dandino instead of Dandini.

By the penultimate scene, everybody was over-excited. The audience was yelling. Children, high on sugar from the sweets thrown to them from the stage, tore up and down the aisles. On stage, the actors weren't behaving much better. Eoin and Dilys had started celebrating early after learning *In the Running* had been nominated for a BAFTA and both were finding it difficult to walk in high heels. The audience roared as Ugly 1 and 2 scuffled over the glass slipper.

'It's *my* slipper,' Eoin bellowed. 'Let me try it on.'

He swung his handbag at Ben. Ben ducked and the handbag hit Prince Charming square in the mouth. Ben cannoned into Kate. Kate felt like she'd been rugby tackled. Sprawled on the floor, she found herself holding Ben's wig instead of the glass slipper.

'I should be the one to try it on,' Ben said snatching back his wig and setting it back on his head, lopsided. He flicked his locks over his shoulders like a shampoo model. 'Because I'm worth it.'

The audience laughed in approval. Kate waited for Frankie to deliver her next line, but the prince looked a little dazed from the handbag blow.

'When I said the prince was a bit of a knockout, I didn't mean you to knock him out,' Ben ad libbed. 'Now, where's that shoe?'

Kate scrambled to find the shoe which had spun into the wings and returned to fit it onto Ben's foot. She looked up at him and winked. 'Good save,' she whispered.

* * *

The pantomime ended with Cinderella bagging her prince and more sweets being thrown to the children. The cast were on too much of a high for it to end just yet, so, led by Saskia, they continued the party in Bristol.

Kate found herself in a dark and packed club listening to house music. By one o'clock she could stand it no longer. Unlike Saskia, she still had to get up early to muck out and exercise. She edged her way through the crowds and tapped Saskia on the shoulder. Saskia threw her arms around Kate like they'd been apart for a decade.

'I'm going home,' Kate yelled in her ear.

'Why?' Saskia pouted.

'I've got work tomorrow.'

Saskia rolled her eyes and gave her an unbalanced wave as she took a slug from her plastic cup.

'You were great tonight, Saskia. Thank you,' Kate yelled, but Saskia'd stopped listening. Kate turned and took a deep breath before making the rugby scrum journey to the door. She waved to a couple of other cast members that she saw, and was finally able to breathe easy as she handed over her ticket to retrieve her coat at the booth and made her way out onto the street.

''Scuse me,' she said, tapping a bouncer on his tree trunk arm. 'Where can I find a taxi around here?'

The bouncer was just pointing out directions when Ben stepped out of the shadows, hands tucked deep into his pockets. He looked frozen.

'Come, I'll give you a lift,' he said.

The bouncer glowered at him. 'You just be on your way, mate, and leave this young lady alone.'

'No, it's okay,' giggled Kate. 'I know him.' She looked at Ben. 'Are you sure?'

'Yeah, come on.' Without taking his hand out of his pocket, he offered her his arm and Kate gladly snuggled next to him for warmth.

The bouncer shook his head and turned away to reaffirm his authority by asking a newcomer for proof of ID.

Bristol was aglow with Christmas lights twinkling in the inky black of a clear winter's night. From the warmth of the pick-up's cab, Kate admired the scene.

'So pretty,' she murmured.

'You should see Dad and Nora's place in Leighs Wood. The whole neighbourhood competes to have the best display. God knows what their electricity bills must be like.'

'Is that where you spent your Christmas?'

Ben shook his head. 'I used to when I was a kid. Dad was big on that sort of thing, even though they never went well.' Ben's face was expressionless in the dim glow of the street lighting. He looked across at Kate. 'They weren't so much family gatherings as Borden gatherings with a de Jager hanger on. Dad would bombard me with gifts to assuage his guilt.' He swung the wheel and they took an exit into a service station. 'Just got to stop to put in fuel.'

He left the heater on for Kate while he filled up. She wondered what it must have been like for Ben and Nicholas growing up, of the awkward family get-togethers, where Ben was nothing more than a reminder of Bill Borden's infidelity and, according to Nicholas, the favoured son. But if all Bill had done for him was out of guilt for being an absent father, then his gestures and gifts were hollow consolations. She believed even less that Ben was the 'taker' Nicholas had described him as.

Ben re-hooked the pump and wandered over to the kiosk to pay. She watched the decorations in the glass-walled kiosk flutter and sparkle as the door whooshed open to let him in. Next to the filling station was a McDonalds, equipped with a reindeer drawn mobile ride outside the door.

Kate had a sudden craving for a McFlurry. After an evening of yelling and singing on stage, and drinking watered-down lemonade in smoky clubs, all she wanted was the smooth cool sweetness of ice cream. She grabbed her bag and opened the door to hurry over to the restaurant.

'Thought I'd lost you,' Ben said when Kate finally returned. 'Where did you get to?'

Kate handed him a McFlurry. 'One for you, and one for me.'

Ben laughed. 'Are you crazy? Ice cream in winter?'

Kate plunged her spoon into her tub. 'It's when it's the best.'

Ben shook his head and chuckled, then dipped into his dessert. 'Mmm,' he said, letting his head fall back against the headrest and sucking his cheeks. He was jolted out of his reverie by an impatient honking behind them.

'Damn,' he said, glancing in his rearview mirror. 'Here, hold this. We'd better find somewhere better to park.' He passed his McFlurry to Kate and started up the engine.

'Where're we gonna go?' Kate asked.

They both looked at the car park in front of McDonalds. It didn't look terribly appealing.

'I know.' Ben slapped down on his indicator and put his foot down. They swung back onto the main road and headed west.

'Where are we going?' said Kate.

Ben flashed her a grin. 'You'll see.'

Ten minutes later, Ben pulled up on the edge of the Clifton Suspension Bridge and unclipped his seatbelt. 'Coming?' he said.

The night air was cold and, given their location over a gorge, rather gusty. Thousands of Christmas lights swung from the suspension cables to create a magical display. Kate looked over the edge. The bridge's reflection wobbled on the translucent rope of water winding its way down the gorge.

'So beautiful,' she murmured.

Ben scooped a spoonful of ice cream into his mouth and leaned his arms on the railing. 'Isn't it?'

Below, a thin layer of snow covered the banks and firs, and Kate took her mobile out to take a photo. Unable to resist, she took one of Ben as well with the cable lights in the background.

He looked over at her and smiled. 'Here. Come.' He held out his arm. 'Let's have a selfie.'

Giggling, Kate shuffled closer to him. They held up their McFlurries and pulled over-zealous faces. They fell into each other, laughing, as they examined the result.

'Don't you dare post that on Facebook,' Ben warned, recovering first.

'Come on, it's not that bad,' she argued. 'It's funny.'

Ben shook his head and turned back to the view with a wry smile. Kate put her phone away and joined him.

In companionable silence, they worked their way through their desserts, arms resting on the railing, their bodies hunched against the cold wind blowing up the gorge. Their arms touched, but neither pulled away. There was something exhilarating about the contact, something comforting too.

Kate's teeth began to chatter. Ben pointed his spoon at the snowy ground below.

'How do you find Will Smith in the snow?' he said.

'I don't know. How *do* you find Will Smith in the snow?'

'You look for Fresh Prints.'

Kate snorted and covered her mouth with her gloved hand. 'That is poor, Ben de Jager, even by your standards.'

'You're still laughing though, aren't you?'

'No, I'm not,' lied Kate.

Ben reached out and pulled her hand down. 'Fibber.' His smile broadened. 'Your lips are blue.'

Kate sucked her lips, but couldn't feel them. He was probably right. 'You've still got grease paint on your ear.'

Ben gave a short laugh and ducked his head between his arms to rub his ear. He looked up again, and, as his eyes came to rest on her lips, his laughter faded.

Kate's heart picked up the tempo, and she watched the parting of his lips, the natural upturn of his mouth, baby soft in contrast to the stubble of his beard surrounding it. She let herself wonder what those lips would feel like on hers.

Ben's breath stilled and he leaned forward, pausing for her reaction. Kate closed her eyes and touched her lips to his. A million tiny whizzbangs shot through her body as he increased the pressure. It lasted only a brief moment before he pulled back and dropped his gaze.

Kate's cheeks tingled as her flush reacted with the cold air.

Ben cleared his throat and hazarded a look at her. 'Sorry. I shouldn't have done that.'

For a second, Kate wondered why not, but then realised, of course, he was thinking of his brother. And speaking of siblings, what about Saskia? Ben fancied her, not Kate. There was no way she could compete.

Ashamed of herself, she dropped her gaze and straightened. Her teeth started knocking again as her jaw tensed.

'Saskia did well tonight, didn't she?' she said.

Ben regarded her for a quiet moment then nodded. 'Yes. She did.'

29

KATE LAY AWAKE, trying to relax in her unfamiliar surroundings. Through the single-glazed windows, she could hear The Golden Miller celebrating Saturday night on the opposite side of the High Street, laughter and shouts coming in waves as people stumbled in and out of the doors.

It would be worse in summer, she realised, when the cold wasn't there to keep them inside. Kate pulled her duvet up to her chin. Her tired brain hadn't been able to work out the heating, so she'd piled on the layers, but now that she had stopped moving and her body's thermostat had dropped, a chill was seeping into her bones.

She looked up at the ceiling where the street light from outside cut a yellow rectangle on the plastering. She didn't like her new surroundings. Saskia, on the other hand, was thrilled with their new location, and was currently getting to know their neighbours at the pub.

The move had completely cleaned out Kate's bank account, and to add insult to injury, the rent here was higher than Mrs Singh's. But there'd been no alternative. Well, there was, but Kate didn't fancy sleeping rough. Maybe she could have found a mobile home like Ben's?

Ben. She wondered what he was doing. For all she knew, he could be just a hundred metres away, partying with Saskia. Did he think about that night on the bridge like she did? Did his stomach backflip at the memory of his lips on hers? If only things could be simpler. If only Leonie's dinner party had gone differently, where she hadn't caught Nicholas's eye and Saskia hadn't caught Ben's. *If only...*

Kate snuggled up to the teddy bear he'd won for her at Arcades and Icecapades. Maybe in some parallel universe, there was a Kate and Ben blissfully in love with no siblings to worry about.

She was just drifting off when she heard the front door open downstairs and the sound of Saskia coming in.

But she wasn't alone. Kate recognised Leonie's voice as well. By the volume and the heightened deliberation of their words, it was clear they were both drunk.

'He's a fool, and he's just made the biggest mistake of his life,' Saskia said. 'He's not worth it.'

'But I love him!' Leonie wailed. 'How am I supposed to live without him? I'll die!'

Oh dear, it sounded like Declan had held up the white flag at last.

'Why would he do this to me? All I've done is love him. I love him, Saskia!'

Kate weighed up whether or not she should go downstairs to see if she could help, then decided against it. Not only did Leonie rarely appreciate her presence, but Kate was surprised she and Declan had lasted as long as they had. She'd always thought Leonie much too silly for the smart, reflective – otherwise known as more mature – Irishman. Kate decided going downstairs now would be a bad idea.

Leonie and Saskia moved from the foot of the stairs into the kitchen and their conversation became muffled.

Kate felt a stab of guilt, not only for feeling a lack of pity for Leonie, but also because her break-up with Nicholas hadn't ignited such heartbreak in herself. She'd been angry, certainly, but her world hadn't ground to a halt because of him.

Neither Saskia nor Leonie were up when Kate left the next morning. She hadn't slept well, the unfamiliar noises jolting her awake through the night, but the bright Saturday morning sunshine helped lift her mood.

Bell ringing practice was taking place at the church up at the top of the street and Kate enjoyed the sounds as she walked along to her car. Maybe things weren't as bleak as they'd seemed last night. She'd been tired, after all. Maybe moving house was symbolic of a new beginning, a new year, a new life.

She scraped the frost off her car's windscreen, humming 'Something Stupid'. Harrison took some persuasion to start in the frigid temperatures, but finally they were on their way back to the flat.

By lunchtime, Kate was done. The carpet cleaners had been and gone and the lounge carpet looked better than when she'd first moved in.

She found Mrs Singh waiting for her on the landing, arms crossed over her bosom, bright red lips pursed.

'Hello, Mrs Singh. Everything okay?' Kate said with a cheerful smile.

Mrs Singh stepped forward and peered into the flat. 'That carpet's not looking much better.'

Kate bit her tongue. 'To be fair, it wasn't in the greatest condition when I moved in.'

'You have the keys?'

Kate rootled through her handbag and handed them over. Mrs Singh pocketed them with muttered thanks, still looking suspiciously at the lounge carpet.

Kate waited expectantly. When Mrs Singh gave her a blank look, she clasped her hands and smiled. She hated talking about money owed.

'So, should I expect my deposit to be paid direct into my bank account?' she said.

Mrs Singh sent her a sharp look. 'Deposit? Are you crazy? You think you're going to get your deposit back?'

Kate felt the familiar chill of panic rising through her body. 'But, Mrs Singh, we've done everything required of us. The flat has been cleaned, the last month's rent is paid, and you have your keys back.'

'Ah, you're very good at keeping to the rules now that you are leaving, but what about when you were living here, huh? What about all the conditions that you broke then?'

'Like what?'

'Smoking!' Mrs Singh bustled over to the lounge curtains and sniffed them. 'Here is the proof! Why do you think I asked you to leave in the first place?'

'But, Mrs Singh—'

'Don't try to deny it! I'm not stupid, you know.'

Kate's panic turned to anger. 'You can't withhold the entire deposit over that,' she said.

Mrs Singh's chin jutted out. 'Have you forgotten that stain on the carpet in the bedroom?'

'What stain?'

Mrs Singh led the way through to Saskia's vacated bedroom and pointed to a spot which had been covered by a laundry basket when they had been in residence. The chestnut colour looked suspiciously similar to Saskia's hair tone.

'I saw this last night when I came in. No cleaning equipment is going to get it out. I'm going to have to replace the whole thing.'

Kate stared at the stain, anger boiling inside her. Saskia had deliberately never told her about the stain. Well, now she could bloody well pay for it.

'I can't afford that!' cried Saskia.

Kate banged the kettle back onto the counter, sloshing water out of the spout. 'Well, I can't either! And it's your fault we've had to move in the first place.'

'I don't know what you want me to say, Kate. I do not have any money to give you. It's not that I don't want to. It's that I don't *have* any!' Saskia's eyes sparked with anger. 'And it is *not* my fault we had to move. Mrs Singh has never liked me; she was just looking for an excuse to chuck us out.'

'And you gave her one by smoking!' Kate threw back.

Saskia clutched her head and growled. 'How much more must I take? Declan's gone and broken up with Leonie, so I've had to spend the night mopping her tears, Jack's been giving me a hard time at work – and it's not the hard time I was hoping for.'

'Well, maybe you should concentrate more on doing your job than on trying to seduce our boss.'

'I can never do anything bloody right in your eyes, can I?'

'You think you're the only one with problems?' Kate said, slamming through the kitchen cupboards in search of the mugs. 'If you haven't noticed, I've also taken some pretty hard knocks lately. Have you forgotten about Nicholas?'

'Well, there you go,' drawled Saskia with a flap of her arms. 'If you'd bothered to put any effort into that one, then we wouldn't be in this position, would we? I mean, who the hell splits up with their mega rich boyfriend right when they're about to be evicted?'

Having found the crockery in the far cupboard, Kate pointed a threatening mug towards her sister. 'I could never stay with him for the wrong reasons. I'm not like you in that way.'

'Don't give me that.' Saskia took a step forward. 'I'm just being practical. But you had to go get all sentimental because your stupid horse wasn't ridden the way you wanted him to be. If you had your head screwed on properly, you'd realise that it isn't such a big deal, not compared to what we're stuck with now.'

Kate turned her back on Saskia and threw a teabag into her mug. Her chest tightened and tears threatened to breach the flood walls. Why was Saskia so strong in confrontations and she so weak? Was she just a sentimental fool? With a shaking hand, she poured the water into her mug. Her shoulders sagged when she realised she hadn't switched the kettle on.

'Saskia,' she said quietly. 'This is about you and me and the money you now owe me for the lost deposit. It isn't about me and Nicholas.'

'I wasn't the one who brought him up, was I?'

Kate looked at her with pleading eyes. 'If you can't afford to pay me back now, then fine. But I do need that money. Even if it's a little each month, I need you to pay it back.'

Saskia pouted and for the first time, Kate saw her lower lip tremble. Saskia's eyes sparkled with tears.

'Bloody Mrs Singh,' she said, her voice a-tremble, and turned on her heel.

Kate sighed and leaned against the kitchen counter. Maybe she'd been a bit harsh. If she really was having trouble with Jack then perhaps she was under more strain than she was letting on. Jack could be a tyrant when he was unhappy.

She flicked the kettle switch then washed out her mug and retrieved another for Saskia.

30

STANDING HIGH IN her stirrups, Kate trotted d'Artagnan alongside Frankie and Bold Phoenix in the twelve-strong string warming up on the Round Gallop. The early morning sun tinted the steam rising from the horses' bodies apricot and turned the frosty turf to diamond-encrusted blankets.

'How's the new place?' Frankie asked.

Kate shrugged. 'Okay, I guess. I thought it would be hell living opposite The Golden Miller, but actually, it's not that bad. Turns out it's only on weekends that it gets really noisy.'

'Must be nice living closer to the shops. You can just walk up the road to Sainsbury's.'

'Just as well. Parking is a nightmare. We've paid for permits to park on the High Street and there are signs up saying it's for permit holders only, but nobody pays attention.'

D'Artagnan broke into a canter as the leaders increased the tempo. He gave a little buck, which pleased Kate. It wasn't a malicious attempt to unseat her, just a show of high spirits, so she didn't bother remonstrating with him. She'd been afraid the King George might have damaged his enthusiasm for the game, but he was working well, especially when his routine exercise was interspersed with hacks around Aspen Court's estate.

'How's Rhys?' Kate asked, remembering how the jockey had taken a nasty tumble the day before.

'Sore. He doesn't say so, but you don't get a cracked helmet and a hoof imprint on your back without feeling it.'

'Did he go for x-rays?'

'Not by choice, but yeah. Nothing broken, thank God. I think he's just relieved. What with Cheltenham just around the corner, the last thing he wants is to get sidelined, all for a selling plater at Worcester.'

'Wouldn't want to miss his chance on The Whistler in the Gold Cup, eh?'

'And the rest,' Frankie laughed.

They slowed as the string completed their warm-up circuit and began to file out for another canter up the Gallops. Kate, Frankie, and a handful of others lingered behind, under instruction that they were to do a schooling session over the practice fences instead.

'It's a funny set-up, isn't it?' Frankie said as they stopped to check their girths. 'A pacemaker, I mean. I know they have them all the time in flat racing, but not so often over jumps.'

'I suppose no one wants a mad gallop over jumps.'

Frankie nodded. 'And usually you'd have at least one horse suited to front running. Strange how all the big chasers this season seem to be midfielders.'

'Unfortunate for d'Artagnan,' Kate said.

A flash of misty light further up the track caught her attention and she saw Jack's Land Rover pulling up. His headlights switched off and she gathered her reins. 'Looks like we're about to get going,' she said.

The first fence rose out of the pink mist and d'Artagnan pricked his ears. They met it on a long stride, but Kate didn't need to push him for the extra effort. He flew over with a whisk of his tail and galloped on to the next. The muffled drum of his hooves on the damp woodchip beat in synchronised rhythm with Bold Phoenix beside them.

The pair took off together and, such was d'Artagnan's exuberance, he landed half a stride clear of his workmate. Kate squeezed his reins just enough to allow the dark bay to draw level again. D'Artagnan fought for his head.

They completed two circuits of the practice fences before pulling up. Kate's arms felt ready to fall off. D'Artagnan snorted foggy plumes, but he was far from out of breath. Kate patted his neck, smoothing his wayward mane onto its right side, and grinned at Frankie.

'Can't complain about that, can we?' she said.

'Not by a long shot. Phoenix had to work to keep up.'

Kate's grin widened. Bold Phoenix had won at Cheltenham Festival a couple of seasons ago, so he was no slouch.

'When's his next outing?' asked Frankie.

Kate shrugged. 'Don't know yet. I'll ask Jack.'

They walked their mounts over to Jack's Land Rover on a loose rein.

The trainer wound down his window as they approached and scrutinised the horses' gait for inconsistencies.

'How was he, Kate?' he asked once they were within earshot.

'Fantastic,' she replied. 'Never felt so good. Any plan for where he's headed next?' She held her breath.

'Either the Denman Chase in a couple of weeks or the Ascot Chase the week after,' he replied. 'Probably the Denman. The Whistler could do with that extra week before Cheltenham.'

Kate's enthusiasm was doused by his last comment. She didn't want reminding that d'Artagnan's racing career was dictated by his stablemate.

'If today's workout was anything to go by,' piped up Frankie, 'then I reckon The Whistler'd better watch out.'

Kate sent her a grateful smile, and waited while Jack discussed Bold Phoenix with his rider.

31

WHEN KATE ARRIVED at her mother's house that Saturday to collect Xander, Val was in a surprisingly chipper mood. Her hair was styled and she was wearing make-up for the first time since Kate could remember.

While Xander went in search of a waterproof jacket, Kate sat in the lounge and tried to make civil conversation.

'Your hair looks nice,' she said. 'Did you get highlights as well?'

Val touched her feathered locks and nodded. 'I figured I deserved a treat.'

Kate hoped the treat was for cutting down on the booze. 'Wish I could do something with my hair,' she said, pulling at a strand. 'But there doesn't seem to be any point. There's always a mist on the Gallops, so it's frizzy within an hour.'

Val gave her a well-you-chose-that-career look. 'How's the new house?'

'Okay. Nice not to have to walk up three flights of stairs, but we're right opposite a pub.'

By her expression, it was clear Val saw this as no bad thing. 'Are you going to invite us round for a house-warming party?'

Kate shook her head. 'Sorry, there's not going to be a house-warming. Can't afford it. Mrs Singh decided not to give us back our deposit.'

'Why not?'

'Saskia'd been smoking inside and ruined her bedroom carpet as well.'

Val sighed. 'She's always been so rebellious. She has that same wild streak as your father. When did she start smoking?'

Kate shrugged. She didn't like hearing about her father. As far as she was concerned, he didn't exist. 'Don't know. She's either really good at hiding it or I'm just very inobservant.'

'Probably a bit of both,' said Val.

Contrary to her self-confessed lack of observational skills, Kate noticed her mother looking at her watch for about the tenth time since Xander had disappeared into his room. Kate's eyes narrowed. As well as hair and make-up, Val's wardrobe looked smarter than usual. 'You going somewhere?' she asked.

Val started in her seat, and got up to straighten a picture frame above the fireplace. 'No, nowhere. Why do you ask?'

'You just look like you're going out somewhere, that's all.'

Val didn't meet her eye as she fiddled with the placement of the mantelpiece ornaments. 'Well, I might pop out to the shops while Xander's gone. How's he getting on with your boyfriend?'

'I've broken up with him. Besides, Xander never met him.'

'But you're about to go see him, aren't you?'

This time it was Kate's turn to look flustered. 'You mean Ben? Oh, he's just a friend.'

Val looked dubious. 'That's not what Xander says.'

'He's letting his imagination run away with him,' said Kate, feeling guilty for placing the blame on her brother. Her imagination was just as flighty when it came to Ben.

Xander reappeared, holding aloft a crumpled jacket. 'Found it.'

Kate got up and Val showed them to the door. It felt to Kate as if she was making sure they were going. The only times Val had shown her to the door was when she was being chucked out after an argument.

'Have a good time!' Val called after them as they walked away.

'Say hi for me,' replied Xander with a last wave.

'Say hi to whom?' Kate asked.

Xander turned pink. 'What?'

'You just said "say hi for me". Who's Mum going to see?'

'No one.'

Kate laughed and looked back to where Val had now closed the door. 'Oh, come on, Xander. What's the big secret?'

'No secret.'

'Then why won't—' Kate stopped and stared at Xander. 'Has Mum got herself a boyfriend?'

Xander shrugged and didn't take his eyes of the pavement cracks. 'Maybe.'

If her mother had someone looking after her and Xander then Kate wouldn't have to worry so much. On the other hand, what if she'd picked him up in some seedy bar?

'Is he nice? What's he like? Where'd she meet him?'

'He's all right,' Xander said. He pulled his hoodie up and quickened his step.

Kate took the hint despite the questions queueing up on her tongue. Who was this man? It was a lot of baggage to take on, and Kate didn't envy any man the task.

Given the weather, which had gone from plain miserable rain to sleeting by mid-afternoon, Kate and Xander's day out to Thistle Lodge Stables wasn't a huge success. Even Ben seemed more subdued than usual.

They gathered in Ben's mobile home for hot drinks afterwards and to dry off in front of the electric heater.

'I guess Jerry must be close to being sold?' Kate said, cupping her mug of tea to warm her hands. It was hard to believe he had been a racehorse not so long ago. To her, he was ready for the Olympics. 'It's going to be gutting to see him go.'

Leaning his elbows back onto the breakfast bar, Ben looked reluctant. 'Yeah. But in the circumstances I guess I should be glad.'

Kate gave him a puzzled look.

'Fiona, the girl who rents the house and three boxes – she's moving up north in March.'

'What? Why?'

'I guess she wants to try out the northern circuit. Competition's hot down here in the southwest.'

'Have you found someone to replace her?'

Ben remained expressionless as he took a slurp of his hot drink. 'No. Hence why I need to sell Jerry sharpish. That'll bring me in a bit of money to tide the place over for a while.'

'Isn't your dad, like, loaded?' said Xander from the sofa.

'Yeah, but that's his money, not mine.'

'Could you ask him for a loan?' Kate suggested.

For the first time, impatience registered in Ben's eyes. 'No. He's done enough for me as it is.'

Kate looked away and sipped her drink in thought. She recalled discussing Ta' Qali's Greatwood Hurdle win with Frankie the other morning and the racehorse welfare charity behind the name. 'What if you start up a charity?' she said.

'A charity? Are you kidding?'

'Why not? Greatwood does it.'

'Well, I've only got half a dozen horses for starters. It's not exactly a massive operation.'

'Does it need to be?' Xander asked. 'My mate Paul's mum works at a hospice for old timers and they've only got, like, a dozen patients.'

Ben shrugged. 'I don't know. I should think half a dozen horses cost a lot more than a dozen OAPs. Securing funding would be a mission.'

'Why don't you ride in more races?' Xander asked. 'You could pay for it with the prize money.'

'I'm an amateur,' Ben replied with a smile. 'We don't get paid.'

'What?' Xander looked both disgusted and disappointed. 'How can you be an amateur when you've been riding all your life?'

'In Ben's case it's more of a level of qualification than an actual reflection of his abilities,' explained Kate. 'Ben won the amateur's championship a few years back.'

Ben looked at her in surprise and Kate laughed. 'Don't act so shocked.'

'It was a long time ago,' said Ben, looking apologetic. 'I'd almost forgotten myself.'

'You won a championship title and you forgot?' said Xander in disbelief.

Ben swirled the dregs of his coffee around his mug then pushed himself away from the table to dispose of it in the kitchenette. 'It wasn't as great as it sounds.'

'Seems naff to win a championship then give up,' said Xander.

Ben didn't look round from his position at the sink. 'Yeah, well. When you've got your daddy buying you all the best horses, you don't always get the best reception in the weighing room.'

Kate noted the tense set to his shoulders, his neck muscles taut. She bit her lips together to keep from pressing for details. She so wanted to rule out Frankie's claim that he'd been banned for substance abuse. If Ben wasn't a popular figure with other jockeys then it was very possible that the information given by Rhys was a rumour.

'Do you even enjoy it?' Xander said. 'If the other jockeys don't like you and you don't win any prize money, what's the point in carrying on?'

Ben turned around and blew out his cheeks. 'I owe it to my dad. Now, are you guys going to help me do the feeds before you go?'

Kate nodded, eager to undo any damage their questions might have caused. 'Of course. Xander, get your feet off the sofa.'

They collected their jackets and boots and opened the flimsy door onto the arctic rain.

Following the hunched shoulders of Ben back to the stables, Kate mulled over his words. Far from explaining things and putting her curiosity to bed, they had thrown more questions up. Ben worked his guts out at Thistle Lodge Stables, earning a measly living, doing it all for his grandfather because *he owed it to him*. He rode as a jockey for his father, not because he enjoyed the thrill of winning or the banter in the weighing room, but because *he owed it to him*. For such a straight forward guy, who never seemed to ask anything of anyone, he seemed to be indebted to enough people.

32

THE DENMAN CHASE had Kate's nerves twisting in confusion. Even though she knew d'Artagnan didn't have a hope of winning, there was still a fairy light of hope that refused to dim. It was like watching the YouTube recording of the 1978 Belmont Stakes. No matter how often she watched it, she still willed Alydar to get his nose in front at the wire. It never happened, of course, the race ran out the same result every time, but there was still that something inside her that refused to accept defeat.

Newbury Racecourse was cold and blustery, a biting February wind that whipped through the saddling yard and howled around the grandstand. None of the six runners looked to be enjoying conditions as they were led around the parade ring.

Jack boosted Ben aboard d'Artagnan and hurried away to do the same for Rhys on The Whistler.

'Hey,' Kate greeted the jockey.

Ben looked frozen in his thin blue silks. 'Hi.'

'He's feeling fresh today,' she said, trying to appear upbeat. Just because her horse was certain to lose, that didn't mean she had to sulk. 'A real ball of energy.'

'I'll look after him, don't worry,' said Ben, seeing straight through her facade.

The horses paraded in front of the stands where the wind was fiercest, blowing down the home straight right into their faces. Into d'Artagnan's face, thought Kate, since he would be the one making the running while everything else would more than likely sit in his slipstream.

'Stay safe.' She gave d'Artagnan a last pat and let them go. The grey rocked a couple of strides before realising he was free then bounded forward.

Kate exhaled in relief. There, she hadn't begged Ben to ride d'Artagnan off the pace, she hadn't whined about it all being unfair. She'd sucked it up just like she'd told herself she would all morning.

She joined Frankie by the running rail. 'How're you feeling?' she asked. Frankie's horse at least had a chance of winning.

'Nervous,' said Frankie. 'Not as bad as I was at the King George, though. I'm glad Canyon Echo isn't here. You?'

Kate gave a noncommittal shrug. 'I just want him to get round safely.' What else could she say? D'Artagnan's odds were drifting from thirty-threes out to fifty-to-one on the bookmakers' boards behind them. Even the punters knew he hadn't a hope. 'I see they've got the bypass boards up on some of the fences,' she said, pointing towards two of the fences further down the long home straight.

'Yeah, unsafe ground I heard. Don't know if it's a good thing or a bad thing though.'

'Has to be a good thing for The Whistler. He needs a good rhythm. The less jumps there are, the better.'

'Still fourteen to get over,' replied Frankie.

As predicted, d'Artagnan set off in front. There was a short run to the first fence, and, so buzzed up, he took off a stride early and had to twist his body to make the spread.

Kate pushed on the rail in front of her to propel d'Artagnan over.

The others followed at a more sedate pace – Moroccan Velvet, Lombardo, The Whistler, China Blue, and, bringing up the rear, Valhalla Calls.

D'Artagnan spring-heeled the next fence and lengthened his lead. He swung round the far turn a good ten lengths clear and galloped down towards the cross fence. Again, he cleared it well. To Kate's eyes, he was jumping better than ever. Behind him, Lombardo parted the birch in third, hampering The Whistler.

Rhys seemed to think twice about his rival's chances and pushed The Whistler forward to avoid being hampered again.

Out in the clear, Ben guided d'Artagnan around the fourth and fifth fences to be bypassed and, with the wind billowing his silks, set him straight for the next plain fence. The closest anything was to the leading duo was the ambulance and television van travelling on the inside of the track, splashing through puddles as they raced to keep up.

The crowd gave a cheer as d'Artagnan stag-jumped the water in front of the stands. In second, Moroccan Velvet led by a length to The Whistler. Lombardo made another error and allowed China Blue to move into fourth.

'He's going good,' Frankie murmured, her fingers crossed. 'Come on, Rhys.'

Rounding the turn to take them into their final circuit, The Whistler looked a certainty. At the back of the field, Valhalla Calls was already losing ground. Lombardo had fluffed his lines one too many times to be a serious threat in the finish, and The Whistler already had form over China Blue. The only other horses in his way were d'Artagnan, whom Kate knew wouldn't feature in the finish, and Moroccan Velvet, who had finished a well-beaten third in the King George.

D'Artagnan jumped the next with less exuberance and Kate knew his energy reserves were running low. The gap back to second was reduced to no more than eight lengths with Moroccan Velvet and The Whistler running side by side. They took off together and so smooth was their jump that her gaze moved back to d'Artagnan.

At the cry of the commentator, she spun her attention back to the field. The crowd gasped and Frankie grabbed her arm. The Whistler was nowhere to be seen.

'What's happened?' she cried.

'The Whistler is a faller!' yelled the commentator in reply.

'Oh nooooo,' wailed Frankie.

Holding their breath, they watched the screen and only let it out when they saw The Whistler stagger to his feet.

'Where's Rhys? Where's Rhys?' muttered Frankie, chewing her knuckles.

'There!' Kate pointed as the muddied figure of Rhys Bradford rose into view.

Frankie exhaled. 'It's up to your fella now,' she said.

Kate gasped. Frankie was right. The Whistler was out of the race. D'Artagnan needn't sacrifice his chances anymore. Clutching the rail, she jumped up and down.

The big grey thundered down the back stretch. Ben had lowered his posture and was still ensuring the strong pace.

'No! Oh, bloody hell, Ben,' Kate exclaimed. 'Look behind you. The Whistler's gone!'

Ben's focus didn't waver though. Judging his fences to perfection, he guided d'Artagnan over the three fences along the back.

'Ben! Fuck's sake! LOOK BEHIND YOU!' Kate screamed, feeling like she was back on a pantomime stage.

'Look, look, look!' Frankie pulled on her sleeve. She pointed back in the field.

The Whistler ran loose, his reins and stirrups flapping. Without his rider, he overtook Moroccan Velvet and had his sights firmly fixed on his stablemate.

'Oh!' Kate gasped. 'Yes! Go on, Whistler! Go on, boy!'

The Whistler made an ugly shape over the middle fence, but landed safely. Just ahead, Ben must have heard the thunder of approaching hooves, because he lowered his stance and scrubbed d'Artagnan's neck.

Kate's heart beat wildly. 'Goddammit, Ben. Check your wing mirrors, you fool!'

To her surprise (had she shouted that loud?), Ben ducked his head beneath his arm to check on the progress of his rivals. He did a double take over his shoulder when he recognised The Whistler galloping riderless a couple of lengths behind.

Very gently, he eased up on d'Artagnan. The Whistler strode past and showed the way over the fourth last. They rounded the turn out of the back and rather than taking the next jump, The Whistler spied a run out lane and chose the smoother exit.

D'Artagnan popped over the third last, just brushing his forelegs through the birch. Four lengths back and gaining, Moroccan Velvet followed suit.

'Ooh, they're catching him,' said Frankie, leaning into Kate as the field rounded the turn.

Kate couldn't reply, couldn't blink, couldn't breathe. She chewed her lip in desperation. Had Ben turned off the pressure too late? Had d'Artagnan enough time to refill his lungs before the final challenge? She wound her lead rope over her knuckles until they ached. It would be a test of Ben's horsemanship to wangle a win this late in the race. Would he even try though?

D'Artagnan swung around the home turn and began the long journey past the two bypassed fences. Those who had bet their money on the less-fancied horses yelled their support now that The Whistler was out of it.

Moroccan Velvet pegged back d'Artagnan's lead and even China Blue was beginning to make ground.

Ben sat still as long as he dared. Moroccan Velvet drew level as they came to two out and Ben finally put his foot down. Kate tightened the lead rope around her hands, waiting for d'Artagnan's response. Would her horse find another gear?

Moroccan Velvet battled to get by, but having had a breather, d'Artagnan refused to give up his lead. They approached the final fence in front of the stands together. Kate roared her horse over and swiped at the air with her lead rope. Both runners landed wearily, but both plugged on, heads stretched low, ears flat back. China Blue jumped erratically back in third. In dogged determination, d'Artagnan regained his lead over Moroccan Velvet, and the challenger petered out.

Having not been able to breathe for the past three minutes, Kate found herself hyperventilating all of a sudden. 'Come on, d'Artagnan! Come on, Ben!' she and Frankie screamed.

The run-in was a long stamina-sapping furlong. D'Artagnan's stride faltered and he drifted towards the outside rail. It was a sure sign he was exhausted.

'Come on, fella. Just a bit further,' Kate pleaded.

She looked back to the others. Moroccan Velvet was back-pedalling, but China Blue was anything but. His jockey swung his whip and the horse swept sideways in a burst of energy. Kate checked where the winning post was, making instinctive calculations whether d'Artagnan could hold out.

'Come on, d'Artagnan! Come on, d'Artagnan!' she cried in panic.

D'Artagnan was emptying. China Blue galloped past and went on to win by a widening five lengths. Kate's legs went from under her and only the railing kept her from falling.

'Are you okay?' Frankie said, pulling her up.

Kate nodded. 'Just a bit traumatised.'

Frankie laughed. 'You're traumatised? My goodness, how close was that! Now, I've got to find The Whistler, wherever he may be and check my husband is still alive.'

Kate grinned and patted her on the shoulder. She ran out onto the course to fetch d'Artagnan. Ben had slowed the grey to a walk and both were breathing hard when Kate reached them.

'That's the best smile I've seen from you all day,' he said.

Kate laughed and covered d'Artagnan's vein-popping neck with pats. 'I don't think I've ever been so excited.'

Ben gave her his customary wink. 'Believe me, you ain't seen nothing yet.'

33

KATE WAS TOO tired to make herself a proper dinner. Instead, she slapped some Nutella onto two slices of bread and made herself a cup of tea. The adrenalin of the afternoon's racing had subsided following a torturous journey home when the lorry had been stuck in traffic after an accident on the M4. D'Artagnan had tucked into his feed as soon as Kate had put him back in his stable, only pausing once to lift his head for her to secure his rug straps across his chest.

She padded through to the lounge to eat her makeshift meal. Saskia was curled up on the sofa, plucking her eyebrows.

'Phew. What a day,' Kate said, dropping into the cushiony confines of her armchair.

'How did it go?' Saskia said, not looking away from her pocket mirror.

'Didn't you watch it on TV?'

'Kate, come on. I'm in the office five and a half days a week. Do you really expect me to give up my Saturday afternoons for work as well?'

Kate shrugged and chewed on her sandwich. 'D'Artagnan came second. The Whistler fell.'

Saskia grimaced, not because of the result, but because of a particularly painful pluck. 'How'd Jack take it? I don't fancy dealing with him if he's going to be a grump all of next week.'

'Disappointed about The Whistler, I guess. And I think Rhys has injured himself. He was signed off by the doctor for the rest of the afternoon. But I think he was pleased with d'Artagnan's run. I was.'

'You're always pleased with d'Artagnan. You're like a new mother with her baby. You've even got him as your cover photo on Facebook.'

'Better than your cover photo. Jack'll probably fire you if he sees it.'

Saskia didn't reply. She held the mirror back and examined both perfectly groomed eyebrows.

'Where are you off to tonight?' Kate asked.

'Golden Miller with Leonie. We need to show Declan that just because he's dumped her, doesn't mean she's going to stop enjoying herself.'

'Do you?' To Kate, that sounded like a lot of unnecessarily hard work.

'Of course.' Saskia put her mirror and tweezers down and stood up. 'Declan should know she doesn't need him like he thinks she does.'

Kate thought back to Leonie's late night lamenting and doubted whether that was strictly true.

Saskia wasn't hanging about to be questioned though. She sashayed across the room and skipped up the stairs, fleet on her high-arched feet. Ooh, speaking of boyfriends – 'Hey, Saskia,' Kate called. 'Has Mum said anything to you about a new boyfriend?'

The only response was the bathroom door slamming shut. Kate shrugged and settled back to eat her dinner. Her mobile phone dug into her groin and she pulled it out and put it on the armrest. A green light flashed, signifying an unread message and she picked it up again. There was a voicemail waiting for her.

'Hi, Kate, it's Ben. Sorry to call you like this, but I thought you'd want to know. Jerry's come down with colic. It's not looking good. Call me.'

Kate spilled her tea and upended her sandwich in her haste to find Ben's number. Breathless, she waited for the call to connect. It went straight to voicemail. She hung up before the beep and sat still for a moment. Jerry had colic again.

Stay calm, she told herself. *It's probably nothing.*

But Ben had called her to tell her. Not looking good? What did that mean? Colic surgery? He'd had surgery before when he'd colicked at Aspen Valley. Was it possible to operate again?

She jumped out of her chair and ran for the door. Bouncing on each foot in turn, she pulled on her boots and yelled up the stairs, 'I've got to go out, Saskia. Jerry's—' Oh, what would Saskia care? She didn't even know who Jerry was. 'I've got to go!' She grabbed her jacket and keys, and ran out into the cold.

Thistle Lodge Stables was quiet but for the secretive rustling of the breeze through the trees. By comparison, Kate's heart thumped like a ten-gallon drum in her ears.

She ran past the darkened windows of Thistle Lodge Cottage and around the side of the stable block. A perigee moon lay on its back in the water trough and bathed the U block in a silvery light.

'Ben?' Kate called quietly.

A snort from Suddenly Seymour's stable was her only reply. Her gaze travelled to the next stable along. The black hatch of the open half-door sent an ominous, almost taunting, shiver through her. She stood still for a moment, breath ghosting the air in front of her, and willed Jerry to lift his head over the door to see what the disturbance was about. In her mind's eye she could see his pendant star shining in the moonlight, the flaxen brush of his forelock catching the light between two close cropped ears.

She waited until the non-appearance of the image was too much to bear then ran over to the stable. Next door, Seymour flicked his head, slapping his lips together, but she had little time to pay him any attention. Her fingers folded over the icy metal frame of the lower door and she peered into the gloom.

'Jerry? Are you here, baby?' she whispered.

Her eyes fought to find the horse in the shadows and another chill ran down her spine when she saw the bed of shavings lying in chaotic heaps and dig marks all the way down to the concrete base. She swallowed, and, as soundlessly as she could, withdrew her hands from the door and stepped back.

She didn't know why she needed to be quiet, but her every sensory nerve urged her to not make a sound. Jerry wasn't here, which meant Ben must have taken him to the equine clinic.

She looked around and saw Ben's horse-box anchored in its usual spot. Panic shuddered through her.

Beyond the trailer was the bullring. Of course! Her heart gave a little leap of hope. If Jerry had colic then Ben would more than likely be leading him around, to stop him from rolling. The horse-box blocked her view of the bullring and Kate sprinted in its direction.

The moon went behind a cloud, blotting out the light, as she ran. She tripped over the trailer's toe-hitch, and, with a cry, landed on her hands and knees.

The bullring was empty, but she refused to give up on the idea. She climbed the bars to get a better view of the paddock beyond. She couldn't see very far and she looked up at the sky to see where the moon was. The cloud refused to be rushed.

Kate squinted in the darkness to pick out the movement of man and horse, but there were too many shadows, too many uncertainties for her to be sure.

'Ben!' she called out. 'Ben, are you there?'

A cool breeze blew into her face, making her eyes water. The paddock began to lighten as the cloud continued its serene course across the sky. At last the moon cast a spotlight over the landscape. Kate leaned forward, her balance on the fence precarious. 'Ben?'

A noise behind made her whirl around and almost lose her footing. It was the rickety door of Ben's mobile home opening. A beam of yellow artificial light cut across the shadows.

'Ben!' Kate leapt down from the fence and hurtled across the uneven ground to the house. Ben caught her at the foot of the steps. 'Where is he? He's okay, isn't he? Tell me he's okay.'

Even by the light of the moon, Kate didn't doubt the answer written into the lines of his face. Her knees buckled and she crumpled to the ground.

He pressed her head against his chest. 'I'm sorry, Kate.'

The shock was almost paralysing. Her eyes were open, but she saw nothing, nothing but the churned up bedding in Jerry's stable. An odd sensation crept over her. She should be crying, shouldn't she? The horse that she loved, that she'd been utterly convinced would be an Olympic eventer, was gone. Just like that. No more. Dead. Why couldn't she cry?

'Come on, sweetheart,' said Ben. He scooped her up under her knees and carried her up the steps and into the warmth of the mobile home. Her arms wound around his neck, Kate looked up at him in numbed silence. He carried her through to the sitting area and laid her on the sofa.

'I'm so glad you're here,' he said. 'I was so close to—' He broke off, and, in the lamp light, she saw his eyes were red. And it was the thought of Ben crying that released the tears.

'Did he suffer?'

Ben squeezed his eyes shut. 'They tried to operate, but it was too late.' His voice cracked and he cleared his throat. 'If I'd just got here sooner – if I hadn't had to ride at Newbury...' A tear spilled down his cheek and he brushed it away.

'Oh, Ben.' Kate didn't know what else to say. She reached out and touched his cheek where his tears would have fallen.

Ben closed his eyes and turned his face into her palm. He hugged her close to him. Drawing strength and comfort from one another, Kate found herself so intimately close, not just physically, but emotionally, it seemed completely natural when his lips found hers. The stubble of his day-old beard contrasted with the soft moistness of his mouth, sending alternate sensory shockwaves through her. His kiss became more demanding and Kate's body reacted accordingly. She slid her hand over his shoulder and down the muscular contours of his arm, her breath shuddering in anticipation. Ben hoisted her closer to him until she could feel the heat of his groin against her.

Their kiss ended and they stared at each other for a moment, breathless. Kate recognised a mixture of emotions in his eyes: guilt, the need to comfort and be comforted, and a fiery arousal that she knew must be reflected in her own.

'Come with me,' he said gruffly. He helped her off the sofa and led her into the cramped confines of his bedroom.

Stripped of their clothes, but covered by a thick duvet, Ben arched over Kate. He lowered his head to kiss each of her heavy breasts, his tongue flickering over a nipple, leaving it slick and cold as he transferred his attention to its mate. He ground himself against her, the heat and friction making Kate ache for his entrance. With a small moan, she pushed her head back against the pillows.

Ben rolled onto his side and kissed her. 'Okay?' he said.

Kate nodded, not certain she was capable of speech.

'You tell me if you want to stop and I will,' he said.

'I don't want you to stop.'

Ben slid his hand over her breast, pushing up with splayed fingers, rubbing a calloused thumb around her areola.

Kate shivered as his hand progressed beneath the duvet. She sucked in her breath as his fingers found her. She reached out to kiss him, to touch him, anything to make such pleasure bearable.

'Hold me,' he murmured.

Kate tried to curb her haste, to be more sensual, but her hands shook as they made their way down his body. Her fingers curled around the heat of his erection, and Ben buried his face in her neck. His fingers became more active, making her feel like a toy being wound tighter and tighter. Kate caressed him, exultant in this newfound wealth of sensations.

Ben moved atop her and Kate arched against him, feeling gloriously fulfilled. Like a true horseman, Ben's rhythm and balance were strong and controlled. With each quickening thrust, Kate felt the tsunami tide of arousal gather inside her. Her body seemed to take on a life of its own, instinctive and nerve-sharp. The wave crashed down and she cried out. Clinging to his shoulders, she felt him shudder and slow. They hugged each other, still as one, drowning in a sea of guilty pleasure.

It was still dark when Kate awoke. The digital clock on Ben's bedside table read 05:51. Pressed against her, Ben's body warmed her from the arctic temperature of the room. His breathing was silken on her neck, softly snoring. The events of the previous night filtered back into her mind.

What had they done?

With care, she lifted Ben's arm from where it was draped across her waist and shifted onto her back. Ben grunted and stirred.

'Ben?' Kate whispered.

'Hmm?' Ben rubbed his eyes with a fist. He paused mid-rub, as if he too had just remembered what happened. 'Hey.'

'Hey.' She pulled the duvet to her chest as she sat up, more to protect herself from the cold than any attempt at modesty. 'I've – um – got to go. I've got work.'

Ben cleared his throat and sat up as well. 'Yes, of course.' He shivered. 'You need the bathroom?'

Kate shook her head. He pulled on a pair of shorts as he stood up, and Kate waited for him to leave the room before trying to locate her scattered clothing. It was silly, really, after the intimacy of last night, to feel so awkward about their nakedness, but, Kate thought to herself, when was the morning after ever anything else?

She was just pulling on her boots when Ben came out of the bathroom. He stood, silhouetted against the light, his shoulders seemingly broader in the narrow doorway. He ran a hand through his hair, leaving it askew, and sighed.

'About last night,' he began. 'I – er – I'm sorry if you think I took advantage of you. It wasn't – I mean, I didn't – I was just as upset.'

Kate shook her head. 'You didn't take advantage of me.'

'But we—' He hesitated again. 'We took chances, didn't we?'

'I'm still on the Pill,' she reassured him.

'Still – oh,' said Ben.

Kate curled her toes in embarrassment. She hadn't meant to bring Nicholas up. In fact, she hadn't thought about him until this very moment. Another layer of guilt wrapped around her. What a horrible thing to do to him. Not that they were dating any more, but to sleep with his brother, the one person whom Nicholas had always felt was the favoured one?

'I'm sorry,' she mumbled.

Ben nodded, but didn't move. Kate went to move past him, when she felt a fleeting touch of his hand on her arm.

'I'm not,' he said. 'I don't know where we go from here, but you should know that sorry is one thing I'm not.'

His fingers curled through hers and he pulled her towards him. Kate rested her cheek on his collarbone, closing her eyes to imprint the heat of his touch and the smell of his skin in her subconscious.

The right thing would be to take back her words, to tell him she wasn't sorry either. But it wouldn't be true. Or rather it would only be partly true, and she had neither the courage nor the time to explain the complexities of what they'd done. She wasn't sorry about their night together. It had been glorious and so *wanted*, Kate now realised. But what she was sorry about was the consequences it would have. There was Nicholas to think of, Saskia as well.

His alarm clock made them both jump. It was six o'clock. Kate withdrew from the embrace. 'I'll be late.'

Ben nodded and she walked out of the room. The lamp in the sitting area was still on, and Kate noticed for the first time, a bottle of spirits sitting on the breakfast bar. Her heart ached for Ben as the reason for its presence hit her. As much as their night together had helped, it didn't change the fact that Jerry was still dead and that things at Thistle Lodge Stables were going to get a lot tougher for its owner.

She opened the front door and was treated to a faceful of windblown sleet. 'Ben?' she said, turning back.

'Yeah?'

'I'm sorry about Jerry. He was a diamond.'

* * *

By the time Kate got to Aspen Valley, her emotions were running high. Without saying good morning to anyone, she ran to d'Artagnan's stable and fumbled with the bolts. The grey gelding was up, with straw in his morning mane and manure stains on his rug.

'Oh, d'Artagnan,' she said, flinging her arms around his neck. The sobs came thick and fast as she cried on his shoulder.

D'Artagnan didn't move. Like a rock, he stood quietly, only a couple of times moving his head to press his muzzle against her back.

'Don't ever leave me, you hear?' she said, gulping back her tears. 'Don't you *ever* leave me alone.'

With an excuse to let go, it felt like all Kate's emotions were flooding to the fore. All the grief, all the frustration, all the self-pity and resentment, all the guilt; Jerry, her mother, her up-bringing, Nicholas and Saskia.

'I'm a bad person, d'Artagnan,' she whispered. 'Ungrateful, hypocritical, demanding. I've ruined things for myself by being this way. But you are so good, so genuine. Given half the chance, you would be the best you could be, and it kills me that I can't give you that.'

D'Artagnan butted her with his nose and snorted over her jacket. He stepped away from Kate and picked up his deflated football. He tossed his head, slapping the ball against his chin, trying to make her laugh.

Kate managed a smile, but it wasn't enough for d'Artagnan. He dropped the ball in his water bucket and sprang back when it splashed over the rim. He pricked his ears at Kate again to see if his theatrics had done the trick. The hard ache of tears at the back of her throat lessened enough to let a small laugh escape.

With a sniff, she wiped her eyes on her sleeve and gave her horse another hug. 'You're a clown,' she said, her face pressed against the warm hard muscle of his neck. 'But you're *my* clown, and that's all that matters.'

34

KATE DIDN'T QUITE know how to deal with her and Ben's new relationship status. By the end of a soggy afternoon at work, she'd almost convinced herself that something that felt so right couldn't be a mistake. Perhaps today being Valentine's Day also played a part. She'd never been one to get excited by the fourteenth of February, probably because the last time she'd been the recipient of the day's favour was when she'd been about twelve, but with her love affair with Ben so fresh, it seemed wrong to trample her bliss.

That said, she felt obliged to tell Saskia. Not that Saskia had ever shown any interest in Ben, but he still seemed somehow her territory.

On the drive home, Kate psyched herself up. Who knew how Saskia would react? Perhaps she should wait a while, see where the love affair went before telling all. But, of course, it had to go somewhere. Was she getting ahead of herself? Maybe. Probably. Though how could she feel so strongly about someone for it not to evolve into something more serious?

The thought of her and Ben's shared intimacy made her stomach flip in a surge of gaiety, like a lamb bouncing in a field of daisies, in a way that she and Nicholas never had.

Was she wrong to pursue her feelings for Ben in front of Nicholas? Possibly, but it had been over a month since they'd last spoken. And he hadn't exactly done himself proud by deceiving her about d'Artagnan.

Hmm, d'Artagnan. There was another factor to take into account. If d'Artagnan was to run on his merits in the Gold Cup then her best chance of persuading Nicholas to change tactics would have been if they were an item. That wasn't going to happen now.

But she would have been using Nicholas if she'd stayed for that reason, and she couldn't do that.

On the other hand, if Ben felt the same way about her as she did about him, then what better chance of d'Artagnan running true than to get his jockey on side? Not that that was the reason she wanted to be with him, she told herself sternly, but hey, when opportunity knocks, she'd be a fool to not open the door.

Kate needn't have bothered rehearsing her speech to Saskia. She arrived home to an empty house. She made her way through to the kitchen to make a hot drink, picking up yesterday's mail from the fruit bowl by the window, which neither of them had bothered opening. There was the usual pizza and Indian takeaway flyers, which she dumped in the recycling, and one, addressed to Saskia, looked suspiciously like a Valentine's Day card. For a mad moment Kate entertained the possibility that it might be from Ben. But she dismissed that idea almost as soon as she'd thought it. Ben wouldn't do that. There was also half a dozen letters that had been forwarded on from Mrs Singh's flat. Three of them were for her and none looked remotely romantic. One from her GP telling her it was time to have another smear test. Another was from her credit card provider telling her that she had a 0% rate until the end of April to transfer her debt onto her card. Kate snorted.

'I'm already maxed out on you, you prats,' she muttered.

The last letter was from Inland Revenue and Customs. Kate's stomach seemed to swallow itself. She hated unexpected letters – she'd become especially sensitive since Mrs Singh's eviction letter – and, in her experience, it was a rare day that she got a pleasant letter from the taxman.

Before she could open it, Saskia arrived home.

'Oof, it's cold out there!' she said, pulling off her bobble hat and scarf. 'Hey, what happened to you last night? One minute you were there and the next you'd disappeared.'

To avoid answering her questions, Kate thrust Saskia's mail into her hands. Saskia gave a squeal at the sight of the lilac envelope and ripped it open. On the front was a teddy bear holding flowers and heart-shaped balloons.

'Who's it from?' Kate asked, her thoughts of Ben inadvertently returning.

Saskia pouted as she read the inscription. 'I don't know.'

'A secret admirer, eh?' Kate said, looking over the top of the card. It was signed with a rather erect and elegant question mark. 'Do you recognise the writing?'

Saskia frowned and rotated the card as if looking at it sideways would help. 'No. Oh, I hate it when they don't say who they are. It's so stalker-ish.'

Kate didn't care. She was just relieved that it wasn't Ben's handwriting. At least, she didn't think it was. From what she'd seen on the calendar in his home, he had a rounded and neat hand. The card's writer appeared to have a spikier style.

'Well, whoever it is must know where you live,' said Kate, picking up the envelope. 'It was delivered here.'

Saskia was quiet for a moment then she gave a gasp. She flipped the card upside down and shook it at Kate with an excited squeak. 'I know who it is! It's Jack!'

Kate's heart dropped. 'You're kidding. Really? Is that his writing?'

'Well, maybe not quite like his. But he would change it to disguise his identity, wouldn't he? And look—' Saskia gave the upside down card to Kate and jabbed the question mark. 'That's not a question mark, is it? It's an upside down J!'

Kate looked. She supposed, with a stretch of the imagination, the rotated question mark could look like a lower case J, but even so... 'It's back to front,' she pointed out.

'Not if you look at it in the mirror.'

Kate laughed. 'Seriously, Saskia? Is Jack really the sort of person to send out secret Valentine's cards?'

'He's practically the only person who knows our new address. It has to be him.'

'Wouldn't he just give it to you at work?'

'It wouldn't be a secret then, would it?' said Saskia. She pressed the card to her chest and sighed. 'At last! Oh, I was beginning to have my doubts, but this *has* to mean something.'

Kate didn't reply. It was all well and good her telling Saskia to stop flirting with their boss, but if he was reciprocating her advances, then she couldn't very well take him to task. Could she? No, Jack was a grown man responsible for his own actions. She wouldn't dare. All she knew was that whatever happened, it would end in tears. If not Saskia's, then Pippa's.

In an attempt to deviate away from her sister's bliss, she tore open her letter from HMRC. She winced at the date on the letter. It had been sent the day before they'd moved. Her eyes flicked over the text, but then her hand began to shake and she had to lay it flat on the kitchen counter.

The kettle clicked off beside her, but she ignored it. Fear ran up her spine like a river freezing up suddenly. Kate could almost feel the crackle of the ice particles. This couldn't be happening. Not now.

Saskia finally noticed Kate's distress. 'What is it?'

Kate swallowed and flattened out the letter, running her nail over the creases. 'It's from HMRC. Apparently, I've been taxed wrongly ever since I started work at Aspen Valley. I've been paying too little, it says.'

Saskia frowned and took the letter. She looked up at Kate with wide eyes. 'That's almost a month's salary,' she exclaimed.

'I know, and—' Kate's voice wobbled and she took a deep steadying breath. 'They want it by the end of the tax year.'

'What? How can they do that? That's no time at all.'

Kate gestured to the letter. 'I know. This has been sitting at the flat for the past four weeks, mind.'

Saskia continued to stare at her. 'What are you going to do? Have you got money left on your credit card?'

'No, the move maxed me out. I don't know.'

'Holy shitbags, Kate. Surely you can speak to them, ask if you can pay it in instalments.'

Kate shrugged and examined the letter again to see if there was the option. 'Maybe. I'll have to ring them. But even so, I'm barely able to make the rent here on my income. How am I supposed to make payments on my credit card *and* these tax instalments?'

'You know I'd help if I could,' Saskia mumbled.

Actually, Kate didn't. Saskia had every right to look guilty, but Kate also knew she wasn't exactly flush either, so it was useless to point fingers and start a row.

She stared at the floor where the linoleum was peeling away from the base of the cupboard. She should make a note of that to add it onto the inventory.

'What are you going to do?' Saskia asked again.

Kate went through her options. What could she sell? Some secondhand DVDs, but they would come nowhere close to covering the bill. Could she ask Jack for a loan? No. His mood at work today had been lousier than the weather with the news that Rhys had broken his arm in yesterday's Denman Chase. And even if he'd been in a happier frame of mind, she didn't know if she could ever look her boss in the eye again, much less ask for a loan. Maybe Saskia could nudge him for a loan? No, she couldn't ask her to do that. Could she borrow from her mother? Not a chance, even if her mother had the money, which she doubted, she wouldn't be inclined to loan any of it to Kate. Anyway, pride forbade her from going begging to her mother.

She puffed out her cheeks as she settled on a last resort solution. 'I'm going to have to sell Harrison,' she said.

'But how're you going to get around? Get to work?'

Kate folded the letter back into its envelope and flapped it against her palm. She gave Saskia a resolute look. 'You're going to have to share.'

Saskia looked horrified. 'But...'

Kate could see the obvious objections going through Saskia's mind: the main one being Kate started work a good hour before she did.

But then Saskia swallowed hard and nodded. She also knew she owed Kate. 'Just until you get back on your feet.'

In a rare show of intimacy, Kate gave her sister a hug.

35

CALL HER A coward, but one bombshell a night was enough for Kate to drop on her sister. She wouldn't say Ben paled in comparison to her new wave of financial woes, but he was news that could wait for another day. When Ben texted her the next morning, Kate realised that 'another day' was approaching faster than she'd anticipated.

Can I come round tonight? I have to get away from here.

The poor man must have been suffering terribly over Jerry.

Kate rushed home after work to bath and change. She even beat Saskia back, which had to be a first. Saskia noticed as well.

'What's up with you?' she said when Kate, at last, appeared from the bathroom in a cloud of steam, lobster pink in her towel and smelling fresh from a coconut and shea butter extract-flavoured soak.

'I'm expecting a guest.'

Saskia crossed her arms and wouldn't let Kate pass to her bedroom. 'Who?'

'Saskia, let me through, it's freezing out here.'

'Not until you tell me who you're getting scrubbed up for.'

Another draughty chill swirled up the stairs and settled on Kate's damp shoulders. For someone who had to deal with the bullheaded antics of d'Artagnan every day, Saskia was no match. Kate dipped her shoulder and pushed past her sister.

Saskia followed her into her room and made herself comfortable on Kate's bed. 'Are you going to make me wait until he gets here?'

Kate hooked her arms through her dressing gown sleeves and gave Saskia a devilish grin. 'Maybe.'

'Aha! So it's a he!' said Saskia. 'New boyfriend? Gosh, you have moved quick.'

'Maybe, it's still early days.'

'Who is he? Do I know him?'

'What's with the fifty questions? Are you my mother or something?' Kate replied, imitating Saskia's well-worn phrase.

Saskia took it good-naturedly and held up the clothes Kate had laid out on the bed. Her lip curled in distaste. 'Crumbs, Kate. The nineties called. They want their wardrobe back.'

'It's comfortable,' Kate defended her choice.

Saskia shrugged in an it's-your-funeral way. 'Why is there white fur on all your clothes?'

'D'Artagnan probably.'

Saskia looked sceptical. 'You wear this to work?' she said holding up the blouse.

'No, but his hair gets into everything.'

Saskia dropped the blouse like she'd found it in d'Artagnan's stable. 'So, do I know him?'

Kate sat down at her dressing table and shook out her wet hair. 'Yeah, I should think so. Big, grey gelding. About sixteen three. Would want to be a footballer if he wasn't a racehorse.'

Saskia threw Kate's teddy bear at her. 'No, silly. Your date.'

Kate's grin faded and she looked away. 'Kind of, yes.'

'Then who is he? Come on, Kate!'

Kate switched on the hairdryer and looked at Saskia in the mirror. 'Ben.' Her words were drowned out by the shriek of the hairdryer and Saskia frowned.

'Who?'

'Ben.' Kate didn't attempt to raise her voice.

Saskia sat up, eyes wide, mouth open. She'd spent enough time in Bristolian nightclubs to be an expert lip reader. 'Did you just say Ben?' she yelled.

Kate switched off the hairdryer. 'Yes.'

Saskia didn't reply. She just stared at Kate.

'Are you okay with that?' Kate said.

'But—but I thought he liked me.'

'He did. For a while. But you didn't like him, so he lost interest.'

'But—but—but that doesn't mean he has to go off with you, with my sister.'

'It wasn't either of our intention to get together. And like I said, it's still early days. Like forty-eight hours early days.'

Saskia gasped. 'That's where you were the other night?'

Kate blushed and looked down. Damn, she'd missed shaving a stubbly spot near her ankle.

Saskia clambered forward on all fours. 'You've already slept with him? God, Kate! After it took you about a year to shag Nicholas, you have no hesitation in jumping into bed with his brother?'

Kate blushed even harder. 'Do you have to put it like that? I didn't just jump into bed with him. This has been something that's been – I don't know – *growing*. And it didn't take me a year with Nicholas. I haven't even known him a year.'

'So it's not such early days then, is it, if this has been growing?'

Kate sighed and gave Saskia a dubious pout. 'Are you really upset?'

Saskia slumped back into a sitting position and frowned, but it wasn't a sulky frown, it was more of a puzzled frown. 'Actually, no,' she said, seemingly surprising herself. 'I'm a little disturbed by it all, and especially shocked by you being the one, but no, I'm not upset.'

Kate grinned in relief. 'Good.'

'Anyway, I've got Jack to keep me amused.'

Kate was about to switch the hairdryer on again, but she hesitated. 'So, it *was* him who sent the card?'

'He's still playing it coy, but of course it's him. The more I think about it, the more I'm convinced. I haven't told anyone what our new address is. Who else could it be?'

Good question. Kate turned on her hairdryer and dragged a roll brush through it. 'That reminds me,' she shouted above the roar. 'I wonder if Mum got a Valentine's gift.'

'Mum?' Saskia looked doubtful.

'Yeah. Did you know she's got a boyfriend?'

'What? Since when?'

Kate switched off the hairdryer again. What she really needed were Saskia's straighteners. 'Dunno. Xander let it slip last time I went round. And she did look like she was making an effort.'

'Wow. Wonders never cease,' said Saskia. 'Who is he?'

Kate shrugged. 'Xander wouldn't say. But I got a text from her today asking us both to go round for Sunday lunch, so I'm guessing she's either going to announce it or introduce him.'

Saskia groaned and fell back against the pillows. 'Do we have to?'

'Don't you want to meet Mum's new fella?'

'Eww. I don't want to think of Mum shagging some wrinkly old man.'

Kate grinned. 'You surprise me. After all, Jack must be – what, forty?'

'Yeah, but he's a fit forty.'

Kate looked at her clock on her dresser. 'Shit. I must get a move on. Can I borrow your straighteners?'

The church bells at the top of the High Street had just chimed the seventh hour when there was a knock on the door downstairs. Kate swore as she tried to pull on her skinny jeans. Shackled at the knees, she hopped over to the window. Down below, Ben stood at the door, hunched in a thick winter coat and beanie.

'Do you want me to answer?' called Saskia from the kitchen.

'Yes, please!'

Bouncing up and down, Kate tugged her jeans into place and hoped they'd be easier to remove should the right opportunity arise. Aware of Ben and Saskia greeting each other downstairs, she used a tissue to clean up her eye make-up then straightened to take a last look in her wardrobe mirror. She made a conscious effort to relax her shoulders. The neckline of her blue-grey tunic top slipped lower, revealing a bit too much cleavage for her liking. She wound a patterned scarf around her neck and tried to make it look fashionable. It didn't work and she whipped it off. What was she so nervous about? Ben had seen her drenched through and covered in mud before. Anything would be an improvement on that.

Yes, but those days had been before they'd slept together.

She took a deep calming breath and left her room. On second thoughts, she dashed back inside and moved her teddy bear from her pillow to her dressing table. Just in case the evening took them in that direction.

Saskia and Ben were sat in the lounge making small talk. Kate found it surreal to think Ben was here to see *her* and not Saskia.

'Hi,' she said, shyness overcoming her.

Ben rose to his feet with a wide smile. 'Hi.'

They exchanged an awkward kiss then sat in opposite seats. All three looked from one to the other in weighty silence then Saskia thumped the armrests of her chair with finality and stood up.

'Right, well, I told Leonie I'd be at the pub five minutes ago, so I'll see you later.'

'Hey, is that my jumper you're got on?' Kate said, noticing Saskia's wardrobe for the first time.

Saskia looked too surprised for it to be authentic. 'Is it?'

'Yes and I've only worn it once.'

Saskia look doe-eyed. 'Please let me borrow it. I don't have time to go up and change. Leonie'll be waiting—'

'Saskia,' Kate warned.

'And it goes so well with these earrings. Pleeease?'

'Oh, go on then,' she said with a wave of her hand. 'Just don't spill anything on it.'

Saskia gave a couple of girly claps and skipped out of the room. 'Thanks!' She stopped at the doorway and sent Kate a mischievous wink. 'Don't do anything I wouldn't do.'

With the slamming of the front door, Kate and Ben looked at one another.

Ben raised an eyebrow. 'I guess that leaves an open field of choices then,' he said.

'She's not that bad,' Kate laughed. 'She's just a terrible flirt, that's all.'

'You spoil her, you know.'

'Good grief, I don't know how you could think that. I'm always nagging at her.'

'She told me you're having to sell your car.'

'Well, I'm not doing it to give her the money. The taxman walloped me with a huge bill.'

'Which you probably would have afforded if you weren't bailing Saskia out of trouble the whole time.'

Kate sighed. 'I don't know, Ben. She's had a hard time of it. She doesn't need me making things any more difficult.'

Ben laughed, but his eyes remained sombre. 'Saskia's right. You do act like her mother.'

'Believe me, I act nothing like our mother.'

'You know what I mean.'

Kate shook her head. 'I don't mean to. It's just that she's young and... *vulnerable*.'

Ben laughed even harder. 'She's twenty-three, not thirteen. Big enough to take care of herself.'

Kate tried to see the funny side, but it wasn't easy. 'I'm just afraid she'll turn into our mum, you know? Partying and drinking like she does.'

Ben's laughter faded. 'I'm sorry, it's not funny. If it's any consolation, addiction is usually caused by an underlying problem, rather than enjoying oneself too much, and I think Saskia falls into the latter category.'

'You've changed your tune about her,' she said. 'When did you stop liking her and, well – you know – start liking me?'

Ben shrugged. 'Hard to say. It just kind of snuck up on me. It's like asking when winter started. It didn't happen overnight. The weather just gradually changed.'

Kate laughed. 'Wow, thanks. Comparing me to winter? That's really nice.'

'Spring then. You know what I mean. What about you?'

'Hate to be boring, but it was much the same—although,' Kate raised a finger as a memory surfaced. 'There was the one time when I *really* noticed you.'

'Oh, yeah?'

'Arcades and Icecapades.'

'Ah, yes,' Ben said in dawning remembrance. 'Yes, that was a rather *enlightening* evening, wasn't it?'

Kate laughed, feeling a rush of heat to her cheeks, then sobered. 'How are things going at home?'

Ben pulled at a loose thread on the armrest. 'A bit tough, I guess. Thanks for letting me come round tonight. I had to get away.'

'I wish there was something more I could do.'

'Yeah, me too. Seymour's not making things any easier.'

'What's he doing?'

'He's been – I don't know – restless since we lost Jerry. Box-walking and stuff, but when I let him out in the paddock, he stands at the gate neighing for his buddy.'

'Poor guy.'

Ben nodded. 'Poor Jerry.' He was silent for a moment, still playing with the thread, then he cleared his throat and pulled himself together. 'Anyway, I don't really want to talk about it, if that's okay. What are we going to do this evening? I need something to take my mind off it all.'

'I suppose I could cook us some dinner,' she said doubtfully, trying to think of what she had that was more romantic than a frozen pizza.

'Do you fancy a movie? We can grab a bite to eat there.'

'In Bristol? Aren't we a bit late?'

'Not if we go now. There's that new Christopher Nolan film on that everyone's raving about.'

'Ooh, yes. I do like his films,' Kate said. 'I'll just get my coat.'

Ben waited while Kate fussed around. 'Hey, what did the woolly hat say to the scarf?' he asked, watching her winter up.

Kate shook her head.

'You hang around here while I go on ahead.'

She snorted and led the way to the door. She'd just opened it when Ben reached out a hand to keep it closed. Kate looked back in question. His expression was difficult to read in the darkened hall.

He touched warm fingers to her cheek and stroked her hair away from her face. He leaned forward and kissed her, a long unhurried kiss that pushed Kate against the wall.

'Wow,' she whispered when he finally came up for air. 'What was that for?'

Ben's eyes twinkled. 'I didn't greet you the way I wanted to earlier, that's all. Come, let's get going.'

36

FOUR HOURS LATER, Kate and Ben walked out of the cinema complex into the glare of the food court.

'Are we going to get something?' Kate asked, looking over at Burger King.

Ben looked at the adjoining Italian restaurant and raised an eyebrow at Kate. 'Crikey, you're a cheap date.'

'Not with the price of those movie tickets, I'm not.'

They walked over and stood to peruse the illuminated menu above the counter.

'Have you noticed the meals always look bigger and juicier on the pictures?' said Ben.

'That's because they're not real.'

'Yeah, but neither is half the food.'

They placed their order with the red-aproned till assistant and stood back to wait. Kate noticed a billboard nearby advertising the upcoming Cheltenham Festival.

'Can you believe we're less than a month away from Cheltenham?' she mused.

'You looking forward to it?'

'Oh, yes. I've always wanted to lead up at the Festival. Only—' She hesitated, not wanting to drag the subject of d'Artagnan up.

'Only what?'

'Only I guess I wanted to go with a horse that I could at least *hope* might stand a chance of winning. It feels tainted otherwise.'

Ben nodded. He stepped forward to take their tray of food and led the way over to a plastic table and chairs.

'If The Whistler wins the Gold Cup, then you'll be able to share in that victory, because he won't be able to do it without d'Artagnan.'

Kate sighed and unwrapped her burger. 'It's not the same.'

'Why are you surprised? You said yourself the pictures aren't real.'

A breath of laughter escaped and she shook her head. 'No, I mean if The Whistler wins. I just think—' She paused, uncertain whether voicing her belief in the grey horse would only receive ridicule in return. So far she'd been able to convince herself that she knew d'Artagnan was worthy of running a true race in the Gold Cup because she was his rider. But so was Ben. In fact, he probably had more of an idea since he was his race rider. 'Couldn't you – I don't know—' She stopped herself when Ben shook his head.

'I know what you're about to ask, so I'll stop you there. Please don't say it.'

Kate's cheeks tingled with heat. 'I know. I'm sorry. It's wrong of me to even think it.'

'I'm sorry too. But I couldn't. I'd be going against the wishes of the family.'

'Could you try persuade them beforehand?'

'With what? D'Artagnan hasn't got the form to back up your beliefs.'

'He came second in the Denman Chase,' Kate pointed out.

'Exactly. He came *second*. Dad wants winners, not runners-up.'

'But he might have won if you hadn't had to go hell for leather for the first two miles.'

'He got beat by China Blue, whom Canyon Echo left in the car park in the Betfair Chase. And with The Whistler beating Canyon Echo in the King George, where does that leave us?'

Kate swallowed her chicken and cheese before replying. 'Yeah, I know. It just feels wrong, I guess. I sit on d'Artagnan every day at home and the vibes I get from him go totally against what the form book says.'

Ben frowned and waggled a barbeque-sauced finger at her. 'Why are you so fixated on winning?'

'I'm not. I just believe in allowing someone – whether it be horse or human – to be the best they can be. And making the running on d'Artagnan is not doing that. Why are you so *against* winning?'

'I'm not. I just don't like riding easy winners.'

'It shouldn't matter how easy they are,' Kate replied. 'You're a great rider. Not just a jockey, but a great overall horseman.'

'Try telling that to the boys in the weighing room.'

'Why do you still do it then?'

Ben finished off his burger and mopped his fingers with a paper napkin. 'Because I owe it to my father.'

'Owe him for what though?'

'Does there have to be a particular reason? Can't I be indebted to him for when he was there for me through the years?'

Kate was taken aback by the impatience in his voice. 'Sorry, yes, of course you can. But if it makes you unhappy, I'm sure he wouldn't want that.'

Ben pinched the bridge of his nose and rubbed his eyes. 'Look, it's complicated. I ride because my father needs me to ride for him – ow, shit, I've got barbeque sauce in my eye.' He looked at her through smarting eyes. 'Can we talk about something else? What about the movie? Did you understand half of what was going on?'

Kate shook her head, but didn't mention she hadn't found the plot half as complicated as his riding terms seemed to be. Maybe Bill Borden's need for Ben to ride his horses was nothing more than a father wanting a sportsman for a son, which she knew from Nicholas was what he'd always wanted. Or was it something more sinister? Something illegal? No, perish the thought. She was letting her imagination run wild.

They disposed of their napkins and burger boxes in the overflowing bin and wandered out of the food court, discussing the two and a half hour Christopher Nolan action extravaganza they'd just witnessed. They were just passing the saloon style doors of the Italian restaurant when Ben stopped.

'Hey, isn't that your mother?'

'My mother?' Kate looked where he was pointing.

Sure enough, Val Creswell was sat at the bar, one trouser-suited leg crossed over the other, in conversation with someone.

Kate gasped. 'Ooh, I wonder if she's with her new man.'

'New man?'

Feeling mischievous, Kate tried to glimpse her mother's date, but there was a pillar in the way. 'Yeah, Xander says she's got a boyfriend.'

'How is Xander?'

Kate knew she was in danger of being spotted the way she was standing, framed by the entrance, and craning her neck. 'He's good, thanks. Back at school. Hasn't been expelled as far as I know. I think those weekend visits really made a difference.'

'Horses are good therapy,' Ben murmured, watching her. 'Listen, do you want to go inside and say hello? It might be easier than standing here looking like indiscreet peeping toms.'

As he spoke, the man – Kate had established that much – opposite Val moved into view. He still had his back to them though and Kate tutted. Finally, he turned, only as far as revealing his profile, but that was enough for Kate. She almost lost her balance.

'You want to go in?' Ben asked again.

Kate stepped back, her heart hammering, and shook her head. 'No, no. No. I wouldn't want—wouldn't want to disturb them.'

Ben shrugged and gave her a puzzled look. 'You okay? You've gone a bit pale.'

Kate shook her head. 'Must be the lighting. I'm fine. Shall we go?'

Ben hooked his arm through hers as they walked away and sent her a concerned look. 'You sure you're okay?'

'Yes, fine,' she squeaked.

Of all the men her mother could have picked, it had to be this one.

37

'YOU GOT PLANS this weekend?' Frankie yelled as she and Kate cantered up Aspen Valley's fog-cloaked hill together.

Kate's mount, Chic Shadow, pulled hard against the bridle. The pain of muscle fatigue in Kate's arms was almost enough to rival her state of mind.

'Sunday lunch at my mother's,' she replied. 'Should be interesting.'

Frankie laughed. 'You should come try out *my* mother's Sunday lunches if you want interesting.'

'Somehow I think this one is going to top them all,' Kate muttered to herself. Louder, though, she asked, 'How's Rhys doing? Is he going to be back by Cheltenham?'

Frankie clicked her tongue and nudged her mount to keep up with Chic Shadow. 'The doc reckons not. He says four weeks isn't enough, but you know Rhys and his lot. When he broke his collarbone last summer, he was back in the saddle within three weeks. He'd rather risk breaking his arm again at Cheltenham than not riding at all.'

The fluorescent boards marking the end of the Gallops seeped through the mist and the pair pulled up.

'He'd be missing out on a good set of rides if he had to miss it,' Kate said as they walked back down the hill.

'Exactly. Ta' Qali in the Champion Hurdle, The Whistler in the Gold Cup, Dust Storm in the World Hurdle. Believe you me, Rhys is *not* going to miss Cheltenham, broken arm or no broken arm. Look up stubborn in the dictionary and you'll find his name listed.'

'Poor Frankie,' Kate laughed. 'The perils of falling in love with a jump jockey.'

'Don't do it,' Frankie advised. 'My mother warned me not to and I ignored her. Now I'm paying the price. Don't make the same mistake. Find someone normal, who works a steady job that doesn't require an ambulance to follow him around.'

Kate laughed, all the while thinking, *you might be a bit late with that advice.* 'He'd have to like racing,' she said.

Frankie pulled a reluctant face. 'That's the thing, isn't it? We're all high maintenance. Take you and me, for instance – we're only work riders, yet we work crazy hours, days away from home to go to the races, especially the ones up north or abroad, and when we do come home we've got mud under our fingernails – not that I have any fingernails – and straw in our hair and we stink of stables.'

Kate laughed and batted her away.

'I think Jack and Pippa have got the best deal,' Frankie went on. 'They're both still really involved in racing, but Jack's not in danger of breaking his neck every day and Pippa's got her artsy work to keep her occupied.'

Kate thought back to her meeting with Pippa at Chepstow where they'd sheltered under the same umbrella to watch Fontainebleau's race.

'Do you really think their marriage is as great as all that?'

'Well, sure. What would make you think otherwise?'

'I don't know. I bumped into Pippa at the Welsh National meeting and she just mentioned how distant Jack had become.'

Frankie nodded thoughtfully. 'He has been rather busy this season. I'm starting to think I should apply for the job as assistant trainer. There's no way you can manage an operation this size all on your own, even if you are the mighty Jack Carmichael.'

With Saskia and her Valentine's Day card at the forefront of her mind, Kate asked, 'You think it's only work that's making him distant?'

Frankie gave a short laugh of disbelief. 'You're not suggesting what I think you're suggesting, are you?'

Kate shrugged, wondering if she'd said too much. 'I don't know. There's more than one way to skin a cat.'

Frankie looked ahead to where Jack's Land Rover was parked midway down the hill, its silver paintwork camouflaging it in the gloom. 'Crikey, it never even occurred to me. I guess he's just as susceptible to a roving eye as anyone. I mean, Pippa has been coming out on her own quite a bit lately. Not that she comes out very often, not with Gabby to keep her busy, but when she does, Jack is hardly ever with her.' She looked at Kate. 'But no, that can't be the reason. He's always been working those nights, holed up in his office studying form and what not. He wouldn't have time to have an affair, would he?'

Frankie's look of concern stopped Kate from suggesting any more. The fact that all the hours Jack spent neglecting his wife were instead being spent at the office was no reassurance to her.

She shook her head and smiled. 'You're right. My imagination is just running away from me. I've been watching too many movies – hey, have you seen the new Christopher Nolan film?'

By the time they'd pulled up next to the Land Rover to update the trainer on their horses' workouts, the idea of Jack's potential infidelity had been put to bed.

Kate sat aboard Chic Shadow, reins looped loose around the gelding's neck, and gazed around as she waited her turn. The mist was so thick, it was impossible to see ten metres ahead, and there was no morning sun to warm the air or even make the mist pretty. Instead, it was thick, dark and when the wind howled against the hillside, it was even a bit spooky. It made sounds travel unevenly. Horses whinnying or the crash of a dropped bucket down at the stable yard were swept up and bounced off the hill making it sound like it was happening in the copse of trees above one of the paddocks.

When the first cries of 'Loose horse! Loose horse!' reached Kate's ears, it was difficult to pinpoint where it was coming from. She screwed round in her saddle, but the fog made it impossible to see very far. The erratic thunder of hooves came down from the top of the hill. Frankie and Jack paused in their conversation.

A flash of black on the other side of the running rail lent Kate reassurance. They, at least, would be out of harm's way. But then the next string of horses cantering up the hill came into earshot.

Jack swore and jumped out of his vehicle. 'LOOSE HORSE! LOOSE HORSE!' he shouted, standing on the Land Rover's side step and cupping his mouth.

His shouts echoed around the valley. The string galloped towards them and Kate and Frankie took up the call. Chic Shadow spun around in alarm. The loose horse pounded down the track from the top.

'*LOOSE! HORSE!*' roared Jack, and this time the riders reacted. The leaders sawed at their mounts' mouths to steady them.

'Who is it? Do we know?' said Frankie, looking back up the track.

The horse galloped into view, dark brown with an emblazoned white face.

'Shit. It's Shenandoah,' said Jack.

The string pulled up in line with Jack's car. Shenandoah saw them at the last moment as he burst through the gloom. In a split second, he changed direction, swerving left into the running rail. In a last ditch attempt, the gelding rose up in an ugly jump, breasting the plastic rail and breaking it.

The horse's momentum carried his jump onto the other side of the track and with an almighty thud, he cannoned right into Chic Shadow.

The air was knocked out of Kate's lungs and the world spun round. Too fast to see anything, to register what was happening, there was just noise. Heavy breathing, frightened squeals, the grinding of metal as the Land Rover took a beating, and the shouts of onlookers. Noise, noise, noise. Then nothing.

Kate came to on the backseat of Jack's Land Rover. It smelt of muddy carpet and leather.

'Kate? Can you hear me?' It was Frankie, sitting beside her.

Kate shifted upright and winced as a sharp pain tweaked her shoulder. 'I don't know. What happened? Was I unconscious?'

'No, just a bit spaced out. Have you broken anything?'

Kate looked around her. The shattered windscreen hung over the dashboard. Jack stood outside, supporting himself against the driver's door.

'The horses,' she said in sudden urgency. 'Is Chic Shadow okay? Shenandoah?'

'The vet's on his way, but I think they've done more damage to you and Jack's car than they have to themselves,' Frankie said, pointing out the window to the horses being held nearby.

'Are you okay?' Kate asked.

'Not a scratch on me. Have you broken anything? You were right underneath it all.'

Slowly the images of chaos returned. The impact of Shenandoah knocking them sideways, the ludicrously close view of the muddy treads on the Land Rover's front wheel.

'I—I think I must have been thrown under the car. I don't think...' She moved her fingers and hands and arms. They all worked. She touched a bump on her head and grimaced. 'Ow. I think I must have hit my head. Are you sure the horses are fine?'

'Let's wait until Declan gets here. I'll just let Jack know you're compos mentis.' Frankie climbed out of the car. 'She's okay, Jack.'

Jack looked in, his face contorting with pain as he bent. 'You sure?'

'Just a knock on the head, I think,' Kate replied. 'Shoulder's a bit sore, but nothing broken, I don't think.'

'Good. That's good. Someone will take you to A&E just to be sure.' He winced again as he breathed.

'Are you okay?' she asked.

'Yeah, just got caught behind the door,' he said, gingerly touching his ribs. He looked ruefully at his Land Rover. 'Can't say the same for the car though.'

'Sorry.' Kate didn't know what else to say. She looked at his pained expression tightening with every breath he took. 'Maybe you should come to A&E as well.'

Jack shook his head. 'Declan O'Keefe's on his way over to check the horses. Can't leave.'

Kate tried to flex her shoulder. 'So much for having the safest job.'

'What?'

'Frankie and I were discussing our jobs just before it happened. We agreed you had it best as trainer.'

A wry smile touched Jack's lips. 'Danger comes in many forms, Kate, many forms.'

A couple of hours later, Kate was regretting her decision to suggest that Jack should accompany her to A&E. They sat in the waiting area alongside a construction worker holding a grimy dressing to his forehead, a child who'd come off his bicycle and whose mother seemed more upset about the damaged Christmas present than she was about her son, and various other walking wounded.

Jack was not happy, especially as he was meant to be racing that afternoon and the triage nurse had refused to change the channel on the television in the waiting area, so they'd had to endure back-to-back episodes of *Antiques Roadshow* and *Cash in the Attic* instead of the 1.30 and 2.05 at Lingfield.

Now that the adrenalin had worn off, Kate was also discovering new tender points on her body. With her riding gloves removed, she found her knuckles were split and turning a dark shade of blue, her shoulder was stiffening up and the bump on her head had turned into a full blown

223

headache. All she wanted was some painkillers and long hot soak in a bath.

Jack was muttering about NHS waiting times when the entrance doors whooshed open and Pippa rushed in, steering Gabrielle's pram like a rally driver.

'Jack? Are you okay?'

Jack tried to stand, but grimaced and slumped back in his chair, eyes clenched shut. 'Fine.'

'Declan thinks he's cracked a couple of ribs,' Kate said.

As well as looking over the horses and diagnosing their wounds as superficial, he'd checked Aspen Valley's human residents as well and had packed them both off to hospital.

'Oh, Jack, you poor thing,' Pippa said, kissing him on his head. 'And your Land Rover. It's totalled.'

'Probably time I got a new one,' Jack grunted.

Kate had to stop herself from saying she had a car they could buy. Jack wasn't the sort of man to drive a Ford Escort. Besides, Harrison wouldn't last a week going up and down the Gallops every morning.

They sat together and waited. Pippa rocked Gabrielle's pram with her foot on the wheel. Her cheery chatter went on apparently unnoticed by Jack, who continued to glower at the television. If he was grateful for his wife's presence then he was certainly playing his cards close to his chest. Except for one of course, Kate thought, remembering Saskia's Valentine's Day card.

38

KATE HAD LOOKED forward to dentist appointments more than to Sunday lunch at her mother's. The extra place setting at the dining room table was the first hint that her suspicions were correct. Val was basting the roast potatoes when Kate walked into the kitchen. The aroma of roasting beef hung in the air.

'We expecting another guest?' she forced the words out.

Val wiped her brow with an oven glove and hesitated. Her eyes were a little wild, verging on fearful. 'Yes. I've invited a friend to join us.'

Kate leant against the kitchen counter and tried to ignore the half empty bottle of vodka hiding behind the recipe book. 'A man friend?'

'For your information, yes.' Val shoved the baking tray back into the oven with a clatter and closed the door in a whoosh of heat.

'Who is he?'

Val took off the oven gloves and took a swig of her drink. 'You'll find out soon enough.' She looked at the clock on the wall. 'In about half an hour to be exact. He's coming at two.'

Kate felt a wry sense of anticipation. 'Do you want some help?'

'You can help me with the Yorkshire puddings,' replied her mother. 'I can never get them to rise. I want to see if you can do any better.'

'Doubt it,' Kate replied. Nevertheless, she measured out the flour and helped find the whisker at the back of a dusty kitchen cupboard.

'Good grief, did you get into a punch-up?' Val exclaimed when she noticed Kate's blackened knuckles.

'No. Had a bit of a run-in with a horse and a Land Rover earlier this week. That's all.'

'That's all? Good God, Katie. That job is going to get you killed one of these days. How can you be so aloof about it?'

'I got off fairly lightly. Jack broke three ribs.'

'Who?'

'My boss. And his car's a write-off.'

'And the horses?'

'They're fine. A few bumps and scrapes, but nothing serious. You got eggs?'

Val rummaged through the fridge and came out with a half-dozen tray. Kate couldn't stop herself from checking the use by date. She was impressed. They still had five days to go. Val was obviously pulling out the stops for today.

Two o'clock came and went. Kate took her time carving the roast, but even so, by the time everyone was seated and the food was ready to be served there was still no sign of Val's mystery guest.

They sat in silence for a while. Saskia and Xander tinkered on their mobile phones. Val watched the clock. Kate watched the steam over the food dissipate as it cooled.

'We may as well start,' she said.

'I'll try him once more,' said Val, getting up to fetch her phone. 'He's probably caught in traffic or something.'

Kate berated herself over her expectations. She wouldn't even call them high expectations, but she had expected something, or some*one* to be more accurate. She should have known better.

'Still going to voicemail,' Val said, returning to the table. She sat back down, her shoulders hunched in disappointment, staring at her empty plate. With a deep breath, she straightened up and beamed at her children. 'Let's eat, shall we? No point in letting it spoil.'

In one fluid movement, Xander put down his phone and scooped four Yorkshire puddings onto his plate.

'Hey, don't take so many,' Saskia said. 'I want some as well.'

Kate almost laughed. Just like old times.

Midway through their meal – which, to give Val credit, was pretty good – it was obvious that their guest was not so much running late as not coming at all.

'So where did you meet this guy, Mum?' Saskia asked, nodding to the vacant chair.

'Oh, I don't know. We've known each other a while now,' Val said airily.

Kate cut through her beef with a vicious screech of her knife. 'Come on, Mum. Who are you trying to kid? We'd have to find out eventually.'

'What do you mean?' The fearful look was back.

'I mean Ben and I saw you when we were out on a date the other night.'

Xander choked on his food. 'You're dating Ben?'

Kate ignored him. 'We saw you at that Italian bar.'

Val's hands shook as she put her knife and fork down. 'You shouldn't spy on people, Katie.'

'I wasn't spying on you. I just saw you.'

'Who is he?' said Saskia.

'He's got a really cool car,' Xander said.

Kate hesitated. 'Xander, have you met him?'

Xander shrugged. 'Yeah, sure. A couple of times.'

Kate's gaze swept back to Val, appalled. 'Does Xander even know who he is?'

Val opened her mouth, but no words came out.

'Who is he?' said Saskia again.

Kate glanced at Xander's uncertain and innocent face. Fierce protectiveness rose inside her. She shook her head in incredulity. 'I don't believe you, Mum. Are you trying to mess him up even more than he already is?'

'I'm not messed up,' Xander said.

'I thought today I could make the proper introductions,' whispered Val.

'WHO IS HE?' shouted Saskia.

'He's Dad! All right?' Kate shouted back.

Saskia sat back in her chair, dumbstruck. Her knife slithered off her plate and splattered gravy onto the table cloth.

'Dad?' Xander whispered. He stared at Kate for a moment more before looking at his mother. 'Is she serious?'

Val's eyes filled with tears and she shook her head at Kate. 'You can be a little bitch sometimes, you know that? Why did you have to break it to him like that?'

'How else were you hoping to break it to him?' she replied. 'You think that man was going to walk in and we'd sit down to a nice family meal and everything would be fine?'

Val gave a non-committal shrug. 'If you made an effort not to make a scene then perhaps, yes, it would have been fine.'

'Don't make this my fault. What are you doing wasting your time with that scumbag, Mum?'

'Don't talk about your father like that!'

'He's not been much of a father to me. He's been even less of a father to Xander. He'd bloody scampered before Xander was even born. Why's he back? What does he want?'

'Everybody deserves a second chance,' Val replied through gritted teeth.

'You've given him plenty of chances.'

'He's my dad?' said Xander.

'He promised this time would be different,' Val said. 'He's changed.'

Like a volcano ready to erupt, hot anger rose inside Kate. 'Bullshit! Where is he now if he's changed so much? He's not here. It wouldn't surprise me if he's halfway back to wherever he came from. He's never been here!'

'He was so young when you and Saskia were born,' Val said.

'And when Xander was born? Why are you making excuses for him? Have you forgotten what he did to you? He deserted you. Not once. Not twice. *Three* times, Mum. He turned you into an alcoholic. He—'

'I am *not* an alcoholic!' Val shouted, thumping the table with her fist and making the plates jump.

Kate tore the napkin from her lap and stood up. The ground beneath her feet felt as stable as a tight-rope. She looked around the table. Saskia looked in shock. Xander was trying hard not to cry. Val's mascara was already running.

'It's his fault you are the way you are,' Kate said, pointing at her mother. 'It's his fault *we* are the way *we* are. He does not deserve the time of day from any of us, least of all you.'

She flung her napkin down on the table to solidify her point and walked out of the room.

'Good!' she heard Val scream after her. 'Go on, then! Since you're too good for us, go! If your time's so precious, go!' Her voice rose as she followed Kate out of the room.

Kate gathered her bag and winter accessories in the sitting room. 'It is and I am,' she shouted back.

Val appeared in the archway, her lips drawn back in a vicious snarl. Kate brushed past her to the front door.

'But if you go, what makes you any better than him?'

Val's icy words of comparison pierced straight to her core and twisted its barbs around her heart. Kate's hand paused on the lock. She stared at it for a moment, seeing the bruised and scabbed skin, thinking how her childhood had felt just as ugly and damaged. It was an injury that time had done a poor job of healing, yet here her mother was trying to reopen the wounds.

She wasn't a coward. She wasn't running away. She was being *driven* away. And this time it was about survival.

She looked back at her mother. Val was hyperventilating, standing with her arms held out to allow for her heaving chest. Her hands were trembling uncontrollably. She looked a mess, and by the look in her eyes, the turmoil extended in as well as outside.

A small part of Kate did wish her father was back – not the one she knew to be real, but the fantasy her mother believed in – just so Kate didn't have to feel so responsible for her.

'If you bring him back into your life,' Kate said quietly. 'Then I will no longer be a part of it.'

39

'DID YOU MEAN it?' Ben asked.

Kate held her head in her hands and blew out her breath. 'I don't know. I just don't want *him* in my life. Mum's bad enough on her own. God knows what'll happen if he comes back. You just have to look at her now to see what he did last time.'

'What *did* happen last time?'

Kate sat back and waved a vague hand. 'Oh, he messed her around. Always leaving, always coming back. And then he left for good when Mum had Xander. Or so I thought.'

'Come on, you know I don't mean a brief summary of events. Tell me what happened *to you*.'

Kate gave him a hesitant look, and Ben nodded in encouragement. Kate took a deep breath. 'I remember the first time I saw her drunk, not that I knew what that meant back then.' She paused to think back. In her mind's eye, she saw it all from the viewpoint when everything in the world was big. 'Saskia was in her cot, screaming her lungs raw, and Mum was passed out on the bed. I thought she was dead at first. Who could sleep through that racket? I tried to wake her up and she wouldn't. So I went and filled my beaker – you know, one of those infant cups with a spout. Mine was yellow.' Kate smiled as the memory resurfaced. 'I filled it with milk and tried to give it to Saskia. But she spilt it all over her bed. I remember her face: this deep red – almost purple – from yelling and her eyes all teary.' Kate shook her head and Ben held her closer. 'Mum was so mad with me. I tried to tell her I'd been trying to help, but that just seemed to make her madder.'

'Probably felt guilty,' said Ben.

Kate thought about it for a moment and nodded. 'I suppose so. I never thought of it like that.'

'How old were you?'

'About four or five maybe.'

'So you were four when you became a parent?'

'I don't know. I don't think it was so bad back then. Mum would binge, I guess, thinking back now.' Kate gave a mirthless laugh. 'Then one day this man knocks on the door. I remember his smile, this huge laughing smile, and him telling me he was my dad. I remember him standing on the step, holding his arms out wide, that smile on his face, and thinking *who is this guy?* He stayed around for a while, but then what happened? Of course, Mum got pregnant with Xander and he was out of the door faster than Frankel.' She shook her head, a cheerless smile on her face. 'And this time Mum really went to pieces. I hated her for it. While all my friends were out partying and hooking up with boys, I was stuck at home, babysitting. I flunked my exams.' Kate looked at Ben for his reaction. 'We had a row and she—' Kate hesitated. She'd never told anyone this much and it was scary. Her courage failed her. '—well, we had a row and I took off. A friend at school was going to the Racing School in Newmarket, so I went too. The rest you already know.'

Ben pulled her close and kissed her hair. 'Poor Kate,' he murmured. 'What a childhood you had to endure.'

'I ran away from my problems though. I'm still running away from them. Mum's right. I'm no better than he is.'

'I doubt she really meant it.'

'How can you know that? She can be vicious sometimes, Ben.'

'Exactly,' he replied, pulling away so he could look her in the eye. 'And she does it because she's hurting too.'

'So why doesn't she get help? If she got help, if she refused to take my father back for once, then she wouldn't feel so hurt. Yet she still does it.'

Ben sighed. 'Alcoholism's a disease, Kate. It's difficult to understand because it's not like having a blood test and seeing you've got diabetes or having a biopsy and seeing you've got cancer. Sometimes, because of that, it's also difficult for the person suffering it to realise it too.'

'But how can she not realise it?'

'She's in denial. If she were to admit to it, she would feel ashamed, a failure, and then there's all the guilt that she's been hoarding over the years.'

Kate frowned at him. 'How do you know all this?'

Ben rested his chin against the side of her head. 'I used to know someone who had the same problems.'

'Did they seek help?'

She felt Ben nod. 'Yes. You mustn't be too hard on your mum. She's not thinking straight. Sooner or later, she's going to need help, and when she does—' Ben paused when Kate evaded his gaze. He tucked a lock of her hair behind her ear and made her look at him. 'When she does, she's going to need your support.'

40

FOR THE NEXT couple of days, Kate was still too angry to feel supportive of her mother. Sitting in the tack room with the electric heater on full blast, she rubbed saddle soap into Fontainebleau's saddle and listened with half an ear to the others talking about the upcoming Cheltenham Festival.

'It'd better not rain,' said Frankie. 'The Whistler hates heavy ground. Hey, Kate, did you see the Ascot Chase on Saturday?'

Kate nodded. Anything pre-Sunday lunch seemed a lifetime ago, but it was near enough for her to remember how Canyon Echo had annihilated the opposition. 'I hear Canyon Echo's been cut to six-to-one for the Gold Cup.'

'I know,' Frankie replied, wrinkling her nose in disgust. With her fingernail she scraped away the dirt under the stirrup skirt. 'What do you think of that Kipling horse? Word is he's gonna be the dark horse in the race.'

Billy snorted. 'Yeah, right. Kipling has got more Fs in his formbook than a Tarantino script.'

'What about that Irish horse, Thunderclap, then?' Frankie countered. 'He's unbeaten this season over fences. Hacked up in the Lexus Chase.'

'Hasn't been to Cheltenham yet though,' replied Billy. 'The hill on the run-in's a killer. Don't trust a horse until he's run at Cheltenham.'

'Well, The Whistler won at the International meeting when he was a novice. Has d'Artagnan ever run at Cheltenham?' Frankie asked.

'No,' Kate said. 'It wouldn't make any difference anyhow. He's not going to win.'

'Gosh, I knew we could count on you to be optimistic,' said Frankie with a laugh.

Kate shrugged and got to work on her stirrup leathers. 'He's only in it to make the running for The Whistler.'

'Yeah, but...' Frankie's words faded as she failed to find anything hopeful to counteract Kate's negativity. 'I've seen pacemakers win before. It's not like in the old days when you could have a pacemaker and then pull him up when the more fancied horse comes through. These days the jockeys have to ride them out to the finish, otherwise they'll get done for race-fixing.'

'It's a bit of a grey area in the rule book, don't you think?' said Kate. 'Pacemakers are required to be ridden to achieve the best possible placing at the finish, yet starting out at a hundred miles an hour for the first twelve furlongs on a horse that benefits from being held up is hardly trying for the best possible placing.'

Frankie shrugged. 'Hmm, maybe. But until they change things, it's still within the rules of racing.'

With a sigh, Kate put her saddle back on its rack and had just taken down d'Artagnan's bridle when her mobile phone vibrated in her jacket pocket. Kate looked at the caller ID and her fingers inadvertently tightened around the handset.

It was her mother. How did she find the audacity to call her?

She looked over at Frankie and Billy. They had moved on to discussing Jack's and Rhys's broken bones and comparing their own injury histories. She switched off her phone and pocketed it. Out of sight, out of mind.

'You ever broken anything, Kate?' Billy asked.

Kate had a flashback to upending her mother's dustbin of empty booze bottles into the sink and the crash of fractured glass.

'Kate?'

Kate blinked herself back to the present and filled her lungs with air. Billy and Frankie were looking at her with concern. She smiled.

'Does my bank balance count?'

That evening, Kate bade a sad farewell to her old friend, Harrison. She handed the car keys over to the dealer, feeling stupidly emotional. The old Ford wasn't the snazziest set of wheels, but it had been her first and she remembered the pride with which she'd driven around in it those first few weeks.

The man counted out a few crusty fifty pound notes and handed them over. Kate felt even worse that Harrison should witness the exchange.

'Righto, I'll be off then, love.'

Kate nodded. 'Yes, okay... Take care of him,' she couldn't help adding.

The man laughed at her like she was joking. He got in and adjusted the seat then slammed the door. Kate winced. She touched the bonnet once in a silent goodbye and walked back down the High Street to her door before the dealer had even started the engine. She couldn't bear to watch Harrison being driven away by somebody else.

Back inside, Kate fingered the notes as she waited for the kettle to boil. Saskia wandered in, head bent to the illuminated screen of her mobile.

'You want tea?' Kate asked.

'Oh, wank,' Saskia muttered.

'What's wrong?'

'Odus fell off the moon again.'

'*What?*'

Saskia looked up at Kate's confusion and flapped a hand at her. 'Forget it.' Her eyes alighted on the money in her hand. 'Ooh, you're rich. You treating us to drinks tonight?'

Kate stuffed the money back in her pocket. 'No, it's money for the taxman.'

Saskia sagged. 'Oh. Pour me some will you?'

Kate took down another mug and dropped a teabag into it. 'You haven't said much about Sunday,' she said.

Saskia shrugged. 'I say let them get on with it. It's her life she's ruining.'

'Do *you* want him back?'

Saskia paused for thought. 'I don't know. I don't remember him very well. All I remember is him holding me by my wrists and spinning me around.' She smiled then quickly swallowed it. 'Sorry, that's probably not what you want to hear.'

'No, I don't mind,' Kate replied. 'I just want to make sure you're okay.'

Saskia batted a hand at her. 'Pff, don't worry about me. I'm all right. Thanks for running Jack over with your horse, by the way. I've made some brilliant progress fussing over him.'

Kate sighed in resignation. The kettle clicked off and Kate poured the hot water into the cups. 'What kind of progress?'

Saskia tapped the side of her nose. 'That's between me and Jack.'

'Are you having an affair?'

Saskia fiddled with her phone and didn't quite meet her eye. 'Well, maybe not physically. He's got three broken ribs.'

Kate shook her head and slid Saskia's tea towards her. 'You know what shit you're going to stir up if you ever get found out.'

'Nobody will find out, not unless you tell them.'

Saskia took her tea and walked out of the kitchen, leaving Kate with just her thoughts. She couldn't wholly believe Saskia's blasé attitude. She must surely be bothered by these things and Kate was afraid bottling it all up would only end in tears.

She was reminded of her own tears, of the patience Ben had shown, listening to her lament. Leaning against the worktop, she took out her phone to call him. It was still switched off from earlier. She sought out a packet of biscuits while it switched back on. It buzzed, and Kate saw half a dozen missed calls listed, one from Ben, one from Nicholas of all people, and the rest from her mother.

'Damn,' she muttered and tapped in her voicemail number.

'You have two new messages,' said the automated voice. 'First message: message received today at sixteen thirty-nine.'

'Kate? Kate, are you there?' came her mother's sniffling voice. 'Oh, please pick up. Is Xander with you?'

Kate stood up straight at Val's panicked message.

'Katie, I don't know where he's gone. He just left. Oh God, it's all my fault. Katie, please help.'

Kate instinctively reached for her keys and swore as she realised she no longer had them.

'Saskia!' she yelled. 'I need to borrow your car. Where are your keys?'

'Already?' Saskia said from the lounge.

Kate strode through to the other room, her phone still to her ear as she waited for the second message to play. With any luck it would be her mother telling her not to panic, Xander was safely home.

Saskia was curled up on the sofa, blowing on her tea and watching TV. 'Couldn't you have run errands before you sold Harrison?'

'Xander has gone missing. I need to go find him.'

Saskia frowned. 'Missing? Missing where?'

'I don't know. That's why I need your car. To go find him. He might be at Paul's—' She stopped as Ben's voice cut through her panic.

'Hi Kate. It's Ben. Just thought you'd like to know Xander has come to visit—' Kate cut the call and gestured to Saskia to give her the keys.

'He's at Ben's place.'

236

Saskia looked mildly annoyed. 'They're in my bag, on the table. Just don't wreck it. You're not insured to drive.'

Kate paused. She didn't much fancy the idea of being caught driving without insurance. She considered asking Saskia to go fetch Xander, then thought better of it. If Xander was in a state, then she wanted to be the one to help him. She'd just have to chance it.

41

FORTUNE WAS ON Kate's side and she pulled up at Thistle Lodge Stables without running into any police. She hurried around the corner of the stable block and found the motion sensor security lights ablaze.

'Xander? Ben?'

Ben appeared from the feed room and lifted a hand in greeting. 'Hey, Kate.'

Kate ran over to him. 'Where's Xander? Is he still here?'

Ben moved aside for Kate to see into the room. Xander stood, balancing a sack of bran over a feed bin, looking wary.

'Xander, what happened?' Kate said, falling upon him.

Xander glowered at her. 'Hasn't Mum been looking for me? Stupid bitch doesn't care.'

'Yes, she's been looking for you. She's been leaving frantic messages on my phone all afternoon. What happened?'

Xander shrugged and upended the sack into the bin. A cloud of bran dust billowed up into his face.

'What happened, Xander?'

Xander ignored her, folding up the sack and adding it to the pile.

'Xander—'

'Hey, Xander,' said Ben, 'why don't you give the horses their alfalfa?'

Xander nodded and pushed past Kate out into the yard. Kate watched him go, dismay rising in her throat. Ben placed a hand on her shoulder and she turned to him.

'Is he okay? Has he said anything?'

'Not to me, no. But Seymour's got all the facts.'

'Huh?'

Ben nodded in Xander's direction. 'He's been here since about four. Shut himself in Seymour's stable and's been grooming him ever since. I heard him talking it over with him.'

'What was he saying?'

'I don't know. I wasn't going to eavesdrop.'

Kate despaired. 'Oh, Ben. Why is everything so—so *fucked* up?'

Ben pulled her into his arms. Kate breathed in his alpha presence, finding comfort in his solidity.

'I'm so glad he came here though,' she whispered into his jacket. 'What am I going to do? I can't let her ruin Xander's life like—like this.' She stopped herself from saying 'like she did mine'. She didn't want be that wet self-pitying rag.

'Things'll get better,' Ben said, rubbing her shoulder blades.

Kate pulled back to look at him, wanting so much to believe him, but stuck in a rut of pessimism. 'How can you know that?'

He brushed her hair behind her ear and smiled. 'Because they can't get much worse, can they?'

'I don't know about that. My whole family seems to be coming apart at the seams.'

'Which is why you need to be strong for them. Take Xander home and talk to your mother—'

'She's impossible to talk to, though. And, after the way I left on Sunday, it wouldn't surprise me if she never wants to talk to me again.'

Ben raised an eyebrow. 'She called you today, didn't she?'

'Yes, but that was just because she couldn't find Xander.'

'Exactly. Because when she needs help, you're the one she turns to. When the time comes for her to seek help with her drinking, who else will be there if you've turned your back on her?'

Kate sighed and hugged Ben tight.

The car ride back to their mother's house was made in silence for the most part. Against her instincts, but taking Ben's advice, Kate didn't press Xander to pour out his heart.

Sat in Bristol's rush hour traffic, however, Xander broke the silence.

'Is Ben your boyfriend?' His face was expressionless, lit red by the brake lights of the car in front. He didn't take his eyes off the road.

'Um, yes, he is.'

'Are you going to marry him?'

This time he did look at her and Kate tried to mask her surprise.

'I don't know,' she said. 'It's a bit early to be thinking about that.'

'You should.'

Kate didn't know how to respond. Xander made it easy for her by staring out his side window and saying no more. He'd given her plenty to think about for the next twenty minutes though.

Using Xander's key, Kate opened the front door to her mother's house.

'Xandie, is that you?' Val called from within the house.

Xander curled his lip. 'I'm not speaking to her,' he said and stomped up the stairs to his bedroom.

'Call me if you ever need to talk, okay?' Kate called after him.

Val appeared from the lounge, her face tear-stained, her eyes swollen and bloodshot. 'Katie, you found him.' She threw herself into Kate's unsuspecting arms and burst into tears.

The smell of vodka was so pungent, Kate was beginning to think even her mother's tears were laced with alcohol. She patted her on the back with an uncertain hand.

At last, the sobs subsided and Val withdrew. Kate handed her a tissue paper from her pocket and Val blew her nose.

'Where did you find him?' she said, mopping her face.

'He was at Ben's.'

'What was he doing there?'

'He likes it there. He looks up to Ben.'

Val shook her head and sniffed. 'Oh, Katie, I've been such an idiot, a bloody, *bloody* idiot.'

Kate struggled not to agree with her. Instead, she gestured to the lounge. 'Why don't we go sit down?'

'He's gone, Katie. He—he left,' Val babbled as they reconvened on the sofa. 'He was never coming back.'

Kate stiffened. 'We're not talking about Xander anymore, are we?'

Val shook her head miserably. 'He only came back because he wants a divorce. Why now? Why, after all this time?'

Kate had a mind to suggest alimony might have something to do with it, but bit her tongue.

'I think he's met someone else,' Val continued. 'He told me I was a wreck. But I'm only a wreck because of him!'

Kate got up to retrieve a toilet roll from the mantelpiece and placed it beside her mother. Val didn't seem to notice.

'He said I have a problem, just like you said,' Val carried on. 'He didn't believe me when I said I didn't. But then he told me to prove it to

him; told me not to have a drink for a week to show that I wasn't an –
that I didn't have a problem.' Val sniffed louder. 'And the thing is, Katie,'
her voice crumbled to a whine, 'I couldn't even last the day. I thought I
could do it. I thought if something meant enough to me to stop then I
could do it. But I couldn't.'

Kate gulped as a knife of hurt twisted inside her. Obviously, her
children's wellbeing hadn't been enough for her to want to stop, but that
tosser of an absent husband was.

'I'm sorry, Katie. I'm such a failure.'

'You're better off without him,' she said gently. 'Now he wants a
divorce, you can have closure and you can get on with rebuilding your
own life.'

'Oh, Katie, what have I done? All this time I've waited for him to come
home. I've made you all hate me.'

'No one hates you, Mum,' Kate said. 'We just find it frustrating when
you won't accept our help.'

Val whimpered into her tissue. 'Katie?' she hiccupped.

'Yes?'

'Will you come with me?'

Kate's heart leapt into her throat. 'Come with you where?'

'To that place. To St Paul's Community Centre. To – you know.'

Kate daren't breathe. 'Alcoholics Anonymous?'

Val sniffed pitifully. 'Yeah.'

A sad smile crept over Kate's lips. 'Course, Mum. I'll be there.'

42

KATE MET HER mother outside St Paul's Community Centre at midday. Val wrung her hands as she looked up at the grey stone building.

'Ready?' Kate asked. 'We don't want to be late.'

Val didn't answer. She looked back at the passersby. 'Do you think they know?' she whispered.

'I doubt it.' Kate placed a hand in the small of Val's back and guided her through the gate into the small recess area.

'Just give me a sec,' Val said, sitting down on a bench. She looked up at Kate with anxious eyes. 'You know, I could really do with a drink to steady my nerves,' she said with a mirthless laugh. 'This AA thing is a bit counterproductive.'

Kate waited, tucking her hands under her armpits to warm up. In the flowerbeds surrounding them, daffodils, swinging in the blustery wind, hinted at the start of spring. In the past, they had always acted as a type of drumroll heralding the upcoming Cheltenham Festival. In moments when she'd forget, the canary yellow blooms would catch her eye and her stomach would flip in excitement. '*It's here!*' they seemed to whisper. '*It's springtime! It's Cheltenham time!*'

A well-dressed woman in a stylish coat and leather boots smiled as she walked past and entered the building.

'Do you think we've come to the right place?' Val asked. 'She doesn't really look like...'

'Maybe she's the therapist,' Kate suggested.

With a gulp, Val stood up and nodded. 'Okay. I'm ready.'

The meeting room wasn't exactly well sign-posted, so it took them a couple of minutes of wandering about to finally find it. Kate hadn't realised she'd had any preconceptions of what an AA meeting consisted of, but it certainly wasn't the poky disjointed room, no bigger than a couple of stables, that she found herself in. A middle-aged Indian man was making a welcome speech.

The well-dressed woman, sat beside the door, caught her eye and Kate took a hesitant step towards her.

'Are we in the right place?' she whispered. 'We've – um – come for—' She stopped. She didn't want to blow her mother's cover if they were in the wrong room.

'AA?'

Kate nodded and she smiled.

'First time?'

'Yes. It's not for me, exactly,' she babbled, stepping aside to reveal her mother.

The woman smiled and patted the vacant chair beside her. 'Take a seat, we're just getting started.'

The room was so oddly shaped with little nooks and cupboard corners that it was difficult to tell how many people were present. Kate could see the faces of maybe five people, but the legs of at least half a dozen more.

The woman passed her and Val a couple of booklets. Kate read the opening inscription.

God, grant me the serenity to accept the things I cannot change, the courage to change the things I can, and the wisdom to know the difference.

She flicked through the booklet, noticing the heavy slant on religious support, and hazarded a look at her mother. God hadn't played a particularly strong role in their lives. The only Sunday excursions they'd had were to Tesco.

'Okay?' she whispered.

Val looked up from her booklet with wide eyes. 'I feel like a fraud,' she whispered back.

Kate patted her hand. 'Believe me, Mum. You're not a fraud.'

The floor was opened for the members to share their stories and for a moment the room fell quiet. Just someone coughing and birdsong outside the window interrupted the silence.

Just out of sight, a chair scraped back and its owner stood up. But the person didn't speak immediately. Kate sat forward to try catch a glimpse of whomever it was. The person took a step forward and out of the shadows. Kate stopped breathing. The person looked up.

'Hi, I'm Ben, and I'm an alcoholic.'

43

KATE DIDN'T STOP running until she was on the bus. She didn't even know where the bus was headed. Muffled by the hiss of air brakes came Ben's shouts in pursuit.

With chest heaving and heart pounding in her ears, she clung to the grab rail and willed the bus to pull away before he reached it. With a jerk, they set off. People turned to stare as Ben banged on the side of the bus.

The driver looked at Kate in his mirror. 'Friend of yours, love?'

Kate shook her head. 'Don't stop, please.'

The driver nodded and pulled into the Bristol traffic. 'You best go sit down,' he said.

Kate tripped up the steps onto the upper level, legs weak, and swung into the nearest seat. She looked out of the window at the traffic down below.

Ben stood by the roadside, arms clasped behind his head in a helpless gesture, his stance that of desolation.

Kate spun round to face the front again. She couldn't watch, couldn't bear to look at him.

She held her face in her hands and closed her eyes. Had that really happened? It felt too surreal for it to be true. Ben, an alcoholic? But he didn't even drink – Kate mentally kicked herself. It made sense now. But she'd never even contemplated it. Lots of jockeys avoided alcohol. They were athletes, after all. And not everyone who abstained from drinking was a recovering alcoholic. She was a prime example, and, without really thinking about it, she'd just presumed he was the same.

'How could I not tell?' she said aloud. Her own mother was an alcoholic, she should've been able to spot the clues. Kate jerked in her seat and spun around. 'Oh God. Mum.'

But St Paul's Community Centre was already out of sight and she sunk back down again. So ashamed of herself for deserting her mother in such spectacular fashion, she wanted to curl up into a ball in the corner and be left to die alone. She prayed that she hadn't disrupted her mother's path to recovery.

Anger overcame her and she bit into her fist. If she had, then it would be Ben's fault. How could he do this to her? The betrayal, the mockery he'd made of her, the breach of trust when he knew how she struggled with her mother's addiction. It was unforgivable.

The knock on the door Kate had been expecting came a couple of hours after she'd got home. She sat in her chair in the lounge, back rigid, fingers tapping on the armrests. She didn't know if she could answer the door. Not *should*, but could. She didn't know how she'd react to seeing his face. It was a toss-up between sobbing and going mental with rage.

The knock came again, making her start. She felt juvenile for ignoring him, they'd have to confront one another at some stage, but did it really need to happen so soon? When her emotions were so fresh?

There was another insistent knock then the scuffling of the letter box being opened.

'Kate?'

Ben's voice came loud and clear into the house, making her tremble even more. She held her breath and tried to be as still as possible.

'Kate. Come on, I know you're in there,' came Ben's voice again. 'I just want to talk.'

'Well, I don't, so go away!'

'Let me in, please. Let me explain.'

Kate couldn't bear it any more. She jumped out of her seat and strode through to fling open the front door. She opened her mouth to rebuke him, but, noticing the number of people around, thought better. She grabbed his arm and pulled him inside. She slammed the door then turned to face him, arms folded. 'Okay, then. Explain.'

Ben looked astonished by his abrupt entrance and stood, speechless, for a moment. 'Um, okay. Right. Well, let me start by saying sorry. I had no idea you were there. It was the worst possible way for you to find out.'

'What, that you're an alcoholic?' Even saying the words felt foreign. It was too much to get her head around.

'Yes,' he replied quietly. He took a deep breath. 'I'm an alcoholic. I've been sober for six years now though. It's not a problem like you think it is.'

'But you still go to AA meetings. What does that tell me other than it's still a problem?'

'Well, yes. But going to meetings helps me manage it, to make it less of a problem. That's what they're there for.'

Kate shook her head in disbelief then turned on her heel and walked back into the lounge. She couldn't stand in such close proximity to him in the hall. 'I don't understand, Ben. I thought I knew you. How can you be an alcoholic?'

Ben followed her through. 'I wanted to tell you, believe me. But I'd seen the damage your mother's alcoholism has caused you. How could I tell you "Oh, by the way, I'm also an alkie?" That would've been the end of us.' He took her arm and turned her to face him. 'That day I bumped into you and your mum in Bristol?' he said. 'I'd just come from a meeting with the person I sponsor. And when you told me about your mum's problems, I *so* wanted to tell you, to show you I understood, to be there for you.'

'So you were just going to keep on lying to me?'

'I would've told you. When the time was right.'

'When? When we're six months in? A year? When we're in so deep that you reckon I can't get out?'

Ben pulled a face. 'Not when you put it like that. But yes, I was waiting until such a time that you knew me well enough to know that this isn't going to change things.'

'Except when you fall off the wagon. Things'd change pretty damn sharpish then, wouldn't they?'

'I'm not going to fall off the wagon,' he said through gritted teeth. 'I promise.'

'How can you make such a promise? What about when times get really tough? When something beyond your control happens—' She stopped herself as she realised such an event had already happened. 'You liar,' she said. 'You've already fallen off the wagon.'

'No, I haven't. It's been six years—'

'Six years, my arse!' Kate exclaimed. 'The night Jerry died, the night that we – there was a bottle of something sitting on your kitchen counter.'

Ben stopped short. He looked at Kate, his mouth slightly ajar, then he exhaled in resignation. He leaned his arms up against the wall and hung his head. 'I didn't drink any of it,' he mumbled. He looked up with reproachful eyes. 'I never opened it.'

Kate tried to recall how far down the liquor was. It had been fairly full, but she couldn't say for certain whether or not it had been opened. 'It doesn't matter. You were going to. And that just proves my point. When things go wrong, you're going to fall off.'

'No, Kate. Don't you see? I didn't drink any of it because *you* arrived. I knew I needed a stiff one.' He tried to lighten the atmosphere with a smile. 'I just didn't realise which type I'd get. *You* are what stopped me. That night and every night since.'

Kate shook her head and wagged a finger at him. 'Oh, no, you don't. Don't you dare try to make *me* responsible for your sobriety. I get enough of that from my own family, thank you very much.'

'That's not what I'm saying,' Ben said with an impatient sigh. 'Look, can we just sit down so I can explain things right from the start?'

Kate's heart hardened. He thought she was a soft touch, worming his way through the door, now wanting to sit down for a cosy heart-to-heart. 'I don't want to hear your sob story, Ben,' she said. 'I think you should leave.'

For a moment they stood facing each other. Kate crossed her arms to hide her trembling hands. Ben looked at her defensive stance then nodded slowly.

'Okay. If that's how you want to leave things.' He stepped back towards the door, but paused by the archway. He looked back at her, his expression bitter. 'I thought more of you, Kate. I really did. I thought, okay, sure, maybe I have fucked it up for us, but I thought you'd be big enough to hear me out.'

Kate breathed in a lungful of courage. She couldn't give in to him. Not this time. If she did, then he'd talk her round, and one thing would lead to another, then where would she be?

Her nerves were so strained, she felt physically sick. She caught her reflection in the mirror and flinched. Her face was pale and pinched, but what she noticed most was the tiny scar above her right eye.

She remembered in flashes, like an action film preview, how she'd got it. The fight with Val, the shame and disappointment of having just failed her A levels, the screaming and blaming, and then Val's hand whipping round. The sting, the shock, the realisation that the wetness wasn't just tears, Val's horrified expression as she looked down at her fingers where her wedding and engagement rings had slid round so the stone faced inwards. Kate had left for Newmarket the same day.

Giving in to Ben meant returning to an environment that had almost destroyed her, that she'd fought so hard to leave behind. What sort of future was she setting herself up for? She couldn't raise a family – have children – with the threat that things could turn sour at any moment, lurking in the wings.

Gathering herself for one last effort, she raised her chin and opened her eyes. She met his gaze with steel and pointed at the door. 'Please leave.'

Ben gave one mirthless laugh. 'Yeah, I'm going.'

44

D'ARTAGNAN'S HOOVES BEAT a rhythmic drum on the woodchip track as Kate guided him towards the first of the practice fences. *Bdrmm, bdrmm, bdrmm, bdrmm, bd* – silence only interrupted by the wind as he sailed over – bdrmm, bdrmm, bdrmm.

Kate lost herself in the speed, blotting out the pain with the power of her mount's stride, replacing the chaos of her personal life with the adrenalin of facing the five walls of birch. D'Artagnan's mane stung her face. The rest of the string paled into insignificance in their wake.

The second fence loomed and the grey pricked his ears. Kate pushed for a long stride and he responded with a mighty effort.

He pecked on landing, shooting Kate up his neck, and for a split second she thought gravity would get the better of her. She dug her knees in and grappled for a hold on his neck. D'Artagnan recovered before she did, raising his head high to rebalance, and enabling her to wiggle back down into the saddle.

'Sorry, fella. My fault,' she whispered, re-gathering her reins. But the momentary rush of danger was like a tonic and again she pressed on towards the next jump.

D'Artagnan met it on a perfect stride and gave it plenty of air. He needed no urging approaching the fourth and fifth, bounding over them both like he could do this steeplechasing lark in his sleep.

Kate slapped his damp neck in praise as they slowed to a jog.

Moments later, Frankie pulled up beside them. Bold Phoenix was blowing hard, propelling plumes of foggy air from his dilated nostrils.

'Crikey, Kate. Did you have the devil on your tail or something?'

Kate patted d'Artagnan with renewed pride. 'He's better than we've had him all season. Fit as a flea.'

'And jumping like one too. Made poor old Phoenix here feel like a selling plater.'

Jack met them by the fence, looking stiff and cold since he'd left his new Land Rover parked well away from the horses.

'That was a bit faster than I was after, Kate,' he said, studying the horses' breathing.

'I know. Sorry. He was having too much fun to act lazy.'

Jack stood back and frowned at d'Artagnan. 'Well, doesn't seem to have done any harm. He's not blowing. Keep going like this and we'll have him spot on in two weeks' time.'

Kate swallowed and nodded. In two weeks' time they'd be on the lorry to Cheltenham.

'All right. Take 'em back,' Jack said with a dismissive wave. 'Oh, by the way, Kate. Next week, I've got Ben de Jager coming in to ride.'

Kate stiffened in her saddle. 'Okay.'

'I want him to sit on d'Artagnan before the Gold Cup.'

Kate and Frankie moved on when he turned his attention to the next pair. Kate wondered if she could come down with 'flu sometime next week. She'd have to find out what day Ben was coming in.

'Frankie?' Jack called after them. 'You've got The Whistler up next, right?'

'Yup.'

'Put a hood on him today, okay? I want to see if blinkers'll make any difference.'

'Difference for what?' Kate asked once they were out of earshot.

Frankie shrugged. 'Rhys says The Whistler was thinking up his shopping list in the Denman Chase. That's why he fell. Hopefully a set of blinkers will make him concentrate a bit more on his job.'

Mention of the jockey reminded Kate of the conversation she and Frankie had had while clipping The Whistler. Rhys had claimed Ben was suspended from racing for having alcohol in his system. Well, that made sense now, she supposed. She shook her head at how naive she'd been.

'How's Rhys getting on?' she asked.

'He's drawn a countdown on his cast,' Frankie replied. 'He's determined to be fit for Cheltenham.' Her laughter faded when she saw Kate wasn't joining in. 'Are you okay?'

Kate smiled. 'Yeah, sure.'

Frankie didn't look convinced. 'Hey, we're having a party this weekend if you'd like to come.'

Kate hesitated. Seeing shiny happy people laughing would only make her more miserable. 'I don't think so. Thanks anyway.'

'Please. It's for my birthday.'

'I thought your birthday was on Valentines' Day?'

'It is, but what with Rhys breaking his arm and various other dramas, we didn't get to celebrate. Please come. Mum's suggested I have a murder mystery party. She and Dad went to one last year and she hasn't stopped raving about it. She was the murderer and I think she enjoyed it a bit too much.'

'Anyone I know going?'

Frankie looked thoughtful. 'Tom, you know from Am Dram, and Rhys of course. Otherwise none that I can think of. A couple are still to confirm.'

Well, it didn't sound like Ben would be there. 'I—I don't know, Frankie. I've just had to sell my car.'

'Saskia still has a car, doesn't she? Invite her along too. She's always up for a bit of fun.'

'Are Jack and Pippa going?' Kate said cautiously.

'Crumbs, no. I love Pippa to death, don't get me wrong, but I don't fancy making a fool of myself in front of Jack. He's still our boss at the end of the day. Besides, if he turned out to be the murderer, I don't think I'd be able to sleep for a week.'

Kate smiled, reassured, tempted. 'Thanks. I'll ask Saskia.'

Kate informed Saskia of the party on the drive home. Once she'd had the rules explained to her, Saskia was more than up for a party, especially one that required role play and dressing up, so Kate texted Frankie with their RSVPs.

Great! I'll email you your characters tonight came the reply.

Kate didn't put her phone away immediately. She was very aware of the two missed calls from Ben still sitting there. She didn't know what he expected of her. It was crazy for him to think she could just dismiss his addiction after what she'd been through with her mother. *Her mother.* Again, the guilt descended and Kate vowed to ring her to apologise once they got home.

Saskia chattered on about the party, asking if Rhys had any glamorous friends from the weighing room attending.

'I don't know who's going,' Kate replied. 'Nobody I know, except Tom and he's gay.'

'Ben's going, presumably?' said Saskia, snapping down on her indicator and slowing for a corner.

'Er – no. Ben and I broke up.'

Saskia hit the kerb. 'What? Bloody hell, that didn't last long.'

Kate shifted in her seat, glad she didn't have to make eye contact. 'Yeah, well. Turns out he wasn't who I thought he was.'

'Really? In what way?'

She hesitated. Hate him all she wanted, she still didn't feel it was her place to broadcast his addiction, even to Saskia – *especially* to Saskia, given her love of gossip. 'He's just not the guy for me.'

Saskia shrugged. 'Ah, well, better to find out now rather than further down the line. It'd be a whole lot messier if you were in love with him.'

Kate made a non-committal noise. It felt pretty messy already and there were no prizes for second guessing why.

Saskia looked at her as they pulled up at the roundabout at the top of the High Street. 'You're not already, are you?'

Kate couldn't meet her eye. 'The road's clear.'

Saskia dragged her attention back to the traffic and accelerated. 'Wow, Kate. You surprise me.'

'Why?'

'I don't know. It just seems a bit reckless. How can you fall in love in just two weeks? You were with Nicholas for longer than that and you weren't exactly heartbroken over him.'

Kate shot Saskia an irritable glance. 'I was, too.'

'No, you were heartbroken over that horse of his.'

'So? That might've only been part of it.'

Saskia swung the car into a parking space and jerked up the handbrake. She raised a sardonic eyebrow. 'Kate, he'd hardly had time to pick up his spare toothbrush before you slept with his brother. Heartbroken? I don't think so.'

'That's a complete exaggeration,' said Kate as she furiously untangled herself from her seatbelt.

They exited the car and, with Saskia softly singing 'He Ain't Heavy, He's My Brother' beside her, Kate marched down the street to their house.

* * *

252

Kate closed her bedroom door and sat down to ring her mother. She didn't know whether to be relieved or not when it went straight to voicemail.

'Hi, Mum. It's Kate. Um, I just wanted to apologise about yesterday. I – um – I wasn't expecting to see Ben there. Obviously. But you probably already figured that one out... Anyway, yeah,' she said, attempting to keep her tone light. 'I'm sorry for running out on you like that and – I don't know – showing you up in front of everyone. I hope I didn't disrupt things too much.' Kate sighed. 'Who am I kidding? Of course I disrupted things. Sorry, Mum. I hope you found it helpful though – the meeting, that is, not me running out. So, I guess I'll speak to you later.' She was about to hang up when it struck her to add, 'I'm proud of you, Mum. Bye.'

'Saskia,' Kate called out later that evening. 'The email from Frankie arrived.'

Saskia came thumping up the stairs and looked round Kate's door 'Who am I?'

'Come sit,' Kate replied. 'It's still loading.'

Saskia bounced over and sat beside her. In the light of the bedside lamp, Kate noticed a bruise on her neck.

'What did you do to your – Saskia, is that a hickey?'

Saskia stretched her neck to look in the mirror and shrugged. 'Yeah, make up's wearing off now.'

Kate froze in fear. 'Who's it from?'

'Hmm? Nobody you know.'

'Not Jack then?'

Saskia looked at her like she was insane. 'No, God, no.'

'But – I thought you were saving yourself for him?'

Saskia shrugged and took control of the mousepad. 'I got sick of waiting for Mr Right. So I opted for Mr Right Now instead. Why's your computer taking so long?'

Kate laughed, as much in relief as amusement. At last, the PDF document opened and Saskia leaned in.

'"You are Joan of Anarchy,"' she read aloud, '"a gun-running biker chick intent on saving France from British ex-pat domination."' She frowned at Kate. 'What the hell?'

'Well, it's a play on words see, Joan of Arc and *Sons of Anarchy*.'

253

'I guessed that much. So I have to dress up like a biker?' Saskia curled her top lip in distaste. 'Who's yours?'

Kate clicked on the second file. '"Jane Austen-Powers, a screenwriter who is convinced her retro 1960s adaptation of *Pride and Prejudice* is going to be a box office hit if only she can convince someone to produce it."'

Saskia pouted. 'That's not fair. Why can't I be that one? I've those Abba boots that I still haven't worn and they'd be perfect. Instead I've got to be some grotty biker with hairy armpits.' She compared the two character profiles for a moment then gave Kate a doe-eyed look. 'Can we swap?'

'Do you know anything about Jane Austen's books?'

'No, but I've seen all the BBC adaptations. I know squat about Joan of Arc.'

'*Saskia.*'

'Come on, Katie. Be a sport. Please.'

'But what if we mess up the whole party plan?'

'I don't see how we could. What difference does it make which of us plays the characters?'

Kate gave her sister a look of long-suffering. What could it hurt on this occasion? She'd just be being bloody-minded if she refused. Plus, she didn't have any platform boots that she was desperate to debut. In fact, she hated heels, so maybe the biker girl would suit her better anyway. 'Okay, you can be Jane.'

Saskia whooped. 'Me Jane. You Tarzan,' and bounced cross-legged on the bed. 'Ooh, this is going to be great! We're going to look amazing.'

45

COME SATURDAY NIGHT, Kate concluded Saskia had been referring to the royal 'we'. Wearing a biker jacket borrowed from Rhys – whom she still wasn't certain was aware Frankie had lent it to her – a pair of Doc Martens and a poor attempt at body armour using tin foil, she felt anything but amazing.

Saskia, on the other hand, looked like she'd just stepped off the set of Hairspray, hair bouffed and her psychedelic dress acting as high vis as they walked across Helensvale in the dark.

There was much laughter coming from inside the Bradfords' and Kate had to ring the bell twice before any footsteps approached. Moments later, came a commanding, 'Alohomora! Alohomora!'

Kate and Saskia looked at each other. The door was opened by a woman dressed in a witch's hat and cloak.

'Damn thing doesn't work,' she said brandishing her wand. 'Come on in and tell me who you are. I'm Hermione Hydrangea, a botanist who does more with her herbs than put them in a flower press. You ever need a pick-me-up, I've got the potion,' she said with an exaggerated wink.

Saskia snorted into her sleeve. Kate cleared her throat and prepared to step into her role.

'I'm Joan of Anarchy,' she said. 'Um, I'm here to stop the British ex-pat invasion of France.' Maybe she should put on a French accent. 'On my mozer-cycle.' Hmm, maybe not.

'Good for you,' said Hermione in agreement, leading them through. 'Montpelier was crawling with Brits the last time we were there on holiday.'

Hermione Hydrangea showed the way into a reception room where about ten people were killing themselves laughing at one another's costumes and characters. Even Rhys, dressed in bubblegum pink shorts and a loud floral shirt, was laughing, which came as something of a shock to Kate. She'd never seen him even crack a smile before.

'What would you like to drink?' said Hermione Hydrangea. 'You've got some punch over there – I made it, it's really good; wine, and Frankie – I mean Mary Poppin Pills – had the cocktail shaker out a few minutes ago.'

'Anything non-alcoholic?'

Frankie's mother looked perplexed. 'I don't know. Hang on, let's try this.' She waved her wand about and pointed it at the punch bowl. 'Vino vaporus evian!' She took the ladle from the punch bowl and took a slurp. 'No, didn't work. Let's try that again. Vino vaporus evian... No, hmm, still not working.'

Kate looked sideways at Saskia and tried not to laugh. 'I'll go find something.'

Kate found Frankie jigging a cocktail shaker about in the kitchen, dressed in a nanny's uniform with an umbrella hanging from her arm.

'Mary Poppin Pills, I presume?' Kate said.

Frankie grinned. 'Damn, you're good.'

'Someone going by the name of Hermione Hydrangea told me.'

'Ah, you met my mother then?'

Kate laughed and helped herself to a juice carton on the counter and an empty cocktail glass. 'That's your mother?'

'Yeah, I know.'

'Are we the last to arrive?'

Frankie poured out her cocktails, humming 'A Spoonful of Sugar'. 'Yup. I'm going to announce the murder in a minute. Right! There we go. Will you help take these through?'

Back in the lounge, Frankie yelled for quiet. 'Okay, I have a special announcement to make. Is everyone here?'

'No,' someone shouted. 'Christian Pray's gone to the bathroom.'

'Or so he says,' someone else replied suggestively.

'Here he comes – hey, Christian, what were you really up to in there?'

Kate nearly dropped the cocktail she was carrying as the man entered the room. Nicholas, dressed in a priest's habit and carrying a dressage whip in his handcuffed hand, stared back at her.

'Right, I have some breaking news,' Frankie said dramatically. 'Our host, Mr Ted Downing, the popular politician who has just secured his second term in office, has been discovered murdered in his country house—'

'Can't be that popular,' interrupted a man standing beside the fireplace.

'Shut up, Dad.'

'Dad? My name is Fitzwilliam Dicey, the best card shark in Derbyshire.'

'Okay. Well, Mr Dicey, I would urge you to pay attention since you are one of the suspects.'

A dramatic ooh went around the room.

'And since we were all in attendance at Ted Downing's celebration bash, we are *all* suspects in his murder!'

A cheer went up in response and Frankie started doling out secret envelopes that would tell one guest he or she was the murderer.

Kate pulled Frankie aside as she handed over her envelope. Frankie gave a small cry of surprise as she was pulled into the kitchen.

'What's *he* doing here?' Kate hissed.

'Who?'

'Nicholas. Who else?'

Frankie gasped and her eyes went huge. 'Oh God. Oh crikey. I'm so sorry, Kate. I didn't think – I mean it never occurred to me. Shit! He wasn't going to come, but then he made plans with Rhys when Evan cancelled. I totally forgot you two dated. Oh, crap. Are you okay?'

Kate bit her lip, wondering if she could sneak out without anyone noticing. Frankie looked mortified already, though. 'Yeah, I'll be fine.' Frankie looked doubtful and Kate patted her shoulder. 'Truly. Don't worry about it. This is your birthday.'

'Sorry.'

Kate made a hesitant re-entrance into the room. She tried to join in a conversation with Hermione Hydrangea and Mr Dicey, but there was little chance of keeping a low profile while dressed in leather and tinfoil.

Nicholas tapped her on the shoulder. 'Kate.'

'She's not Kate,' said Hermione. 'She's Joan of Anarchy. And you'd better watch out, she's on the war path if you're British.'

Nicholas looked mildly annoyed. 'Well, I'm not. I'm supposed to be from Seattle.'

'Hello, Nicholas,' Kate said stiffly.

Nicholas guided her away from the others. 'How've you been?'

'Fine.'

'I've been trying to call you.'

'I don't want to talk about it,' replied Kate. 'Let's just try to enjoy our evening, shall we?'

'You're not still mad with me, are you?'

Kate thought about it for a moment and honestly, with everything else happening in her life lately, she hadn't felt mad or otherwise about Nicholas for weeks. 'No.'

Nicholas looked hopeful. 'So, we're okay then?'

A mental image of d'Artagnan making the running in the King George surfaced. 'Please, Nicholas. Let's not talk about it here.'

'I'm sorry things went the way they did. I never meant to hurt you or lie to you.'

Kate could feel resentment clawing at the back of her throat. 'Nicholas, I don't want to talk about it. I've come here to celebrate Frankie's birthday, not to argue with you. Can we just forget "us" for one evening?'

'What other opportunity am I to get to tell you how sorry I am? Ben even told me I should try make amends, so here I am.'

Kate felt like she'd been kicked in the gut. 'Ben said that?'

Nicholas nodded. 'And for once, he's right. Let's put all this behind us. When you think about it, it was just a little tiff, wasn't it? We were happy together before the King George.'

'Yes, but—' Kate was about to say he'd betrayed her a long time before that, but they were interrupted by Frankie announcing dinner was ready. 'I don't know, Nicholas. I can't think right now.'

'Of course, of course,' Nicholas was quick to assure her. 'I understand this has all been a bit of a shock.'

They moved with the flow through to the dining room and Kate found herself sat between Nicholas and Rhys, aka James Bondi.

Rhys frowned at Kate's wardrobe. 'Nice jacket.'

Kate tried to keep a straight face. 'Thanks. Nice – um – shirt.'

Rhys looked down in disgust. 'Just wearing it is giving me hay fever.'

Mr Dicey called away Rhys's attention and Kate turned back to Nicholas.

'Why do I get the feeling this hasn't been as much of a shock for you as it has for me?'

Nicholas had the decency to look guilty. 'I was actually invited a while back, and I'd refused. But then I heard you were coming, so I changed my mind. I mean, why else would I be here? Look at me.'

Kate almost laughed. He was right. Nicholas wasn't the likeliest candidate for a murder mystery party, and he did look a little ridiculous in his priest's outfit. He appeared encouraged by her smile.

'I don't even know whom I'm supposed to be. I get yours and I get James Bondi, he's a secret agent under cover as an Australian surfer. But I'm just a priest.'

'That's only half your character though, you know that, don't you?' Kate said. 'The whip is a reference to Christian Grey.'

'Who?'

Kate's ears burned and she cleared her throat. '*Fifty Shades of Grey?*'

Comprehension flooded his face, followed swiftly by a blush. 'Ah. Okay, now I get it.'

With each course served, the guests quizzed each other on their whereabouts when Ted Downing was murdered. By the end of the meal, Kate was still none the wiser. She knew she hadn't done it, her card didn't have the X on it. And Nicholas was so awkward with his character that she'd dismissed him before they'd finished their salmon ceviches. By the time the cheeseboards were making the rounds, she had narrowed it down to either Saskia's character, Jane Austen-Powers, or Frankie's mother, Hermione Hydrangea.

'Everyone decided on their villain?' Frankie asked, popping a wedge of brie into her mouth.

One by one, everyone named their suspect. Like Kate, most had gone for Jane or Hermione, but Rhys had plumped for Kate, which made her strangely happy, even if he was wrong. The only person to accuse Nicholas was Saskia and Kate was sure she'd only done it to throw others off the scent.

'Now, time for the reckoning,' said Frankie. 'Hermione, will you kick us off?'

Hermione Hydrangea squinted at her card and read her final speech. 'I didn't kill Ted Downing. I might have slipped him a few herbal teas and provided him with a charm at election time, but at the time of his murder I was doing a potions deal with the Treasurer for his Befuddlement Draught addiction.'

'Bugger,' said Frankie, throwing down her napkin. 'There goes my theory. Mr Dicey, you're next.'

One by one, each of the guests revealed their innocence, and as the odds narrowed, Kate became more and more convinced it was Saskia. She read out her alibi and and patted Rhys's hand. 'Sorry, not me.'

Only three other suspects remained – Nicholas, Saskia and Tom, once an Ugly Sister until he broke his leg. Saskia looked very coy. Nicholas cleared his throat and read from his card.

'"Ted Downing was a dear friend of mine who enjoyed many of the same passions as myself. The thought of his death brings fear and sorrow to my heart."' Nicholas paused to look around the table. '"But the thought of him revealing my kinky habits to the church brought even greater fear to my heart and so it was *I* who killed him."'

A gasp went around, except for Saskia who gave a triumphant 'Ha!'

'"I waited for Joan of Anarchy to conclude her meeting before sneaking into Mr Downing's private quarters and strangling him with the items that he was otherwise so keen on."' Nicholas dangled a pair of handcuffs for everyone to see.

Kate shook her head. 'How did I not guess?'

Nicholas didn't appear to recognise the subtext of her words. 'What can I say? I'm a man with hidden talents.' His gaze lingered on her and his humour faded. 'Have dinner with me next week?'

46

THE ATMOSPHERE AT Aspen Valley the following week was electric with everyone's thoughts on Cheltenham Festival starting the following Tuesday. Kate had more pressing things on her mind. One – she and Fontainebleau had to be packed and ready to leave for Exeter by eleven o'clock and two – Ben would be paying a visit, so he could put d'Artagnan over some jumps.

Kate thought she had planned everything so that she would be halfway down the A37 by the time he showed up, but for once she was running late and Ben was running early.

She was attempting to put Fontainebleau's travel bandages on, but the gelding, knowing what they meant, was being nappy and wouldn't stand still.

'Do you want a hand?' a familiar voice at the stable door asked.

Kate didn't look up. 'No, thank you. I have everything under control.'

Fontainebleau stamped his foot and the bandage slid down his leg. Kate sighed and began again. The stable door was unbolted and her jaw tightened in annoyance.

'I said I'm fine, thank you.'

'You're going to be late,' replied Ben.

Kate looked up, her eyes flashing with anger. 'Then will you let me get on, please?'

Aware of him standing over her, she rewound the bandage around the fibregee pad, tutting to herself when the pad refused to stay in place.

'Ben, you're putting me off. Don't you have somewhere to be, like tacking up d'Artagnan?'

'Actually, that's why I'm here. I don't know which is his bridle.'

'The one hanging on the peg with his name on?' she said sarcastically.

'It's not there.'

'What?' Kate looked up irritably, then she remembered. 'Oh, shit, yeah. He broke his noseband yesterday. Look on the trunk next to the

261

medical cupboard. I think I left it there. You'll need to pinch a noseband off one of the others, though. Use Chic Shadow's.'

She'd just managed half the bandage when Fontainebleau skipped sideways. Kate straightened up with a sigh.

'Here,' said Ben. He walked around to Fontainebleau's offside and lifted the horse's opposite foreleg off the ground. 'Now try.'

With Fontainebleau forced to balance himself on the leg Kate was working on, she was able to secure the bandage. She stood up and grudgingly thanked Ben.

He moved to Fontainebleau's head, stroking the chestnut whorl under his forelock, and nodded. 'You're welcome.'

Kate took the horse's lead rope and led him to the door. 'I have to go,' she said.

'Kate.' Ben reached out a hand to stall her. 'I'm still the same guy.'

Kate chewed her bottom lip, her conscience wrestling with her heart. 'That may be true, but you're not the guy I thought you were.'

'Cut me some slack, Kate, will you? I'm sorry I'm not perfect. Is that the kind of guy you're looking for? Mr Perfect?'

'No, Ben,' she said through gritted teeth. 'But I am looking for someone who will be honest with me.'

'When have I ever lied to you?'

'There is more than one way to be dishonest.' Kate kicked open the door and led Fontainebleau out into the weak spring sunshine.

Ben followed her out and made no attempt to keep his voice down. 'The way you were honest with me?'

Kate looked around, aware of other staff members pretending not to hear them. 'I have been nothing but honest with you,' she hissed.

Ben's angry eyes didn't leave her. 'So, if I hadn't bumped into you and your mum that afternoon outside St Paul's, you would've told me about her anyway?'

Kate held up a finger to stop him. 'Don't bring my mother into this.'

'It's not about your mother. It's about your guilty secrets. You have them just as much as I do. Does that change who we are, though?'

'Well, excuse me if your "guilty secret" is a bit closer to home than mine,' she replied. Fontainebleau snorted in disgust at being kept standing around and tried to eat his lead rope. Kate pulled it free and tugged him forward. 'I have to go.'

* * *

It was a good day to go racing, if not to meet ex-lovers. Exeter Racecourse was bathed in sunshine, with a haze drifting over from the neighbouring moorland. Midges darted through the air catching the light like fireflies. Fontainebleau was in high spirits and bounced away when Kate let him and Donnie McFarland, Rhys's replacement, loose on the track.

She joined Jack in the paddock. He was watching the horses canter down to the start on the big screen.

'D'Artagnan worked well this morning,' Jack broke the silence. He glanced across at her. 'Just thought you'd like to know.'

Kate set her jaw and nodded. 'Good.'

'I didn't realise you and Ben were seeing each other outside the yard.'

'You saw us this morning?'

Jack shrugged and looked back at the screen. 'Couldn't help it.'

'I'm sorry. Ben and I aren't seeing each other like that, not anymore.'

Jack exhaled a long tired breath. 'I'm not usually the type of person to give advice on relationships, but Kate, I've got to say, if you've broken up over his... *history* then I'd urge you to reconsider. Ben's a decent bloke.'

'It's a bit more complicated than that,' Kate said tersely. Getting advice on her love life from her boss was not what she'd signed up for.

'You talking about your mother?'

Kate breathed through her teeth. Bloody Ben had to go and announce it to the whole of Aspen Valley, hadn't he?

'Saskia mentioned it before,' Jack contradicted her thoughts.

'Then you understand,' said Kate, 'that after growing up with a drunk, and finally getting away from it, I don't intend to take on another.'

Jack looked at her again. 'Ben's not a drunk, Kate. He's a recovering alcoholic. There's a big difference. He's been clean something like six or seven years.'

Kate thought back to the spirits bottle the night of Jerry's death. 'I wouldn't be too sure about that.'

'Believe me, he is. Ever since he got busted, he's had to take regular tests to show he's clean.'

Kate tangled Fontainebleau's lead rope around her hands. 'Well, I'm still not going to be somebody's crutch. I've got enough problems with the rest of my family to have to deal with him as well.'

'You ever considered that maybe he could lend *you* support? He understands the illness, he knows how to deal with it.'

Kate gave Jack an impatient look. 'I appreciate you looking out for me – I think – but Ben brought it upon himself. It's something that he's going to have to live with, not me. I can't deal with his—his *weakness*.'

They fell silent, making Kate regret her harshly spoken words.

Jack opened his mouth to say something then hesitated. He cleared his throat and frowned at the ground. 'I—I used to date a girl, you know, before Pippa. Her father was my best patron. You ever heard of Ken Mardling?'

Kate shifted uncomfortably, not knowing where this conversation was headed. 'You won the Gold Cup with his horse, Virtuoso.'

'Well, long before Virtuoso was on the scene, I was a small-time trainer, scraping the midweek meetings to get winners. Then Ken came along, filled my stables with some very classy horses. And suddenly I'd shot into the limelight – winners, not just runners, in the big Saturday meetings. But there are people out there, armchair experts, who sit there and criticise your success.' Jack paused to think back and gave a wry chuckle. 'I can't tell you how angry it made me when people said that my success was only down to Ken's patronage. It's hurtful, Kate, and harmful. You begin to doubt your own worth. And you can either do one of two things, you can keep going and prove them wrong, or you can self-destruct.

'Ben faced the same problem riding his father's horses, and unfortunately, he went into self-destruct mode. But you know what? He came back, straightened himself out and walked back into a weighing room that had never liked him. Weakness?' Jack raised an eyebrow at her. 'I don't know if I'd call that being weak. I'd call that bloody brave. But, hey, each to their own opinion, right?'

Kate stared at him. In the space of a minute she'd learnt more about her boss than she'd done in the last two years. Jack wasn't exactly renowned for opening up to people. He must think a great deal of Ben.

But that was different, Kate told herself. For starters, Jack wasn't romantically involved with him. Secondly, he'd known all along about Ben's alcoholism, whereas Kate had had to find out the hard way. She wondered what things would have been like if her mother hadn't decided to go to AA, or even picked a different day. Would she and Ben still be together, she still none the wiser? Maybe. Probably.

Kate touched her finger to the scar above her eye to remind herself she'd made the right decision.

* * *

The starter mounted his rostrum and Kate knocked her knuckles together for luck.

'Where are Font's owners?' she asked.

'They've got a box up in the stands. I try to avoid watching with them. He goes so close so often, their disappointment kills me.'

The starter raised his flag, the amber light before the green. The tape snapped back and the horses charged forward like a cavalry regiment. It was a short run to the first of the eighteen fences and not much time for jockeys to find a position. Fontainebleau was lost in the field as they took the first.

Unable to find her horse, Kate's gaze lingered on the rear of the field where any fallers would soon be revealed. The first fence claimed no victims.

Onto the second plain fence, and Donnie found a spot with a clear view, six wide. Fontainebleau bounced over and Kate clenched her fists in hope. Fontainebleau, who had about as much rhythm as she did on a dance floor, had found his stride barely two fences in.

The third was an open ditch. Fontainebleau made a mighty effort, twisting in midair to clear the spread. He landed safely and headed for the right-handed turn. Others weren't so lucky and swinging into the home straight for the first time came a reduced field of fourteen horses.

Four more fences followed, close together, and Kate punched a fist into her palm with each nimble leap her horse took.

'He's going well,' she murmured as they galloped past.

Jack grunted in reluctant agreement. 'He's still got plenty to find against Morning Mr Magpie and Paradigm Shift—*oh*! Maybe not,' he said as Morning Mr Magpie blundered at the water jump.

Up the side of the course where the thick border of skeletal trees were dotted with new buds, the field stretched out. Fontainebleau travelled well for Donnie, but he was losing ground with every stride that he took wide.

Another open ditch claimed two more runners, depleting the field to twelve. Kate had the feeling they weren't done yet. There were still eight fences to take and a mile and a half still to cover. When fatigue set in and lactic acid burned through their muscles, Exeter's stiff fences would become harder to navigate. Fontainebleau was fit, but he was also thirteen years old.

The horses passed their point of departure, headed by Egyptian John. Fontainebleau galloped eight lengths back, half a dozen horses behind. Paradigm Shift closed on the leader and the pace lifted. Kate bit her lip as another ingredient, speed, was added to the dangerous mix. The horse towing Fontainebleau tipped up over the thirteenth, and Kate knocked shoulders with Jack as she instinctively swerved to avoid the faller.

'Sorry,' she muttered, not able to tear her eyes away from the race.

Ahead was the open ditch and for the first time Kate noticed the canvas screens erected on the landing side. She grimaced, hoping the screens were just precautionary. Stewards waved their flags to direct the runners around the inside of the jump, but such was their proximity from the last, there was a mad scramble to duck inside the wing of the jump.

Fontainebleau, kept wide by Donnie for most of the race, was caught out worst. Donnie pushed down in his stirrups and sawed at his right rein. Fontainebleau threw his head and cocked his jaw.

Kate balanced on her right foot, leaning in like a tight rope walker, willing Fontainebleau to make the corner before he reached the jump. Jack staggered sideways.

Fontainebleau half-leaped, half-crashed through the wing, sending the white plastic rails looping off its posts like pool noodles.

Kate clapped her hands over her eyes then peeped through her fingers. 'My God, he's still going!' she gasped.

Now only two from the rear, Donnie pushed Fontainebleau along to make up lost ground. Egyptian John surrendered his lead to Paradigm Shift. From off the pace, Morning Mr Magpie made a move. Donnie spotted the favourite gunning up the inside and manoeuvred his horse into his slipstream. He slapped Fontainebleau down the neck with his whip and scrubbed with his hands.

The long run around the turn and into the home straight for the final time was in their favour. Fontainebleau rallied to the task and stuck with Morning Mr Magpie as the favourite slipped by the field.

'If he stays on, we might still get placed,' muttered Jack.

'Come on, Font,' Kate whispered, feeling the crackle of adrenalin rise up her spine.

Four from home, and Fontainebleau passed the fifth-placed horse in mid-air. The three remaining fences came fast and furious. Fontainebleau stood off the third-last and put in a wild leap that had him down on his nose on landing. Egyptian John back-pedalled, forfeiting fourth position.

Morning Mr Magpie appeared to have the race at his mercy as he jumped the second last upsides Paradigm Shift. His jockey's body language was insistent, but not yet desperate. Donnie, by comparison, was flat to the boards. Fontainebleau stuck out his mud-spattered face, his thin neck stretched low, ungainly legs plugging through the deep ground.

Kate squeaked in excitement as he jumped over the last and into third place. Four lengths ahead, Morning Mr Magpie was getting the better of Paradigm Shift. Whips flailed and jockeys rocked in desperation. The front two refused to give way to each other. But to Kate's surprise, Fontainebleau was gaining on them.

'Pull him wide! Pull him wide, Donnie!' she screamed as she suddenly realised they had a chance of winning. That surely couldn't be true though. Fontainebleau hadn't won in almost a decade. It just wasn't something he did.

A quick glance at the finish line told Kate Donnie didn't have time to pull his horse around the others. She gasped. He was going between them, through a gap barely wider than his stall door. Fontainebleau pinned his ears and steamrolled his way between his rivals. Donnie didn't even have space to raise his whip. Twenty yards to go and there was nothing more he could do to urge his horse into the lead. It was up to Fontainebleau.

Fontainebleau wasn't the biggest of horses, but his heart was mighty. Gripping the bit between his teeth and closing his eyes to the mud, he strode forward. The three horses flashed past the post, but one thin chestnut head reached further than the others.

'He won!' screamed Kate. She whirled round to face Jack. He looked just as stunned as she. 'Fontainebleau won!' she screamed at him.

Jack laughed loudly (so *that's* what it sounded like). He scooped Kate up in a bear hug and spun her round. Still laughing, he planted a smacker of a kiss on her temple then grimaced, placing a hand on his injured ribs. The pain wasn't enough to wipe the smile from his face though.

'What a horse,' he said. 'What a way to bow out.'

Kate stopped mid-celebration. 'Bow out? What do you mean?'

Jack gave her a sad smile. 'Come on, Kate. You knew it was coming. He's thirteen now. This was always going to be his last season, and what better way to end a career than on a high?'

Kate bit her lips together and fought the ridiculous tears that sprang to her eyes. She watched Fontainebleau trot back down the course to the gateway. His ears were pricked, his eyes bright, his face and chest were caked in mud, but no horse had ever looked happier.

'I know,' she said. 'It's just really bittersweet. Does he have a home to go to?'

She instinctively thought of Thistle Lodge Stables and her tears swelled. Jack put an arm round her and guided her towards the gateway to meet the victors.

'The owner's daughter wants a horse to do a bit of dressage on. I reckon Fontainebleau would like that.'

Kate nodded and wiped her nose on her sleeve. She was getting soft. 'Yeah, he would.'

47

'SASKIA!' KATE CALLED up the stairs early that evening. 'That landlord agent guy is going to be here in a minute. Is your room tidy?'

Saskia replied something inaudible, but Kate couldn't wait. She hadn't even had time to shower since getting home from the races, and she'd totally forgotten about their rent inspection.

She plumped the cushions in the lounge and threw a shawl over the back of the sofa to make it appear more presentable. Her phone rang as she was disposing of some very dead flowers. Kate's stomach clenched. It was her mother.

'Hi, Mum. Everything okay?' she answered.

'Yes, I think so, thanks, Katie.'

Phew, she didn't sound mad for being stood up. Kate looked around the kitchen to see what else needed cleaning. What was that smell? She looked down at the bin. Maybe she should take the rubbish out. Collection wasn't until Friday, but still, something smelt horrible in there and she didn't want the agent to think they were living in squalor.

She pinned the phone between her cheek and shoulder and wrestled the bin bag free.

'What are you doing?' asked Val. 'All that bumping and grunting.'

'We've got a house inspection in a minute and I'm still cleaning. I'm sorry about the other day, Mum. I left a message on your phone.'

'It's okay, Katie. I understand. I just wanted to tell you I've been going to meetings every day this week. I haven't touched a drop.'

Kate paused, praying to God that her mother was telling the truth. 'That's great. Hey, I'm really proud of you.'

'Yeah, me too.' Val gave an embarrassed laugh. 'Look, Katie, the more I've been going to the meetings the more I've come to understand how it affects everyone around me, like you and Xander, and Saskia.'

Bugger, Kate bet Saskia hadn't cleaned her room yet. 'Sorry, hold on, Mum.' She dropped the bin bag and returned to the bottom of the stairs. 'Saskia! Your room had better be clean when the agent gets here!' she yelled.

'And I was wondering if you would like to come along to a meeting with me?' continued Val.

Saskia's door was yanked open and she stuck her head round the corner, purple face pack in place and hair wound in a towel. 'It's clean, Kate. Jesus! It's not like we're going to get kicked out for me having a messy room.'

The door was slammed shut again and Kate breathed out through her nose. 'Sorry, Mum, what did you say?' she asked, hurrying back into the kitchen to get the bin bag.

'I want you to come to an AA meeting with me.'

Kate stopped short. 'I don't think that's a good idea.'

'No, Katie, you're wrong. It would be a really great idea. The people I've spoken to—'

'Mum, if Ben is there then it will not be so great, I promise you.' Noticing dust on one of the kitchen shelves, Kate grabbed a disinfectant wipe.

'I haven't seen him at any of the meetings I've been to,' said Val.

'He was there the first time.'

'Well, he hasn't been since.'

Had he fallen off the wagon? Kate sighed and gave the shelf one last flick with the wipe. She hoped not. 'When do you want me to come? I've got work, remember.'

'Next week?'

'No can do. It's Cheltenham next week.' Saying the words out loud made the hair on her neck stand on end. This year she wouldn't be watching it on the television in the racing office. This year she would be there, in the thick of it, leading up d'Artagnan.

'Is the Festival all week?'

'No, Tuesday until Friday, but—' Kate was interrupted by the doorbell ringing. 'Shit, he's here. I've got to go, Mum. The estate agent's here. I'll speak to you later.'

'So you could come on Monday?'

Kate went to throw the disinfectant wipe in the bin only to find it without a bag inside and a half-full one squatting by the door. 'Yeah, okay, Mum. Monday it is, but I can only take a couple of hours off, three at the most. I'll meet you there. Gotta go. Bye.'

Kate threw the bag out the kitchen door onto the small courtyard behind the house and blasted the room with air freshener. The doorbell rang again.

'Hi, come in!' Kate exclaimed, breathless in her haste. 'Mr Llywelyn, right?'

The estate agent gave her an odd look, making Kate consciously draw in her panic.

'Jensen, please,' he said, stepping over the threshold in his patent leather shoes. 'Everything going okay?'

'Yes, splendid! No problems whatsoever.' He didn't need to know that the kitchen windows had been sticking. Not yet, anyhow. She didn't want to be the overly demanding tenant that every landlord hated.

Jensen smiled in approval and gestured forward. 'Okay if I take a quick look around?'

Kate ushered him through then stood feeling like a spare part as he nosed around the lounge and dining room. 'Would you like something to drink? Tea? Coffee?'

'I won't, thanks.' He scribbled a couple of notes on his clipboard and wandered through to the kitchen. 'No problems with the boiler? Heating working okay?'

'Yes, no problems. We've been very comfortable here,' Kate assured him.

'Good, good.' He sniffed the air, still heavy with the scent of jasmine and vanilla, and sneezed.

'Bless you.'

Jensen searched his pockets for a handkerchief and came up empty. Kate went into overdrive, pulled out the dirty disinfectant wipe from her pocket then stuffed it back in again. She tore off a couple of sheets of kitchen roll for him. Jensen blew his nose, sounding like a trumpet that had been run over by a car. Kate had the insane urge to laugh.

'Your sister home?' he asked, pocketing the paper towel.

'She's upstairs.'

Jensen beamed. 'Great, I can say hello when we're up there.'

Kate followed him up the stairs. He detoured via her spotless bedroom and bathroom then knocked on Saskia's door.

'Kate, for fuck's sake, I've cleaned—' Saskia wrenched open the door and stopped mid-sentence at the sight of the estate agent. Her face pack cracked as she smiled.

'Hello, there. I didn't hear you come in.'

Jensen looked flustered. 'Sorry to disturb you. I just need to do a quick spec.'

Saskia stood aside. 'Spec all you want,' she said in a husky voice. How she managed to turn men to jelly, even with a purple face and wearing Peppa Pig pyjamas, was beyond Kate.

She took a reluctant step forward to see into Saskia's room. It didn't look too bad, considering. At least the bed was made and most of her laundry was in the basket.

Jensen stood in the middle of the room and looked around. His gaze paused over Saskia's dressing table which was awash with make-up and hair products. Her month-old Valentine's Day card was clipped to the mirror.

'I see you have a secret admirer,' he said.

'I do love a bit of mystery,' murmured Saskia.

Jensen turned pink and averted his gaze to scribble more notes. He dotted the page with a conclusive tap and beamed at them both. 'Everything seems to be in order. And I'm glad you've settled in well. I'll leave you to it.' He tore off a sheet of paper and gave it to Kate as he passed. 'A copy for you.' He paused by the door and turned back to Saskia. 'You going out tonight?'

'Just to the pub to meet a friend.'

'A boyfriend?'

Saskia looked amused. 'No, a girlfriend, actually.' She gave him a coy smile. 'You should come along.'

Jensen looked down at his clipboard and gave an embarrassed laugh. 'I don't know.'

Saskia feigned disappointment. 'That's too bad. But if you're too busy—'

'No! I'm not too busy. In fact, I'm all finished for today. You going to The Golden Miller?'

Saskia nodded.

Jensen tucked his clipboard under his arm, still looking awkward. 'Maybe I'll see you there then.'

* * *

After seeing Jensen out, Kate ran back up the stairs to Saskia's room.

'I don't believe you,' she said, laughing. 'How on earth do you do it?'

Saskia was sat back at her dressing table, wiping off her face pack with a cotton ball. 'Do what?'

'How do you manage to pick up men when you've got a face like a radish and your hair in a towel?'

Saskia shrugged. 'Just sheer natural magnetism, I suppose.'

Kate snorted. 'Well, if you do start dating him just be nice, okay? I don't want to get kicked out of here too.' The Valentine's Day card on Saskia's mirror caught her eye and she paused. 'I wonder if...' She tugged the card free and looked at the inscription inside. Her mouth fell open and she looked from Saskia to the card to the door.

'What?'

'Do you think maybe it was *him* who sent you this?'

Saskia batted her away. 'I'm telling you, it was Jack.'

'But look.' Kate pointed to the question mark. 'If that really is an upside down J, then it could be him. And he was the only other person who knew where we lived.'

Saskia gave her a dubious look. 'What's his name again?'

'Jensen. Jensen Llywelyn.'

Saskia glanced at the card again. 'I still think it was Jack.'

Kate shook her head in exasperation. Then she remembered the copy of the inspection sheet Jensen had handed to her. She whipped it out and compared the writing. 'It is him! Look, Saskia.'

Saskia looked, then looked again with more urgency. 'Oh my God, it is!' She looked at Kate and they howled with laughter. 'Wow, that's—that's a little creepy, don't you think?'

'Not as creepy as Jack sending you a card.'

Saskia didn't look convinced. 'Oh, well,' she said with a shrug and turned back to the mirror.

'Are you going to tell him you know?'

Saskia looked doubtful. 'Maybe I shouldn't encourage him. I don't really fancy dating a Welshman.'

'Why?'

'Have you seen their language? It looks like a dictionary sneezed.'

The doorbell rang and they stared at each other.

'Do you think it's him again?' Saskia whispered.

Kate tried not to laugh. 'Maybe.'

'Go see.'

Kate thundered back down the stairs and opened the door. Her laughter faded when she saw who it was. 'Nicholas,' she gasped. 'What are you doing here?'

'Er, hi.'

Kate stared at him then remembered her manners. 'Come in, come in. Um, were we supposed to be meeting tonight?' She was pretty sure she'd turned down his dinner offer at Frankie's party.

Nicholas stepped through the doorway, hands clasped, a nervous smile frozen on his face. 'No, I thought I'd surprise you.'

'Well, you have. How did you know where I lived?'

'I bumped into Leonie the other evening. She filled me in on – you know – what you've been going through lately.'

Kate narrowed her eyes. 'Oookaaay. What exactly has she told you?'

'Just that you've had a rough time and, well, that's really why I'm here. I've – um – got a surprise for you. Call it a belated Christmas present, even though that's passed. Obviously.'

Kate held out her hands to resist. 'Nicholas, I don't want anything. I can't accept—'

'It's to do with d'Artagnan.'

Kate shut her mouth. Maybe she should hear him out. 'D'Artagnan?'

'Yes.' Nicholas stood, tense in the middle of the dining room, still bundled in his coat and scarf. 'I like you, Kate. Very much. And I would like us to try again.'

'Nicholas—'

He held out his hand to stem her objections. 'I got to thinking. The reason we broke up in the first place was because of d'Artagnan, so it makes sense that if we race d'Artagnan like you want then we have nothing to fight about.'

Kate's jaw hung slack. 'You'll let him run on his own merits?'

Nicholas nodded pensively.

'In the Gold Cup?' She couldn't allow for any confusion this time.

Nicholas nodded again. 'In the Gold Cup.'

Kate didn't know how to react. Exultant joy fought with a sorrow that still pined for Ben. Nicholas searched her face for an answer, looking more and more doubtful the longer she stayed silent.

'That is, if you're not seeing anyone already,' he said, wringing his hands.

Oh, God. He didn't know about her and Ben. Of course not. Why would he? He and Ben were hardly on the best of terms, and it wasn't the sort of things that was just popped into a casual conversation. Maybe she should tell him? She didn't like the idea of keeping secrets. But what good would it do? It would just damage the brothers' relationship further. And, Kate hated to admit it, Nicholas might be so upset that he'd change his mind about d'Artagnan.

Kate realised she'd already made her decision.

'I'm not seeing anyone,' she said.

Nicholas beamed. 'Then maybe we can try again?'

Doubt snagged inside her. She couldn't use Nicholas like this. 'I don't know, Nicholas. I don't know if I'm ready.' She sighed. 'I can't change how I feel, just like that,' she said, snapping her fingers.

'That's okay, that's okay. You take all the time you need. We can take it slow,' he assured her.

Kate chewed her lip as guilt slunk up to her. Nicholas must think her terribly ungrateful. She gave him a weak smile. 'Thank you?'

'You're welcome.' Nicholas was all smiles. He gestured to the front door and in the general direction of The Golden Miller. 'Do you fancy celebrating over dinner?'

Every enzyme in Kate's body shot in reverse. 'I've already eaten—' She gave herself a mental kick when his face fell. 'But we can have a drink together, right?'

Nicholas turned apple-cheeked again. 'Great. Shall I wait while you doll yourself up?'

Kate stopped short. She'd forgotten she was still wearing her clothes from the races. 'Oh. Oh yes. Of course. If you don't mind.'

48

'SO, LET ME get this straight,' said Frankie as they walked their mounts back down the hill. 'You went out with Nicholas last night, but you're dating Ben?'

'No, I'm not dating either of them.'

'But Nicholas offered to change d'Artagnan's racing tactics on condition you get back together.' Frankie looked confused.

Kate lifted her hands in a helpless gesture. 'Yes.'

'But you're not back together.'

Kate squirmed in her saddle. 'No. I just thought – I don't know what I thought. He just showed up out of the blue, said "Here's the deal, Lucille. How about dinner?" and I couldn't very well turn him down.'

'How was dinner?'

Kate looked shameful. 'I lied and said I'd already eaten. But we had a couple of drinks, and actually, it was okay. Nicholas isn't a bad guy. I mean, when he's not stitching d'Artagnan up and not telling me, he's really quite pleasant. I could do worse.'

Frankie looked dubious. 'Quite pleasant? Could do worse? Kate, that's not exactly a shining report on a man you're considering dating.'

Kate sighed and wound d'Artagnan's mane around her finger. 'I know. Maybe it's too soon after Ben, you know? What I had with Ben was – I don't know. I want to say "special", but that's just corny. I had fun with him, I could be myself with him. I—' She paused to find the right words. 'I'd look at him, or he'd touch me, and it felt like the world burst into song.'

'And Nicholas doesn't make you feel that way?'

'Nicholas is different.'

'Huh,' said Frankie, sounding less than convinced. 'Remind me again why you broke up with Ben?'

They pulled up in the yard and dismounted. D'Artagnan whipped Kate across the face with his tail as she unhitched his girth. 'Ow. We broke up because he wasn't who I thought he was.'

'Can you be more specific?'

They met at the saddle rack and lumped their tack onto the rail. Kate hesitated. Frankie was her best mate at work, and she trusted her not to spread the word about Ben's problems, but it still didn't sit right with her conscience.

'No. He just left out a few key details about himself.'

Frankie rolled her eyes. 'So you were able to be yourself when you two were dating, but he wasn't?'

Kate rested her hands on the rail and shook her head. 'My life is turning into a soap opera, isn't it?'

'Can't you forgive him for what he's done? Look at Rhys and me. We didn't exactly get off to the best of starts thanks to Peace Offering, and look where we are now.' Frankie wiggled her wedding-ringed finger at her.

'It's not as simple as just forgive and forget. Not that I think what you went through was simple or anything,' she added hastily. 'The details Ben left out are ongoing. They're always going to be there and I don't think I could handle it.'

They led their horses over to the hosing bay and Frankie switched on the tap while Kate cooled down d'Artagnan.

'Can you really not tell me what these "details" are? You're making my imagination run riot,' Frankie said. 'Is it some weird fetish?'

Kate laughed. 'No! Nothing like that. Sorry. It's not my story to tell.'

'And Nicholas doesn't have any dodgy details going for him, does he?'

'Not that I know of.' She stepped back as d'Artagnan gave a full body shake.

Frankie took the hose from her to get to work on Bold Phoenix and shrugged. 'Well, seems pretty clear to me which brother you should go for.'

'Ben?'

'No, not if you can't live with whatever he's got going on. Nicholas. He's straightforward, more or less. He's safe. And I don't mean to sound shallow, but let's face it, he's got money. He's "pleasant".' Frankie tried to use air quotes and yelped when she splashed herself.

Kate nodded in reluctant agreement. 'That's what Saskia said, even though she said boring rather than safe. Said he had more to offer.'

'In my experience, it's not always what a man can offer that's important, but what he's willing to sacrifice.'

Kate's shoulders sagged. 'Nicholas is potentially sacrificing the Gold Cup for me.'

'And what's Ben sacrificing?'

She shook her head sadly. 'There's nothing he *can* sacrifice.'

'And by the sounds of it, nothing to offer either.'

Kate felt queasy at the thought of turning her back on Ben completely. 'Except love,' she murmured under her breath.

She led d'Artagnan over to the horse walker, her thoughts a tangled wool ball.

'I don't know, d'Artagnan.' With a defeated sigh, she swapped over his bridle for a head collar and secured him on the walker. 'There you go,' she murmured with a final pat. 'Your turn to go round in circles.'

Kate walked back to her boxes to get her next ride ready when she noticed Fontainebleau's door open. She rushed forward, imagining Jack's reaction if he saw one of his horses joyriding up the Gallops, but stopped short when she reached the entrance. Of all people, Ben was inside, putting a travel rug on her horse.

Kate had to steady herself against the doorframe. 'What are you doing?'

Ben turned at the sound of her voice. They stared at one another, countless unspoken words passing between them, then he resumed his task. 'Taking him home.'

'Home? This is his home.'

'Not any more, it isn't.' He clapped the chestnut gelding's shoulder and ducked under his neck to untangle the rug ties. 'Here, grab this, will you?'

Kate automatically stepped forward and took the ties Ben was holding out beneath Fontainebleau's belly and buckled them into place. 'What do you mean?'

'He's been retired, didn't you know?'

'Well, yes, of course, but he's going to the owner's daughter to do dressage.'

Ben came back around and double-checked the horse's tack. 'Apparently she didn't think much of him when she came to see him.'

Kate was outraged. How dare anyone disrespect her horses? 'What? The cow. So they're just going to throw him on the scrapheap?'

Ben gave her a patient smile. 'No, he's coming to me. And we'll see where he goes from there.'

Thoughts of Fontainebleau going to Thistle Lodge Stables brought back painful memories of South of Jericho.

'But—'

Ben led Fontainebleau out of his stable, making Kate take an evasive step back.

'How are you able to take on another horse?' she asked. With his tenant moving away and Jerry's death, his business had to be floundering.

Ben stopped and looked at her. 'You've given me plenty to think about these past couple of weeks and I think I've found a solution. Who knew anything good could come of it?'

His words stung and Kate lifted her chin in defence. 'Fine, just don't let the gate hit you on the way out.'

Ben walked away, Fontainebleau at his side. Kate couldn't bear to watch them go. She slammed the stable door shut and marched in the opposite direction.

Saskia was unusually quiet on the way home. Only as they neared Helensvale's outer reaches did she speak.

'So, I was thinking maybe we should see if any of the Aspen Valley staff who live in Helensvale want to do a liftshare thingy.'

Kate blinked at her. 'Oh. Um, yeah, that sounds like a good idea. You could halve your fuel costs if we got a couple of people involved.'

'I was thinking more along the lines of *you* finding a lift with *them*,' said Saskia, not taking her eyes off the road.

'Oh.' Kate didn't want to say that that hurt, but she was a little disappointed. 'Not keen on the early mornings?'

Saskia shrugged. 'I just think it's best not to rely on me alone for lifts to work.'

'You're not thinking of pulling a sickie over Cheltenham, are you? Saskia, I know those are busy days, but all the more reason—'

'Calm down. I'm not pulling a sickie. I'm just saying plans might change, that's all.'

The overly light tone to her voice set alarm bells ringing in Kate's head. 'Saskia, what aren't you telling me?'

'I've just been thinking lately that maybe I'm not cut out to be a racing secretary.'

'You're only figuring this out now?'

Saskia sent her a dark look. 'Just because I'm not interested in horses, doesn't mean I couldn't do the job.'

'What about Jack? I thought you and he were going to ride off into the sunset together.'

Saskia shrugged. 'Yeah, I'm having second thoughts about him too. Like, do I really want to be with a man who's married to his job?'

Kate felt a weight lift her shoulders. One less thing to worry about. 'And another woman,' she murmured.

'And seeing what Leonie went through with Declan just reinforces that feeling. Declan was always at work. He totally neglected Leonie.'

Kate made a conscious effort to stay silent.

'So I've given up on the idea of Jack.'

'That's good. Be sure to have another job lined up if you're going to quit, though.'

'Hmm, bit late for that,' Saskia mumbled.

Kate looked at her sharply. 'You've quit already?'

Saskia pulled into a parking space and took a deep breath. 'Actually, I got fired.'

With the engine turned off, the silence was engulfing.

'You got fired? Why?'

Saskia looked sulky. 'Jack didn't think I was suited to the job, said he needed someone in the office "whom he felt comfortable working with". Stupid prat. Thinks he's above all of us plebs. I tell you, his ego could have its own postcode, it's so big.'

'You made me believe you were having an affair with him, though.'

'That might have been wishful thinking on my part,' Saskia mumbled.

'Oh boy, okay, keep calm, keep calm,' Kate breathed. Saskia didn't look like the one needing to be calmed. 'Did this all happen today? How much notice has he given you?'

Saskia nodded. 'I've got 'til the end of the season, so a couple of months, but to be honest I don't think I'm going to stick around that long. I mean, I don't owe him anything.'

'But you must. Or at least find another job first.'

Saskia unbuckled her seatbelt and opened her door. 'Leonie and I are going to London.'

Kate scrambled out of the car after her. 'Is that wise? You should be saving money, not spending it on weekend trips to London.'

Saskia slammed her door and smiled at Kate over the car roof. 'Who said it was just for the weekend?'

Over tea, Kate listened while Saskia laid out all the adventures she and Leonie were destined to have. Most of them sounded like they should come with a health warning.

'Where will you stay?' she asked.

'Dunno. We'll find somewhere. We've got friends we can crash with to start with.'

'And money?'

'We'll get jobs.'

'But—' Kate took a deep breath to steady herself. She didn't know how Saskia could talk so nonchalantly about such a huge undertaking. Was she missing an enzyme or something? London was big and dangerous and full of all the wrong temptations. A naive twenty-three-year-old with a wild streak and a penchant for 'adventure' would be swallowed up in seconds.

'And then once we've made some dosh, we're going to go travelling. I'm thinking Australia, but Leonie wants to go to South America. What do you think?'

Kate was sure she'd read somewhere that Australia housed the most venomous animals on earth, and she'd seen photos on the internet of spiders the size of dinner plates found in Peru. Then there were all the drugs and kidnappings and organ theft. What was wrong with Helensvale? It wasn't like it was a boring town. There was Aspen Valley and Bracken Fields to put it on the horseracing map, and The Golden Miller could get quite rowdy if one was after a little danger.

'What do you think, Kate?' Saskia asked again.

Something in her eyes told Kate that Saskia wasn't feeling as gung-ho as she'd have her believe. 'I think—' Kate muscled a smile onto her face. 'I think you'll have a fabulous time.'

49

KATE FOUND HER mother sheltering from the rain on the steps of St Paul's Community Centre the following Monday.

'Nice weather,' Val said, holding a palm out as Kate ran for cover.

'Tell me about it. All we need is for Cheltenham to be waterlogged. You okay?'

Val nodded. 'I've been clean for twelve days now,' she said proudly.

'Seriously? Not even snuck a swig?'

Val shook her head. 'No, Xander helped me get rid of it all. I needed his help. I didn't trust myself.'

'How's he doing?'

'Hard to say, really. Better, I guess. He's been asking about going to see Ben.'

Kate brushed the rain off her shoulders and held the door wide for them to enter. 'Not going to happen. Ben and I aren't exactly on speaking terms.'

'Is it because of his addiction?'

'Mum, I really don't want to talk about it. Are you sure he's not going to be here today?'

Val shrugged. 'No, but he hasn't been to any midday meetings since the day you made a getaway.'

Heat stole over Kate's cheeks as she realised she would probably have to face many of the people who had witnessed the drama.

Unlike her last visit, they were early today. Kate followed her mother over to a corner where a table was laid out with teas and coffees. Kate dared to look around.

On first appraisal, it didn't appear Ben was here, but what she did see covered her with shame. The people that sat around chatting weren't the scraggy drunks on park benches that she'd hurry past at night. They all looked *normal* – clothes clean and pressed, hair and faces groomed.

With their teas in hand, they bagged a couple of seats in a corner next to the window. The rain was lashing down outside, fat rivulets running down the glass, obscuring the view. Sipping on their teas, they waited while the room filled up. Kate was impressed to see her mother so relaxed.

At last, silence fell as everybody shuffling for a seat found one, and a middle-aged man, handsome in an old-fashioned movie-star way, stood up.

'Looks like that's everybody, so we'll get started. Thank you all for coming to today's meeting—'

He was interrupted by the door opening. Kate spilled her tea down her front as she recognised the latecomer. Val's hand shot out to still Kate's instinct to flee.

'No, you don't,' she murmured. 'Not again.'

Ben stared at Kate for a moment, frozen in the doorway, then, with an apologetic smile to the speaker, closed the door behind him and took a seat. Kate's throat felt like it was closing up. She knew this would happen, it was sod's law, but this time she was on the other side of the room from the door and Ben stood between her and freedom. Her cup rattled back onto its saucer and her mother reached out to take it from her before she dropped it.

The speaker continued his introduction, but Kate didn't hear him. A nerve ticked beneath her eye. Ben frowned at his boots, knuckles white and shoulders rigid.

'Well, since I'm up, I might as well start,' said the speaker. 'I'm Eric and I'm an alcoholic.'

Kate jumped when the room responded with an accumulative, 'Hi, Eric.'

Her eyes widened. This was bizarre. It almost felt like she was in a movie, but only as a spectator, and everyone else were actors playing their part.

'I used to doubt myself,' said Eric. 'When I first came to AA, I wasn't even sure that I *was* an alcoholic. I could go without a drink, I could function. I worked a nine-to-five job without a problem, but then I'd go home via the pub or pick up a bottle of whisky at the off-license and I'd spend my evenings drinking. I didn't see it as being a problem, quite the opposite. It softened the blows of reality. It helped me to unwind after a stressful day at work. That couldn't be a bad thing then, could it?' Eric gave a small laugh and shook his head. 'But the more often I did it, the more I seemed to become immune to it. I had to drink more to get to that same state of relaxation. I started going to the pub *and* the off-license. I'd promise myself just the one bottle, but then three quarters of the way through I'd start to panic. I couldn't bear the thought of being dry. So I'd go out again, visit a different off-license, so I wouldn't be recognised...'

As Eric continued with his story, Kate became less aware of Ben. She became overwhelmed with guilt. These weren't actors putting on a performance for her entertainment. They were real people with real problems. Battling alcoholism was their reality, to be lived every day.

Eric finished his story and sat down. A pause ensued as they waited for another person to speak. Kate's eyes locked with Ben's. Eyes that she'd always thought of as laughing showed no trace of humour. His Adam's Apple bobbed as he swallowed. With a deep breath, he stood up.

'Hi, I'm Ben and I'm an alcoholic.'

Kate looked away, hating the sound of those words. Tears stung her eyes. Beside her, Val joined the others in greeting Ben.

'I've been sober for six years and three months,' said Ben. 'I'm twenty-nine now, so being an alcoholic aged just twenty-three wasn't something I'd envisaged for myself.'

Kate could feel his words directed at her, but she couldn't look up. She dug her fingernails into her palms. Ben's voice came through louder, clearer and more painful, though.

'I had it all going for me. I was brought up in a loving family environment by my grandparents, my father visited often, provided well for me, too well it would seem. My mother died soon after I was born, so I never knew her, never missed her. Of course, I missed *not having a mother*, but my nan and opa were very good to me. I became a jump jockey and my father couldn't have been prouder. He provided me with the best horses in training and I won the amateur's championship title in my first season.'

He paused and Kate looked up to see why. Ben chewed his lips, still frowning at his feet. He lifted his gaze and looked straight into Kate's eyes.

'It should have been the best moment of my life, but it wasn't. I was ridiculed, labelled an armchair rider, and being just nineteen, I didn't know whether to believe them. I began to hate my father for doing so much for me. He didn't understand – *couldn't* understand – what was wrong. I was winning, what could possibly be the problem? I started drinking, first as a way of escape, then when I had to give a sample at the races and got a three week suspension, I continued to drink as a means of getting caught again. The safety aspect of it all – I didn't care about that. I wanted to self-destruct, so it worked pretty well.' Ben gave a wry chuckle. 'I got canned more often than tuna. I went out one night, did some coke, drank myself into a stupor because I knew I'd be riding the next day. I was in no fit state to ride. This time I was given a two-year ban.'

Kate stared at him in horror. She couldn't imagine the mind-set one had to be in to be so self-abusive.

Ben gave her a pained look. 'I bolted. Cut ties with my family, my friends, hooked up with a bunch of bums and proceeded to drink myself past any coherence. I wasn't prepared for the guilt that came with it. I knew my father would be confused, definitely disappointed, and, to my mind, pretty angry. I convinced myself that I was doing the right thing. He hadn't asked for me as a son. He already had a family, one which my presence always seemed to disrupt.' Ben took a deep hesitant breath. 'I have many regrets, but the one that kills me is that my grandfather died not knowing where I was, if I was still alive even. I couldn't even attend his funeral. How could I when I knew my father would more than likely be there? I was ashamed of what I'd become, but the fear of giving up the bottle was greater.' Ben bit his lip as his voice broke. He looked down and tried to compose himself.

Tears rolled down Kate's face. She couldn't breathe. All she felt was Ben's agony over his grandfather.

'Not going to Opa's funeral was the last straw. I OD'd. I don't remember much of what happened in the days following that, but from what I've learnt since, I had my stomach pumped. I was put on dialysis. The hospital called my father, told him to come say his goodbyes.' Ben looked up and splayed his hands. 'I made it, obviously. My father put me in a rehab clinic, a place out in north Wales. I did three months there, but it's hard when you've got nothing to fill your days with and you can't stop thinking about having a drink. It's the first thing you think of when you wake up and the last thing when you go to sleep. The clinic had a work scheme where patients could get jobs while still in rehab. Working in garden centres, on farms. Because of my background with horses, I was offered a job at a charity, a racehorse rehabilitation centre. And something inside me clicked, it gave me direction. I wanted to run my own rehab centre for horses – and that's what I do, kind of. It's not the easiest of ways to earn a living. A lot can go wrong.' He looked at Kate, seemingly through to her soul. 'But a lot can go right too. My father still doesn't really understand what happened, so I still ride his horses – some of them at least. I won't take the armchair rides. I can't go back to the abuse in the weighing room and the media. But I owe it to him after he picked me up and got me help. He's never complained, never used it as a weapon against me. It's also a reassurance to him. I get tested pretty much every time I set foot on a racecourse. If I did fall off the wagon, then my father would know about it.

'And that's pretty much where I'm at now. Some days are easier than others. Some days much harder. But I know the bottle is not my friend, regardless of what my brain might try to tell me.' Ben blinked, and looked around at the silent room. 'Thank you for listening,' he mumbled and sat down.

50

CHELTENHAM FESTIVAL BEGAN with a bang the next day. The Champion Hurdle was the big race of the day and Aspen Valley Stables were double-handed with Dexter and Ta' Qali heading the betting market.

Crammed into the office to watch the race on the television, the staff were torn between the two.

'My money's on Ta' Qali,' said Woody, sitting on Saskia's desk. 'He's the one on the up.'

'How can you say that?' argued Billy. 'If Dexter wins, this'll be his *third* Champion Hurdle title. He'll join an elite club.'

'That's the thing though,' piped up June, who Kate noticed always took Woody's side. 'His *third* Champion Hurdle. He's got a lot more miles on the clock than Ta' Qali.'

'And a lot more experience. You need experience to handle Cheltenham. Ta' Qali's never been there. He'll boil over.'

'He handled Punchestown okay last year. And he whipped Dexter and that Kickstart Murphy.'

'Hardly. He won by a nose. Besides, that was last season. Dexter beat him in the Christmas Hurdle ten weeks ago by a lot further.'

'Rhys has chosen to ride Ta' Qali. That's gotta mean something.'

'Yeah, it means his wife owns a share and he won't get laid for a month if he doesn't ride her horse.'

'Is he fit though? His arm's kept him out for almost a month. If the finish is as tight as it was at Punchestown, he's going to need to be a hundred per cent to win it.'

'Rhys is better than Donnie even when he's only fifty per cent.'

Saskia covered her ears and groaned as the argument became more heated. 'Christ, will you listen to yourselves? It's just a horse race!'

Twenty pairs of eyes swung round to stare at her. Silence, apart from the tinny voices on the television, hung heavy.

'*Just a horse race?*' spluttered Billy. 'Saskia, how can you say that? This isn't just a horse race.'

'This is *Cheltenham!*' Woody exclaimed. 'This is—this is—'

'The greatest show on turf!' shouted someone from the back.

Saskia rolled her eyes. 'Fine. Whatever.'

The argument between the Dexter and Ta' Qali camps continued until the horses were circling behind the start.

'Zip it, will ya?' someone yelled. 'I can't hear what they're saying on the TV.'

A few grumbles lingered, but, for the most part, the lads and lasses of Aspen Valley turned their attention back to the screen. There were just four horses on the presenters' lips: Dexter, Ta' Qali, Kickstart Murphy and another up-and-coming Irish superstar, The Troubadour. It was as if the other ten runners didn't exist.

'Here we go,' someone said. 'Saskia, turn it up.'

The tension in the office was palpable as the runners were called forward. The tape whipped back and the fourteen horses plunged forward. A few members of staff, unable to contain their excitement, gave whoops and cheers.

'And they're off and running in the Grade One Champion Hurdle,' drawled the commentator. 'Looks like Dexter's going to make the running. Yes, Dexter takes a keen hold and spearheads the field alongside Jaipur. It's a short run to the first of eight hurdles and Dexter isn't hanging about. In third, Ta' Qali gallops on the outside of Best Picture, further back to Flintstone, The Troubadour, You Zulu Warrior, and Kickstart Murphy is held up in about tenth at this early stage.'

There was a long run to the second flight and Dexter bowled along in front with ears pricked and toe pointed. The horses streamed over the obstacle in front of the stands almost in Indian file, rapping the hurdle with a *rack-a-clack-a-clack.*

The stable staff all leaned to their left as the field swung round the bend into the back straight.

Still Dexter led, but he appeared to have settled under Donnie's persistent restraint. Beside him, the thirty-three-to-one outsider, Jaipur, matched strides while Ta' Qali ran in their slipstream.

'And now approaching the third, there's little change to the order,' the commentator droned. 'Dexter still leads to Jaipur. A great jump from Ta'

Qali and he now moves up to contest second. Back in the field, a scrappy jump from The Troubadour, gets a flick of the whip from Paddy Flanagan. Kickstart Murphy still bides his time, now in eighth place on the inside of Kalon and Hurricane Winds.'

The field galloped hard over the undulating ground and Kate noticed Ta' Qali drop back a bit, so Dexter and Jaipur had a clear advantage. By the top of the hill though, the leaders were reined in a wrap to give them a breather, and the field began to cluster together again.

Jaipur's jockey became more animated and someone in the office groaned.

'Oh no, don't leave Dexter up front alone. You know how he idles!'

The horses flew the fourth without mishap and rounded the dogleg turn that led uphill.

'Dexter leads now by two lengths to Jaipur being hustled along. In third, Ta' Qali moves to the inside, The Troubadour on his tail in fourth.'

The cluster of horses swung round the top turn and thundered downhill towards the fifth. Dexter's lead remained undiminished, but behind him, Jaipur gave way to Ta' Qali. Runners back in the field were niggled at, their jockeys pressing for more effort.

'Look at that!' someone shouted.

Kate noticed it at the same time. The grey Kickstart Murphy sliced through the field like a ghost, Finn O'Donnaghue barely moving a muscle on his back. The commentator's voice rose an octave.

'Still Dexter leads, but now push comes to shove, and the challengers are a-comin'. Kickstart Murphy makes his move! Dexter is joined by Ta' Qali over the third last. Jaipur is hanging in there in fourth. The Troubadour makes another mistake and forfeits his place. Here comes Kickstart Murphy!'

The nervous tension in the office cranked up another notch as the horses rounded the long sweeping turn for home, and they began to yell for their favourite.

'Rhys Bradford still hasn't made a move on Ta' Qali,' cried the commentator. 'Dexter is beginning to show the strain. It's a long way to the second last. Ta' Qali's sitting pretty on his outside. The Troubadour makes up ground into third. Kickstart Murphy moves into fourth place. Here is the rematch, everyone! Dexter and Ta' Qali, over the second last, joined at the hip. Clear by two to Kickstart Murphy on the outside of The

Troubadour. O'Donnaghue raises his whip on Kickstart Murphy! The Irish superstar comes under pressure for the first time!'

The commentator's voice was drowned out by the shouts in the office. The horses swung round the turn into the home straight and the last Kate could hear of the commentator was his frantic shout 'And Ta' Qali throws down the gauntlet! He takes the lead!'

She was up on her feet with the rest of them, jumping up and down, using the lad in front of her as a push-off.

Under a strong drive from Rhys, Ta' Qali pulled two lengths clear of Dexter. Kickstart Murphy and The Troubadour galloped in hot pursuit. But no Cheltenham race was ever won until after its stamina-sapping hill. And Ta' Qali was yet to experience it.

Meeting the last fence, his brief lead was sucked up by his pursuers. Dexter picked up again and Kickstart Murphy was not stopping.

'Go on, Ta' Qali!' Kate yelled. 'Go on!'

They jumped the last, three in a row. Heads down and whips fanning, the three jockeys rocked back and forth in their saddles. Slowly, slowly, with the rail to help keep him straight, Ta' Qali edged ahead. Dexter stuck close, but couldn't match his stablemate's stride. The staff gave a mighty roar as Ta' Qali nodded over the line, half a length clear of Dexter and two lengths clear of Kickstart Murphy.

Woody leapt onto Saskia's desk and gave a triumphant warrior cry, beating his chest like a silverback gorilla. Saskia glared up at him and tried to remove her paperwork from beneath his dirty socks.

By the end of the first day of racing, Aspen Valley Stables had one winner, one second and a fourth to their name. And, while the staff trooped out of the office for the seventh time to get on with evening feeds, Kate couldn't help lingering behind. On television, the riders in the amateurs' race were pulling up, and she longed for the camera to focus on the sixth place finisher. Ben had ridden a longshot trained up north.

'Can I switch it off now?' said Saskia, aiming the remote control at the screen.

'Just a minute. I just want to see...' She shook her head. She didn't know what she wanted to see. Ben, obviously, but she didn't know what she was hoping to achieve in doing so.

The screen blacked out and Kate turned to Saskia, who arched her eyebrows at her. She sighed and hitched a bum cheek onto the desk.

'Saskia, do you ever feel like your life is taking you in a direction that you're not sure is the right one, yet you're powerless to stop it?'

'Sure, half the fun is finding out where you're heading.'

'But if you *know* where you're heading?'

Saskia pouted at her and tapped the remote control against her chin. 'Are you in love with him?'

'Who?' Kate cringed at her own words.

'Wow, you're in more of a mess than I thought. Either of them, I guess.'

'I don't know. How do you know?'

Saskia held up her hands. 'You're asking the wrong person. I imagine you'd just *know*.'

Kate thought for a moment. 'I feel like Nicholas is someone whom I could grow to love. Maybe. Possibly.'

'And Ben?'

'Ben—' The words dried in her throat. 'Nicholas is a good guy though. Look at everything he's done for me.'

Saskia narrowed her eyes at her. 'Are you going to start dating him again?'

Kate looked at her sister, her expression pained. 'I kind of feel like I already am. Ever since he said he'd let d'Artagnan run on his merits, I was pretty much his. I couldn't turn that down, could I?'

'But what have you turned down instead? Are you putting d'Artagnan ahead of Ben?'

'But Ben and I had already broken up—'

'Rubbish. You had a falling out. You're in love with him, for goodness' sake! You don't just split after one tiff.'

Kate sighed. 'You don't understand, Saskia. It was hardly a tiff. And even if it were, what am I supposed to do now? I doubt whether Ben even wants me back.'

'Why do you say that?'

Kate looked down at her lap and mumbled, 'Apparently he told Nicholas to make amends.'

'And who told you that? Nicholas?'

Kate's expression conceded the dubiousness of this claim. 'But also, when he found out about me selling Harrison, he offered to buy me a new car. And if you leave, I'm going to need some wheels. I just – I just feel like I'm beholden to him. That I need him, but for all the wrong reasons. I'm *using* him.'

Saskia regarded her for a long moment then with a reluctant sigh, reached beneath the desk for her handbag. She hooked out her keys and tossed them to Kate.

Kate caught them in surprise. 'What's this?'

'My car keys. Take them. And the car, obviously.'

'But Saskia—'

'No, don't argue or I'll change my mind. Take it. Then you won't have to accept anything from Nicholas.'

'But you can't give me your car!'

'Course I can. I owe it to you, anyway. And besides, when I'm in London I won't need one.'

Kate stared at her. Saskia had never done anything so selfless. Her fingers curled around the cold metal. She jumped off the desk and scooted round to give her sister a hug. 'Thank you,' she said, squeezing her from side to side.

Saskia laughed. 'So now you're going to break it off completely with Nicholas, aren't you?' She groaned when Kate hesitated. 'Kate, come on. I don't want him for a brother-in-law. He'd bore the Christmas stockings off the wall if we ever had family get-togethers. He'd definitely drive Mum back to drink.'

Kate was excused from answering by the hollering of her name from outside. She realised she was probably holding up the feed queue.

Five minutes later, Kate tipped d'Artagnan's dinner into his manger. She barely had time to remove the bucket before he dove his nose inside. He snorted, sending up a cloud of bran particles, and Kate smiled at his unsavoury table manners. She stroked his neck and planted a kiss on his temple. Her hand stilled on his mane and she squeezed her eyes shut to block the tears.

'I'm sorry, fella.'

Reaching into her pocket, she withdrew her mobile and opened a fresh text message to Nicholas.

Are you free tonight? Need to talk.

51

NICHOLAS HAD TAKEN the news with composure. He'd sat in dignified silence as Kate had babbled out excuses and reasons why she had to forsake d'Artagnan.

'Is there nothing that will change your mind?' he'd said, at last.

'I'm sorry, Nicholas. I don't—' She'd hesitated, not wanting to be blunt. 'I don't *feel strongly enough* about us to let you do this. You need to run d'Artagnan how *you* want to run him, not how I want.'

And that was it. He'd accepted it and they'd parted ways. Today was Friday and she hadn't heard a word from him since. Today was Gold Cup day and there was no turning back.

Kate was dumbstruck by the sheer volume of people trying to get into Cheltenham. They spilled out from the town's pubs and pavements in their thousands, all cheering at the lorry when they recognised the name. By the time they pulled up outside the red brick racecourse stables, she was nauseous with nerves.

Kate hopped out of the cab after Frankie then had to steady herself against the door when her world see-sawed.

Frankie laughed and reached out a supportive hand. 'You okay?'

Kate let go of the lorry and tested her balance. She nodded. 'A bit of an adrenalin overdose.'

'I know it's tough,' said Frankie, wrenching open the ramp bolts with a clunk. 'But try to think of it as just another race day. You won't be doing d'Artagnan any favours if you're a bag of nerves.'

That was easier said than done.

'Hey, fella.' Kate stepped up the ramp and greeted her horse with a touch on his nose. D'Artagnan's ears were pricked and his nostrils were wide as they scooped in the unfamiliar sounds and smells of the racecourse. Beside them, Frankie led The Whistler down the ramp. The partition was swung open and Kate took a deep breath. Calm. Calm. Calm.

She led her horse down the ramp, and was nearly pulled off her feet when d'Artagnan chose to spring-heel the last three feet. For the first time, she noticed the television cameras and photographers gathering. They called for her and Frankie's attention, whistled to the horses, backed into one another as they searched for the perfect angle for their shot.

Kate looked around, slack-jawed. Green and gold banners flapped in the wind announcing that *this* was Cheltenham Festival, the home of champions. It was like going from a Helensvale am dram production to the Hollywood premiere of a blockbuster film.

'Come on, Kate,' called Frankie.

Kate jerked back to the present and realised she and d'Artagnan were in danger of being left behind. They followed the other seven Aspen Valley horses into the stable yard where, with press, media and public forbidden access, a deceptive calm prevailed.

Jack was waiting for them by their allocated boxes and he took care to check all the horses over for any injuries incurred on their journey. D'Artagnan was last in line. Jack ran a hand down a hindleg then straightened, his mouth grim, but his eyes glittering with energy.

'All set then.' He puffed out his cheeks and gave Kate a rare smile. 'T-minus six hours.'

Those six hours stretched into an eternity for Kate. She took lunch with Frankie and a couple of other lads. Billy, who was leading up Shenandoah in the Foxhunter Chase, leaned over his lamb curry and said in a conspiratorial voice, 'Word on the wire is Canyon Echo's gonna start favourite. The Whistler's weak on the exchanges and the on-course bookies are gonna have to match their prices.'

'Like how weak?' said Frankie.

Billy swiped through a couple of pages on his phone. 'Was six-to-four, now you can get him at two-to-one.'

'How's d'Artagnan's price looking?' Kate couldn't resist asking.

Billy tapped and swiped then looked hesitant. 'Twenty-to-one. But you know how exaggerated the exchanges can be,' he added quickly.

'And it's not impossible for a twenty-to-one shot to win,' said Frankie. 'Look at Lord Windermere. That wasn't so long ago.'

Kate nodded. She wanted to add that Lord Windermere hadn't been anybody's pacemaker that day. She smiled and got to her feet to dispose of her untouched lunch. 'It's okay. It's really quite a good price for a pacemaker. It would probably be higher if he wasn't grey.'

Kate began to understand what shaken champagne must feel like when, finally, she led d'Artagnan into the amphitheatre-style paddock. The racegoers that stood shoulder to shoulder at the ringside seemed different to any other crowd. She could almost see their anticipation hovering in the atmosphere like heat waves, even though the temperature was probably in single figures.

The sun flashed off something high above the right of the parade ring and Kate recognised the statue of the great Golden Miller, whose namesake she now lived opposite.

D'Artagnan walked beside her with his head held high, snuffling and snorting, jogging every few steps when he could no longer keep to a walk. Ahead of them was Canyon Echo. It was the first time Kate had seen him in the flesh and, particularly from this angle, he looked a powerhouse of muscle. He had a backside like an elephant and he made The Whistler look a wimp in comparison.

The centre of the ring was so full of people that she hadn't a hope of spotting Nicholas and his father, but she knew they must be there, somewhere. And when the jockeys spilled out of the weighing room, she knew Ben must be among them too.

The bell rang for jockeys to mount. Kate was too preoccupied with keeping their distance from Canyon Echo's rear-end to think about her inevitable meeting with Ben.

Jack legged Ben into the saddle, making d'Artagnan jump into a crab canter. Ben wrapped his legs around the grey's barrel sides, loose of his irons, as he waited for his mount to settle down. He was pale, his mouth thin and tense, a muscle leaping in his jaw.

'All right?' she said.

Ben nodded. 'You?'

'Nervous. First time at Cheltenham.'

'Make the most of it.'

She was tempted to ask what his riding orders were, but decided against it. Why upset herself?

Ben inserted his gum guard as the twelve runners exited the parade ring, effectively ending their awkward exchange, and Kate concentrated on the job at hand.

China Blue slotted in between them and Canyon Echo to take his rightful place in the order. The rangy bay was awash with sweat. He fought his handler, acting like an unbroken yearling as they walked out onto the course for the parade in front of the stands. D'Artagnan picked up on his rival's nerves and snatched at his bit.

'Easy, fella,' Kate murmured. She felt a tap on her shoulder and turned back to Ben.

He pointed to their left and smiled.

She looked and her breath caught in her throat. The grandstands, bearing the names of the late greats, and the expansive grounds spilling down to the track were filled to capacity. A flash of green here and there marked Ireland's representatives, die-hard fans who had made the journey over especially. Her skin prickled at the sheer awesomeness of the sight.

Up ahead China Blue's lad could hold him no longer and the horse broke rank, plunging out of line and bolting down the track. Canyon Echo's lads (he had two, plus another walking close by) let their charge go as well.

Kate's pulse quickened as the course opened up in front of her. The infamous Cheltenham hill seemed to stretch forever. Endless miles of white rails sparkling in the sunshine set off the lush emerald turf.

She knew what lay ahead, that when the starter raised his flag, she wouldn't be on tenterhooks like Frankie and the rest of the grooms. But even so, the atmosphere around her was so electric, so full of positive energy, it was difficult not to hope for the impossible.

She unclipped d'Artagnan's lead rope. 'You know what you've got to do,' she said with a last guilty pat on his shoulder. She looked up at Ben and tried to smile. Tears sprang to her eyes. Where the hell did those come from? It had to be the whole shebang making her emotional. 'Good luck,' she mouthed.

Ben nodded. He gathered up his reins and stood up in his stirrups as d'Artagnan broke away. Kate stepped aside, so she wouldn't get run over by the horses following, and watched the grey gelding gallop further and further away from her. She felt like a mother sending her child away to school, but this was no school for the faint-hearted. Lung-bursting uphill fences with open ditch spreads and tricky upright fences on steep downhill curves made sure every obstacle was a challenge.

* * *

296

Sixty-five thousand cheers sent sixty-five thousand goose-bumps washing over Kate's body. The race for the Gold Cup was on. Kate leaned on the rail beside Frankie, balancing on tiptoes for a better view. Easy to spot, d'Artagnan was just one of two greys in the race, the other being the French raider, Sacre Coeur, and she glimpsed the flash of white spearheading the field.

It was a short run to the first of the twenty-two fences and all horses navigated it safely. The blood pounded in Kate's ears as the horses galloped past the stands for the first time with two more circuits ahead of them. Out in front, d'Artagnan galloped with Kipling for company on his outside. The pair matched strides over the second fence and swung left away from the stands to head out into the country.

A little piece of Kate's heart broke as she realised the impossible was indeed a hope forlorn. She glanced across to where Nicholas and his parents were stood alongside Jack further down the walkway.

'And we have an early faller!' the commentator exclaimed.

Kate's attention whipped back to the race. On the landing side of the second fence, she saw the fifty-to-one outsider, Song of Hiawatha, lurch to his feet and gallop away. She scanned the rest of the runners, noting The Whistler held up in midfield and Canyon Echo stalking him. Her nerves already fraught, she jumped when Frankie grabbed her arm.

'Kate, look! Is he pulling up? What's he doing?'

Kate switched from real time to the big screen in front of the stands. The picture showed d'Artagnan losing ground on Kipling, his mouth agape as his rider restrained him.

Kate's heart bounced into her throat. Oh God, here she was lamenting the fact her horse wasn't being ridden the way she wanted him to be and not even contemplating that he might succumb to injury.

But he couldn't be injured. Ben still aimed him at the next fence. They took it three lengths adrift of Kipling. She gasped, not daring to hope. She darted a look at the Borden party, but couldn't keep her eyes off the race long enough to gauge their reaction.

Over the water jump and d'Artagnan was passed by the Irish horse, Thunderclap. The following three fences followed in quick succession with Kipling showing the way at a brisk gallop. They rounded the top of the hill and swung left to head back towards home, Kipling out in front, d'Artagnan steadied into fourth, The Whistler still held up with Canyon Echo his shadow.

Kate gripped the rail as the horses thundered downhill towards the seventh. D'Artagnan jumped big and nodded on landing, making Kate throw her weight back and nearly pull over the rail. Kipling led the field past their point of departure, ears pricked and head held high.

The crowd cheered louder as the horses tackled the first in the home straight. D'Artagnan put in a short stride and lost a length on landing. On his outside, Sacre Coeur, the other grey, moved up to share fourth.

The ground reverberated beneath Kate's feet as the horses passed the stands for the second time. Despite drifting back, Ben was riding confidently aboard d'Artagnan. Further back, Rhys let The Whistler out a notch and began to pick off a couple of the runners already showing fatigue.

Again, the horses swung left, sweeping past the rows of white corporate marquees. Kipling made a mistake over the next, allowing Thunderclap and the free-running China Blue to close in on his lead. Sacre Coeur passed d'Artagnan over the next plain fence and cut in front of his rival.

Kate winced as Ben was forced to snatch up his reins. He only just had enough time to pull his horse into daylight before the next fence was upon them. D'Artagnan twisted over, but stayed on his feet.

The water jump was next and all eleven remaining runners cleared it fluently.

'Ooh, here we go, here we go!' cried Frankie, jumping up and down.

Kate searched out The Whistler and saw the reason for Frankie's excitement. Rhys had lowered his body and The Whistler was gaining on the front runners. Intent on remaining his shadow though, Canyon Echo was right behind.

The horses streamed over the open ditch, only Esprit de Sivola, the back marker, making any serious blunder. The Whistler jumped up alongside d'Artagnan over the next fence and Kate saw Ben turn his head. She wondered if he and Rhys were saying anything to each other. Rhys didn't look like he was in the mood to chat.

Reaching the top of the hill and swinging left, the race hit top gear. The commentator's voice rose in anticipation and the crowd roared in excitement. The horses thundered towards the downhill fence, and Kate's stomach lurched as a tired Kipling crumpled on landing. D'Artagnan and The Whistler rose together, their shoulders bashing as the latter drifted off a true line.

Kate blew out her cheeks as both horses landed safely. The rest of the field followed in their wake and Mr Mistoffelees, hindered by Kipling, unseated his rider. The race took on a new urgency as the horses tackled the next fence with d'Artagnan and The Whistler bridging the gap between them and the front three. China Blue emptied quickly and the two Aspen Valley horses had to take drastic action to avoid his deceleration, passing him on either side.

Swinging into the home straight for the final time, Sacre Coeur was the next to crack. The crowd roared louder than Kate thought possible, the noise making her eardrums quake. Thunderclap soared over the second last. The Irish contingent raised the roof of the grandstand. Still stride for stride, their jockeys shovelling in tandem, d'Artagnan and The Whistler lifted off together. Canyon Echo followed in their slipstream.

Ruthless, the Aspen Valley duo closed in on Thunderclap. Approaching the last, Canyon Echo's jockey pulled him wide and the four horses jumped it together.

Kate was delirious with excitement. She and Frankie clung to each other, screaming home their horses, jumping up and down in ungainly embrace. The commentator yelling at the top of his lungs could barely be heard for the noise of the crowd.

'Four in a row! Just the Cheltenham hill to conquer! Thunderclap gives way! The Whistler draws ahead! D'Artagnan's going with him! Here comes Canyon Echo! Canyon Echo down the outside under a strong left-handed whip!'

D'Artagnan's grey head nodded into the lead. In a relentless drive, he pulled ahead of The Whistler, a head, a neck, a length, two lengths. Kate nearly climbed on top of Frankie, so hysterical was she. Her horse was keeping on. The Whistler was beat. Only Canyon Echo thundering up the centre of the course threatened his Gold Cup victory.

Cheltenham's hill wasn't infamous for nothing. It sapped the stamina from the stoutest of stayers, and d'Artagnan, willing as he was, began to lose the battle.

With a hundred yards to go, Canyon Echo stuck his nose in front. Kate could see it happening, as if slow motion, as her horse ran out of puff and the super-engine that was Canyon Echo slowly, but unerringly, stamped his authority on the race.

The big bay galloped over the line, his jockey rising high in his stirrups and punching the air. D'Artagnan followed four lengths adrift. In third,

Thunderclap found his second wind too late and only just managed to demote The Whistler to fourth.

Kate and Frankie fell onto one another, gasping for breath. Sobs racked Kate's body as her emotions got the better of her. Through sparkling tears she saw Nicholas walking towards her. He gave a shrug of wry disappointment, and held out his arms.

Kate stared at him for a moment. *This was his doing?* Kate was overwhelmed by gratitude and pride. She stumbled into his arms and hugged him tight.

'Thank you,' she said. 'Thank you, thank you, *thank you.*'

Nicholas's shoulders shook, but it difficult to tell if he was laughing for the noise as the crowds cheered in the winner. Nicholas cupped her damp face with a gloved hand. His gaze flickered over her shoulder to where the horses were making their way back down the chute. He smiled and leaned in to kiss her. Kate jerked back in surprise. Oh dear, maybe she'd come on a bit strong. She hadn't meant to give him the wrong impression.

'Nicholas—'

'Kate!' Jack's voice was hoarse, but stern, and demanded immediate acknowledgement. He pointed to the returning horses. 'Go see to your horse, will you?'

With an embarrassed smile, Kate extracted herself from Nicholas's arms and ran to meet Ben and d'Artagnan jogging back down the chute. She'd speak to Nicholas afterwards and make sure they were reading from the same hymn sheet. She couldn't concentrate on him right now, there was too much going on, too much adrenalin pumping through her body, too many emotions pulling her off-balance.

D'Artagnan threw up his head as Kate descended on them. She flung her arms around his slick neck, and patted him until her hand stung.

Ben looked down at her, a sad smile on his muddied face. He looked pointedly in Nicholas's direction. 'I guess I'm too late.'

Kate didn't know what to say except a feeble, 'I'm sorry, Ben.' How was she supposed to react? Was she meant to be bowled over by him following orders? She couldn't hold his eye any longer. She dropped her gaze in frustration, and only then did she notice d'Artagnan's off foreleg stained red amidst the mud. 'He's bleeding.'

52

D'ARTAGNAN'S INJURY TURNED out to be nothing more than a minor overreach, and by seven o'clock that evening, he was tucked up in his stable back at Aspen Valley and vacuuming up his feed.

Kate leaned her arms on his stable door and watched him in the darkness. 'I'm proud of you, fella. We all are. You ran the best race of your life today. Thanks to Nicholas,' she added. 'And I'm sure he would want to be here to congratulate you too, but he and his dad are hosting some corporate dinner or other. They were all there today, you know. All watching you, all cheering you on.'

She'd tried to talk to Nicholas after the race, but everything had been so manic, there literally hadn't been a spare moment. She supposed she could just text him and set him straight, but after what he'd done for her today, he deserved to be told face-to-face. The lorry had just pulled into Aspen Valley's front yard when she'd received a text from him, suggesting she come over the following morning. It made Kate wince to think of his blissful ignorance, but what could she do before then? He was buttering up rich clients at some black-tie affair all night. Tomorrow morning would be as early as she could make it.

She reached out a hand and d'Artagnan turned to see what she had to offer. She wiped the crumbs clinging to his whiskers. 'I'll leave you to your dinner. And I'll see you on Monday.'

Kate set off across the near-deserted stable yard, but detoured via The Whistler's stable. She poked her head over the door to find Frankie double-checking her horse for leg-heat.

'Hey,' she said quietly, so as not to startle either of them. 'I'm out of here.'

Frankie didn't look up from her task. 'Okay. See you tomorrow.'

'No, Monday. I've the weekend off. Oh, and Frankie?'

Frankie looked up.

Kate grinned. 'Congratulations on being made assistant trainer.'

Nicholas opened the door the next morning with a spatula in his hand and a wide smile on his face. 'Come in, do,' he said, waving her through.

Kate hesitated as he aimed a kiss at her cheek. 'Um, morning.'

'And what a pleasant one it is too.' Nicholas looped his arms around her and kicked the door closed. 'You okay?'

Kate didn't think he wanted the literal answer just yet. 'Yeah, fine. Thanks. How was your dinner thing last night?'

'Lonely without you.' The smoke alarm interrupted his reply. 'Oh – bacon's burning.'

Kate followed him through to the kitchen. Nicholas reached up and silenced the alarm. 'No, it was all right, really. Dad's clients seemed to have a good time yesterday. Mike Weitz was even talking about buying a couple of horses.'

Kate wondered what it must be like to have so much money that one could just decide on a whim to buy a couple of racehorses.

'Nicholas, there's something I need to talk to you about.'

'Tell me over breakfast.'

'No, I—'

'Come on, I've cooked for both of us. You can't let it go to waste. Why don't you dust off the table and chairs out on the patio so that we can eat outside and enjoy the sunshine.'

He turned back to the stove without waiting for a reply, leaving Kate to stand, curling her toes.

'Nicholas—'

'It's going to be ready in a couple of minutes.'

Kate gave in. It'd probably be a better idea to tell him when he'd finished cooking anyway.

Five minutes later, they were both seated at the wonky table in the fresh spring breeze, listening to bird song and the faint growl of traffic from the road. Kate told herself she'd have built up enough courage to tell him by the end of one rash of bacon and a fried tomato.

Nicholas took out his mobile phone and took a picture of her.

'Nicholas!' Kate cried. 'I had my mouth full.'

Nicholas grinned and studied the picture, tapping on the screen for a brief time. 'Perfect. That was a real money shot.'

He put his phone away and resumed his breakfast. Every time either of them tried to cut into their food, the table jiggled and spilled their orange juices. Nicholas laughed and disappeared inside to get a cloth and to find some cardboard to balance the table.

Kate sat back, wondering what the hell was happening. She'd come here to set the record straight with Nicholas, yet here she was enjoying a home-cooked meal out in the sunshine? She looked up at the pagoda of mulberry vines and a memory pinged. Patting her mouth with her napkin, she got up to investigate the vines beneath the upstairs bedroom window.

'Hey there, what are you up to?' Nicholas said, stepping out through the French doors.

'I was just looking for something.' She looked back to where Nicholas was crouched down, sliding a folded piece of what looked like a Christmas card under one table leg. 'You remember that bird's nest that was up here? I can't find it.'

'Hmm, yeah. I got rid of it.' He jigged the table then stood up and dusted off his hands. 'There, that should do it. Come, your food's getting cold.'

Kate thought she must have misheard him, or at least, misunderstood him. She looked up again just to make sure the bird's nest wasn't there then retook her seat. 'You got rid of it? Had they abandoned the nest?'

Nicholas shook his head, and covered his mouth as he chewed on his bacon and eggs. 'No. They were making such a mess of the paving. They don't shit like normal birds, because they've been guzzling on the mulberries. I have a hell of a time getting the stains out of the stone.'

Kate stared at him. 'But what about the chicks?'

'Oh, I threw it out before they hatched, don't worry.' He looked at her dumbstruck expression and laughed. 'Come on, Kate. You're not getting upset over some silly bird's nest, are you? It's not like I shot them or anything. I'm sure the mother bird has built a nest somewhere else and laid more eggs.'

'But Nicholas—'

'Don't you think you're being a bit hypocritical?' he interrupted. 'You're getting upset because I threw out a bird's nest, yet you're sitting here eating eggs and bacon. What about the pigs and chicks that had to die for your breakfast?'

'That's different,' she replied. 'They died so I could eat. Those eggs in the bird's nest died because you didn't want to clean up their purple poo anymore.'

'God, you're as bad as Ben,' he muttered.

Kate didn't want to think about Ben. 'Leave him out of this.'

Nicholas ignored her. 'Harping on about one thing then doing the exact opposite. He's at the front of the animal rights brigade, but it doesn't stop him from being a jockey. Claiming he's not in it for the winning, or for the glory and then pulling a stunt like yesterday—'

'Nicholas, I said I don't want to talk about B— wait.' She narrowed her eyes at him across the table. 'What do you mean, pulling a stunt like yesterday? What stunt?'

'Nothing.' He busied himself with spreading jam onto his toast.

'No, come on, tell me.'

Nicholas sighed and put down his knife. 'Well, I was hoping you and I could carry on a while longer, but I suppose you'd have to find out eventually. Doesn't really matter now.'

A cold wind seeped through Kate's skin. 'Find out what?'

'You know what. Ben disobeying his orders and sabotaging The Whistler's race.'

Kate sucked in her breath and her knife fell through the table slats to the ground. 'That was Ben's idea? Why did you let me think it was yours?'

Nicholas's eyes glittered as he patted his mouth with his napkin. Kate was taken aback by how sinister he could appear.

'More fool you for making such assumptions.'

Kate's cheeks burned. 'But up until Tuesday night you were—'

'Kate, what planet are you living on? D'Artagnan was never going to win the Gold Cup, as he has since proven. I was never going to go along with it.'

'So, you were lying all along?' Kate's voice shook in anger. 'What did you think would happen once the Gold Cup was run?'

Nicholas gave an indifferent shrug. 'That wasn't the point. Actually, I thought my plan had failed when you went all noble and told me to race d'Artagnan however I wanted.'

'Your plan? What *plan*?'

Nicholas picked up his knife, making the sun's reflection flash off the blade. 'Did you see the look on Ben's face when you ran into my arms?'

He shook his head and chuckled. 'He set himself up without even realising it, the muppet.'

Kate gulped. 'I don't understand.'

'Come on, Kate. Do you really think I want my "brother's" leftovers?'

Kate's heart jumped in her throat and she stared at him.

Nicholas gave a patronising nod. 'Oh yes. You kept that one quiet, didn't you? Didn't think to tell me you were hopping into his bed behind my back.'

'I never—'

'Bullshit! I'm not a fool, Kate! Did you think I was just going to lie down and take it?'

'Then why am I here?' she replied. 'Why go to all this trouble when you don't want me?'

Nicholas chucked his napkin onto his plate and gave her a sly smile. 'To teach Ben – and you – a lesson. Give me a break, Kate. I've got my pride. You, on the other hand, seem to live in your own little self-absorbed fantasy. The way you didn't even question my motives when I said I wanted us to get back together. You thought that I was just some poor schmuck crawling back to you. I wasn't going to let you two get away with it.'

'I never cheated on you, Nicholas. We'd broken up long before Ben and I got together.'

'Yeah, right,' said Nicholas with a mirthless snort. 'You were always "Ben this" and "Ben that". Anybody would think he was God's gift. He's not. He's an alcoholic, Kate. Did you know that?'

Kate took a deep breath. 'Yes, Nicholas. As a matter of fact, I did know that. He's a *recovering* alcoholic.'

'Recovering? Recovering from what? His hangover from that stupid Halloween party you made me go to? You remember you saw us arguing? That was because he'd been boozing! Splashing all that champagne around, acting an idiot.'

Kate sat stiffly in her seat. 'No, he hadn't.'

'How can you be so sure?'

'Because he was racing the next day – he was riding Laughing Stock – and he would have needed to take a piss test. Any alcohol would have shown up in his sample.'

Nicholas looked disgruntled. 'You think he's still sober after yesterday? It'll be your fault if he's not, you know.'

'How can you be so cruel?' Kate said with a gasp. 'He's your brother, for goodness' sake!'

'He's no brother to me,' Nicholas said, holding up a warning finger. 'He's been a parasite on my family. You deserve each other really.'

Kate's temper was too hot to feel the insult. 'So, this is all a farce. All this Mr Nicely Does It act was just a way to rub Ben's face in it.'

'Revenge is a dish best served cold.'

Kate stared at him in silence, unable to comprehend the loathing that he must feel towards Ben, and towards her, to concoct such a hurtful vendetta.

She swallowed and made an effort to compose herself. She picked up her knife from the floor and put it back on the plate.

'You should know that I never had any intention of coming back to you,' she said primly as she stood back up. 'I came here today to set the record straight.'

Nicholas grinned. 'I figured as much.'

'Then why the big charade?'

'Because Ben doesn't know it's not real.'

Kate shook her head. 'Ben doesn't know I'm here at all.'

Nicholas raised an eyebrow. 'Doesn't he?'

Kate paused by the French doors.

Nicholas looked up at her, relaxed in his chair, and picked up his mobile phone. 'He will have just received a picture of you having breakfast at my place. A picture can tell a thousand words, isn't that what they say?'

53

I T WAS CLOSE to midday before Kate pulled up outside Thistle Lodge
Stables in Saskia's car. With the engine stilled, she gripped the
steering wheel and took a deep breath. She didn't know what she was
going to say – well, she had an idea, but it was if Ben was willing to
believe her, or even listen to her, that would be tricky.

With a last summoning of her courage, she got out of the car and
walked around the stable block. Ben was washing down Suddenly
Seymour.

She pulled back her shoulders, exhaled, and walked forward. Ben
didn't hear her coming. She was about ten feet away when Seymour
spotted her and spooked.

'Whoa there, whoa,' responded Ben, nearly pulled off his feet. 'What's
the—' He turned and saw Kate. '—problem. Hey.'

'Hey.' Kate flapped an awkward arm.

Ben resumed his hosing duties. 'What do you want?'

'You got Nicholas's message?'

Ben nodded. 'Not that I needed it to know what was going on. Come
to rub it in? Hmm?'

'No.' Kate shook her head. 'It's not true. I came to apologise. And to
ask if we could start again.'

Ben chuckled to himself and directed a particularly sharp flow of water
at Seymour's muddy hindlegs. Seymour skittered to the side and rolled
his eyes.

'You going for a record?' asked Ben. 'See how many times you can
ping-pong between me and Nicholas?'

'I didn't get back together with Nicholas, you must believe me. I'd
gone over there this morning to tell him we would never work. Please,
you have to believe me.

'I *have* to believe you? Really, Kate? Because you make it bloody
difficult to do so sometimes.'

'Nicholas let me believe he'd changed d'Artagnan's tactics.'

Ben raised an eyebrow at her and shook his head. 'Sounds about his style. Seems to me, though, that things were getting quite cushy between the two of you before then. A table for two at the pub, going to parties together—'

'We didn't—'

'Frankie Bradford's? Yeah, I heard about it. Don't bother denying it.'

'I didn't know he was going to be there. It was the first I'd seen him since Boxing D—'

'Why didn't you stop it there then?' he cut her short.

Kate sighed, a shawl of shame wrapping around her. 'I wanted d'Artagnan to run on his merits in the Gold Cup, and I knew if I told Nicholas there was no chance for us then d'Artagnan would have suffered.'

'But Nicholas still didn't agree. My orders back there in the parade ring at Cheltenham were to jump out in front and gallop him into the ground,' said Ben through clenched teeth. He jabbed himself in the chest. 'It was *me* who held him up.'

'I know. I told Nicholas on Tuesday that I couldn't go through with it. I couldn't force myself to be with someone for the wrong reasons. Then in the Gold Cup—' She gave a helpless laugh. It was too complex to explain when time felt so constrained. 'He lied about it all. Right from the start. He lied about the race, he lied when he sent you that message this morning.'

Ben gave a mirthless snort. 'What? You gonna tell me that's not his backyard you're sitting in using the china and cutlery Nora gave him?'

'It's not what you think, Ben. You have – *please* believe me. I'd only arrived about ten minutes before he took that picture. I hadn't stayed overnight. I didn't sleep with him.'

'But you would've.'

'No!' she cried. 'I'd gone there to tell him there could never be anything between us. At the Gold Cup, he made out that we were back together since he'd changed tactics. But we never were. He knew it too. He did all that to hurt you, don't you see? To hurt us.' She looked at him in desperation. 'But it backfired on him,' she carried on quietly, 'because it made me realise just how much I don't want to see you hurt...' She took a deep breath, trying to gauge which way Ben was leaning. '*You* are the one who makes my heart skip. *You* are the one I'm in love with.'

Ben stopped hosing Seymour. He let his hand fall to his side, the water spouting out and wetting his boots. He looked at Kate with doubtful eyes. 'Love me. Love my addiction.'

Kate nodded. 'I'm sorry. It scared me, Ben. *Terrified* me. I was dealing with my mother at her worst. I couldn't contemplate a life with someone with the same problems. But then I went to that AA meeting – the second one – and I heard everyone's stories and I think I began to understand it a bit more. Things are always so much scarier when you don't understand them.' She took a step closer. 'I listened to your story too.'

'Sounds like you took a lot out of that meeting.' Ben turned to let Seymour drink from the hose-end. 'Turn it off, will you?' he said, nodding to the tap.

Kate hurried to oblige. Then she stood, not knowing quite what to do next, as Ben set to work scraping the excess water off Seymour's body.

'You know why I rode d'Artagnan like I did?' he said without looking around.

Kate was hesitant to say it. She closed her eyes. 'Because you loved me?'

'No. The thing that made me decide to do it for certain was when you let us go. You said "You know what to do".'

'I—I was talking to d'Artagnan.'

'Yeah, I know, but it felt like you were talking to me too.' He stopped scraping to look at her. For the first time he smiled. 'And because I loved you.'

Kate's heart felt like she'd hit the jackpot on the slots. 'Do you still love me?' she whispered, hardly daring to breathe.

Ben dropped Seymour's lead rope and scraper and bridged the gap between them. With damp and dirty hands, he cupped her face and kissed her. Kate let herself soar, like the thrill of riding the drop jump on Jerry, a full body experience that removed all sense of space and gravity.

Ben withdrew. 'That answer enough?'

Kate nodded, finding difficulty in speaking. 'And you forgive me?'

'What's there to forgive? You were being had. I'm just sorry we didn't win yesterday.'

'Winning wasn't what was important.'

'I know, I know. You just wanted d'Artagnan to be the best that he—' He paused, his smile widening. 'I've just realised something.'

'What's that?'

'All this time, you've been pushing for d'Artagnan, I couldn't understand it. I thought it was because you wanted to win the Gold Cup, but it's not. You wanted to give d'Artagnan the chance you never had.'

'Sounds a bit pathetic, doesn't it?' Kate said, turning her tingling cheeks into his palm to hide her blushes.

'Not really. I'm just sorry you didn't win.'

Kate rested her hand over his. 'I did.'

Ben laughed. 'You call this first prize? Half a dozen stables to muck out and six muddy horses to clean?'

Kate looked around at the set-up. 'Are you going to be able to keep this place going?'

'Well, I might need some help. But I did what you suggested. I applied to be a registered charity, and thanks to Xander, I've got funding to open it to troubled teens.'

Kate gasped. 'Oh, Ben! That's a fantastic idea.'

'And I've got qualifications in social work and therapy from when I was working at that rehab place in Wales, so it'll be a proper set-up.'

Kate hugged him hard. 'Oh, I'm so pleased. What about your race-riding? Are you going to be able to manage both?'

'I spoke to my dad after the races yesterday. Told him I was quitting race riding.'

'How did he take it?'

Ben looked undecided. 'Not sure. He was a bit disappointed, I think. Maybe apprehensive is the better word. He thought I was quitting because I was back on the booze, but I think I've convinced him that's all in the past. He liked the charity idea of running this place as a charity.'

'Racing needs places like Thistle Lodge.'

'It's a two-way street. Anyway, it means I can move out of that tin can and take up residence in a proper house. Fiona's moving out in a couple of weeks, so.' He raised an eyebrow at her. 'Would it put you and Saskia in a bind if I asked you to move in with me?'

Kate pinched her tongue between her teeth with glee. 'Saskia's moving to London.'

'And you're letting her go?'

Kate nodded. 'She's a big girl now.'

Ben squeezed his arm around her. 'That, she is.'

He kissed her again and Kate's head spun. It seemed too surreal to be kissing Ben. Too much like a fairytale.

Lips barely apart, he whispered. 'You want the other news?'

'There's more?'

'Dad was so up for the idea that he said he'll send all his horses through Thistle Lodge.'

Kate gasped and jerked back so that she could look at him properly. 'So d'Artagnan will live here one day?'

Ben nodded. 'And if he's a good boy, he might even stay on. I'm going to need some stalwarts to rely on. Seymour's sticking around.' He motioned to the horse, and only then did they realise he was no longer stood there. 'Seymour?'

'Where's he gone? Seymour?'

The clip clop of hooves on the walkway gave the gelding away. Trailing his lead rope, Seymour was off to chat to his mates.

'Shouldn't we go get him?' Kate asked when Ben didn't make a move.

Ben fobbed him off with a vague wave of his hand and looped his arms around Kate. 'The feed room's closed. What harm can he come to?'

And with that, he bent to kiss her again.

Suddenly Seymour turned to look at the couple, wondering what on earth was up with them. *Pah!* They didn't look like they'd be bothering him any time soon and he had a mission to fulfil. He was going to find his old pal, Jerry.

He clopped past Miranda's door, ignoring her tossing head and snapping teeth. She was too uptight for his liking. He rounded the corner to the isolation stable, where he'd heard noises these past few days of a new resident going by the name of Fontainebleau.

Seymour stopped dead in his tracks as the most beautiful chestnut he'd ever clapped eyes on lifted his head over the stable door.

A clarion whinny of newfound love echoed around the yard, but did little to disturb Kate and Ben still locked in each other's embrace.

THE END

KEEPING THE PEACE
(ASPEN VALLEY SERIES, BOOK 1)

London waitress Pippa Taylor has no interest in horses or country-living. But when she inherits Peace Offering, a hopeless racehorse, she embarks on a career change in order to see her late uncle's wish to run him in the Grand National come true.

But having talked her way into a job as racing secretary to champion National Hunt trainer Jack Carmichael, and moved to the West Country, Pippa finds herself facing more daunting obstacles than even the Grand National can throw at her....and that's before her tempestuous relationship with her new boss can be considered.

Moody, fiery-tempered and particularly easy on the eye, Jack's moral code is threatened by Pippa's arrival. After a Christmas they would both rather forget, love and deception buffet Pippa's new rural lifestyle and as her time at Aspen Valley Stables draws to its conclusion she discovers Peace Offering is not the only thing she will want to keep.

Amazon #1 Bestseller

'The book is well paced and the kooky characters absolutely believable. I laughed a great deal.' ***** *The Romance Reviews*

'Keeping the Peace has everything from a great storyline to some hot romance! The female Dick Francis.' ***** *The Filly Forum*

'Evocative imagery and crisp writing sets this story apart from the competition.' ***** *Natalie Keller Reinert, bestselling author*

GIVING CHASE
(ASPEN VALLEY SERIES, BOOK 2)

There has only ever been one man in Frankie's life: her father, Doug Cooper. That is, until she takes the job of amateur jockey at Aspen Valley Racing Stables. Here, in the rolling countryside of southwest England, she crosses paths with star rider, Rhys Bradford. Her crush on him would be made so much simpler if they didn't both have their hearts set on the same prize: the coveted ride on Grand National favourite, Peace Offering.

In the turbulent run-up to National Hunt's biggest event, questions are raised. What exactly does Doug have against the Bradfords? Is Rhys playing games with her heart? Will Ta' Qali show his true potential in time to warrant his place at Aspen Valley? Why do there have to be so many blasted calories in strawberry cheesecake? And lastly, who exactly *is* Francesca Cooper?

Frankie's curiosity unearths some long-buried secrets that their keepers would rather remain buried. And on a journey of self-discovery that takes in Britain's fiercest steeplechase courses, love will prove her costliest stumbling point.

Amazon #1 Bestseller
Winner of the SKoW Awards' Best International Romance.

'Reminiscent of a Tom Sharpe novel but funnier.' ***** *The Racing Post*

'A pleasure to read. This book's a winner!' ***** *Equestrian Trade News*

'Montlake should consider signing Hooton.' ***** *Amazon reviewer*

SHARE AND SHARE ALIKE
(ASPEN VALLEY SERIES BOOK 3)

Tessa thought buying a share in the dysfunctional Ta' Qali Racehorse Syndicate would be the perfect distraction from a life best forgotten. Some are willing to distract her with words of woo, while others are able to distract her with just a nonchalant look.

But neither Hugh's flirtations nor Sin's disregard are diversion enough when their horse, Ta' Qali, is found deliberately injured. Someone close is responsible and Tessa finds herself questioning the innocence of everyone around her.

With his nobbler still at large, the race is on to get Ta' Qali fit and on course in time to prove himself the champion Tessa's always believed him to be. But he isn't the only one up against the clock. Love is threatening to leave without her; and win, lose or draw, Tessa's in for the ride of her life...

Winner of the Katy Price Prize, 2014
Finalist in the RWA Marlene Contest, 2014

'A great combination of mystery, thrill and romance. Get this book. Seriously. You will not regret it.' ***** *Forging Fiction*

'Punchy, expressive and easy to read – a perfect holiday read.' ***** *Kick On!*

'Think Dick Francis, but lighter and funnier.' ***** *Oh Gingersnap!*

AT LONG ODDS

When Ginny Kennedy returns home to Newmarket to revive the family's racing stable, she has just one thing on her mind: winning the coveted Dewhurst Stakes at the end of the season.

Not only is she faced with the challenges of making her way in a man's world, but she must also cope with her next door neighbour, rival trainer Julien Larocque.

Sharing the same ambition as the suave and successful Frenchman is just part of her problems though. She must resist his magnetism if she is to succeed, but the more she steels herself away, the more she is drawn to him. When her world takes a sinister turn, Ginny must decide who she can and cannot trust.

Come Race Day, she realises that there is a lot more at stake than just a trophy...

'If you haven't read Hannah Hooton, start now! Wonderful romances with a bit of mystery.' ***** Amazon reviewer

'Great characters, believable story lines... unable to put it down.' ***** Amazon reviewer

'A true and classic romance with great plot twists, unexpected villains, and a delicious love interest.' ***** Amazon reviewer

Lightning Source UK Ltd.
Milton Keynes UK
UKOW04f1141170515

251693UK00001B/139/P

9 780992 985356